Praise for
Highland Obsession

"Watch out for your fingers. . . . *Highland Obsession* is on fire—a scorching page-turner from cover to cover! Sexy Highlanders and wickedly erotic romance, Dawn Halliday is the HOTTEST new voice in Scottish romance."

—Monica McCarty, *USA Today* bestselling
author of *Highland Scoundrel*

"Dawn Halliday blasts onto the erotic romance scene with a well-written, passionate debut certain to keep readers up all night."

—Jess Michaels, author of *Taboo*

**Praise for the Other Novels
of Dawn Halliday**

"I found myself eagerly reading through the pages waiting to find out what would happen next . . . a wonderful summertime read."

—Romance Junkies

"Joyfully Recommended! There was nothing about this novel that I didn't like. Well, other than the fact that it made me sweat. Ms. Halliday gets two thumbs up . . . impressively awesome."

—Joyfully Reviewed

"Passionate . . . a wonderful read."   —Just Erotic Romance Reviews

continued . . .

HIGHLAND
OBSESSION

DAWN HALLIDAY

A SIGNET ECLIPSE BOOK

SIGNET ECLIPSE
Published by New American Library, a division of
Penguin Group (USA) Inc., 375 Hudson Street,
New York, New York 10014, USA
Penguin Group (Canada), 90 Eglinton Avenue East, Suite 700, Toronto,
Ontario M4P 2Y3, Canada (a division of Pearson Penguin Canada Inc.)
Penguin Books Ltd., 80 Strand, London WC2R 0RL, England
Penguin Ireland, 25 St. Stephen's Green, Dublin 2,
Ireland (a division of Penguin Books Ltd.)
Penguin Group (Australia), 250 Camberwell Road, Camberwell, Victoria 3124,
Australia (a division of Pearson Australia Group Pty. Ltd.)
Penguin Books India Pvt. Ltd., 11 Community Centre, Panchsheel Park,
New Delhi - 110 017, India
Penguin Group (NZ), 67 Apollo Drive, Rosedale, North Shore 0632,
New Zealand (a division of Pearson New Zealand Ltd.)
Penguin Books (South Africa) (Pty.) Ltd., 24 Sturdee Avenue,
Rosebank, Johannesburg 2196, South Africa

Penguin Books Ltd., Registered Offices:
80 Strand, London WC2R 0RL, England

First published by Signet Eclipse, an imprint of New American Library,
a division of Penguin Group (USA) Inc.

First Printing, August 2009
10 9 8 7 6 5 4 3 2 1

LIBRARY OF CONGRESS CATALOGING-IN-PUBLICATION DATA

Halliday, Dawn.
  Highland obsession/Dawn Halliday.
    p.   cm.
  ISBN 978-0-451-22701-0
  1. Triangles (Interpersonal relations)—Fiction.   2. Highlands (Scotland)—Fiction.   I. Title.
  PS3608.A54835H54   2009
  813'.6—dc22   2009003849

Set in Goudy
Designed by Ginger Legato

Printed in the United States of America

*This is for my husband: my best friend, my muse, and my partner,
whose never-ending love and support remind me
every day how lucky I am to have him.*

ACKNOWLEDGMENTS

With thanks to my super agent, Barbara Poelle—your support and enthusiasm inspire me to be the best writer I can be.

Thanks to my amazing editor, Becky Vinter, for your insightful guidance and for your belief in this story.

Thanks to all the writers who helped me so much in crafting this book: Anya Delvay, Evie Byrne, Moira McTark, Elayne Venton, and Maya Banks. I appreciate your tough critiques and your honesty as well as your hand-holding and friendship. You're the best!

Finally, huge thanks to my family and friends for being so supportive and understanding, even when I lock myself in my office and write till midnight on weekends. I love you all, and I couldn't do it without you!

HIGHLAND
OBSESSION

CHAPTER ONE

C am dismounted and tethered his horse to the spindly trunk of a juniper. Though a full moon had brightened the night sky earlier, clouds had gathered and now a soft mist fell. The horses' heavy breathing steamed the air and their intermittent snorts contrasted with the whisper of water on the bushes and grass.

Ignoring the needles scraping his arms, Cam glanced back at Mac-Lean, who remained mounted, waiting for Cam's instruction. The man and his horse formed an inky shadow in the increasing gloom.

The ground sank under Cam's feet and leaves rustled as he moved to take measure of the small valley below. He scanned the stables and few dark outbuildings hardly visible through the rain, but his gaze came to an abrupt stop when it collided with the largest dwelling in the enclave—Alan MacDonald's two-room cottage near the banks of the loch.

Sorcha and Alan were inside. Alone at last on the first night of their marriage.

Hours ago, from behind an old cairn, Cam had watched the villagers dance around a bonfire as the lively tune of their fiddles and pipes echoed through Glenfinnan. Cold to the marrow of his bones, he'd stared past the stones down at them, at *her*. Sorcha smiling shyly as

Alan led her in a reel, her skirts swishing around her calves. She looked as a young bride should: beautiful, happy. Innocent.

But she wasn't innocent.

Her father had tried—and failed—to keep a tight rein on her. Now it was Alan MacDonald's job. Cam knew Alan would do it better.

Smoke puffed in small clouds from the chimney and light spilled out from the cottage windows onto the water, making it glitter as it splashed gently against the pebbled shore.

Again Cam glanced at MacLean, who sat patiently upon his horse, reins held loosely in his meaty hands. "Wait here. Come only if I call for you."

MacLean nodded. Cam didn't allow his gaze to linger on the big man—he didn't want to see any sign of disapproval, though logic told him MacLean followed him blindly with no interest in separating right from wrong. If Cam saw disapproval in MacLean's expression, he'd be conjuring it from a blank slate.

Swiping the back of his hand over his stinging eyes, Cam stared at the cottage. He had no choice but to go down there. He had to see it through to the end. Maybe then his obsession with her would end.

"Stay out of sight," he murmured to MacLean.

"Aye, milord." MacLean's rough voice came from behind him, but Cam hardly heard. He was already striding down the wet slope toward the cottage.

Sorcha. Her name rose in his mind, peaked and receded like a delicate wave. How had it happened this way? And why, for God's sake, did it even matter? He'd thought Sorcha was a toy, an entertaining plaything. A dalliance. Nothing more. How wrong he was.

Over a month ago, her father had left Cam's service and moved his family to Glenfinnan. The day before she'd gone, she met him in his bedchamber. After they made love, she'd clung to him, and her eyes had glistened with tears as they'd murmured their farewells.

Cam assumed he'd forget about her. He predicted he'd easily find another skirt to amuse him. Instead, he'd thought about her daily. He ached to see her, to hold her again. To touch her silken skin. To see her generous smile, then kiss her into submission.

When he learned of her upcoming marriage to Alan MacDonald, something had snapped in his consciousness. Thoughts of her began to occupy his every waking moment. He'd tried to stop. He'd schooled himself to restraint and resolutely kept out of her affairs.

Today was her wedding day. And, God help him, today he hadn't been able to stay away.

He reached the edge of Alan's cottage and placed his palm flat on one of the cold, wet stones. Slowly, he walked around the back to the closest window, dragging his fingers across the jagged surfaces of the stones as he went. Now completely hidden from MacLean's sight, Cam peered inside.

There was Sorcha, closer to the window than he'd expected, facing away from him. She stood still, her dark hair a satin waterfall cascading down her back. Beyond her, the large, cluttered space contained a rough-hewn dressing table, several chairs and chests, a long bench, and a bed built into the wall. A peat fire flickered in the fireplace at the room's far end. Rustic, but comfortable. Nevertheless, far below Alan's means.

Cam sensed movement deeper within and ducked away, his pulse surging to a frantic cadence.

Breathing heavily, he leaned back against the wall. Out of all the men in the world, why did it have to be his closest friend who'd taken her to wife?

Cam turned his face up to the rain and savored the feel of the stones digging deep into the flesh of his shoulders. What in the devil was he doing, slinking about like a common low-bred thief? Longing for something he could never have? He hated himself for it.

Yet he couldn't stop.

He turned and looked in the window once again. Alan sat on the edge of the bed now. He'd removed his plaid, and his white linen shirt covered him to midthigh. He spoke softly, much in the same way Cam had seen him calm a jittery horse.

Sorcha took a step away from the window. Cam couldn't see her expression, only the dark fall of her hair shimmering in the light of the tallow candles as she moved. She wore a thin linen nightdress that shifted provocatively with the sway of her hips.

Alan was ignorant of Cam and Sorcha's previous carnal acquaintance. If he knew, he never would have married her. Cam was familiar enough with his friend's personality to know this as absolute fact. It was clear Sorcha hadn't revealed anything of her experience during the short period of their engagement.

Ultimately, Cam couldn't blame her for hiding the truth. Her father had placed her in this position, and she would die before dishonoring him. Furthermore, her blasted Highland morals wouldn't allow her to embarrass or anger Alan, her laird and future husband.

And now they were married. Joined together . . . as one . . . until death. Cam winced. *Bloody hell.*

Would she continue to play the part of the timid virgin tonight? Would she cry out as she had when Cam took her maidenhead? After she had made that small, frightened noise, he had frozen in place, hating to have caused her pain. But she'd clutched him tight and whispered to him, saying it was all right and encouraging him to continue. Soon she had arched up to meet him, making a little sound of pleasure with each thrust.

Cam would never forget that night. When he had broken through the shield of her virginity, her reaction had been honest. With Alan, it would be a deception. Cam tried to take some comfort in that, and failed.

Sorcha sat on the edge of the bed beside Alan, turning so Cam could see her profile. Her eyes were downcast. A lock of hair fell across her face, and she reached up to brush it away with trembling fingers.

So she did choose to play the pious fraud. Cam grimaced, clutched the windowsill, and watched.

* * *

Sorcha couldn't stop shaking. It wasn't that Alan MacDonald didn't appeal to her—in fact, the opposite was true. He was handsome in a rugged, fierce way, yet there was a kindness about him that inspired trust. Only a month had passed since his return to Scotland after a nearly twenty-year absence, yet the MacDonalds of the Glen already respected their laird as if he'd never left at all.

She was not as quick to trust as her kinsmen. She didn't know this man at all. Alan had spent so many years on English soil, he was little more than a stranger to her.

She possessed only one memory of him before he and his mother had gone. They'd visited Camdonn Castle to see her parents. Sorcha had been just a small child and he'd paid her no attention, but she'd clung to her mother as he'd cast narrow, furious glances at everyone, his lips turned down in a scowl. Later, she'd been told the poor lad was angry because he didn't want to leave Scotland. Nobody blamed him.

He'd finally returned to acknowledge his birthright—his lands on the southern side of Loch Shiel, bordered by the Earl of Camdonn's property on one side and the village of Glenfinnan on the other.

Within a week of his arrival in the Highlands, Alan had met with her father and negotiated their betrothal. Her father was delighted, but Sorcha had never been so afraid. And Sorcha was not the kind of woman who frightened easily.

"Come, Sorcha. Lie beside me."

Trying to calm her roiling tension, she turned to him and lowered herself to her side on the bed, her body rigid.

Alan scooted down beside her. Facing her, he stroked her hair behind her ear. She shuddered at the intimate contact. Only one other man had touched her like this before, but that was such a different man. Dark where Alan was light. Whipcord lean while Alan's body rippled with muscle. Everyone was suspicious of the Earl of Camdonn and approached him with anything from guarded wariness to outright hostility, while Alan had earned the clan's trust in a matter of days.

"Such beautiful hair you have, Sorcha," Alan murmured. "Soft and silky, and black as a raven's."

Would he still think so in ten years when it started to go gray, like her mother's had? Mama had died giving birth to Sorcha's brother . . . would Sorcha die in childbed too?

The years stretched before her, brimming with the unknown and now under the control of the man lying beside her. She forced a smile and pushed out a response to his compliment. "Thank you. That is very kind of you to say."

"I'll go slowly," he said. "I know you are frightened."

Sorcha blew out a breath and nodded, but she couldn't meet his eyes. Yes, she was frightened, but not for the reason he imagined. She had experienced sexual congress in many different forms, in many different places and positions, and she had taken great pleasure from it.

She didn't fear this man's inevitable invasion of her body. No, she feared the future. Living with a stranger day in and day out. Would they grow to love or despise each other? Would he be kind to her or cruel? Years down the line there might be a brood of children for her to care for. What would her life be like then? Would Alan take mistresses? Most of the men she knew did. Even her father, though he was always discreet, kept a woman on the mountain.

She would never take another lover. She didn't know what her life with Alan would be. Nor did she know whether he'd rule her body as Cam had, though she supposed she'd learn soon enough. In the end, it didn't matter whether Alan satisfied her. She was married now, and she would honor that to the death. She would never bring shame upon herself or her husband.

She feared for her future. For her life. Surely it was not so odd to do so. Would she die a year hence, in this very cottage, in childbirth? Or would she survive it to birth a dozen babies? Would Alan ever return to England? Would he take her with him?

She knew nothing, and it frightened her.

His fingers, warm against her skin, paused at her temples. "Sorcha, we are hardly acquainted with each other, and I was thinking it would be best to wait awhile before I got you with child."

Sorcha's breath caught, and she spoke without thinking. "What?"

His palm cupped her cheek. "Are you anxious to have children, lass?"

"No." She drew in a breath and shook her head, stumbling over her words. "What I mean to say is that I should very much like to bear your sons, of course, but . . ." Her voice dwindled. She felt so awkward, so green and uncertain in her own skin.

He shook his head, reading her easily. "Don't tell me what you think I want to hear. Be honest with me. Speak the truth."

"My mother died in childbirth when I was ten years old," she blurted. She clamped her lips shut. How to explain that she'd held on to her younger sister as her mother suffered horrifically? That she'd always feared a similar fate?

"Aye, I'd heard that, and I'm sorry for it." Alan's hand moved to her shoulder and stroked down her arm. Tiny hairs rose in a line on her skin, following the path of his fingers. "It is natural you'd fear it after losing your mother in such a way."

"But don't you want a son?"

"I do, eventually." Alan's fingers laced through hers, coaxing her clenched hand to open. His soothing touch was beginning to calm her. "I would like sons *and* daughters. But we have the rest of our lives for that, don't we?"

Sorcha swallowed hard. "Aye, we do."

He spoke gently. "How much do you know of how children are made, lass?"

She blinked at him. She knew he thought her a virgin, but surely he didn't mistake her for a complete innocent. Perhaps he'd languished in sprawling English mansions for too long and forgotten that the people of the Highlands lived in close quarters. She formed her words carefully. "I know everything, I think. Before my mother died, we lived in a one-room cottage. I am the eldest of four children."

He sighed—it sounded like a sigh of relief. "I don't want to hurt you. Or surprise you."

After her experiences with the earl, not much Alan could do to her body would surprise her. "Thank you," she said in true appreciation for his kindness.

This was so different from her first time with Cam. That joining had been rushed and surreptitious, on the floor of an unlocked closet, where anyone could walk in at any moment. Cam had slowed only after he had first thrust impatiently into her, and she had whimpered at the sudden, sharp pain. Stricken with guilt, he had apologized over and over for hurting her as he'd rained kisses upon her face and neck.

This time the circumstances were different. Premeditated, slow, calm. She and Alan were husband and wife, taking their time, in the private comfort of their own home. Alan moved at a leisurely pace, as if he had the rest of his life to make love to her. She supposed he did, after all.

"I will spend outside of you, for now. But you must realize that's not as fulfilling for a man. And it's certainly not guaranteed, though it will reduce the chances of my seed taking root within you."

To keep from saying "thank you" like a fool again, she merely nodded. Cam had spent on her belly and in her mouth most of the time, though in his fervent haste he did come against her womb more than once. She was lucky he hadn't gotten her with child.

More than lucky. She knew her dalliance with the earl could have cost her everything. Yet at the time, even that knowledge hadn't stopped her. She had lived her days desperate to see him again, to feel his hands on her body, to succumb to the sensation of him inside her.

She'd known her actions were impulsive and foolish. Perhaps that had been part of the pleasure in it—the innate excitement in furtive trysts and secret rendezvous.

When her father had taken her from Camdonn Castle to live in Glenfinnan, she'd secretly mourned losing Cam, but their separation was for the best. She'd never been enough of a fool to think there was a future for them—she was a factor's daughter and he an earl, for heaven's sake.

Alan grinned suddenly, jolting her attention back to the here and now. This man was her future, not the Earl of Camdonn. She'd best remember that.

"It seems odd that one of our first conversations should be of such a personal nature. But I want to be candid with you, Sorcha. I believe honesty to be the basis of a strong marriage."

She smiled back at him, and this time it was real. "As do I."

And then her own hypocrisy struck her. She truly believed honesty was important to a marriage. Yet she lay here, deceiving her husband on their first night together, playing the part of the virgin wife. What a liar she was.

She hated lying. It was no way to start a marriage based on trust. Yet if she revealed her past with the Earl of Camdonn, it would only bring pain to them both. Alan would be furious that she wasn't an innocent as her father had promised.

Her father had told her that her virginity was important to Alan, and though she'd opened her mouth to blurt the truth a hundred times in the past weeks, she hadn't been able to force the words out. The truth was too painful, too raw, and in the end, she couldn't bring herself to disappoint her family. The laird honored them by his wish to marry her, and she couldn't bear the pain she'd cause if the truth were revealed.

In any case, the men had been too distracted to pay her much attention. The country was rising in rebellion, and her upcoming nuptials were overshadowed by talk of whether the MacDonalds would join the effort to remove King George from the throne of England and replace him with King James, who currently languished in exile in France.

She'd never thought herself a weakling but now realized she was. She'd either dishonor herself by lying or dishonor herself by speaking the truth. Both ways, she would lose.

A shudder shook her shoulders, but she stilled them, resolute. Only tonight would she pretend to be something she wasn't, and henceforth she would be true to her husband. It was for the greater good. When honesty would serve only to cause needless suffering for all of them, what was the point of it?

Alan's fingers touched hers, then traced the curve of her hip. His touch was so warm, so gentle. "You are lovely, Sorcha."

He was stroking her again, trying to calm her. His efforts made her like him all the more. "You—" Her voice broke, but she tried again, unused to offering compliments to the opposite sex. "You are quite bonnie yourself, Alan MacDonald."

Tentatively, she reached up to trace his square-shaped jaw with her fingertips. She brushed her thumb over his nose, running over a small bump on its ridge. Continuing upward, she stroked his broad forehead and skimmed his hairline, touching the soft, burnished gold hair that curled around his temples.

She stared into his eyes. By far, they were his best feature. A crystalline blue, they were framed by pale but impossibly long lashes and thick eyebrows, and their edges crinkled when he smiled. When she gazed into them, she felt as if she dove into his soul only to find a perfect sapphire, pure and real. It was no wonder that every person he met instinctively liked him.

She ran her fingertip across his full bottom lip. Quick as a flash, he grasped her wrist, holding her hand in place, and his mouth closed around her finger. His eyes fluttered closed as he suckled her finger gently, reverently. The warm, moist sensation traveled under her skin and down her body to her center. Her blood rushed there, heating her, making her flush and open for him.

When her breaths became shallow, he released her. "You taste like sunshine, Sorcha."

She laughed shakily. "How does sunshine taste?"

"Like a hot summer's day, blooming heather, sweet wheat." He didn't return her laugh. His eyes narrowed into thin blue slits as he stared at her. When he spoke again, his voice emerged low and rough. "I'm going to kiss you now."

Her chest tightened, and she could scarcely draw in a breath as his lips came down over hers. He tugged her shift upward and cool air brushed over her buttocks.

Her hands clenched and unclenched at her sides. Her finger was still wet from his mouth. Her skin was fired with sensitivity from head to toe. She felt the smoothness of the quilt beneath her. The rough scratch of the linen as her shift inched up her waist. The heat of his body clashing with the chilled air. His lips, so soft, warm. His tongue pressing inside her mouth, exploring her as if she were a delicate treasure. His hand slipping beneath her shift and closing over her breast, teasing her peaked nipple until she released a low gasp with every breath.

Her nails dug into the skin of her palms, and the sting of pain forced her to open her hands. She moved one arm around his waist, aware of his nudity beneath his shirt. Was he hard for her yet? Did she dare touch him?

No. No, not yet. He thought her a virgin. But oh, how she wanted to stroke Alan's cock, feel him grow stiff in her hand. She gasped again, stunned by the sudden strength of her desire for him.

Alan drew away, no doubt misinterpreting her noise. His eyes flared with concern. "I'll make it feel good for you, Sorcha. Open yourself to me." His hand slid away from her breast, moving down her belly to the vee of her thighs.

"Let me touch you," he continued softly, gazing at her. She knew without feeling him that he was hard indeed, erect and desperate for her, but he also wanted to make her comfortable, so she wouldn't feel too much pain when he broke through her virgin's barrier.

Slipping his fingers between her legs, Alan groaned. "You're wet for me already, lass. I can help ease the way. Let me."

"Aye, Alan," she murmured, closing her eyes. "Please."

He moved down her body, nudging her knees wider apart. She was glad Alan's cottage was away from the village and the surrounding structures were empty of servants tonight. There was no other soul within a mile, and she could bare herself to the window and scream her pleasure as loudly as she desired—something she could never do at Camdonn Castle.

Alan was still for a moment, and she looked down at him. His eyes gleamed as he stared at her quim. Using his thumbs, he spread her wide, then with the flat of his tongue, bent his head and licked her from top to bottom. She froze, stunned by the sheer carnality of the act. Then she jerked away, but he clasped her thighs, pinning them against the quilt.

Cam hadn't done this. He'd used his fingers, explored everywhere, but he had never touched her there with his mouth.

Alan raised his head and smiled at her, his lips shiny from her juices. "Yes," he confirmed. "You are the sun."

And then he proceeded to devour her. Sorcha fisted her hands in the green and blue blanket and allowed herself to fall into the pleasure.

He played with her clitoris, using his tongue as a tool to tease it and stroke it until it was so engorged, Sorcha was certain she would burst.

"Please," she panted. "I want, I need . . ." But she couldn't voice it. A part of her held on to a small measure of sanity and prevented her from saying any more.

Alan chuckled against her sensitive skin. "Yes, lass. I know."

Without removing his mouth from her, he inserted one finger inside her, working her, though Lord knew she didn't need to be worked.

"More," she gasped. Her demand bordered on folly, but she couldn't bring herself to care.

He hummed against her, and she would have bucked off the bed had he not held her down. He drew his finger out and pushed a second one in. Now he pumped her wholeheartedly, without reserve, as if he knew she could take what he had to give. His fingertips stroked her inner walls, ramping up her pleasure with every thrust. He lowered his head again, and when his tongue swiped over her sensitive bud, an uncontrollable moan of pleasure erupted from her throat. Spasms racked her body, intense and overwhelming. Her channel clutched at his fingers, holding them deep within her as if she'd never let him go.

"My wife is a wanton," Alan murmured.

She panicked. She'd been too lustful, too amorous. Surely he had discovered her secret. Every muscle in her body tensed, abolishing the languor brought on by the orgasm. *Please, God, let Alan believe this is all new to me.*

In a way, in fact, it was. Alan was so different from Cam.

Keeping his fingers buried inside her, Alan moved up her body, spreading kisses over her skin. He had hiked up his shirt and his cock rubbed against her thigh before settling against her mound. His expression softened at her distress. "I meant that as a compliment, Sorcha. I want you to be a wanton. I want you to lose yourself. I want you to scream from my touch. Every day, if possible." He smiled. "It is just as I had hoped. We will do well together, I think."

She gave a jerk of a nod, unable to shake the fear rooted deep inside her. But then he began to stroke her again, making her passage tighten and shudder around him.

He buried his face in her hair and his lips brushed against her ear. "Are you ready for me, wife?"

With tears welling in her eyes, Sorcha nodded. She opened her legs and sank her teeth into her lower lip, bracing herself for his invasion.

Cam observed it all, unable to tear his gaze from the scene unfolding before him. Alan touching her, tasting her—something Cam had never done. Why?

There was no time to ponder his oversight at the moment. All Cam knew was that he wanted to taste her, he wanted it desperately, and he wanted to kill Alan for being the only one who could.

From this vantage, he could see flashes of Sorcha's sex, glistening red and ripe. How could she give herself over to Alan so easily? Could she have forgotten all those nights she'd spent with Cam? *No. No, it was impossible. She couldn't forget him. He wouldn't allow it.*

Cam brushed his hand over his breeches in an attempt to soothe his aching cock, to no avail. He was stiff as a pike, and as long as he watched Sorcha, panting and flushed, with her shift pushed up high around her waist, it would remain so.

Her scream as she came pierced through the windowpane. Cam shifted uncomfortably and unbuttoned his breeches in an attempt to relieve some of the pressure.

Alan had crawled up alongside Sorcha, his fingers still buried deep inside her. He murmured something into her ear. Christ, but Cam wished he knew what the man had said. Sorcha squeezed her eyes shut and opened her pale legs, revealing her shiny, slick folds to Cam. Alan withdrew his fingers from her and pressed them to her lips, speaking softly. Her tongue darted out, and her eyes widened as she tasted herself on his skin.

Cam slipped his hand into his breeches and grasped himself, biting back a yelp at the coldness of his palm against the hot skin of his cock. The shock faded, though, the heat quickly overwhelming the cold.

Alan shifted himself over Sorcha, reached down to position himself at her entrance, and inched forward. Cam supposed the halting movement was an unnecessary effort to diminish Sorcha's pain. Beneath Alan, Sorcha arched up and cried out.

Good work, Sorcha love. That should convince him.

Cam jerked on his cock, blinking back tears. God, he was pitiful. The last time he'd wept he was seven years old and his father had beaten him for running away from home to chase after his governess, who was to marry and leave him forever.

He hated Alan. This wasn't fair. Sorcha should be his. She *was* his. Why did he have to be born into this godforsaken position in life? He hated the earldom. He wanted his own picturesque cottage. He wanted to be the one joyfully fucking Sorcha for the first time.

Alan pumped into her now, the muscles in his arse flexing with every thrust. Shivering with cold, lust, and barely contained emotion, Cam tugged on his cock in time to each of Alan's thrusts.

Sorcha's fingers dug into Alan's muscled back, so hard that little pinpricks of blood seeped through the coarse white material of his shirt. Her head moved back and forth as Alan's thrusts built in frequency. He fucked her deep, and though she wasn't a virgin, it looked as though he pushed her to the limit.

Damn him. Damn him for giving her pleasure. Cam pulled on his cock, groaning as his fingertips scraped over the delicate skin of the head. Alan moved at a frenzied pace now, and Sorcha's head whipped from side to side. Her legs wrapped around Alan's thighs, her toes curled. And then, to Cam's surprise, Alan wrenched out of her. Cam came, spurting over his hands and his breeches, just as Alan released onto Sorcha's stomach.

Alan and Sorcha stared at each other for a long moment before Alan leaned down and kissed her gently on the lips. Then he gathered her close and held her, his seed smearing between their bodies as they lay pressed against each other, their chests rising and falling with their heavy breaths.

But it was not a release for Cam. It was a call to action. Though his hands and breeches were slick with come, his body remained tense and unfulfilled.

He would not be this pitiful creature, standing in the rain and frigging himself while he wept. He was the bloody Earl of Camdonn, not some inexperienced lad with his hand to his heart pining over a lost love.

Sorcha MacDonald belonged to him first, and by God, he'd bloody well have her again. Alan MacDonald was a nobody, a lowly Scottish laird of little means. He didn't deserve her.

Curse the repercussions to hell.

Turning away from the window, Cam buttoned his breeches, wiping his sticky hands on the wool as he rounded the corner of the cottage and made a low, trilling birdcall to summon MacLean.

As soon as Cam saw the shadowy figure thundering down the hill leading Cam's mount by the reins, he drew his sword and ran to the front door of the cottage. He tried pushing it open, but it was bolted from the inside, so he stepped back and kicked through the weak planks, gaining strength from anger and need.

He barreled inside to see Alan rushing through the doorway of the bedroom, naked, Sorcha at his heels. He reeled to a stop as Cam stalked toward him, sword held at the ready.

"Stay back, Sorcha!" Alan bellowed. Sorcha halted at the threshold, her green eyes wide and her face pale with shock.

"What the hell are you doing here?" Alan thundered. He glanced at Sorcha, who stood in all her naked glory in the doorway, and then whipped his glare back to Cam. "Damn you, Cam," he ground out, teeth bared. "Get out of my house. *Now.*"

Just the thought of Cam seeing her naked had driven Alan into a fury. What would he do if he knew Cam had seen that body time and again, if he knew how frequently, how wildly Cam had possessed it?

Cam narrowed his eyes. Remembering the look of adoration Alan had given Sorcha after he came, Cam lunged closer, allowing all his righteous fury to show on his face. Before the man could react, Cam kneed him, hard, in the balls. Alan's breath exploded in a whoosh, and he doubled over with a groan, clutching his crotch. Making a small sound of dismay, Sorcha leaped toward Alan.

Keeping his sword trained on Alan, Cam flicked a glance at Sorcha, stalling her in her tracks. "You're coming with me," he said flatly.

Understanding flared in her green eyes, but just as she turned to scramble away, Cam lunged at her, hooked his arm around her waist, heaved her over his shoulder.

"No!" Alan roared. White-faced, he dove for them, but MacLean, who'd been standing by the splintered remains of the front door, drew his sword and rushed between Alan and Cam.

Sorcha came alive as Cam wheeled around and took his first step toward the exit. "What are you doing?" she shouted, pounding his back. "What are you doing, Cam? Stop it! Put me down, now!"

He grimly wondered whether she was aware of the informal way in which she'd addressed him. If Alan had heard, surely he would realize there had been something between them. She kicked and screamed and scratched at him, but Cam held her firmly. He expected such treatment—he already knew that as deliciously submissive as she was in bed, she could be a wildcat when she considered herself wronged.

"Hold him off," he shot over his shoulder to MacLean, who held his broadsword steadily trained on Alan's neck.

Cam sheathed his own sword as he strode outside. Mounting his horse with a fuming, slippery, naked woman wasn't the easiest thing to do—it would be nigh impossible one-handed. He managed it without grace, flopping her over the docile gelding, then pinning her down as he mounted behind her. When he had her seated in front of him, still trying to squirm away, he threw his plaid over her shoulders to cover her nakedness. Then he grabbed his reins and slid his arm between the edges of the cloth to lock around her bare waist, still wet with Alan's semen.

Alan's enraged shouts sounded from the doorway behind him, but Cam did not spare him a glance. Instead, his lips twitched. *Sweet victory.* She would be his once more.

He turned the horse toward Camdonn Castle just as Sorcha's teeth sank into his arm.

CHAPTER TWO

"**G**oddamn you!" Alan ignored the searing pain in his balls and the nausea boiling low in his stomach. Fury swept through him, angry, hot, and painful. He tried to dodge past the enormous man blocking his way, but the tip of the sword nicked Alan's shoulder, and a hot line of blood trickled down his chest. "You bastard," Alan growled. "Let me pass!"

Beyond the man's bulk, he saw Cam toss Sorcha on a horse.

The unreality of the situation slammed into him. Impossibly, unbelievably, the Earl of Camdonn—*his friend Cam*—had just broken into his home and abducted his new wife. What in the name of God did Cam think he was doing?

Raindrops shimmered over her pale, bare skin. Cam threw a red tartan plaid over her, his movements clumsy because she writhed and squirmed in his grasp. She put up one hell of a fight with her small body, but her attempts proved ineffective against the height and strength of the Earl of Camdonn.

As Cam urged the horse to a gallop, Sorcha's eyes met Alan's for the briefest of seconds. The wild look of fear he saw there made him roar in frustration. His wife was being abducted—by Cam, of all people—and Alan, damn besotted fool that he was, couldn't protect her.

Alan had let his guard down. The pleasure Sorcha brought him had made him soft. He had allowed this to happen. He had failed to protect what was his. It was his fault and his responsibility to make things right.

Alan turned his glare to the brute blocking his exit. He knew the man—Angus MacLean. MacLean trailed everywhere after Cam like a damned lap dog.

"Get the hell out of my way."

MacLean shook his head, and his pockmarked face twisted into a sneer. "Nay."

Alan shifted to a fighting stance. He was naked and vulnerable without a weapon, but goddammit, he wasn't about to let that prevent him from going after Sorcha.

MacLean didn't move his sword tip from Alan's chest. "You just stay put there, MacDonald, and sit tight till his lordship finishes with yer wife and brings her back." He paused and frowned, his brow furrowed in confusion. "Make that *if* his lordship brings her back."

Alan's lip curled. "Go to hell, MacLean." He offered up a silent prayer that MacLean was as idiotic with a sword as he was with everything else. Alan was certain Cam kept MacLean near only to intimidate, because intimidate he did—he was a giant of a man, half a head taller than the doorframe and almost as wide.

MacLean waved the sword menacingly. His movements were clumsy and ungraceful, not the precise swipes of a skilled swordsman.

"I dinna want to kill ye, MacDonald."

"Well, that's a good thing, MacLean, because I've no desire to die by your hand," Alan said evenly.

MacLean lowered the sword, and a grin played about his lips. No doubt he actually believed Alan would give up and passively allow his onetime friend to carry off his naked wife on their wedding night.

Alan ducked his head and rammed his body into MacLean's, using every ounce of power he could muster.

"Oof!" MacLean's breath wheezed out of him. He reeled backward until his beefy body slammed the edge of the doorframe, causing the cottage to shudder and the sword to slide from his fat fingers. It crashed onto the wet flagstones just as MacLean's feet slipped out from under him. He landed flat on his back, half inside the cottage, half out. Alan leaped on top of him and slammed his fist into the big man's jaw before he could regain his bearings.

Alan scrambled for the sword, grabbing the hilt just as MacLean thrust a giant fist into his wounded shoulder. Gritting his teeth against the jarring pain, Alan smashed the sword hilt into the giant's soft stomach.

Groaning, MacLean wrapped his arms around himself and curled into a ball. Alan leveled two punches at his torso, but MacLean suddenly possessed no interest in fighting back. As a disgusted Alan jumped off him, the big man brought his knees into his chest and rocked back and forth, whimpering about his abused belly. "Curse ye, MacDonald. You've busted my gut. Now I'll die and 'twill be yer fault," he sobbed.

It'd be a blessing to humanity if he did die, Alan thought, but kept his mouth shut as he jerkily donned his shirt and plaid. In a few seconds, he had mounted MacLean's oversized bay and urged it toward Camdonn Castle.

The castle rested on the flat top of a high spit of land jutting into the loch. Cam slowed his horse as they followed the twisting, narrow path that led up to the castle gates. The drizzle had stopped and the moon once again spilled light over the countryside. The grounds shimmered and glistened in the silvery beams.

Consisting of a medieval keep now used as the living quarters, a dozen outbuildings, bountiful gardens, and a wide, green courtyard, Cam's family seat was not only imposing, but magnificent. A testament to the power his family held in the Highlands.

Sorcha sat in front of him, quiet now, as tense as a bowstring pulled taut. She couldn't fathom what Cam thought he was doing by stealing her from her husband's bed. But fear and panic had given way to calm, and a slow, simmering anger.

It was over between them. Over for nearly two months, and sealed today by her marriage to Alan MacDonald. Did Cam honestly think she'd come willingly?

No Highlander should dishonor a woman in this way, and most Highlanders wouldn't dare to for fear of reprisal from their clan. But Cam was an earl, above reproach. He wielded the strongest authority in this region of Scotland, his power rivaled only by the Duke of Argyll far to the south and the Earl of Seaforth to the north. Cam could do anything he pleased, and he knew it.

Sorcha had drawn blood with her fingernails and teeth in at least half a dozen places on Cam's body, and that gave her some consolation. But fighting him was like fighting steel. When he'd yanked her against his warm, solid body and informed her casually that struggling was no use, that she should save her strength for his bed, she had fallen into a state of rigid calm. She conceded defeat for the time being, if only to conserve her energy for the larger battle ahead. And for that, she needed to let go of her fury and panic and think rationally.

She could smell the whisky on his breath, and she feared he was in his cups. The way he had taken her from Alan's bed—it was either the act of a madman or someone who was completely sotted. Cam had never given her any indication that he would do something so utterly insane as to abduct her on her wedding night. If he was capable of going to such lengths, there was no telling what else he might do.

As one of his men came running toward them carrying a lantern, he drew on the reins and waited. Sorcha pulled away from him and sat a little straighter, staring directly ahead. She yanked the plaid tightly around her frozen body. She was warm only where his legs encased her buttocks and outer thighs.

"Rouse some of the men," Cam told the approaching guard. "There might be trouble."

The man nodded, and she could see from the corner of her eye that he doggedly kept his gaze averted from her. "Aye, milord."

Cam glanced back at the path they had just climbed. She followed his gaze and saw no evidence they'd been followed. Where was Alan? Surely he would do something. Surely he wouldn't let Cam get away with this.

But what could he do? Alan was a minor laird, and while his men were loyal, they were few, and he had little recourse against a powerful lord like Cam.

"Send six men to MacDonald's and bring MacLean home. If he's under attack"—Cam paused, frowning—"try your damndest not to shed too much blood," he finished.

Sorcha's body convulsed, and a strangled sound emerged from her throat before she could prevent it. He tightened his arm around her waist in warning, and his plaid slipped from Sorcha's forehead, revealing her face to the guard. His jaw went slack and recognition flared in his eyes.

"Go now," Cam growled.

Dropping his gaze, the man recovered and made a quick bow. "Aye, milord." Straightening, he risked a final glance at Sorcha, who lifted her head and glared daggers at him, before he turned and strode away.

"Too much of a coward to kill him yourself, Cam," Sorcha whispered, staring after the man, "that you must order your henchmen to do it for you?" She wrapped her arms tightly around her body to prevent herself from shaking.

"Hush." He dismounted and lifted Sorcha off. She was stiff in his arms as he set her down and straightened the plaid over her shoulders. "Alan MacDonald can take care of himself. It's clear you don't know much about him."

She pressed her lips into a thin line and remained silent. Inwardly, she raged at him, cursed him for a fool. What had he done? In one fell swoop, he had put her well-being in jeopardy. He was so self-absorbed, he'd probably not even considered the repercussions this mad abduction would have in her life. Her marriage was in jeopardy—Alan would likely reject her now. And her position as a respectable woman . . .

"Now, it's your choice, Sorcha. You can walk inside on your own power, or I will carry you slung over my shoulder like a sack of grain. Which shall it be?"

She met his gaze full-on, letting her anger show in her eyes. "You may trust that you will never carry me like a sack of grain, for I will scratch your eyes out before I allow you to throw me over your shoulder again."

Cam shrugged carelessly, rousing her ire even more. She clenched her fists at her sides. *Arrogant bastard!*

"Very well, then. You will walk." He gestured gallantly at the living quarters, a rectangular stone building with a square tower rising from one end. "After you, my lady."

She surveyed her surroundings rapidly, calculating her odds at escape. It was hopeless. Even if Cam didn't catch her, and given his long muscular legs he could easily do so, the gates were closed and well guarded.

Tossing her head, she turned and marched toward the building, holding the plaid tightly wrapped around her body. Her feet were bare, but she didn't wince as she walked proudly across the stone clearing. The wool covered her only to her knees, and the heat of Cam's gaze simmered over her bare calves as she stepped onto the landing and opened the front door.

A servant appeared in the doorway leading to the cellar stairs but slunk away upon glancing at Cam's face. Sorcha resisted turning to see his expression.

She hesitated as a sudden, unwelcome despair flooded through her. She knew this building so very well. She had explored every part of it during her childhood. Until August, her father had served as the old earl's factor, and they had lived in a cottage on the grounds along with her younger brothers and sister. When Cam's father had died last winter,

Cam had returned from England to manage his inheritance. After helping Cam straighten out his affairs, Sorcha's father had left the earl's service to spend the remainder of his days with his clansmen in Glenfinnan.

"I suppose I am not expected to return to my old bed in the cottage, my lord." She hated the defeated, pleading quality in her voice.

"You will go to my bedchamber," he said softly. He came up behind her, set his hands on her shoulders, and pulled her back against his solid chest. He bowed his head and took in a deep breath against her hair. His lips brushed over her ear. "You know where it is."

"Aye, I do." She stiffened under his touch, and he pushed her forward, turning her toward the staircase that led up to his bedchamber.

Sorcha sucked in a breath, but then calmed herself as she released it. He wouldn't hurt her. That rare balance in Cam—the edge between stark, unpolished strength and generous tenderness—was what had attracted her to him to begin with. Cam possessed an innate compassion and kindness he hid from the world but had revealed to her in their lovemaking. She had always felt safe with him, from their first touch. As mad as his actions had been tonight, she couldn't believe Cam would use violence on her.

She glanced at him over her shoulder and spoke softly. "I don't fear you. You may think you have power over me, my lord. That might have once been true, but no longer."

His dark eyes hardened. "Go."

She turned back to the stairs and stared at them but didn't move. "You dishonor me on my wedding night," she said dully. He already had shamed her, and now he would make it worse by bedding her not two hours after she'd lain with her husband for the first time.

"Honor has naught to do with this."

Oh, it had everything to do with this.

"You intend to rape me in your bedchamber. You wish to make my husband a cuckold." Even as she said it, she could not bring herself to truly fear him raping her. But she did fear his bedchamber, the memories it possessed, the power he had once held over her. He stood close enough that she could smell him, spicy sandalwood with a raw, masculine musk beneath. Lord help her, but as much as her heart rebelled against him, her body remembered his touch, even after his crazed behavior.

Cam tightened his hands on her shoulders. When he spoke, his voice was husky. "It is me you want, Sorcha. I am the one you desire in your bed. Not Alan MacDonald, and not anyone else."

A tremble rippled down her spine. Yes, she'd wanted Cam, but that was in the past. Earlier tonight, she had wanted Alan. Wanted him badly.

Even if her body still desired Cam, she'd vowed to stay true to Alan until death. She could not live with herself if she broke that promise.

She spoke, forming her words carefully. "I gave Alan MacDonald my vow under God tonight. The instant I made that vow, everything else ceased to matter. I am his now. No one else's."

"No."

"Yes. I belong to him and no other."

"It isn't too late."

Sorcha laughed bitterly.

He slid his hand down her back over the rough wool of the plaid and gave her a soft nudge at the base of her spine. "Go upstairs."

She stepped forward. One foot in front of the other until she stood at the bottom of the staircase. He remained still, watching her, but then closed in behind her as she began to walk up. He followed her to the landing at the top and they progressed down the long hall. Floorboards creaked under their feet. When she reached the door to his bedchamber, she stopped and stared at it. Images of what had happened between them inside flashed through her mind. He had taken her on the green and black silk counterpane, on the hard planks of the floor, against a woolen wall hanging, on a bed of furs before the fire. In every position—her on top, on her knees, on her back, her legs wrapped around his waist . . .

Very deliberately, he set his palms flat against the door, boxing her in with his arms. "Do you remember how we loved in there, Sorcha? The pleasure we shared?"

Oh, she remembered, but she would not admit to it. She tilted her face at him with false bravado. "You are speaking of the fornication we indulged in? The sin?"

"But it didn't feel like sin to either of us, did it?"

She looked back to the smooth, glossy planks of the door. "If I rot in hell for my sins, for certain it is God's will."

Cam tensed. "I imagine God desires us to reconcile our feelings for each other before he sends you to a life of servitude to a man you don't know."

"I have already reconciled my feelings. I thought you had too."

"You have entered into a marriage under false pretenses, so surely nothing is set in stone. You may have played the innocent on your wedding night, but when Alan learns of your lies—"

Her head whipped around. "How do you know—?" she gasped.

He smiled, nuzzling her ear with his lips. "I watched, beautiful Sorcha. I watched you spread your bonnie legs for him and play the innocent."

Her body shuddered violently. She snapped her mouth shut, but her lips wobbled at their edges. He had eavesdropped on her tentative coming together with Alan earlier. She felt violated, the beauty of her joining with Alan forever sullied.

Finally, she forced herself to speak through her tight throat. "How . . . dare you?"

"If you do not want to be watched, perhaps you should consider having curtains made so passersby cannot witness how sweetly you open your legs for strangers."

She hated him, hated his arrogance. It was so . . . *English*.

He reached down and pushed on the handle. The door swung open. Cam's manservant jumped to his feet from the wing chair beside the fire.

"My lord?"

"Go, Duncan. I've no need of your services tonight."

Duncan bowed and met Sorcha's horrified gaze, his eyes widening as he recognized her. Cam nudged Sorcha inside so his servant could pass.

"He is my father's friend," she whispered, looking after him as he disappeared down the hall. Tears sprang to her eyes, but she wouldn't let them fall. "Duncan MacDougall will make certain all of Glenfinnan hears of this." Her body quaked and she dropped her face into her hands. "Everyone will know I came to your bedchamber tonight, on the night of my wedding, that I— Oh Lord, I am disgraced. Alan will be—"

"Alan can bloody well take care of himself!" Cam spat. "Why do you care so much about Alan when he is nothing to you?"

Seeming to require something upon which to vent his fury, Cam slammed the door shut.

She looked coldly up at him. "Alan is an honorable man. And he is my husband."

He gave her an equally frosty stare. "I know Alan MacDonald's character far more intimately than you."

"You have offended him. He will demand satisfaction."

Cam gave a harsh laugh, drew aside a delicate embroidered green and black silk bed curtain, and brusquely tied it to the post before sitting on the edge of the mattress. "What can he do? He knows he cannot rise against so lofty a personage as the Earl of Camdonn." He said the last with bitterness, pushing his hand through his short dark hair.

She remained in place standing just inside the bedroom door, her eyes narrowed at him. "And what do you plan to do, my lord? Keep me locked up here forever? Again, I ask, what is it you want from me?"

Something passed over his face, an emotion she couldn't comprehend, but he blinked it away and let his eyes rake over her, resting on her breasts beneath the plaid. The chill in the room had hardened her nipples, and they pushed against the wool.

"I want you." Staring at her chest, he took a step toward her. "I know the taste of you so intimately, it is part of me. I hunger for you, Sorcha. I've missed you. It's been too long."

"You cannot have me," she said with all the conviction she could muster, and was rewarded with Cam's subtle flinch. "I'm married . . . I am an honorable lady, married to the laird—"

Cynically, he raised a brow.

He was right. She wasn't honorable—she'd lied to her husband on her wedding night. She threw up her hands. "Why, Cam? Why now? Why the night of my marriage?"

"I don't know." By the bewilderment in his expression, she sensed that he truly didn't understand his own motivation.

"It has been weeks since I left this place. Why didn't you come to me before?"

"I wanted to. I thought about you constantly." His lips thinned. "I thought it best not to interfere with your father's plans. I was a fool. I didn't know how strongly I'd feel about it until it happened, until I actually saw you—" His face settled into a hard mask of determination. "I won't stand by and watch someone take what is mine."

She hissed out a breath. "I'm not yours. I never was."

"You *always* were. I was the one to take your maidenhead, was I not?"

She turned away from him and strode to the window, a narrow, tall opening in the stone, probably once an arrow slit. She had to get away from him, from his handsome, brooding face, and the roiling emotions that passed over it in waves. She should still be in a murderous rage, but, as always, his emotion affected her. The dark eyes the villagers called cold she saw as soulful. Everyone assumed that his tight bearing and upright carriage signified arrogance and disdain, but she interpreted his posture as a mask for deep-seated insecurity and a need to be loved.

Cam had appealed to her on such a basic level from the very beginning. Power, money, dashing good looks—those were things that drew women to him but that Sorcha had always imagined herself immune to. No, she had been attracted to the intense feelings and strong soul-deep emotion buried behind the facade of the jaded debauchee.

Right now, he hurt . . . It was written across his face like words on a page. He wanted her badly, and for the first time, she realized he truly believed himself in love with her.

Yet as much as her heart panged in sympathy for him, she knew Cam only wanted her for selfish reasons.

"Aye, you took my maidenhead. You took that which is so precious to most women, and indeed, was precious to me. But did you ever have a mind to give anything back?"

He frowned at her from across the room. "What do you mean?"

"I cared for you. More than a little." She rested her forehead against the stone sill and closed her eyes.

Seconds later, his hands settled on her shoulders, gentle this time. "I won't let you go, Sorcha. I want you with me."

"That's impossible." She straightened her spine even as her body yearned to relax against the hardness of his chest. Her throat constricted and she opened her palm against the cold glass.

She belonged to someone else. She'd slammed the coffin's lid on her relationship with Cam when her father had laid her hand in Alan's today, when the minister had bound them for life, literally and symbolically. She sighed. "I was never meant to be the mistress of a great man—I was meant to be the wife of a humble one."

"I never asked you to be my mistress, Sorcha."

"No. You merely assumed, with your typical arrogance, that I would not conceive of saying no."

"If you didn't desire me, you would have refused my advances."

"That is true." She turned to him, forcing him to release her shoulders. "But now it's different. Whether I desire you is of no consequence. I must refuse you. I have a sacred obligation to Alan MacDonald."

His lips turned down, and his eyes glinted in the meager light. "A man you know nothing of."

"I made a vow, and I must honor it regardless of how little I know of him." She sighed. Before tonight Alan had been a virtual stranger to her. But now she felt like she knew Alan rather better than Cam might think. Alan was gentle and honorable. He made her feel safe, as safe as Cam once had.

More than anything, though, something powerful had happened between them when they'd joined. She couldn't name it, but remnants of it still trickled through her, firing her nerves.

"I know Alan MacDonald." Cam's voice was soft. Dangerous. His eyes took on a predatory gleam. "I can tell you all about him. What would you like to know, Sorcha?"

"I don't understand—"

"I met Alan in London. Later we went to Oxford together."

"You did?" She regretted the question instantly, for it revealed her ignorance.

"Aye. He was fulfilling his mother's legacy at the university. Did you know she was an English lady?"

"Of course."

"Disowned by her family for falling in love with a Highland barbarian. Yet her father must have retained some affection for her, because he held in trust a legacy for Alan. It was due to her health they returned south when Alan was a lad. A delicate Englishwoman, she could not endure our harsh climate once Alan's father died."

Sorcha resisted covering her ears. It seemed blasphemous to be learning details about her husband from her ex-lover. "I do know all this," she said tightly.

Bracing one arm on the window, he leaned forward, his lips brushing her temple. "Alan MacDonald taught me everything I know about how to pleasure a woman."

Sorcha stiffened. She didn't want to hear about Cam's past exploits. Or Alan's.

But Cam didn't stop. "Our goal was to visit every bawdy house in Oxford, to see how many women we could buy, how many we could take at once and in how many different ways. We wished to experience the ultimate debauchery. With my money and Alan's charm"—Cam's lips twisted in a sneer—"it wasn't difficult to accomplish."

Sorcha turned to stare out the window into the darkness. Far off in the distance past the castle gate, a light flickered. Might Alan be out there, coming after her? But what could he do? Even if the whole population of the glen rose up to save her, Cam could order every soul slaughtered with a flick of his wrist.

"I don't want to hear any more." She glanced back him. "What will you do with me, Cam?"

His jaw twitched. "I'm not letting you go. You will not leave Camdonn Castle."

"Alan MacDonald is my husband."

"He will seek an annulment once he hears the truth. Then you may stay by my side with a clear conscience."

So that was how Cam saw her future—as a spurned wife, as his mistress. And when he tired of her, she'd be finished. Relegated to the mountain with the other whores and discarded women. "What do you believe will cause Alan to abandon me so quickly?"

A smile played on Cam's lips. "Alan doesn't abide liars. He values honesty above all else. And your fate will be sealed when he learns how you feel about me. When he sees what I can make you do. Perhaps we should let him watch us together, Sorcha. Perhaps if he sees how you respond to me, how eager you are to open your legs for me—"

"Never!" she spat.

"It would be nothing new to him. He's watched me fuck women before."

"Not his wife, I daresay," Sorcha said thickly.

Cam smiled, but the smile did not reach his eyes. "True. I imagine it will only add to the excitement."

"Stop it."

"Knowing Alan as I do, I think he would enjoy watching me with you, Sorcha. He wouldn't want you to be his wife any longer. Oh no, he only wants an innocent, an angel, to occupy that position. But we both know you're neither, don't we?"

"Please stop."

"Perhaps he'd want to join us." His fingertip trailed a path down her arm.

"No," she whispered, but she could not deny the sinful response her body had to his terrible words. Cam knew her too well—he knew that speaking to her coarsely made her mad with lust. Images of kneeling before Alan's muscular body with Cam taking her from behind suddenly flooded her mind.

No . . . She had to stop. Staring out into the darkness, she pressed her thighs together, hating Cam all the more for taunting her like this.

"Or perhaps we could fuck you together. Would you like that, sweet Sorcha?"

She froze as his hand wandered over the curve of her buttocks, tugging the plaid down as his fingers drifted lower.

"Stop it, Cam," she burst out. "Please, stop." She pressed her forehead against the windowpane in a vain attempt to cool the fire in her blood, but she could not stop the illicit thoughts. They roared through her, mixing the reality of both men with the fantasy of having them together.

His madness must be catching. But then, he'd always had this effect on her.

He leaned closer to her, and the stiff rod of his cock nestled between the cheeks of her buttocks.

"I think you still want me, Sorcha."

"I hate you," she whispered.

Gently, he pried the edges of the wool away from her fingers and pushed it from her shoulders. "You are so beautiful. Let me show you."

"No."

The plaid fell to the floor, leaving her bare and exposed against him. His clothes were still wet from the rain, and she shivered.

"Go to the bed," he ordered softly. "Wait for me there. You will see what man you truly honor."

She stole a glance at his bed. It stood there, quiet and inviting, piled high with warm blankets. The hairs on her arms and legs rose, and she shivered again, not only from cold but from fear.

"No."

His fingertip stole around her body and brushed over her puckered, sensitive nipple, eliciting a low groan from her.

She hated him. She'd left their relationship with fond memories of him, and now . . . now he was on the verge of destroying her.

He cupped her jaw in his hand, and the heat of his skin shot through her. "I need you, Sorcha. More than any other man in this world. I wish to keep you here with me, forever. Tonight I will show you."

"No." She moved her lips, but only the subtlest sound emerged. She doubted he heard her at all. She glanced at the door. He had her trapped in his home, in his bedchamber, and had attempted to weave her in his spell of lust and need. There was no way she could escape.

She had made a promise to Alan, under God. She belonged to Alan now.

"Let me take you, keep you, hold you against me. You want me, Sorcha. I know you do. You always do."

She made a sound of dissent.

"And I want you. I need you." He ground his cock against her buttocks. "Can you feel it, Sorcha?"

Sorcha closed her eyes.

Cam's voice lowered to a harsh whisper. "I need you tonight. Now. Go to the bed."

She moved away from him and took a step toward the bed, clutching her arms around her naked body. Her hand brushed over her stomach, still sticky with Alan's release.

"Go to the bed, Sorcha."

She nodded and took another step. Behind her, she heard the rustling sound of Cam kneeling to remove his boots.

She closed her eyes, allowing the battle to rage within her, her fists clenching and unclenching at her sides.

She knew what she had to do.

Taking a deep breath, she steeled herself. Then she spun around and sprinted for the door.

Grasping the handle, she yanked it open and leaped out into the hall.

CHAPTER THREE

The castle, like Alan's own lands, abutted the southern shore of the loch, and within the hour his mount turned down the twisted path leading to the castle grounds. As Alan neared, lights flickered through the scrubby trees, and approaching hoofbeats sounded from the direction of the gates. A shout filtered through the brush; someone must have spotted him. He drew MacLean's horse to a halt and waited in the middle of the path. The animal pranced anxiously, picking up on his mood.

Riders rounded the nearest bend and emerged from the mist. Alan counted six of them, all heavily armed, wide-awake, and wary. Sent by Cam, no doubt.

A man Alan didn't recognize led the group. He stared up at Alan, his dark eyes round as marbles in the dim light. "You're trespassing on the Earl of Camdonn's lands. Who are you and what business have you here at this hour?"

"I am Alan MacDonald. I've come to fetch my wife." Alan felt the weight of his broadsword, comfortably heavy at his left hip, and his dirk sheathed on his right. He scanned the men rapidly.

"You'll not find her here," the leader said.

"Sure yer not some Jacobite bastard come to murder our lord in his sleep?" asked another, his rawhide face drawn tight with suspicion.

"This has naught to do with politics. All I want is my wife." Alan pictured Camdonn Castle in his mind. Across the courtyard and through the parting mist, its white stone walls would gleam dimly in the pale moonlight. Yellow light would shine from the tall, narrow top-story windows. It was Cam's home, where his friend felt safest. Alan had heard stories of Cam's happy childhood here before his mother died and his beloved governess had left him. Before his life had turned lonely and unhappy, with a father who didn't understand him and who sent him away to England at the earliest opportunity.

No, Cam wouldn't have taken her anywhere else.

He returned his focus to the men, who had formed a straight line before him, their mounts sidestepping nervously.

He'd barrel through them, and if he survived, make a dash for the main gate. The castle was surrounded on three sides by the loch and steep cliff walls, and the iron gate was the only way in. He'd have to fight his way past the guards there, then run for the living quarters. Cam kept a barracks on the castle grounds. Theoretically, Alan could be forced to battle through a hundred men before reaching Sorcha.

His chances were slim, but what choice did he have? He wouldn't stand by and allow Cam to ravish his wife, as unreal as the notion was. In all their years of friendship, Alan had witnessed Cam tupping many a woman, but never one with any connection to Alan. And he had never seen Cam force a woman. What madness had infected him?

Alan had seen the look on Cam's face when he had taken her, and he could not mistake the man's intent. Cam wanted her. He valued her. Far more than he valued his lifelong friendship with Alan.

Alan had visited the earl just last week, and nothing had seemed amiss. They'd spent most of their time together lounging in Cam's comfortable drawing room and contrasting their lives in Scotland and England. They'd resolutely stayed away from the topic of politics—in that regard they'd never seen eye to eye—and Alan's upcoming marriage. Alan remembered now that each time he'd brought up Sorcha's name, Cam had quickly steered the discussion in another direction.

Placing his hand very deliberately over the hilt of his broadsword, Alan cast the guards a hard look. "She's my wife," he said softly. "I know he brought her here."

The leader was undaunted. The men surrounding him sat straight-backed in their saddles, on high alert. Tension radiated from them.

"Where's Angus?" one of them asked. He looked like a shrunken version of MacLean, pockmarks and all. Definitely a close relation.

Alan stifled a grimace and gestured in the general direction of his lands. His balls still ached from Cam's blow. His shoulder throbbed and smarted where MacLean had hit and pricked him with his sword.

"Did ye kill 'im?"

"No. He'll be along soon enough, I imagine. He'll be right as rain once he sleeps it off."

"Our orders are to turn you back, MacDonald. No soul is allowed entrance to the castle grounds this night." This came from the leader.

"She's my wife," Alan repeated. No sane, honorable man would fail to understand his motivation, or his intent.

"Go home, MacDonald," another man said in a grating voice. Focused solely on the leader, Alan didn't know which of the clustered men the words came from.

Not without Sorcha.

Horses shifted restlessly, and a gap stretched between the leader and the man to his right. Alan didn't hesitate. Sinking his heels into the horse's sides, he drew his weapon with a whoosh of steel against leather. As the six men rushed to unsheathe their swords, he galloped toward the center man, aiming the sword at his heart. Unable to draw quickly enough, the man tried to veer his horse away, but Alan was too fast. Alan's broadsword sank into his side. Crying out hoarsely, he slumped forward as Alan withdrew.

If the man died, Alan could be hanged for this act alone. But there was no time to think on that now. He had to get through them. To reclaim his wife.

Someone shouted, but Alan couldn't make out the words. Thanking God for the clearing sky and the full moon, he pressed the bay into a full run. The horse thundered toward the castle gate. He ignored the hoofbeats pounding close behind him. Ahead, another group of men had amassed at the entrance.

But he wouldn't give up. He'd rather die fighting than sit scratching his arse while his innocent wife suffered at the hands of an earl in the grip of madness.

As he neared, the men at the castle gates drew their weapons. Alan counted another five guards on foot. Added to the four pursuing him, that made nine men, most of whom looked familiar, though he hadn't visited Camdonn Castle often enough to know them by name.

His horse sprinted at the gate, then shied as it encountered the obstacle of the men and metal blocking its way. Alan swayed in the saddle, struggling to stay mounted.

"Halt!" One of the standing men raised his musket and aimed it at Alan.

The four mounted men behind approached the gate in a flurry of hooves, reining in their horses as they neared.

Regaining control of his mount, Alan straightened his spine and held his broadsword at the ready. "I'm here to fetch my wife. Permit me to enter."

"Blast it, MacDonald, can ye not see yer outnumbered?" shouted one of the mounted guards.

"Give it up, man." A grizzled guard stared up at Alan, his hand on his sword hilt, his silver brows furrowed. "Go on home, MacDonald. None of us wants trouble tonight."

"Nor do I. So let me by or I will be forced to fight my way through you."

A few of the men snorted derisively.

He'd have to be on foot to pass through the gate. Alan dismounted carefully, keeping his senses attuned to any movement.

"She's my wife," he repeated as his feet struck the muddy path. "What the hell kind of husband would I be if I were to allow another man to rape her?"

"The wise kind," one of the men muttered.

"The living kind," added another.

Though they jested, they all remained wary and on alert. There was no way to compel them to let down their guard. Alan had to force the issue.

He lunged for the gate, knocking down the musket of the man barring his way and kicking another in the leg.

Alan turned to the man on his right, the man who'd told him to give it up. He drew his sword with a whoosh, his silver brows snapped so closely together they looked like a straight line over his eyes. Steel clashed, once, twice, then a searing pain sliced down Alan's back, nearly causing his legs to buckle.

He regained control of his legs and spun around. One of the mounted men had struck him. Two swords slammed against his one, and someone caught his wrist, wrenching the steel from his grasp. Blood streamed hot down his back. His arm was twisted behind him, forcing him to his knees. Words penetrated through the muddle of Alan's mind. "Ye'll not have her back if yer dead, MacDonald."

Now both his arms were yanked behind him. A man looped rough twine around his wrists. His flesh was on fire.

"Alan."

Blinking away the film of pain and frustration blurring his vision, Alan looked up into the kindly face of Duncan MacDougall, Cam's manservant and a secret Jacobite. The servant breathed heavily, and sweat beaded upon his brow even in the coldness of the night.

"Duncan," Alan gasped. "Sorcha . . ."

"Aye, lad, I heard the ruckus out here. I've just come from the castle. She's with his lordship."

Alan closed his eyes. He knew it was so, but to hear it confirmed felt as painful as a sword slicing him in two. He groaned. Stars swam in his vision. His head throbbed. His shoulder ached. His back burned.

"Why?" he whispered.

Duncan knelt before him and clutched his chin, forcing Alan to meet his wizened eyes. "Ye must keep yer strength, Alan. This is folly. They'll kill ye, sure as not."

"No. I have to get to her."

Cam was no rapist, but his expression had been that of a desperate man, a man who'd do anything to get what he wanted. Images flashed in Alan's mind. Cam forcing Sorcha onto her back. She was naked, her pale skin stark against his darker flesh. Black hair against black hair . . . tears streaming down her face as he held her down . . .

Alan made a final attempt to lunge to his feet, but the guards held him firmly down.

Duncan's kindly face swam before him. "Use your head, Alan MacDonald. Go to her father—he has a history with his lordship."

So did Alan—his past with Cam was more extensive than any of the surrounding men could imagine—but what good was that to him right now? Alan blinked. Duncan was telling him to leave? He shook his head. "It's too late for that. I've injured men in Cam's—his lordship's—service. And Sorcha"—his voice cracked—"my wife . . ."

He'd kill Cam for this.

He struggled against the men who held him. "Let me go to her, damn you."

Duncan leaned toward him and spoke in low tones. "They understand, lad. Go home now, and there'll be no more bloodshed. If ye persist, they'll either have ye in chains or dead by night's end."

"I can't—" Alan's lungs constricted. He could scarcely breathe. Could he turn his back on Sorcha . . . allow Cam to have his way with her?

What would she do? From what he'd seen of her tonight, she was no helpless chit. She had fire within her. Was she still fighting him? Alan squeezed his eyes shut.

"Ye'll be no good to her dead," Duncan said gently. "Go, lad. Go to Stewart. He'll help ye."

He was no good to her defeated, either. Mustering all his strength, he lunged forward again, breaking away from the men who held him down. He sprinted to the iron gate and rammed his shoulder against it. The hinges groaned, giving slightly under the force of his blow.

But someone shouted, something slammed into the back of his head, and everything faded to black.

Cam was too fast for Sorcha. He leaped to his feet as she flung open the door, and he sprinted forward, catching her arm and jerking her around as she ran into the hallway.

She screamed, and though the noise was loud enough to wake half of Scotland, nobody ran to her rescue.

Cam hauled her up against him, wrapping a hand around her lower back. She fought him. Writhing in his embrace, she again sank her teeth into his arm as she scored his face with her nails, all the while screaming bloody murder. "Let me go. Let me go, damn you! I hate you! You bastard!"

His biceps stinging from her bites, he locked her wrists in one of his hands and dragged her back into his bedchamber, kicking the door shut behind him. Once he reached the bed, he tossed her onto it. She flipped her body over and made to scramble away, but he jumped beside her. He grabbed her ankle and yanked her toward him. He swung his leg over her, straddling her hips, holding her down with his weight and pinning her arms overhead.

Blast it, he didn't hurt women. He hoped to God he wasn't hurting her. By the twisted look of rage on her face, she wasn't feeling it if he was.

He shook her. "Stop it, Sorcha. Do you hear me? Stop! Have you gone mad?"

"Have you?" she spat. "Do you think I'll just lie here while you rape me? Make a cuckold of my husband as I simper in approval?"

"You will come to me on your own accord," he said flatly, though he was beginning to wonder. Her vehemence shocked him.

Didn't she love him?

"I'd rather rot in hell." She tugged her arms as if to test his strength, then held still, staring up at him. Hostility flared in her green eyes.

Then again, what had he expected from her? Thankfulness? Perhaps from a lass less spirited, less honor bound than Sorcha. He was foolish to have thought Sorcha would fall into his arms, despite what they had once shared. She was a married woman, and he had forgotten how indomitable the bonds of marriage were to Highlanders.

Yes, she had cared for him once. He'd seen it in her eyes when he'd made love to her. Hell, she'd stood at the window and admitted it, not ten minutes ago.

"Let me go, damn you."

She was beautiful, vibrant, alive. His cock swelled in his breeches. He raked his gaze down her body. Her bare breasts were tipped with dusky nipples, pebbled into hard little points, making his mouth water in anticipation of suckling one as he touched the other, rousing her passion . . .

Yet perhaps the state of her breasts had nothing to do with arousal. It was more likely due to the cold draft in the room.

He wanted her, but he could not take an unwilling woman. His code of honor wasn't quite as rigid as hers, but it did know certain limits. Though those limits begged to be redefined at this moment.

"You want me." It came out as a near growl.

She shook her head. "No! No, I do not."

With his free hand, he reached behind him, gently slipping one finger between the silken lips of her sex. He found her slippery, open, ready for him. She jerked under his touch and let out a squeal of dismay.

He removed his hand and held his finger up before her, showing her the glistening proof of her arousal. "But you do."

She stilled beneath him and stared up at him with hard, determined jade-colored eyes. Only her fingers moved—curling and releasing relentlessly above her head where he pinned her wrists.

She spoke quietly. "My body remembers you, Cam. It remembers this place, this bed, the nights we spent here."

He nodded in understanding. His body remembered too.

"The flesh doesn't know right from wrong. It doesn't understand honor. It has no conscience. But my soul does, Cam. My heart does. To take your pleasure with me now will destroy all the memories I have of you, all the affection I've held for you over time. Please." A single tear escaped her eye and traveled down the side of her face, but she didn't blink.

"You want me, Sorcha. You love me, and it is me you desire, not Alan MacDonald."

"I beg you. Please don't do this. Don't force me to do something that will make me hate you forever. Please don't destroy me. I haven't the strength to resist you, but if you do this now, know that my heart and soul will never succumb. Is that what you want?"

Struck dumb, he merely stared at her. What *did* he want from her? First and foremost, he wanted her body. But he wanted more. He wasn't the kind of man who'd accept anything less than the whole, especially from a woman he cared for so deeply, who occupied his thoughts night and day.

He was a bloody fool to have waited until her wedding day. If only he'd understood his feelings before he'd seen her with Alan tonight.

Nevertheless, she'd given herself to him freely once, and she would do so again.

Alan came to slowly, the throbbing in his head and body guiding him through a haze of pain back into reality. He lay on his stomach, and his shirt was gone. He crawled onto his knees, gripped his head in both hands, and took stock of his surroundings.

He was at home, and there were people all about. Sorcha's family—her father and brothers and sister. A fresh, cheerful fire crackled in the hearth, and the smell of peat smoke wafted pleasantly through the air.

Someone smacked him on the shoulder. "Aye, we can see that yer awake, but Stewart willna release me to me bed till I've stitched ye up nice and tight."

He turned to stare at the woman who'd spoken. As shrunken and wrinkled as a dried-up apple, Mary MacNab gazed at him with cruel, ice blue eyes, small pinpricks of light nestled in the tanned-leather skin of her face.

Alan winced as his head pounded harder. Mary MacNab. What in God's name was she doing here? She was the town healer, well-known for her poor bedside manner toward men. It was rumored a man had wronged her once, and she held a grudge against his sex ever since. While she was ever kind and gentle with women, she seemed to relish a man's pain.

He rubbed his temples, and the memory of the night's events slammed into him. *Sorcha*. His hand in hers as the priest married them. Her dark, silky hair. Her parted, panting lips as he'd thrust inside her. Spilling his seed over her belly. Holding her afterward, loving the feel of her slight, warm body pressed against his as she'd snuggled into him. The sweet smell of her.

And then . . . Cam. Attacking him, grabbing Sorcha. The encounter with MacLean and the later, hopeless battle against Cam's men.

It took Alan several moments to reach the conclusion that it was not some bizarre dream.

Mary MacNab waved a large, menacing needle at him. "Unless ye wish me to sew up that gaping mouth o' yers, ye'd best lie down."

He scanned the occupants of the room in rising panic. She wasn't here. The bastard still had her.

"Sorcha!"

He made to scramble off the bed, but a strong hand closed over his shoulder. "Nay, lad. You'd best let Mary sew you up. Then we'll worry ourselves over my wee daughter."

He looked into the hard face of William Stewart, Sorcha's father. Stewart was a strong, stalwart man, always fair, who doted on his four surviving children. He'd lost the youngest—and his wife—in childbirth. Sorcha's brothers, James and Charles, and her sister, Moira, stood behind Stewart, staring at Alan with varying shades of blue and green eyes. They all looked alike though. Their close familial ties to Sorcha were unmistakable.

"How did I get here?"

"Duncan MacDougall and some of Lord Camdonn's men brought you home and put you to bed. Then they sent a messenger to say that you were injured, so we came straightaway. You were soaked in blood, lad. Mary just arrived to sew you up."

"How long?"

James, younger than Sorcha by five years, took a step closer, peering at him through narrowed green eyes. He was a handsome, dark-haired youth, but tonight his anger showed through in his stormy expression.

"You've been home a good two hours," the boy gritted out.

"Hell," Alan muttered. He covered his face with his hands. Behind his palms, he closed his stinging eyes. Surely it was too late by now. He'd failed her. God, they hadn't even been married a full day, and he'd failed her.

"Lie down, lad. You'll be no good to Sorcha if the wound festers."

He wished people would stop telling him he'd be no good to Sorcha if. He was no damned good to Sorcha as it was. He pushed a frustrated hand through his tangled hair.

James nodded curtly, agreeing with his father's wisdom. "That's one hell of a gash, Alan. You'd best have Mary see to it."

Stewart flashed a quelling look at his son for his language, and then turned back to Alan, his face grave. "Aye, it's a deep cut indeed."

At the time, it had stung, but he'd thought it little more than a scratch. Now it was hot and flowing fresh blood, and it hurt like hell.

"You'll not be fit to join Lord Mar in Perth, then," James muttered. "We were hoping to march south next week."

Despite his men's enthusiasm, Alan wasn't convinced joining the Jacobites right now would be the best course of action for his people. If King James landed in Scotland with a French army at his back, that would be a different matter altogether. But the king had given no indication that he'd be arriving anytime soon, which left the Earl of Mar to lead his cause.

Alan had known the Earl of Mar briefly in England, and he'd found him to be a self-serving sort whose loyalties swayed toward those who offered him the most compensation. He was not the kind of man who inspired Alan's trust, and Alan hesitated to risk his own men to the whims of such a commander.

Stewart frowned at his son, and James turned away in disgust, fists balled. Alan sighed. The lad was too eager for battle. Then again, so were most of the MacDonalds.

Stewart turned away from James and lowered himself into the chair nearest Alan's bed. "You'll be scarred for life, I'll wager." For a long moment, he simply stared at Alan as his three children bustled about, heating water and gathering cloths to clean Alan's wound while Mary MacNab snapped instructions at them.

"Lie down now." Stewart's voice was firmer this time, and Alan obeyed. He was in no mood to argue with his father-in-law, and his back burned like fire.

"This'll hurt like you've fallen into the rivers of hell," Mary MacNab pronounced gleefully.

"It already does," Alan grumbled.

If he managed to survive her brutal ministrations, at least it was likely the wound wouldn't fester. Despite her cruelty, the villagers believed Mary MacNab's magic could ward off all manner of infection. For that reason only, he'd suffer through whatever torture Mary MacNab had planned for him. He needed his health in order to rescue his wife.

Mary snorted. "Like all the sniveling members of yer sex, ye have no understanding of true pain."

He turned his head to the side to see her sneering at him.

"Is that so?" he mused aloud, wondering if the agony of watching your wife being dragged away by your closest friend qualified as true pain. He'd never experienced anything so brutal. The thought of a witch like Mary MacNab stabbing a needle into his flesh suddenly didn't seem so daunting.

"Indeed. You men weep like babes at the merest twitch."

He sighed. "Just get it over with."

Mary glanced across the room at Sorcha's sister, who was busy near the fire. "Moira, lass. Ye wanted to learn more about stitching deep wounds. So watch. And you, boy"—she pointed a crooked finger at Charles, the youngest of the Stewarts—"get to boiling that butter as I directed ye."

Charles retrieved a pot and hurried to the hearth, and Moira, Stewart's second-eldest child after Sorcha, nodded and came to stand beside Mary. Moira was a cheerful, freckled splash of sunlight with long, dark auburn hair. She watched in fascination as Mary began to scrub away the blood with a coarse cloth. Alan gritted his teeth against the pain.

At the first jab of the needle into his skin, Alan stiffened and closed his eyes. He would not think on the agony of it. Instead he'd think about Sorcha dancing at their wedding earlier tonight, her green eyes sparkling, her skirts lifted up past her ankles. Just looking at her had made his heart soar to new heights.

When Alan was eight years old, his father had died. By the time he was nine, his mother had decided to return to her childhood home in England. Alan had grown up there, raised by his mother and his

English grandfather, but he had always known one day he'd return to the Highlands, where he'd acknowledge his birthright as laird of the MacDonalds of the Glen.

He'd gone to school, suffered the taunts of the English boys, and then he'd met Cam. . . .

"That's it, lass."

Moira's needle gently burrowed into his flesh. Somehow the idea of her wielding the nasty-looking implement was more comforting than the thought of Mary MacNab with it.

Cam and he had made quite a pair of dissolute bachelors in Oxford. They'd indulged in all manner of debauchery and enjoyed every second of it. They had drunkenly dragged each other out of brothels more times than either of them could count. They'd shared women, passed women back and forth, fucked one woman together. . . .

And then Cam's father had died in January, and Cam returned here to assume his duties as the new earl. After Cam left London, Alan heard from his uncle, who'd taken on the duties of laird while Alan remained in England. While his uncle hadn't said anything outright, Alan had read between the lines. His uncle was aging, and his duties growing too heavy to bear. The quickly escalating political tension was simply too much for him to manage.

Alan's return was long overdue. He was no longer a dissolute young buck of London; he was a man with a legacy and the responsibility that came with it. That meant going home, leading his clan, marrying, and producing heirs.

Alan had first traveled north from London to finish some business at his grandfather's estate. In August, his uncle succumbed to a fever and in September Alan finally came to claim his birthright.

"Good, now tug the thread tighter—it's necessary to close the wound as tightly as ye can so it doesna fester."

Moira pulled hard on the thread, and a gasp leaked from Alan's throat before he could stop it.

"Oh no!" she exclaimed. He raised his lids to see her looking down at him, her brow furrowed. "I'm so sorry, Alan."

"It's all right, lass," he said from between his teeth.

Mary MacNab snorted. "Don't allow their whining to stop ye from what ye must do, Moira. For if you do, ye'll be ineffective, and they'll rot from the inside out." She yanked on the thread, but Alan was prepared and merely released a harsh breath.

He squeezed his eyes shut again and saw Sorcha, with her piercing eyes and black hair, in his mind's eye. She was small and lithe, dark-haired and pale-skinned, with those wicked, beautiful, cat-shaped green eyes. The first time he'd seen her, she was leaving her father's house with her sister as he was dismounting at the gate, planning to visit her father, his own father's old friend. He'd stared after her in awe, scarcely able to breathe.

Later, when Stewart had mentioned that he was searching for a husband for her, Alan leaped at what seemed like a perfect opportunity. She was six years younger than him, at twenty-two, with the proper background and Highland pedigree—her mother was a daughter of the MacDonald of Keppoch, and her father descended from the MacLeods. And the way her eyes flashed when she looked at him—*perfect*.

Her family loved her unconditionally, that much was clear. Alan didn't know her well, but beyond her beauty she did not seem a vapid creature like so many of the young ladies he'd known in England.

"Now tie off the end like this," Mary said. The women had worked all the way across his back, down from his right shoulder at a steep angle. His muscles spasmed as Mary tugged and pulled brutally at his flesh. At Mary's command, Moira used her light touch to smear warm, melted butter along the entire length of the wound. Then Mary smacked him on the arse. "All right, MacDonald. The worst of it is done."

Alan groaned softly and rolled to his side, watching as Mary opened a pouch full of smooth pebbles, which she and Moira silently placed in a circle round his bed. When he raised an eyebrow in question, she snapped, "Dinna give me that superior English look, lad. These are enchanted stones, soaked in silvered water. They'll be warding off the evil wee beasties that wish to kill ye through the wound."

After the circle was in place, she intoned a brief charm, and finally nodded in satisfaction. As Moira collected the stones and stored them in the pouch, Stewart led Mary outside, no doubt to discuss an exchange for her services. Alan rubbed at the bristle on his jaw. He'd take care of Mary's payment later, in a way so as not to embarrass Stewart. Though they held a high status in Glenfinnan, Sorcha's family possessed little real money, whereas Alan's inheritance from his grandfather had made him rich—by Highland standards, that was. Though certainly not nearly as rich as the Earl of Camdonn.

Stewart sent the boys to escort Mary home and came back inside. Moira placed warm bowls of barley broth before them, and though it seemed odd to Alan to eat at this hour, Moira insisted it would help him heal. He had to admit, the tasty, fragrant soup warmed him.

The sun would rise in another hour. What was Sorcha doing now? The thought made his gut ache with misery.

Her father sat across the table from Alan, eating silently. When he finished, he set his spoon in his bowl and pushed it away. Then he clasped his hands on the tabletop and met Alan's gaze.

"What happened tonight, son?"

Alan clenched his fists beneath the table. God, to make this admission, to admit to his incompetence at keeping her safe, nearly killed him. Stewart would surely hate him for failing to protect his daughter.

This was his penance, he supposed. He must admit to his failure, then remedy it.

Shame coursed through him, but he couldn't let Stewart see it. Alan would get her back. No matter what horror Sorcha suffered at the earl's hands, Alan vowed to never cast her off. A violent shudder ripped down Alan's spine at the thought of Cam defiling his young, pure wife.

Moira had seen his body quake. "Are you still cold?" She reached to remove his bowl, offering him a sympathetic smile. "There's more broth."

"No thank you, lass." He tried to return her smile but failed. He glanced back at the older man. "Sorcha and I had—" He cut a glance at Stewart's daughter and shook his head. "We were—uh—about to go to sleep, when Cam—his lordship—crashed in, flung her over his shoulder, and rode away, leaving one of his henchmen. I fought him, then pursued the earl a few minutes later."

Stewart dropped his silver-topped head in his hands. "I should have known."

"Should have known what, sir?"

He looked up at Alan with a bleak expression. "That was why I left the earl's service. I am getting old, and I suffer from aches and pains. It was a valid enough excuse to leave my position at Camdonn Castle. There was also the problem that the earl's political beliefs don't particularly align with my own. But the true reason was that I didn't like what I could see developing between him and my daughter."

Moira paused in her step as she walked past the table. Stewart glanced sharply up at her. She returned his stare, eyes wide, her guilty expression speaking volumes. She knew something. A secret had just been revealed.

And suddenly, in the unspoken conversation between Moira and her father, it became crystal clear.

"What are you doing, Cam?" Sorcha had cried as Cam tossed her over his shoulder.

She had addressed him as Cam. She knew him well enough to speak to him informally, which meant she knew him very well indeed.

She'd been so deliciously wanton in Alan's bed, and although there was a shyness to her, she possessed none of the timidity he might imagine from a virgin. He hadn't known what to expect, really, never having taken a virgin before, but he hadn't felt any resistance from her maidenhead. He hadn't seen any blood . . .

Alan's gut twisted. Goddammit. She'd played him false. She was no innocent.

He needn't worry about Cam defiling his wife. The bastard already had.

After an hour spent in his study drinking whisky, Cam hesitated at his chamber door, clutching at the door handle as his body swayed unsteadily. He'd left Sorcha earlier, needing to straighten his twisted thoughts before doing something to her he knew he'd later regret.

He would sleep elsewhere tonight; sleeping beside her would present a temptation he was powerless to resist. But he wished to check in on her once more, perhaps watch her in slumber as he had in the past. Her sweet red lips parted as she breathed deeply, her body relaxed, her dark hair cascading over the snow-white pillow.

Slowly, so as not to wake her, he unlocked the door and pushed the handle. Well oiled, it swung open silently.

He stepped inside. Saw his bed, with the curtains still open. Her back to him, Sorcha lay curled in a ball on top of the green and black silk counterpane.

He stopped in his tracks. Had she made a noise? And then he saw her shoulders shaking as sobs racked her small body.

He'd never seen her cry like this. She'd let a tear escape earlier, but that was one single tear trailing down the side of her face, and that had nearly broken him. Now she cried with her whole body—great, wrenching, heaving sobs that made his blood run cold.

He wanted to go to her, to comfort her. How could he, though, when he was the source of her grief? He remained rooted to the spot, his hands fisted at his sides, frozen with indecision.

He wanted Sorcha. He needed her. She was his. Damn it, he *loved* her.

And she might have loved him too, once. But she would never forgive him for this, for the wrong he had done her tonight. And by God, it tore him apart to see her suffer.

It struck him, in a moment of clarity in his whisky-muddled mind—the only way he could hope to win her love was to let her go.

But that didn't make any sense, damn it! He wished he hadn't drunk so much. Sluggishly, he brought a hand up to rub the bridge of his nose. Deep in her grief, she still hadn't noticed his presence in the room.

If he let her go, she'd return to Alan MacDonald.

Alan MacDonald, once his closest friend, would never forgive him either.

Cam shook his head. His obsession with Sorcha had eclipsed his friendship with Alan, as if it were absolutely meaningless. They'd been like brothers . . . and in one brazen move, Cam had obliterated years of companionship. Severed the bonds of friendship formed long ago by two Highland lads in the midst of hostile English schoolboys.

Had he lost both the people he loved most in this world? With one foolish action?

How he wished he could go back in time. After watching Alan come over Sorcha's stomach, instead of barging in on them, he'd turn away and ride up the mountain to slake his lust on a welcoming whore.

But no. That wouldn't have worked. Then neither Alan nor Sorcha would know his heart. He couldn't have kept it from them forever, could he?

God, he couldn't let her go. It would surely kill him if he did.

But he must.

He knew it. He would not keep the woman he loved against her will, threatening her with rape every minute of the day. It would drive him mad, and she'd only grow to hate him, despise him with all the formidable strength contained within that small, lovely body.

He couldn't do this to Alan. Couldn't throw his power in Alan's face and dishonor him in the eyes of his clan so soon after his friend had returned to claim his legacy.

Quietly, he turned around and retraced his steps back into the hall. Feeling as though he'd left part of his soul inside the room with her, he closed the door. Then he leaned against it and sank to his arse on the cold planks of the floor, dropping his face in his hands.

He had no choice. He had to release her.

He'd take her home in the morning.

Damn it to hell.

CHAPTER FOUR

Sorcha froze. The door had just shut, she was certain of it. But she couldn't feel a presence nearby. Gulping back a sob, she swiped the back of her hand over her damp eyes and slowly turned over.

Nobody was in the room. Which meant someone had come in and then left, while she had been too absorbed in her misery to notice. She sat up stiffly, clutching the plaid to her chest, her mouth tight with frustration. She was too weak. Her weakness made her vulnerable, and she couldn't allow herself to be vulnerable.

For long moments, she stared at the door. Made of thick planks, it concealed most outside noise, and she heard nothing. Yet she imagined the intruder was just beyond, debating whether to interrupt her.

Was it Cam? Most likely. Heat prickled through her cheeks at the thought he had seen her cry. She had never wept in his presence before. In fact, she couldn't recall the last time she'd wept.

He'd left her over an hour ago without explanation, though his face had been twisted with some dark emotion. She couldn't fathom what he'd been thinking, but his departure had stunned her for a long while. Cam had never left her naked in bed before. Thank the Lord for whatever had possessed him to do so tonight.

She'd tried to find a way out, but the door was bolted from the outside, and jumping from Cam's window was impossible—even if she could fit her body through the narrow slit, she'd likely break a leg, if not her neck, on the craggy rocks below.

Overcome by the hopelessness of her situation, she'd collapsed on the bed and wept. For the loss of Cam, of her reputation, of the carefree life she'd lived before tonight. For her hopes of a future with Alan.

Staring at the door, she realized she hadn't heard the smooth sound of the bolt sliding into place, nor had she heard the solid click as it was locked. Knowing Cam, it wasn't likely that he'd neglected to bar her in, but then again he could be even deeper in his cups by now. She wouldn't be surprised if he'd gone directly from her to his whisky. He'd looked like a man who could use another drink.

But if he was drunk, why hadn't he come in and ravished her? Given his earlier behavior, that was what she'd expected. The man made no sense at all.

She continued staring at the door, every nerve in her body on edge, waiting for the telltale sound of him locking her in again. But there was only silence.

Could it be possible? Could she just walk out of here? Cam would have guards posted at the entrance gates and in the guardhouses speckled over the grounds, but they wouldn't hinder her. She'd grown up at Camdonn Castle. She knew a better way out.

She thrust the covers aside and swung her legs over the edge of the bed. Gooseflesh rose across her skin, and she shuddered. Though she'd be wet and chilled through by the end of this night, she might as well try to keep covered.

She stood, padded over the thick carpet to Cam's wardrobe, and opened the door. The hinges creaked loudly, and she stood still for a long moment, waiting. When nobody stormed in wondering at the noise, she turned her attention to the piles of clean, crisply folded shirts, stockings, and drawers. Surely he possessed more clothing than all the men of the glen combined.

She grabbed the top shirt and pulled it on, faltering as she smelled Cam on it—musky and male, with a hint of sandalwood spice. Her body heated instantly in reaction. Her flesh had been too well trained, but she was grimly determined to untrain it. Rolling the sleeves up to her wrists, she decided it was useless to try a pair of breeches or trews. Stockings were also out of the question. She'd never be able to keep them on. Cam's shirt covered her to her shins, and it, along with the plaid, would have to do until she arrived at Alan's cottage. Her new home, if her husband would still have her.

Sorcha glanced at the door. She should run. If there was any possibility of escaping from Cam, she must take it.

It was not regret that tightened her chest. Surely it was something else. Anger. Yes, it was certainly anger. Not fear of never seeing Cam again. Not pity for how her escape would make him feel. Certainly not that. The wretched man didn't deserve her pity.

Anger was the only emotion she could encourage, the only feeling she could accept with a clear conscience.

Pressing her lips together, Sorcha walked to the bed to wrap the plaid around her body. She found a simple iron pin in a chest beside the wardrobe, and she used it to attach the edges of the plaid at her chest. Then she walked to the door leading to the hallway. It glided open without a sound.

She glanced both ways. The passageway was dark, lit only by the dim candlelight cast from Cam's room behind her. All was quiet. By this hour, everyone had gone to bed save the guards on overnight duty. Yet dawn couldn't be far away. Soon the castle would be abustle with servants going about their morning chores.

Closing the door behind her, Sorcha scuttled down the hall on tiptoe. Except for the creak of a floorboard that nearly made her leap out of her skin, she moved silently on bare feet.

Once down the stairs, she rounded the corner to enter the entry hall. As quietly as possible, she drew the bolt on the front door and let herself out into the chill of predawn.

Now it would be dangerous. She cast a glance at the barracks, thankfully still dark. Yet some of the men were awake, keeping watch over the grounds. She had to be as silent and careful as a wraith to prevent them from seeing or hearing her. The moonlight was waning, but the feel of dawn was in the air, and the earliest hint of a morning glow softened the nighttime sky.

She flattened her body against the stone wall and inched around the building. A crunch of footsteps on gravel sounded nearby, and she froze.

Quickly, she wedged herself behind an outcropping and prayed. Half her body hung out in plain view, but she was in shadow and covered by the dark reds and blacks of the plaid. The man would not see her unless he turned. Sorcha held her breath as he crossed the courtyard and disappeared into the barracks.

She moved faster now. Keeping her back pressed against the wall, she shuffled around the corner, down the long end of the building, and around the back. A guardhouse stood at the end of the spit, but if she was lucky, she'd be fast enough and they'd miss her.

She sprinted across the grass, ducking low as she reached the two bushes she always used to mark the entrance to the path down the cliff. Here the incline to the water was not quite vertical, and rock formations in the face of the wall created natural steps. They were too dangerous and too steep for most to bother with, but Sorcha had clambered down them often as a lass. A tiny cave stood at the waterline—no more than a deep impression in the earth—where she'd gone to escape the constant tension she felt living on the grounds of a loyalist lord in a family and community that covertly sided with the Jacobites.

Tonight the steps were covered in mud and slippery with moss. Clearly it had been a long time since anyone had made use of this method of climbing down to the water. She clutched at small outcroppings as she nudged her body downward, grasping for the rocks with her toes. Her foot landed on a sharp edge, and she yelped as it jabbed into the most tender part of her arch.

"Did you hear that?"

The voice had come from the guardhouse, not ten yards away. Scrabbling for purchase, Sorcha ducked beneath the lip of the cliff and pressed her body against the earth, hanging on with her toes and fingers and gritting her teeth against the tingling pain in her foot.

"Anyone out here?"

"Likely just an animal, Will."

The second voice sounded sleepy, as if Will's sudden jump to attention had awakened its owner.

"Sounded like a person to me," Will groused.

Again, Sorcha heard footsteps. This time the steps were soft—the person was walking over wet, springy grass. It sounded like only one pair of feet—probably Will come to investigate the noise.

He stopped just above her. Sorcha knew if she looked up and around the ledge she'd be able to see his boots. But she didn't dare move. Her lower lip trembled, and she bit down hard on it.

"Sounded like a woman." Will's voice rang clear just overhead.

Sorcha hoped beyond hope that he hadn't heard about his master abducting the newly wed Sorcha Stewart.

The second man still sounded far away. "P'raps a rat," he said on a yawn.

"Huh. Ain't never heard the sound of a rat compared to the sound of a woman before." Light descended around her as Will crouched overhead, lowering his lamp to peer over the edge of the cliff. Sorcha held her breath.

"Aye, Will." The other man gave a mocking laugh. "'Tis all that squeaking they do when ye bed them. You just wouldn't know."

Will didn't answer, but the light disappeared and his footsteps sounded again, this time receding back toward the guardhouse.

Sorcha released a shaky breath. Carefully, she continued making her way down, facing the cliff. The steps seemed to have changed since she'd last come down this way. Now they felt more dangerous than they had before. Perhaps it was because of the darkness, though she'd descended these steps at night on occasion. Most likely it was just that she'd simply become more cautious. She felt much older now than the last time she'd descended to the loch, although not even a year had passed.

Finally, she reached the cave that had once served as her secret place. She stepped into it, though she didn't really have the time. A twig had caught a tiny piece of linen at the level of her waist. Sorcha took it and rubbed it back and forth between her fingers, remembering her last visit here. The new earl had just arrived from England and the staff had lined up to wait for him. Sorcha had escaped to her secret spot and was caught up in her daydreams when the housekeeper had called for her. She'd scrambled out and had met the earl—Cam—breathing heavily with exertion and with her skirt torn. He had noticed, too. His eyes had raked over her, pausing when they reached the tear, and then he'd met her gaze for a brief, electric moment before moving on. She'd felt flushed all the way to her toes for hours afterward.

It was the beginning of the end. A month after that, he'd kissed her in an alcove, and by March, she'd become Cam's eager bedmate. She couldn't steal away from her father's watchful eyes often, but when they came together, she and Cam had made every moment count.

Sighing, Sorcha turned toward the loch, dreading what must come next. She could skim along the edge of the bank for a time, but then she'd have to wade into the water and walk the short distance to shore. Though she'd been taught to ignore superstition, the water looked eerie, like an undulating blanket of velvet, and she sent up a quick prayer for the kelpie to be sound asleep in his nest.

She traveled along the water's edge for as long as she could. Mud and reeds squished between her toes. She tied Cam's shirttails in a cumbersome knot just below her breasts and hiked the plaid onto her shoulders. If she could keep the fabric dry, it might help to warm her later. The loch was cold as ice. If she wasn't careful, she might freeze to death before arriving at her husband's cottage.

Trying to convince herself that it was a better fate than dying as the Earl of Camdonn's whore, she waded into the water. She gritted her teeth against the shock of it as she progressed down the slope and immersed herself to the waist. After the initial painful bite of cold, her skin numbed in all the places the water touched.

The rocks of the pebbled beach ahead glowed dimly in the dusky predawn light. Focusing on the shore, she tried to take long, smooth strides so she wouldn't splash. A mixture of rocks and mud and slimy water weeds covered the ground, and she moved slowly to find her footing.

Finally, she emerged from the water. Frigid air collided with her body, and she shuddered violently. She brushed the wetness from her legs before untying Cam's shirt and allowing it to drop down to her shins. The fabric clung to her damp skin. Clenching her teeth to keep them from chattering, she unfolded the plaid and draped it around her body.

She glanced back to Camdonn Castle. Word had not got out that she was gone. Everything was silent, the buildings still dark. A shadow moved near the guard gate, and she slipped behind a low, spindly alder for cover.

The difficult part of her escape was over. Now she merely had to walk the few miles along the shore until she reached Alan's cottage.

Would Cam come after her once he discovered her missing?

Perhaps she should run.

Over an hour later, a glorious morning had arrived. The sun shone brightly, but frost still clung to the eaves, and the arrival of the sun hadn't heated the earth.

Sorcha straggled down the path to the cottage. Her teeth chattered so hard she hoped they were rooted strongly enough in her mouth to withstand the battering.

Scratches and bruises covered her feet. Every cut burned, especially a rather bloody one on the bottom of her arch, and each time a rock nudged against one of the bruises on her soles she felt the deep, aching pain. She was grateful she hurt—it meant she would be all right. If her feet had gone numb, she'd have greater cause for worry.

Nobody came out to greet her, and she paused at the closed wooden door, now cocked haphazardly on its hinges. As of yesterday, this was her home, but she'd spent only a short amount of time here. It didn't *feel* like home. Not like Camdonn Castle did.

Bracing herself with a deep breath, Sorcha pushed on the door, and it swung open crookedly.

The first person she saw was her father. His head snapped up from where he'd rested it on his arms at the table. He lunged to his feet. "Sorcha! Thank God."

People seemed to emerge from the walls themselves. Her sister and brothers. Last of all, Alan, standing at the doorway to the bedroom, his eyes narrowed like blue arrow slits.

Uncomfortably aware she was dressed in naught but a damp, finely tailored man's shirt and a rucked-up, dirty plaid, she straightened her spine and nodded at her father. "Da."

Then she bravely met her husband's gaze.

Alan had changed. The gentle, kind expressions of last night had hardened to stone.

"What happened, lass?" Her father strode toward her. She never thought to see so many emotions rage across his face. He'd seemed melancholy yesterday at her wedding, but today there was so much more. Anger, fright, annoyance, disgust, worry, concern. He stood before her and reached out to clasp her shoulders. He shook her lightly.

Sorcha licked her lips. "I escaped from Camdonn Castle." When his facial expression didn't change, she added, "By way of the loch."

Everyone stood still, staring at her, expecting her to say more.

"Nothing happened," she blurted. "The earl didn't harm me."

In a blink, Moira nudged Sorcha all the way inside and closed the door as best as it could be closed behind her. "Oh, Sorcha. You must be half dead with cold. Let me have a look at those poor feet, then."

Her teeth chattering, Sorcha let her sister lead her to a chair beside the fire. Moira rattled off instructions for warm water and rags while her brothers fetched what she needed, and Sorcha thanked the Lord she hadn't been asked to offer more details. Yet.

Someone draped a clean plaid over her shoulders, and she wondered whether her father or her husband had done it. By the time she collected enough strength to turn around, both men had faded into the room's shadows, but James stood behind her. He curled his hand on her arm and bent down to her ear. "I'll kill him for this, I swear it."

Alarmed, she glanced back toward her father and Alan. They were quiet behind her, but she could feel the heat of their gazes—the concerned father and the . . . what? How was her husband feeling? What did Alan think about all this?

She gazed dully at the fire as Moira cleaned the cuts and bruises with painstaking slowness. It hurt more than Sorcha had expected, and she gripped the edge of the table, clenching her teeth against the pain. Finally, Moira held her right foot high, inspecting the underside. No wonder it had bled so profusely—a rock had sliced a gash right across the center of her arch. Moira's forehead creased in a frown. "This'll need stitches."

"Can you do that, Moira?" Sorcha looked from her bloody foot up into her sister's freckled face.

Her sister nodded. "Aye. Mary MacNab was here earlier, and she taught me how."

Sorcha's heart began to race. "Mary MacNab was here?" She forced herself not to look at Alan. Had Cam's henchmen hurt him?

"Aye." Moira flicked a glance beyond Sorcha's shoulder. "Alan was cut as well, but we sewed his back up nice and tight."

She felt weak. Nausea boiled in her stomach. Alan had been injured because of her. She looked at her sister in despair. "I—I need to dress first."

"Of course." Moira supported her as they withdrew into the bedroom, where Moira helped her with her stays, shift, and petti-coats, and the striped blue plaid dress she'd worn to her wedding. When she returned to her seat before the hearth, her father nudged a glass filled with amber liquid against her elbow. "Would you like a nip, lass?"

She raised her brows at the whisky, but then she saw Moira rotating a needle over the fire.

Sorcha's foot hurt terribly, and she winced at the thought of that needle piercing her tender flesh. They'd not see her falter, not if she could help it. She took the proffered glass and tossed back the burning drink in one big gulp.

Chewing on her lip in concentration, Moira threaded the needle, then looked up at their brothers. "Charles, James. Hold her leg down, will you?"

Sorcha closed her eyes, pretending she was somewhere else. Anywhere but in her husband's room surrounded by her family, with thread being forced through the ticklish part on the bottom of her foot and her new husband staring dagger holes into the back of her head.

No, she was at Camdonn Castle, down in her cave by herself. Daydreaming.

It was there she'd read the volumes of books she'd discovered in the library after she'd insisted to be taught to read like James. She'd found the books so exciting, so full of exotic places, adventure, and romance and . . . lust.

It was there, in the cave, that Sorcha had discovered her body. All by herself, with the loch swishing at her toes, she'd learned how to make herself come. It took only a few moments. Two fingers rubbing vigorously above the part of her body Cam had later fully penetrated, and a ripple of delicious sensation would pulse through her whole being, making her gasp in delight. . . .

"There now. All finished," Moira said.

Sorcha blew out a shaky breath, realizing she was trembling. The whisky swirled through her, muting the pain spiking up her leg from her arch. Resting her foot on her knee, she squinted at the tight loops of thread. They felt awful—scratchy and strange—but they were tiny and tight and expertly stitched.

She smiled at her sister, impressed. "Well done, Moira."

The younger woman beamed at her with pride, but then her smile faltered. "I haven't the charm stones Mary uses."

Sorcha shrugged. "Ah well, I think Mary's skill is just that—skill. It has naught to do with charms or pebbles, I daresay. I'd not put too much faith in that nonsense."

Moira released a breath of relief. "I thought so too, but somehow the charm seems to finish it." She narrowed her eyes a little, then rose and embraced Sorcha. "I know what we must do. I'll be right back."

She turned away, disappearing momentarily into the other room. When she returned, Sorcha saw that she carried her aunt's wedding gift, a kertch—the headdress of a married woman. Her aunt had embroidered a beautiful old-fashioned trinity knot on the snowy white linen.

Moira knelt before her, and tears pricked Sorcha's eyes. Sorcha and Alan had intended to return to Glenfinnan in the morning, where the wedding festivities would continue, and Sorcha and her sister had planned to have the kertch ceremony in their father's cottage before they began.

Given last night's events, surely the celebrations would be canceled. Sorcha didn't even know whether Alan would have her now.

She groaned in despair. "Moira—"

"You're married, Sorcha." Understanding softened her sister's blue eyes. "We must do this."

"But—"

Moira's expression firmed. "No matter what happened last night. You're married to Alan MacDonald, and it's your duty to wear the kertch."

Moira could be stubborn at times. She had that look on her face now—her shoulders squared, her lips pressed into a line, and a challenge sparked in her eyes. The men were silent—apparently none of them dared counter her. Even Alan. She reminded Sorcha of their mother.

Blinking back tears, Sorcha nodded.

Moira smiled. "I wish Mama could be here to do this."

"So do I," Sorcha whispered.

Moira combed out her hair and then prayed aloud for guidance and wisdom for the new bride. She placed the kertch on Sorcha's head so the embroidered point went halfway down her back. The men watched in silence as she tied the other two points beneath Sorcha's chin. She finished by securing their mother's circular silver brooch at her chest. "God bless you, sister. And your marriage too."

"Thank you." Sorcha focused on her sister, too afraid to look at her kinsmen's expressions and petrified of what Alan's face might reveal.

Moira flattened her hand against Sorcha's chest and the sisters exchanged a smile. The moment was broken by their father, who cleared his throat. "Can you walk, lass?"

"Walk?" she breathed, turning to him.

So that was it. Her father would take her home. No sooner had she become a matron than her husband had discarded her.

"Wait just a moment." Alan's voice was as hard and brittle as glass. All the eyes in the room riveted to him. "Why should she need to walk?"

Her father stared at Alan, then said in a low voice, "She'll be coming home with us, and we've no horse or cart to carry her."

"No," Alan said shortly. "She will remain here. With me."

Thank the Lord. Sweet relief, as cool as the waters of the loch in the summertime, swept through Sorcha.

Moira wrung her hands. "She will need someone to look after her injuries. And so will you."

"We will care for each other's injuries," Alan said.

A strange thrill bubbled up from Sorcha's core as the image of him with her foot cradled in his lap flitted through her mind. But it disappeared as his frown deepened. He was furious. Would he beat her when her family left? Judging from his scowl, it seemed likely.

Her father glanced at her, his expression brimming with questions. She knew if she told him she wanted to leave with him, he'd fight for it.

But she didn't. She wanted to stay with Alan. To explain what had happened with Cam. To face his wrath, if it should come down to that. She was his wife, and she would not slink away with her da like a spineless maiden.

"I will stay here with Alan. Tell me what to do, Moira."

Her father looked mildly horrified, and his expression almost made Sorcha smile. She'd kiss him on the cheek if she didn't know it would embarrass him.

Moira left instructions for the care and cleaning of their wounds and said she'd walk out to check on them later this afternoon. Until then, she commanded both of them to rest. Sorcha, she said, must stay off her feet, and Alan must refrain from strenuous work. A woman and a group of boys were coming later to attend to the chores and the cooking, so neither Sorcha nor Alan possessed any excuse to leave the cottage.

With that, her brothers and sister hugged her. After James said his goodbye and kissed Sorcha's forehead, Alan took him outside. She watched as Alan thrust aside the lopsided door and closed it with a rattling bang behind them.

Sorcha's father knelt beside the chair. "I'll check on you soon, lass."

"Thank you, Da."

After they all left, Sorcha sat in silence. She warmed her toes before the fire, dreading what might happen next.

Then the door squealed open and wood scraped over the flagstones as Alan drew one of the chairs closer to the fire. He situated it beside hers and, with a low groan, lowered himself into it.

Another long silence.

Finally, Sorcha couldn't bear it a moment longer. Biting her lip, she turned to her husband. "What did you say to James?"

"I told him he's not to touch the earl or demand any sort of retribution. You're my responsibility now, and I'll manage the situation as I see fit."

Sorcha swallowed. "How—how did he respond?"

Alan shrugged. "He'll do as I say, whether he's happy about it or not."

He was right—James would do as his laird said. He was hot-headed but not reckless enough to go against a direct order from Alan. Yet another long stretch of quiet ensued while Sorcha gazed down at her hands clasped in her lap. Finally, she looked up at him. "Are you all right?"

He stared at her for what felt like an eternity. Fury was the only expression she could decipher on his face, and her throat thickened in fear.

"You fucked him," he said, his voice rough.

"No!" Sorcha winced, not so much at the harshness of his words, but in remembering her vow to be honest to him always. "Not last night," she amended.

He turned to stare broodingly at the fire. "You are lovers, then?"

"No. Not anymore." It hurt to tell the truth, especially after the gentle lovemaking they had shared. It hurt to admit she was less than what he had believed her to be. She knew well that such a revelation might destroy everything.

He raised an eyebrow. "For how long were you fucking him?"

"Nigh on seven months." She brushed an errant tear from her cheek and kept her gaze fixed on the fire. "It ended before you returned home."

From the corner of her eye, she saw Alan's lip curl in a sneer. "Not to Cam, apparently."

"I suppose not." She wrapped her arms around her body and rubbed vigorously. It was unbearably cold today. Sorcha wondered if she'd ever be warm again.

"But you say he didn't cuckold me last night? After seven months of sharing his bed, you refused him?"

"Aye."

Alan let out a harsh breath and ran his hand over his head. His fingers curled at the top of his scalp and clenched a clump of hair. "You lied to me, Sorcha."

"No, Alan, I—"

"You pretended to be someone you weren't."

Again, tears pricked at her eyes. "Aye. That I did."

"After that, why would I believe anything you tell me? How can you sit there and tell me Cam didn't take his pleasure on you after carrying you naked from my home?"

Sorcha clenched her arms, tightening her fingers until she knew they'd leave pink marks. "I won't lie to you again, Alan."

He made a disbelieving noise.

"It is all I can offer. You've no reason to trust me after I deceived you, but please believe me when I say I wanted only to make it good for you. I didn't mean to hurt you. I couldn't touch Cam last night—I wouldn't. He wanted to bed me, but I fought him. He locked me in his bedchamber and I escaped. To come home . . . to you."

"Were you aware I knew Cam in England?" Alan asked.

"He—he told me."

"For once, I wanted to bed a woman who hadn't been thoroughly debauched—by him or by some other Englishman. I wanted a pure, innocent Scottish lass to share my bed. To be my wife. Someone who could bear my children and be by my side."

"I can do all that. I will be by—"

He raised his hand to stop her from speaking. "No. I thought I'd achieved all that when I wed you, Sorcha. But you lied to me. Your father lied to me."

"My father knows nothing of this."

"He suspected. Why do you think he moved you and your family from Camdonn Castle?"

She stared at him, stunned.

He nodded. "Aye, he suspected what Cam was doing to you. Fucking you. Stealing you into his bedchamber at night? Taking you in the closets and in the cellars during the day?" Alan rose abruptly. "He taught you well, I imagine. Last night you offered yourself to me like a frightened virgin, but there's more to you, isn't there?" His eyes narrowed further. "Was it an enjoyable game to play, Sorcha? Playing the innocent to fool your poor besotted husband? Were you laughing inside at your clever deception?"

Poor besotted husband? She was flabbergasted. Until now, he'd given her no indication that his feelings for her went beyond kindness.

"No." Sorcha hung her head. *Truth.* Only the truth from now on. "I . . . didn't enjoy it. I wasn't laughing."

"What then?"

"The deception—it made me feel terrible. But last night was . . . special. You—you made me feel . . ." She took a deep breath. "*Desired.*"

"And Cam?" Alan said harshly. "How does Cam make you feel?"

"He makes me feel nothing. Not anymore."

"How did he make you feel, then? When you were fucking him?"

"Please don't ask me that."

He knelt before her and took her chin in firm fingers, forcing her face to tilt toward his. "Tell me, Sorcha. What did he do to you? How did he make you feel?"

"No," she whispered.

"Did he make you slick between your legs? Did he make your nipples hard? Did he make you ache for the feel of him thrusting inside you?"

"Alan," she begged.

"Did he make you do things for him? Suck his cock? Stroke his balls? Go on your hands and knees and tilt your arse at him so he could take you from behind? Take you over his knee so he could spank those firm cheeks?" His fingers tightened over her chin. "Open your eyes, *wife*, and tell me. Tell me everything."

Her vision swam. It was obvious he and Cam had once been close, because he described exactly what they'd done. "What do you want me to say?" she cried.

His hand dropped away from her chin. "I want you to say he never touched you. I want you to tell me this is all a nightmare and that I'll wake in the morning with my beautiful, unsullied wife lying beside me."

"I can't," she groaned.

He rose again and strode to the window. Facing away from her, he said, "Then tell me about your first time. Your real first time. With the earl."

"Please . . . no."

"Why not? If I couldn't have been there for my wife's loss of innocence, I think it's within my rights to hear about it, at least."

"He took me in a closet," she murmured, her cheeks flaming.

"And?"

"We were both fully clothed," she said in a monotone. "He'd flipped my skirts up. I couldn't see anything because they were covering my face." She remembered the scratchy feel of wool covering her nose. Cam had pinned her arms overhead, and unable to breathe, she'd turned her head to the side so the fabric wouldn't asphyxiate her.

"What happened?"

"He was . . . in a hurry. Rushed, because the door was unlocked and servants were passing by outside. I don't think he knew I was"—she licked her lips—"untouched."

"Did you make a noise, Sorcha? Did you scream, even with the threat of discovery?"

She pushed the words out. "I did."

"Did it hurt?"

"Aye, it did."

"But then you did it again after that, didn't you? Why?"

Humiliation swept through her, threatening to drown her, but she clawed herself up, grasping at the crumbling walls of her pride. "Because I wanted to." Her voice was hardly above a whisper.

"Because Cam made it feel good, didn't he? Even through the pain?"

She closed her eyes, remembering that day. The smell of cedar wood and lavender surrounding them. Her backbone pressing into the hard planks of the floor. The feel of a man's body on top of hers for the first time. And then the pain, so sharp, but then dulling to be replaced by something exciting and wonderful.

"Aye," she breathed.

"Did Cam realize it was your first time after he penetrated your body?"

"Aye, he did." And he'd begged for her forgiveness for being rough.

"What did he say?"

"He said sorry. He said he'd make it better next time."

"And did he?"

"He did." The second time they'd been in Cam's bed, and he'd gone slow, taking his time to arouse every part of her body before he'd taken her. It was the first time she'd come for him.

"I should hate you for this," Alan said in a low voice.

She rose from the chair and hobbled over to him. Her swollen feet were tender all over. She stood beside him at the window, gazing out over the glistening green of the lawn separating the cottage from the loch.

"Do you hate me?" she asked, too afraid to look at his face. Tension radiated from every pore of his body, creating a force that made her fear moving closer.

"I don't know."

"But do you believe it when I say nothing happened between me and Cam last night?"

"I don't know that, either. I don't know if I believe a word you say."

She understood. She looked up at him, seeing for the first time a terrible lump on the side of his head. Emboldened by empathy, she reached up to touch it, but he cringed away.

"What happened?" she whispered.

"I was in a fight."

"With whom?"

"Cam's guards."

So he had come after her, fought for her. A feeling she'd never experienced surged up from her chest. "Thank you."

"You're my wife. I will protect you, even if . . ." He didn't finish, so she did it for him.

"Even if I betrayed you."

He didn't answer.

She wished he'd let her touch him, because the sudden desire to lay her head on his shoulder was almost more than she could bear.

He glanced down at her. "You shouldn't be on your feet."

"I don't care."

His lips firmed. "Get some rest, lass. You probably didn't sleep at all last night."

"Neither did you," she murmured. "Will you come to bed with me?" Perhaps there she could be brave enough to embrace him, to show him how thankful she was for his acceptance, however tentative, of her. How grateful she was he'd tried to save her from Cam.

"No. I'll make up a pallet by the fire. You take the bed."

Her heart sank. "Alan, I—"

He raised a brow at her.

"I wish you would sleep with me. I am your wife."

"For now, Sorcha." His face was hard as carved marble.

"What do you mean?"

He eyed her, and she'd never seen anyone peruse her body so dispassionately. As if she were a broodmare and he assessed her for her ability to bear foals.

"I haven't decided what I'm going to do with you," he said finally, his voice cold. "Maybe I should send you back to the Earl of Camdonn. You are perhaps better suited to be his mistress than my wife."

CHAPTER FIVE

Cam awoke flopped over the desk in his study with a half-empty glass of whisky beside his hand and a headache from hell.

"Christ," he muttered. He rose unsteadily on shaky legs and squinted at the morning light sifting in between the cracks in the curtains. How much had he had to drink last night? Apparently far too much.

Sorcha.

"Christ!" he exclaimed, louder this time.

He remembered everything. *Almost* everything. The important bits, at least. The fact that he'd left Sorcha alone in his bedchamber, weeping in misery. The fact that he'd planned to release her this morning.

Maybe that wasn't a good idea, he mused, rubbing the bridge of his nose. Alan was a proud man—would he take her back after what had happened? Cam couldn't be sure. He'd seen Alan with women often enough. But he'd never been bound to anyone in the way he was bound to Sorcha. And Cam had never before interfered in Alan's relations with a female.

Perhaps Cam should simply lay down the facts and let her decide. He'd made a mistake by abducting her, but it was too late to undo it.

Through no fault of her own, her marriage to Alan was in jeopardy, but Cam would offer her a good life. He'd keep her here at Camdonn Castle. He'd support her and protect her and offer her an income large enough to make any Highlander swoon. He'd even have his lawyer draw up some favorable terms, if she desired.

If, after all that, she still wished to return to Alan—well, Cam would no longer hold her against her will.

At least, he'd try his damndest not to hold her against her will. He swallowed down the cotton in his throat and glanced longingly at the pitcher of whisky, but it was too early to get drunk.

The thought of chaining her in the castle dungeon was far preferable to the thought of returning her to Alan MacDonald's bed. But seeing her crying last night . . . He couldn't do that to her. As much as he wanted her, it killed him to see he'd caused her pain.

He dragged his unwilling body to his bedroom. He took a deep breath at the door, remembering the heartrending scene of her sobbing in his bed. What would her mood be this morning? Would she be angry? Still in tears? Accepting of her fate?

He opened the door to silence. His bed, though rumpled, was empty. He stepped inside to scan the room. "Sorcha?"

She was nowhere to be found. In desperation, he checked the window—it was locked, and in any case, she'd be a fool to try to squeeze through it—and searched the wardrobe and under the bed. Nothing.

It hit him like a brick in the gut. Clutching his stomach, he turned slowly toward the threshold. He'd walked right in. He'd been so bloody sotted last night, he hadn't locked the door.

She'd escaped.

Alan stood at the window as Sorcha rested. He wasn't tired, though he hadn't slept at all last night.

He could join his men in their duties. It was a busy time—not only was it the middle of harvest, but they were still herding the straggling cattle down from the shieling where they'd been taken to graze for the summer.

He could read one of the books he'd brought with him from England. He could go out and work, though Moira had forbidden manual labor. He could fix the damaged door, which was allowing a frigid draft to waft in from the outside.

He could take off his clothes, lie beside his wife, and make love to her. She was his, after all, to do with as he pleased.

No. His pride wouldn't allow him to touch her. He'd opened his heart to her far too easily, and now he paid the price. He wouldn't let her know how her deception cut him to the quick. Couldn't let her know he cared.

He shouldn't be feeling so strongly about this. But he was shaken to the core, flooded with disappointment and the bitter taste of betrayal. Out of all the men in the world, why had it been the goddamned Earl of Camdonn?

He walked to the partition separating the two rooms and gazed at the bed. She lay curled on her side, covered by a plaid with her pale arm wrapped over it. She was relaxed, her wine-red lips parted in slumber, her long eyelashes arcing at the bottoms of her eyelids. Her hair swept around her head like a midnight-colored fan.

If only he could bury himself deep into her sweet warmth again. Start over, from the beginning.

But as he'd told her earlier, she wasn't what he wanted, wasn't what he'd looked for in a wife. God knew for once he wanted a woman completely separate from Cam's influence. He'd thought she'd be that woman.

Yet . . . as cold as he felt toward her, something about her behavior nourished a seed of hope somewhere inside him. Maybe it was her pained honesty when he'd so brutally questioned her about her relations with Cam. In that, he knew intuitively, she hadn't lied.

But why? After deceiving him so smoothly last night, why wouldn't she try to continue the charade? He didn't think it was sheer fear of him discovering her secret. She'd been afraid to tell him everything, but resolute. Determined.

She was an enigma, this pale Scottish woman. One he didn't know how the hell to approach. She brought out a vulnerability in him he didn't like at all. Never before had a woman had the ability to hurt him. He'd been married to this one for less than a day, and the wound she'd inflicted on him pained him far more than the slice down his back.

Alan blew out a breath. Hell. All of his hopes, his dreams for a happy life in Scotland with his new wife, had gone up in smoke. Nothing was as it should be.

Memories washed through him, of the times he and Cam stood side by side, friends through good times and bad. In England they'd been inseparable through school and university. Together they were invincible, or so they'd thought as young men.

When Cam returned to Scotland, their communications had dwindled. Alan had been busy with his grandfather's estate, Cam had been busy assuming his duties as earl, and neither of them were faithful letter writers. And when he'd finally returned to Scotland eight months after Cam, Alan had been overwhelmed by clan business and his upcoming nuptials. He'd seen Cam on only a few brief occasions, the visit to Camdonn Castle last week the longest . . . and in retrospect, the strangest. He realized now Cam hadn't been quite himself. He hadn't looked Alan in the eye, and he'd drunk whisky steadily throughout Alan's visit.

Alan had missed his friend, thought about him often, mulled over how odd it was he saw him less in Scotland than he had in London, even though they lived closer to each other now. Alan planned to visit again once the political crisis had calmed. He'd admonished his Jacobites to live peaceably beside Cam's loyalist men. He'd considered asking Cam to join with him on an investment he planned to make in cattle.

Their duties had forced them apart, but in Alan's mind, their friendship was as solid as ever. If he ever truly needed anything, he knew Cam was just a few miles away.

But Cam had severed the tight bonds of their friendship last night when he abducted Sorcha. The sense of loss left Alan feeling winded. He felt as if two people close to him had died.

Sorcha shifted, made a low sound in her throat, then stretched and rolled to her back. Her eyes opened and slowly came to focus on him.

"Alan," she murmured. Her voice was like honey, smooth and sweet and sliding under his skin like a warm balm. "What time is it?"

"After noon."

"Have you slept at all?"

"I'm not tired."

She rose to her elbows. "I'll make you something to eat."

He stood silently, watching her as she left the bed, her shift falling to her shins. His cock swelled at the way the linen draped over her body, clinging to the pert breasts, the flare of her hips. She hobbled to the table in front of the silver-edged mirror he'd given to her as a wedding gift and ran a brush through the silky cascade of her hair. With deft fingers, she made a single braid down her back and then, with a shy glance at him, pulled a plaid over her shoulders and limped past him, slipping on her shoes set beside the front door.

Reminded that she'd escaped from Cam to come home to him, Alan winced at the clear pain in her movement. That simple fact warred with the bitterness of the betrayal swirling in him.

"No," he said.

She looked up at him, blinking in surprise.

"You're not to walk."

"But—but I need to—" A flush pinked the slanted angles of her cheekbones.

Alan could not abide the thought of her walking outside on those swollen, damaged feet. It could worsen her injury, open her sutures . . . worse, it could cause her more pain.

In two long strides, he was at her side. Kneeling, he reached behind her knees and pulled her into his arms. She gasped and stiffened, but when he settled her against his body, she relaxed. Still, her expression was alarmed.

"This will hurt your back."

"No." His stitches pulled slightly, but they held. He looked down at her face, so close to his own. Her skin reminded him of English ivory rose petals—soft, supple, smooth, with a tinge of pink. "Will you be warm enough?"

"Aye." Her voice was husky. "I'll only be a moment."

With her body nestled against his own, he carried her outside to the privy. The midday sun had risen high and peeked out between puffs of clouds, melting the earlier frost.

Within a few moments, she opened the wicker door and hobbled out. He swept her into his arms again and carried her back inside, where he gently set her beside the dining table so she could use it for support.

She unwrapped a meat pie brought from the wedding festivities last night. After she'd set the small table, she glanced up at him. "Would you like to eat?"

He shrugged and sat across from her, silent as she poured claret into their cups.

His wife shouldn't be waiting on him like this. He'd wanted them to be out here alone for the first days of their marriage, unencumbered by servants, so he'd arranged to have fresh food brought to them daily. Soon his three small outbuildings would be brimming with families come down from the shieling.

He'd wanted these few weeks alone with her. He hadn't thought about her serving him.

He groaned inwardly. Again, the need to take care of her, to protect her, nearly overcame him. It didn't make sense, given that he now knew what she was.

He tossed down his wine. She looked up from beneath her eyelashes, and anger flushed through him again. He detested the innocent glances, the false primness in the way she sat across from him.

"More?"

He pushed his cup forward. Eyes downcast, she refilled it with the red liquid.

How would she sit for Cam? Naked, most likely. Had Cam made her touch herself for him? Squeeze those delicate fingers over her nipples while he watched? Press them between the lips of her sex and rub frantically until she came?

Alan blew out a breath. Such thoughts would drive him mad. His comfortable cottage suddenly felt oppressive. Anger and pain and arousal swirled within him, heady and hot and . . . Hell. He stood abruptly, his chair scraping the floor as he pushed it backward. "I'll be outside."

She rose too. "May I go with you?"

He raked her body with his gaze—the long braid, the clinging shift, and finally the swollen, injured feet that made his chest clench. "You cannot."

Hurt flared in her expression before her eyelids lowered so he couldn't see the emotion behind her hooded eyes.

He pushed his chair away, pausing at the sound of her soft voice. "When will you return?"

"Later." Tucking the edges of his plaid under his belt, he strode out of the warmth of his cottage and into the cold.

In a haze, Cam went through his morning routine. After he ate breakfast, he met with his factor and his steward to discuss castle business. He listened to Duncan natter about London fashion as he shaved Cam and adjusted his wig. The old man prattled on as if he hadn't seen Cam shove his friend's newly wed daughter into his bedchamber last night.

Had Duncan aided her in her escape? Cam studied his manservant. No, he doubted it. Quick-witted, brave Sorcha had accomplished the feat all on her own while most of the castle inhabitants, including Duncan, were fast asleep.

Cam studied himself in the mirror as Duncan powdered his wig. Sorcha, ever frank with him, had stated she liked him without it. She loved to run her hands through his short-cropped hair. The wig made him look like a haughty English aristocrat, but she preferred him *au naturel*. She preferred his earthier, baser attributes. She'd always regarded his more manly features with something like openmouthed wonder.

Women often lusted over Cam, but Sorcha was different—she'd liked him as a person too. She understood him in a way nobody in his life ever had. She knew what gave him pleasure, but even more important, she intuitively understood what gave him pain. Her reaction to him—not to his money or title, but *him* as a man and a human being—had made him puff up like a peacock flaunting his plumage. Whenever she was near, he'd felt valued. He'd felt loved.

Besides Alan, Sorcha was the only person who liked him unconditionally. God knew his family didn't, especially his father, who on his infrequent visits to London had spent more time with Alan than he had with his own son.

"Did Alan MacDonald come here last night?" he asked his manservant abruptly.

Only the slightest falter in his movements marked Duncan's discomfiture. "Aye, milord. Whilst you were here with . . . Mrs. MacDonald."

Cam gritted his teeth at the implication Duncan made by stating her name in the precise way he did. "What happened?"

"The guards attempted to turn him away. He injured Rory Mac-Adam, milord."

"Will he be all right?"

"Aye. The doctor has seen to him. MacDonald's sword pierced a bit o' fat in his side."

Damn it. His own mad actions had caused blood to be shed. "And what happened?"

Duncan shrugged. "Alan would have gladly brought about his own demise to gain entrance. So I convinced him to go home."

Cam raised a brow. "How?"

"I only needed to point out the stupidity of his approach"—Duncan's lips quirked—"and then direct one of the men to cudgel him over the head."

Cam sighed. Knowing Alan, it shouldn't be surprising that he would fight to the death for his new wife. But would he have been so willing to die for her if he'd known how long she'd shared Cam's bed?

Duncan chewed his lip. "If I might ask, milord. Where's the lass now?"

Cam tried to appear unaffected. "Gone home, I imagine." He thought of several addendums to add to that comment, words like, "I was finished with her, you see," but not only were they lies, they made her look like an object, a whore.

He thought of the defiance in her eyes. No, Sorcha was neither object nor whore.

God, how he needed her.

When Duncan finished with him, Cam left his chamber and headed for the stables, determined to mount his horse and fly back to Alan's. He'd take her again, capture her from her bed if he had to kill Alan to do it—

Cam's step faltered, and then he paused on the gravel path, staring bleakly at the gray stone wall of the stables. As prideful and arrogant as he was, he saw those features in himself and understood them for what they were. He knew, unlike many of his station, that there existed better men in the world than he, and that many of his betters were born into stations below his own.

Like Alan.

Just then, a flurry of activity pulled his attention toward the entrance to the adjoining kitchen. He turned as MacLean appeared from behind the heavy wooden door, holding a dripping cloth to his face and looking rather the worse for wear.

"What happened to you, MacLean?" Cam growled.

"The bastard broke my jaw," the big man whined. "And my gut too."

Cam resisted rolling his eyes heavenward. Goddamn if MacLean wasn't imposing as hell, but he possessed the pain tolerance of an infant.

"I doubt that, MacLean. Has the doctor taken a look?"

"Aye, yer lordship. He says they're naught but bruised. But I know he's wrong. I know it!"

"Tell me what happened."

"Quick as a sprite on his feet, he is," the big man grumbled.

Cam almost smiled. Alan was by no means the faster of the two of them, but the man possessed a mean skill with his fists. A Highland youth was forced to be a fighter when sent away to England and faced with the cruelty of the schoolboys. Cam had rescued Alan only once—when he first arrived in England, a group of boys jumped him and broke his nose. After that, Alan had quickly learned to fight and was soon Cam's equal in skill. By then, though, Alan had earned the boys' respect and admiration, and brawling was no longer necessary.

Cam nodded soberly. "Yes, it's true he's quick. You're lucky he didn't kill you."

MacLean looked abashed that Cam had dared use him to fight Alan at all, and Cam put a hand on his shoulder. "You did well, man. Take pride."

MacLean straightened, giving him a gap-toothed smile. "I did well, milord?"

"You did indeed. Now go fetch a fresh cloth for your bruise. You may take the rest of the day for your leisure." With another pat on his back, Cam let the giant go.

He turned back toward the stables, then paused again.

Alan could have killed Angus MacLean but he'd shown mercy. Honorable Alan. His friend. They'd been closer than brothers for nearly twenty years.

Cam flattened his palm against a cool, flat stone and closed his eyes, listening to the nickering of horses inside.

Sorcha.

He must let her go. Alan's strict code of honor wouldn't let him give her up, even if he did discover the truth of her past with Cam. Even if he never cared for her like Cam did, he'd hold on to her until death, if only for his blasted Highland honor.

Cam had been out of his mind last night, and what he'd done was wrong. He'd caused them pain, and only because of his own spoiled, selfish need for her.

He *did* need her.

But she was Alan's now.

Repeating that to himself over and over like a papist's Hail Mary, he turned away from the stables and went to the barracks to see to his injured guardsman.

"Hold your hands up."

Dusk settled over Loch Shiel, quiet but for the soft swoosh of a misty rain falling on the water. All was serene except the simmering tension inside Alan MacDonald's cottage. He'd been absent the first day of their marriage, leaving Sorcha to her own devices. Unfamiliar with the aching feeling of loneliness tightening her chest, but not one to sit idly, she'd oriented herself in her new home. She had tidied the bedroom, scrubbed the already spotless hearth, and set about baking bannocks. Cooking was not a skill she knew well, having been raised at Camdonn Castle with its skilled kitchen staff.

The first batch was hard as bricks, but she'd coated the second with custard, and they'd come out edible, even rather delicious. Smiling at her achievement, she'd set them aside for later.

In the afternoon Moira came, along with their brothers, to bring food and see to her foot. No sooner had Moira given up on Alan and gone home than he'd reappeared, tired and wet to the bone. He'd eaten supper, making no comment on her bannocks but eating all of them, a fact that gave her a small measure of pride. Then he'd gone to sit on the edge of the bed to remove his shoes, and she'd made the command for him to hold up his hands.

He dropped his ties and looked up at her. "What did you say?"

Sorcha licked her lips. She might not be virginal, but she was no cocky whore brazenly flaunting her wares, either. She desperately wished to please this man. He was her husband, and she wanted to bring him back to her side.

Alan looked at her with disdain. When he focused those sky blue eyes on her, she felt like a parched flower withering in bright sunlight. As if he scrutinized her, stripped bare, exposed and naked . . . and found her lacking.

Cam had never looked at her this way. He'd gazed on her with interest. With lust. Even with affection. But it seemed too much to ask from her husband. It hurt, but she deserved it. In his place, pride would compel her to behave the same way.

Sorcha plunged ahead. "I said, lift your hands. Moira was here earlier, and she said I must clean your wound and change the dressing. I'll remove your shirt."

He studied her in silence for a long moment, and she realized he was exhausted. His eyes drooped slightly at the corners, and deep lines were etched into the sides of his mouth. His color wasn't as bright as usual, and his thick curls hung limply at his shoulders.

Last night he'd been married, taken her in carnal relations, had her stolen from his house, defeated Cam's henchman, ridden to Camdonn Castle, and tried to fight Cam's guards before finally being subjected to Mary MacNab's brutal doctoring. Moira had told Sorcha the whole story. He hadn't slept, except for the hours he'd been unconscious due to his head wound. And from the looks of it, he hadn't slept all day either.

He tore his gaze from hers, turned his back to her, and rigidly lifted his arms.

She rushed to help him with his shirt, trying not to wince at the dull pain when she added weight to her foot. Moira had brought her a crutch, but in her haste, she forgot to use it.

Standing behind him, she reached around to untie the strings holding the neck of his shirt closed. Her fingers fumbled and tightened the knot, and his hands closed over hers, gently prying her fingers away. Allowing her arms to fall to her sides, she clenched her teeth. How many times had she easily stripped Cam's shirt off him?

Best not to think of that now.

Alan finished loosening the ties, and she grasped the hem of his shirt. He shifted to take his weight off the fabric so she could lift it. She inched it up his wide torso, trying not to ogle his body. He was a beautiful specimen of a man. Strong, solid, his muscles defined in relief. Like Cam, he had very little fat on his body, but whereas Cam's muscles were lithe and sleek, Alan's bulged, etched under his skin as if by the blade of a sculptor. His innate strength almost frightened her, and would have had she not already seen his gentle nature. Both Alan and Cam exuded masculinity, but in such different ways.

She tugged the shirt over his head and set it aside. She untied the linen bandage and unwrapped it from his waist, slowly peeling the final layer, which had stuck to his wound. He didn't move—didn't make a noise. As she tugged the last of the fabric away, her eyes locked on to the mean-looking gash, and her breath caught.

"Oh sweet Lord," she gasped.

He didn't say anything, didn't move.

She just stared at it. The cut was deep and long, with scores of tiny black stitches sealing it shut. It slashed across his lower back, slightly diagonal, from low on his waist across to his shoulder on the other side.

She spoke dully. "You needn't have done this. You needn't have risked your life for the likes of me."

He whipped around so suddenly she flinched. "You are my wife. I would have risked my life—and more—to keep you safe."

Anger sharpened his tone and hardened his features, and it didn't escape Sorcha that he'd said the words in past tense. She clenched her fists at her sides and closed her eyes. *And now, Alan? Would you keep me safe now? Knowing I am not the virgin you desired? Knowing I am a liar?*

She was far too cowardly to utter the words.

She opened her eyes to find him staring at her. Shuttering his expression, he turned away and muttered, "Clean it, then."

Biting her lip and tensing her muscles to keep them from trembling, she fetched a clean rag and the water she'd warmed over the fire. She dipped the cloth and began the slow, painstaking process of cleaning out the wound, gently scrubbing away the blood and sweat that had accumulated throughout the day. In the silence, she was aware of every move he made, from his deep breaths to the heartbeat pulsing beneath his skin. As she rinsed the cloth, she looked at the blond hair softly curling over his shoulders and down past his nape. He'd tied it back in a queue yesterday, but today he'd left it loose and flowing. What would it feel like to comb her hands through that thick mane? Biting her lip, she squeezed out the cloth and refocused on her task.

She tried desperately to keep from hurting him. Holding her hands steady, she cleaned over the sutures and between them, more than Moira had said was required, but she wanted to be thorough. If he died from infection, it would be her fault.

The only noises were of the water sloshing in the pot, the gentle rustle of fabric as she shifted on the bed, and the soothing sound of the gentle rain falling outside.

She rinsed the cloth again, watching his broad shoulders rise and fall with his deep intakes of air, watching the muscles ripple beneath the taut skin. She moved her gaze over each contour, imagining running her fingers, then her tongue over every dip and curve.

She remembered his taste from last night. Warm and earthy. Like a blade of grass on a hot summer's day, but mixed with his own essence. She wanted to lick him all over.

It was a bad impulse, a wicked, debauched thought. One she should banish immediately. One she might have considered during her wild affair with the Earl of Camdonn. But Alan would be disgusted if he could read her mind.

He'd said he wanted a good wife. An innocent.

She'd been innocent once, and she could regain her innocence, if that was what he wanted. Not in body—no, that was impossible—but in her mind and heart. She'd curtail her rampant lustful imaginings.

When she had almost finished and had reached the area where the cut rounded his side, he gasped and flinched away.

"Did I hurt you?" Her voice broke the extended silence between them and sounded unnaturally loud.

"No," he said stiffly. Then, "It tickles."

She stared at the back of his head, fighting a smile. "Well, forgive me. I didn't mean to tickle you."

"Nothing to forgive."

"I haven't finished yet."

He released a breath through pursed lips. "Continue, then."

"You mustn't move."

"I'll try."

Before she thought about it, she slipped an arm around his waist, resting her palm flat on the indent of his chest just beside his heart. "Focus on my hand here and perhaps you won't feel the other so much."

She cringed, realizing her touch was brazen, and not something an innocent, newly married maid would have done.

She started to move away, but his hand came to rest over hers, heavy and warm, pinning her palm between his fingers and his chest.

Raising the damp cloth to his wound, she continued to clean its edge. His muscles tensed under her hands, but he didn't cringe again, and she finished in a few swipes. She threw the cloth into the dirty water in the pot.

"It's clean now. I'll give it a few moments to dry."

"Aye."

For a long moment, he held her hand pinned against his heart. Sorcha's breaths grew shallow, and her heartbeat surged. Then he withdrew his hand from hers, and she let her arm fall away.

She wanted to touch him again. Run her fingers along the outsides of his bulging arms. Feel the muscles flex and move and heat under her touch.

She ruthlessly squashed the wanton thought and glanced at the dwindling fire. "Are you cold?"

"No."

"Will you sleep in bed with me tonight?" She immediately regretted the question, for it, too, had sounded forward. Could she say or do nothing without second-guessing herself?

"I think not. I'll lay a pallet on the floor."

She was glad he was turned away. He wouldn't be able to see the shining tears of hurt pricking at her eyes. "Aye," she said, her voice rough with emotion. "I understand."

"Do you, Sorcha?"

"I do." Pride would keep her upright. It was all she had left to hold on to, as fragmented and ruined as it had become in the past hours. She rose from the bed and took the pot of water to dump down the drain in the wall that led to a cesspit outside. When she limped back into the bedroom, he'd turned so he faced her as she entered.

She tried to smile at him. "The clock says it's half past six. We've been married a full day."

He glanced at the clock on the mantel. "Aye. So we have," he said, his tone flat.

Perhaps the longest day of her life. When his gaze returned to hers, it was emotionless.

"Don't you want to ask me where I was all day, Sorcha?"

She stared at the floor. "It's none of my business where you were."

The bed creaked as he shifted his weight, and when he spoke, there was an edge to his voice. A hint of challenge. "Isn't it?"

A shiver of dread began low in her belly, traveled up her spine. From the base of her skull it spread down her arms, making her hands tremble. Had he gone to the mountain? Where the prostitutes and lemans lived?

"I would like to know where you went . . . but perhaps"—her voice shook when she continued—"I don't deserve to know."

"Perhaps you don't."

She glanced back up at him. His eyes reminded her of ice chips floating at the edge of the loch.

It was one of her worst fears. That she wouldn't be enough. That one day her husband would tire of her and slake his lust upon someone else.

Long ago, when she'd seen other abandoned wives despair over the loss of their husbands, and again when she'd watched her own dear father ascend the mountain, she'd promised herself that no matter what it took, once she married, she'd hold on to her husband.

How naive she'd been. They'd hardly been married a day, and he was already indifferent. Worse, she'd brought it on herself by her thoughtless, impulsive actions, her cowardice, and her lies.

She knew Alan imagined her with Cam. She knew Alan pictured Cam's cock entering her, pictured their hands on each other's bodies, their limbs entwined. The images rolled off of him in invisible waves, and along with them, his anger seethed. Her betrayal and her deception were boiling within him, and the likelihood he'd take a mistress in retaliation was very high indeed.

She drew in a lungful of air. "Last night you told me it was important for a man and his wife to be open and honest with each other."

"Aye," Alan said on a sneer. "I have observed how long that 'honesty' lasted."

"But I agreed with you," she protested. "I promised myself that after that one deception—which I believed would save us both from unnecessary pain—I would never betray you again." She took a step closer to him. "And I meant it. It has been so difficult, but I have been honest with you, completely honest, about everything from that moment until now."

"Will you continue to be honest with me, Sorcha?"

"Aye. Forevermore. No matter what happens."

He raised an eyebrow, and his lip curled in sarcastic disbelief. "Really?"

Sharp, cutting pain sliced through her at his expression, his mocking words. How could this man wield such power over her? And so quickly?

She almost wished he'd beaten her.

CHAPTER SIX

I f not for the fact that the Jacobites had taken Inverness in the weeks before, Cam would have left Camdonn Castle to visit his favorite establishment tucked away on the banks of the firth. Once there, he would have proceeded to tumble a few slight, dark-haired wenches while imbibing half the place's stock of whisky to help him pretend those wenches were Sorcha.

But given the volatile political climate in his part of the world, it would not be wise. Cam was a Whig like his father, who'd been aligned with the Duke of Argyll and had been granted a viscountcy in the English peerage. Cam had spent most of his life in England, speaking English and involved in English politics. He was a lord, and ultimately, because of his ancestral and personal bonds, he was a tacit supporter of the government.

The mood of the people in this region of Scotland leaned heavily in favor of the Pretender. Out of sympathy for their cause, Cam turned a blind eye to the Jacobite grumblings on his own lands. Scotland's unpopular union with England eight years ago had done nothing to better their situation, and with the death of Queen Anne and the ascent of the Hanoverian King George to the throne of Great Britain, the time was ripe for rebellion.

Since his return home in January, Cam had maintained tight scrutiny of current events. In the past month, the Duke of Argyll and his government army had holed up in the southeast in Stirling, to protect the crown jewel that was Edinburgh. Meanwhile, the Earl of Mar and his Jacobites had taken most of the northern cities, pausing finally at Perth. Just days ago, a Highland army thousands strong had marched south to join them.

The two sides were on a collision course in the Lowlands, and it was only a matter of time before their ultimate clash.

So far the Jacobites had ignored Cam. If they beat Argyll in Stirling, then Cam might have cause to worry for his title and lands. Until then, he resolved to keep his head low and heighten security on his properties. He made sure his barracks were well stocked—not for the purpose of joining either side of the confrontation, but to protect his own interests. He'd focused so much of his attention on this task that when Alan had arrived in Scotland, he'd scarcely had a moment to welcome him home.

His plan to abstain from rousing unwanted attention meant that he was tied to his land until the uprising was over. There would be no Inverness whorehouses to soothe his aching need. No bawdy taverns to ease his troubled thoughts.

A man could sit and drink in his study for only so many days before it became more of a tedious task than an escape from reality. The only remaining option, though he hadn't ridden up there since his father died, was the mountain.

Cam sat in his study, whisky in hand, and thought of Sorcha inside that tiny cottage with Alan. Him touching her. Her crying out in ecstasy. The two of them, laughing together. Laughing at him.

God. It was like poison coursing through his veins.

He wanted her so badly, his blood thrummed with it. His cock ached for her. His limbs strained for her. His heart was affected worst of all. It had shattered into a million pieces, and Sorcha was the only one capable of gluing it back together.

Every day, he considered taking her from Alan again. Chaining her to the walls of Camdonn Castle so she couldn't escape. Ordering Alan killed the next time he tried to win her back.

Taking what he wanted—what he *needed*—from her. By force.

That was where the fantasy ended. Because as much as he loved sinking his cock into Sorcha's tight sheath, there had been so much more to it than that. Her seemingly unconditional acceptance was the true source of his dependence on her.

Just as he'd been dependent on his governess after his mother died so long ago. He'd thought he'd never survive when she left him. He remembered running away from home to find her, only to be discovered by his father's men a day later, a frightened seven-year-old boy shivering in a ditch on the outskirts of Glenfinnan.

His father had eyed his tear-streaked face with disdain and then ordered a servant to beat him, apparently deeming the task beneath him. A month later, he sent Cam to school in London, where he'd lived in lonely misery until he'd met Alan and they'd become fast friends.

The Sorcha of the other night—angry, defiant, and finally hopeless, her body willing but her mind completely repelled by him—was not who he wanted. He wanted her beside him in bed, but he also wanted her happiness, and her love. If he took her by force, he'd have none of that.

All his other options exhausted, wretched in mind and body, Cam finally gave in.

He rode to the mountain to see Gràinne.

This was hell.

The quiet days Alan had imagined spending alone with Sorcha, learning about his wife, pleasing her and teaching her how to please him, had turned into endless hours of silent, seething tension. Her near desperation to placate him was obvious, but it failed to penetrate the barrier he'd erected around himself as soon as he'd discovered she was a liar.

He'd have been furious to learn she'd given herself to anyone before him, but the fact it had been Cam took him over the edge of hot fury into frozen anger.

As close as he'd been to Cam, an insidious rivalry had always existed between them. What Alan had lacked in the title and funds possessed by his friend, he'd made up for by sheer strength and ability to sway others. When they worked together to achieve whatever ends they sought, they always encountered success. They never clashed. Both knew it would be brutal if it ever happened. But it was there. That oh-so-subtle competition, often seen by one only in the gleam of the other's eye.

And now the game had begun. It was war, it was deadly, and Sorcha was their Helen of Troy.

Cam could return at any moment to try to steal her away, this time with more men. For the first two days, Alan had been on guard, keeping his weapons near and his hand on the hilt of his broadsword. When he went for his first long "ride," he'd called several of his men away from the herd to guard the cottage in the event Cam tried to come back to kidnap her.

Sorcha seemed to think Cam wouldn't return. But why not? As much as Alan wanted to kill the earl for what he'd done, a part of him understood. Alan, too, seemed to be developing somewhat of an obsession with his wife.

"Would you like more eggs?" Sorcha asked softly.

"No." Even that singular word came out harsh, like a punishment, and she flinched, hurt flaring in her eyes.

He looked away. He hated what he was doing to her, but he couldn't help it. The damage had been done. It was eating away at him like a rabid disease, and he didn't have a cure. In a way, he didn't want one. He wanted to punish her. She deserved his wrath, every bit of it. He'd never harm her physically, but he wouldn't quash his anger. He refused to hide it from her. She deserved every cool look, every careless shrug.

Surely she knew most English husbands would have discarded her the moment they learned she wasn't pure. He'd considered it, but ultimately he wasn't prepared to take such a step. Something in her demeanor, her sincere candor since that first morning, her willingness to take responsibility for what she'd done, stopped him.

A part of him knew that if he continued treating her with such aloof disdain, she might be the first to leave. She would run away from him. Probably directly into Cam's waiting arms.

Damn them both.

God help him, he didn't want her to leave. His desire to keep her close was too strong. He was perversely fascinated by her, not just by her appealing form, but by something deeper. *Her.* The woman who would risk death escaping from her lover to return to the husband she hardly knew. The woman who desperately craved his forgiveness for the wrong she'd done him.

It was turning into a test of wills. How much could she take before she broke? Before Alan's anger dissolved into something else? Would it be gentle love or sheer need? Would he surrender to lust and take her again? If so, it wouldn't be like that first night. No, this time, he'd take her like she deserved to be taken.

That pretty mouth rounded over his cock while he fisted his hands in her hair and pumped himself inside her. Feeling her hot tongue slide over his shaft as he asked, "Does Cam fuck you like this? Does he take your mouth, Sorcha? Does he make you gasp for air?"

Alan sucked in a breath. Her nearness was driving him mad. The sweet smell of her permeating the small space of his cottage—a place he had once thought of as his own. A place that had symbolized peace to him. Now it was filled with her confusing, infuriating, intoxicating, beautiful presence.

"Moira will be out later. Mary MacNab is coming too, to check on our wounds."

Alan sighed. He wasn't eager to see the old witch again. "I'll be back by the time they arrive."

"You're leaving again?"

"Aye."

"Will you be riding?"

"Aye."

Pressing her lips together as if to stop herself from saying anything more, she rose to clear the plates. He watched her in his peripheral vision, pleased to see she no longer limped as she walked.

Suddenly, she spun around to face him, clutching the front ties of her stays.

Her fingers trembled as they plucked the strings.

Alan froze in place. She pulled the ends of the stays apart. She pushed her sleeves over her arms and the fabric fell down in a heap to her ankles. Stays, petticoats, and shift puddled on the floor, leaving her bare.

Alan hid the shudder that racked his body at the sight of her. She was absolutely perfect. Lush curves softened her slender form. Her breasts were heavy and plump, with cherry-red nipples topping them, already hardening in the cool air. Her stomach was pale, slightly rounded. Her waist was narrow; her hips flared. At the juncture of her thighs, the triangle of hair was so dark as to seem nearly blue-black in the dimness of the room.

Alan let his eyes skim over her. His own body roared into life, as if her shedding her clothes had lit a thousand fires under his skin. But, by sheer force of will, he kept still, his eyes blank, his expression flat.

He dragged his gaze back up to her face, her pleading, desperate face, and raised a cynical brow.

Silence. Then her voice, shaking with a plea. "Take me to bed, Alan."

He flicked a glance at the window and then back to her. "It is noon."

"Does that matter?"

"It does." Though he couldn't muster an explanation why.

She licked her lips. "I want to please you."

"I know." God, he nearly flinched at the sound of his voice. He sounded so damned cold.

But whether he liked it or not, her sweet penance was chipping away at the ice encasing his heart, and he felt an unwelcome surge of affection for her.

"I want you to forgive me. I want to show that I can be a good wife to you. That we can be happy together." She lowered herself to her knees before him, dragged in a breath, and then continued in a low voice. "I am yours. My life is yours. My well-being is yours. But please, please take me. Take me as a husband takes his wife. Only then will I know you've forgiven me."

She was right. She belonged to him now. She'd made a vow, under God, to be his. She bowed her head against the steel of his gaze.

Struggling not to touch her, Alan spoke. "I freely gave you my trust once. But you destroyed it—you made a mockery of it with your lie."

"I know," she whispered, her head still bowed. "I'll do whatever it takes to regain your trust."

"If I spurn you from my bed?"

"Even then."

"Would you seek out a lover to bed behind my back? Would you return to the Earl of Camdonn?"

"Never," she bit out.

"What if I should take a mistress?"

She glanced up at him, and the heat of possessive anger flared briefly in her eyes. "It would hurt me if you did that. It might destroy me."

"And if I choose to destroy you?"

He was testing her. But she'd made a promise, and he wanted to know that she meant it no matter what.

She clenched her jaw. Her shoulders shook. It was a long moment before she spoke again.

"Then, Alan . . ." she ground out, and he knew she'd given away the final vestiges of her pride, had bared her soul and offered him, a virtual stranger, ultimate power over her. "Then I would be destroyed."

Alan closed his eyes. Maybe he needed to destroy her—destroy them both—and only then could they build something from the ashes.

Gràinne opened the door, and her jaw dropped at the vision she beheld on her threshold.

The new Earl of Camdonn. *Blessed Virgin.* Not the nervous wee lad who'd come knocking fourteen years ago, begging her to relieve him of his pesky virginity. His hair was cut short now, almost to his scalp, but it was still dark as pitch. He was so tall she had to tilt her face up to see his.

It had been two years since Gràinne had last cast eyes upon him, but the image of him most deeply imprinted on her memory was of a fourteen-year-old fumbling youth with the makings of a fine man.

She'd taken him under her wing. Taught him some of the joys of carnal communion.

But he would know more now. He was fully grown, virile, and with a look in his eye that bespoke his power and experience.

"Well, Gràinne. Are you going to let me in?" His voice was low, dark, and dangerous. *Oooh.* Even as jaded as she was, it sent a tremor down her spine.

He'd changed since his days as a youth. He was darker now, not only in appearance but in demeanor. The last time they'd slept together was over five years ago, when they had separated as friends.

He smiled at her, but it was tight-lipped, and the expression in his eyes was deep and haunted. Gràinne was no fool. He wanted something from her. Something she'd be more than willing to offer, given enough silver. She almost chuckled. Cam was never thrifty with his coin, like so many other men were. Probably because he was the richest man within a hundred miles.

She opened the door wider and stepped aside to let him pass. "Come in, love."

The inside of her cottage was warm and cozy. She had no protector now, but Cam did remember on occasion to send her a little something, and as old as she was—nearing her fortieth year—Gràinne was still popular enough among the whores on the mountain. Never knowing who might come by, she kept her home cheerful and welcoming, and herself and her clothing spotlessly clean. After her daily routine of plucking out the few strands of gray that had begun to appear, she brushed her hair three hundred strokes, but never wore a cap or put it up. She left her long red locks to cascade in thick curls down her back. As much as people disparaged red hair, she knew it was nothing but the green-eyed monster rearing his ugly head. Every other hair color was drab in comparison. Her hair was her best feature, and she flaunted it brazenly.

"Please sit." She gestured to the table in the center of the one-room cottage. "Would you like a dram of whisky?"

The earl lowered himself into a chair beside her, and when he looked up at her, sharp intelligence quickly blotted the stark pain in his eyes. "Yes, please. Thank you."

She went to the cupboard to pour the amber liquid into her finest goblet. When she brought it out to him, he took it from her, wrapping his hands around the cylindrical shape. To this day, she remembered what those long fingers felt like inside her. Her cunt grew damp at the thought.

He took a deep swallow of the amber liquid and set the cup down. His eyes met hers across the table. As much as he'd changed on the outside, she sensed he was still the same man underneath. She wouldn't mind exploring the similarities and differences more intimately. She wouldn't mind at all.

"How are you, Gràinne?"

"I'm well," she said. "And yourself?"

He broke the eye contact, turning his gaze to her bed. "I've been better."

Her response was automatic. "I can comfort you, love."

His mouth twisted into a bitter smile, but he didn't look at her. "Can you, Gràinne? I've come to see if you can."

She had already released the clasp on her *arisaid*—her woman's plaid—and was plucking at her stays. She pulled them off her shoulders, pushed her shift down her arms, and proudly naked—for she possessed the body of a woman half her age—she walked around the table to stand in front of him. Deep in his thoughts, he hardly glanced at her as she knelt before him and reached forward to unfasten his breeches.

"Tell me your troubles. Like you used to."

He didn't answer, just adjusted in the chair to give her easier access to his ties.

She loosened the top knot and separated the fabric. His cock lay against the taut, flat skin on his stomach. Not flaccid, but not at a full stand either. She grinned at the sight of the earl's shaft. She'd seen many specimens of manhood—large and small, fat and thin—but the size and girth of Cam's penis had always fit her most pleasantly.

She stroked one long fingernail down the silky length, and to her satisfaction, it twitched and grew another inch.

"Is it the Jacobites?" she asked in a low voice. "Are they causing you grief?"

"No."

She glanced up at him seductively. She had his attention now. He was gazing down at her, studying her every move.

Very deliberately, she licked her lips, then swiped the point of her tongue from the root to the tip of his cock. "Mmm . . . you still taste like heaven."

She looked at him from beneath her lashes. He didn't smile. "You were always very kind to me."

"It isn't kindness," she said, pretending to be affronted. "'Tis the truth." She curled her fingers around him, tightening then releasing. Though outwardly she focused on his cock, she paid close attention to his reaction to her. His chest shuddered as his breath hitched, and then he sighed.

"A lass, then?" she asked, making her voice light. She hoped he would say no. She wasn't a stupid woman, nor was she prone to fanciful dreaming. She knew he'd had many whores and taken mistresses. One day—probably soon—he'd marry some fine lady. It was the way of the world. But it didn't mean she'd stopped feeling altogether. She held a special place in her heart for the Earl of Camdonn. She always would.

She tightened her fingers around his shaft and pumped it lightly, savoring the feel of it expanding in her hand.

He grunted. "Yes. A woman."

Poor, sweet Cam. At that moment, he reminded her of the frightened fourteen-year-old. "Your mistress?"

"Not anymore."

She pumped him again, using her free hand to open his breeches wider, giving her access to his balls. She slid her fingers under them, tickling the sensitive spot at the base. "Why, love?"

"She married."

"Och," she said sympathetically, bringing her lips lower to brush them over his exposed crown.

"She married Alan MacDonald five days ago."

"Ah." Gràinne came down from the mountain infrequently, for women of her status weren't welcome in Glenfinnan, but she lived in a tight-knit community, and she knew of most of the goings-on in the glen.

Alan MacDonald, the Highlander who'd spent his youth among the English, had returned to claim his ancestral right as laird of the MacDonalds of the Glen. Sorcha Stewart, a dark beauty whose father was the old factor at Camdonn Castle, had immediately caught his eye.

Aye, Gràinne knew the whole story. She hadn't known, however, that Sorcha was Cam's mistress. Had Alan MacDonald known?

Gràinne infused her voice with sympathy. "And now you cannot have her."

Cam's fingers threaded in her hair, and he pulled her closer to his pelvis and his seeking cock.

"I took her on her wedding night, but she . . . she rejected my . . . advances. Then she escaped."

That, she couldn't ignore. Pushing against his hand, she looked up at him, eyes wide. "Truly?"

"Yes," he said grimly. "I'm surprised the news hasn't already traveled up here."

She was too.

"I've exposed her secret. I've placed her marriage in jeopardy." He groaned. "Hell, I've destroyed her. And yet . . ." He pushed Gràinne's head down. There was no way she could fight the power of his hand— not that she wanted to. She opened her mouth, taking his cock deep, until the head pushed against the opening of her throat. "And yet I want to do it again. Force her to be with me. Chain her to the walls of Camdonn Castle. Feel her sucking my prick . . . ah . . . like you're doing now, Gràinne."

Moving up to the top of his shaft, she rounded her lips over him and pushed back down slowly, feeling every contour of his cock. He was solid now, hard as granite except for the covering of soft skin and delicate bumps marking his veins. She curved her palm over his balls, massaging gently. He tilted his hips, forcing himself deeper down her throat.

With her saliva lubricating the way, she slid her lips up, then down, making a tight seal over his hot flesh. She closed her eyes. His other hand came to tangle in her hair, and he guided her movements, forcing her lower, then tugging her up only to push her to the base of his cock yet again. She opened her throat and took him. She inhaled him until she felt him to the roots of her hair. Using her tongue, she explored every part of him, gasping when he pulsed, his seed boiling against her lips.

"I want her back, Gràinne. I want her to want me. I want her to love me. I want her to be obedient . . . like you are. Responsive . . . like you are."

Gràinne couldn't stand it anymore. She slid her fingers between her legs and rubbed furiously. She moaned over his cock as he guided her, deep and rough. She scraped her teeth up and down his sensitive shaft, and he growled low in his throat.

Her cunt was dripping, dampening the insides of her thighs. Her clitoris was hot and swollen and eager. She drew slick circles around it with two fingers. Then, when she couldn't bear teasing herself a moment longer, she tapped her middle finger against it. Her whole body shuddered in response. Using two fingers, she pinched it.

She cried out over Cam as spasms jerked through her body. At some point, he hauled her mouth off his cock and yanked her against him as her orgasm surged in deep, rolling waves through her body. His cock was wedged between them like a steel rod cradled by her breasts. His taut stomach pressed against her cheek as he held her to him, his hips moving in tempo with her clenching cunt.

When the storm receded, he rose, hefting her along with him. She stumbled, clinging to him as he kicked off his breeches. He took her waist in his hands and spun her around. Then he pushed on her back between her shoulder blades, bending her over the table.

Gràinne reached forward, clasping the opposite edge of the small table with both hands as he moved behind her, pressing his burning shaft into the crack of her arse.

"Why doesn't she want me like you do?" His voice rumbled down her spine, prickled the back of her neck. "Even when years pass between my visits to you, you're always willing, always ready for me."

She whimpered, but the sharp, ever-analytical part of her mind knew the answer. It was because she was a whore and she knew how to excel in her trade, while Sorcha, even after having played the part of his secret mistress, was merely a young woman seduced by his bonnie masculinity.

The blunt tip of Cam's finger slid down the crack of her backside, followed by the heat of his cock until they settled between her wet folds. Without preamble, he tunneled into her. Gripping the edge of the table, Gràinne arched her back until his mouth touched her neck.

"Take me," she murmured. "I need you. Take me hard." Her intuitiveness helped her to be very good at her trade. She gave him exactly what he wanted to hear—even if she wasn't the woman he wanted to hear it from.

He fucked her. Gràinne could do nothing but hold on and take the battering. She groaned in pleasure. She panted. Her body caught on fire. It was animalistic rutting in its purest, finest form. His solid cock grinding into her as she tightened around him. Her hip bones thrusting almost painfully into the table. The wet sounds their bodies made with the repetitive advance and retreat. Her breasts smashed hard against the wood, and her nipples rubbed gloriously against the rough whorls. Cam's hands clenched her waist so tightly she was certain he'd leave marks. She gloried in each bite of pain that came with the advance of his cock until it slammed against her womb.

His thrusts deepened, hardened. She began to shake deep in her core. The vibrations branched out until she shuddered from head to toe. He was solid and strong behind her, inside her. Rock hard as he reached the pinnacle.

His fingers tightening over her hips, he slammed into her once, twice. Then with a long, low groan, he froze, shaking. Spilling his seed deep within her. Gràinne made a low keening noise, pushing her arse into his pelvis as tightly as it would go. His pulsing cock sparked off her own spasms, and she let herself loose, shuddering as release opened her from the inside out.

They both stilled slowly, emerging out of the orgasmic haze. Gràinne realized with a pang that they'd spilled the expensive whisky, and it was dripping onto the packed dirt floor. Cam leaned over, bracing his weight on either side of her.

"Thank you, Gràinne," he whispered, his voice thick. He moved a strand of hair away from her cheek and his lips brushed over the spot, warm and soft.

After a long moment, he pushed himself off her. Gathering her pliant body into his arms, he carried her to the bed.

CHAPTER SEVEN

Cam stripped off the rest of his clothes and lay facing Gràinne, his body an arm's length from hers. He'd almost forgotten how she pleased him. Physically, he felt sated, but being with Gràinne hadn't sealed the chasm in his heart. If anything, it had grown.

He'd betrayed Sorcha.

A foolish thought, really, considering the fact she was probably sleeping with Alan at this very moment. They were probably fucking like rabbits in their secluded little cottage.

Gazing at him with her intelligent doelike eyes, Gràinne reached up to stroke his cheek.

He groaned. "I want her back, Gràinne. I should never have allowed her to marry."

"Could you have stopped the marriage?"

"Yes, I think so." Why hadn't he tried? Christ, he wished he'd faced his feelings for Sorcha before he'd lost her.

"Does she love you, Cam?"

He closed his eyes, then dragged the heavy lids open. "She did. I think."

"But not anymore?"

He sighed. "It has little to do with love. She has married Alan, so now she is bound to him. Even if she hated him and loved me, she would resist me to her dying breath for the sake of her honor."

Gràinne's lip curled. "I've never been a woman to go on about honor."

Cam laughed out loud. An honorable Gràinne? The two words didn't seem a likely pairing. "Why not?" he asked through his chuckles.

She shrugged lightly. "What is the point? Mark my words, honor always comes round to bite you in the arse."

"Is that so?"

"Always," she said confidently. She moved a few inches closer, and he felt the heat of her. His cock reacted immediately. Thinking of Sorcha . . . with Gràinne's willing flesh so close. A combination his restless, hungry body couldn't refuse.

"But won't you be thinking of marriage soon?" Gràinne asked. "Isn't it time for you to be worrying about heirs and sons and such?"

He rested his hand on her bare shoulder. "Implying I'm getting long in the tooth, are you?"

She huffed a laugh. "I'll never admit to being old, love. And since you're eleven years my junior, I trust you'll always be a mere youth to me."

He cocked a brow. "Is that so?"

"Aye," she said soberly. But her brown eyes twinkled. "A green lad, that's what you are."

He snorted. "Hardly."

The twinkle died. "Perhaps you should be abandoning the thought of pretty Highland mistresses and instead be on the lookout for a wife."

"I don't want a wife," he said stubbornly. "I want Sorcha."

"Would you marry the lass?"

"What?"

"Did you never entertain the idea of marriage to her?"

"I can't marry her." At least that's what he'd thought at the time. He had always comported himself as his station required. When he returned to England to manage his viscountcy, nobody would respect him if he brought along a Gaelic-speaking, *arisaid*-wearing Highland wife.

Like a brick on the head, it finally hit him what an ass he was. She might have fallen in love with him and married him had he pursued it in the proper way. And, of course, he only realized this now. When it was too damned late.

Gràinne pursed her lips. "Because you're a mighty lord and she's a nobody."

He'd never felt such self-loathing as he did at this moment.

"Right." Glancing at her, he blew out an exasperated breath. "Don't look at me that way, Gràinne."

Gràinne stroked a fingernail down his chest, lighting a string of heat in its wake. "Perhaps you should leave her to her MacDonald and begin to think of the high-and-mighty lady you'd wish to marry."

"When the time comes—and please mark it won't be for a while yet—I shall go to England or the Lowlands to find my bride. A rich heiress would be preferable. With a good, strong bloodline." He'd find a woman who was the complete opposite of Sorcha MacDonald.

"Ah," said Gràinne, tapping her finger on his belly. "You prefer to shop for a wife in the same manner you'd shop for an expensive horse."

"Exactly."

"Perhaps it is time to begin your search."

"No," he said softly. "Not yet." That was one step he wasn't ready for.

"You won't be this young"—her fingertip stroked his growing cock—"this virile, forever."

"No, I won't," he said gruffly. "So I'd best take advantage of it now, hadn't I?"

"Aye," she whispered. Her hand left his cock and her fingers entwined with his, bringing them to her mound. "Do you feel your seed leaking from me?"

"I do." He slid his fingers into her wet heat and closed his eyes. "I want to win her back, Gràinne. I want her to come to me willingly. I want her to choose me over Alan."

Damn it, that would never happen. Why couldn't he face the truth?

Gràinne pushed on his fingers, guiding them deep inside her. "Ahh . . . You wish her to choose to be your mistress over the wife of the laird?"

Yes. Yes, that was exactly what his heart desired. He wanted to win her fairly. If only it wasn't too late. And if her marriage to Alan could be dissolved, hell, he'd do it now. He'd marry her in a heartbeat.

"Yes, Gràinne." He scissored his fingers inside her channel, and she took a sharp intake of breath. It was an act designed to please him, but he enjoyed it nevertheless. "I want her to be in my bed, gasping like you just did."

Gràinne's eyes fluttered shut. She tilted her hips so he could press his fingers deeper. "I do so love the feel of you inside me."

He pulled his fingers out and slid them back in. She was sopping wet with the mixture of her sex and his seed. Slick and ready and willing.

"I have an idea," she gasped.

His heartbeat ratcheted upward. Gràinne used to say that before suggesting some new and innovative way for them to find pleasure in each other.

"What's that?" he asked gruffly.

"I know how to make you happy, love."

His heart sank. That, of all things, seemed an impossibility. "How's that?" His fingers pumped into her. Her slick walls tightened over him, and his cock pulsed in response.

"I know how you might win her back."

Yanking his fingers out of Gràinne, he flipped her over onto her back and loomed over her. "Open your eyes."

She obeyed. He ground his cock into the drenched apex of her legs.

"Tell me," he gritted out. "Tell me how."

"Later," she murmured, spreading her legs wide to receive him. "Take me first. Take me hard."

So he did.

Sorcha didn't know how to win her husband's favor. She was inexperienced at flaunting her feminine wiles, and the few tricks she tried had fallen flat. Alan might have wanted her on their wedding night, or maybe he'd just been pretending—as she'd pretended her innocence. Either way, it was clear he didn't want her now.

At night, she tossed and turned, murmured about being cold. Hinted in every way that she wanted him close.

It was no use. He just glanced at her with that chilly gaze and then turned toward the fire and burrowed beneath his plaid.

She was beginning to ache. She watched him, studied him as the days passed with no relief from the uncomfortable, never-ending tension between them.

He was so unlike Cam, but so appealing he took her breath away. His rugged face was so alive, his long blond hair so thick and soft. His bronzed skin glowed in the firelight, his chiseled muscles flexed and rippled, and in response, her own body invariably grew warm and needy. So much so that she actually considered relieving herself of her lust when he went on his long rides.

But would that not be a betrayal, too? She was determined to save herself for him and him alone. Nevertheless, she was beginning to think perhaps she was destined for a life of celibacy—a grim prospect to face given her tremendous appetite for all things carnal. Perhaps this was a just punishment for her sins.

Cam. She sighed. As naive as it might be, she couldn't bring herself to hate him for what he'd done. He'd brought out the truth between her and Alan, something she'd been too cowardly to do on her own. She now knew it was for the best . . . She'd been a fool to think she could have lived her life through with that lie hanging like a curse over her head.

Cam wouldn't try to take her again, because deep in his heart he did care about her happiness and well-being. If he didn't, he would have raped her that night. If he didn't, he would have made sure to lock the door to his bedchamber.

Every night, she prayed for him to find peace. She wasn't the one who could fill the emptiness inside him, and she fervently wished he'd finally come to understand that.

A soft knock on the door heralded Moira's entrance, and Sorcha looked up from the forgotten embroidery in her lap.

"Woolgathering?" Moira asked softly.

"Aye, a little." Sorcha glanced at her brothers, who hung back beyond the doorway.

"We'll just go see about your cow, then," James said. "Have you milked her this morning?"

"Not yet."

Moira reached for the milking tub near the doorway and handed it to Charles. "Good, then. The task is yours. And check if there are any eggs for Sorcha and Alan as well."

"Aye." Charles took the bucket, and he and James disappeared in the direction of the stables.

"I brought you some food." Moira set a large basket upon the table and began to draw out small wrapped parcels. "Should be enough here to last through tomorrow."

"Thank you."

Her sister disappeared into Alan's tiny larder. *Her* tiny larder, she supposed. If Alan didn't intend to divorce her—he still hadn't made his intentions clear.

Moira came back brushing her hands, her blue eyes agleam. "Mary says I can remove your stitches today. Alan's too. Where is he?"

Sorcha couldn't meet her sister's eyes. "On another of his rides."

Moira pulled out the chair beside her and took her cold hand, chafing it in her own warmer ones. "Oh, Sorcha. Is he so very angry with you?"

"Aye." Shame flooded through her, heating her cheeks. Before this disaster, Moira was the only soul alive who knew about her affair with Cam.

Moira frowned. "But why is he angry with you, Sorcha? It wasn't your fault the earl kidnapped you."

She stared at her sister. "Wasn't it?"

Moira dropped her eyes. "Aye, well, I suppose in a way . . . perhaps. But Cam is a man full grown, and he had to have known whatever had happened between you in the past ended once you married Alan. Surely you cannot be held accountable for his actions."

"But I can be held accountable for my own actions before I was married."

"Aye." Moira took Sorcha's foot into her lap. "That you can."

Sorcha curled her toes, fighting a cringe as her sister prodded at her arch.

"You've been keeping it clean, I see. It's healing well."

"Alan hasn't allowed me to leave the house." There was more bitterness in her voice than she'd expected, and she clamped her mouth shut to prevent any more churlishness from escaping.

She wasn't being fair, really. He'd been a true gentleman, fetching things for her and carrying her whenever she needed to venture outside. When he was at home, that was. When he wasn't, he ordered her to refrain from going out and had given her a chamber pot to use instead of the outdoor privy.

Raised in a house constantly filled with happy discussion and debate, she was lonely and alone here in Alan's little valley. Worst of all, she felt disconnected from the world. It had been nearly a week since she'd heard any news about the rising.

Moira pushed against the tender flesh of Sorcha's arch. "Aye, well, you surely can go out now. The wound's fully closed. Just be careful not to step on any more sharp rocks for a time, and you'll be good as new before you know it."

Sorcha blew out a breath as her sister poked at one of the threads, sending a jab of discomfort through her foot.

Moira removed a packet from the pocket in her *arisaid*. She opened it to reveal a small knife with a long, thin blade and a pair of tweezers. "I'll cut the stitches with this, then pluck them out. There's only five, so it'll be quick as can be."

Sorcha bit her lip. "Alan has more."

"Aye, but the foot hurts more than the back. Mary says I'm lucky Alan wasn't the one with his foot hurt, or his complaining would echo in my head for days to come."

Sorcha had to smile at that. "Why do you think it is Mary despises men so much?"

Moira rearranged Sorcha's foot on her lap. "Heaven knows. Rumors say her husband was cruel to her and left her destitute, and she now blames it on all mankind."

"I wonder if that's true," Sorcha mused.

Moira shrugged. "I'm not certain. But I do like her. She's a wise healer, and she's teaching me well."

Sorcha hadn't known what possessed the rough, pagan Mary MacNab to take Sorcha's Christian, educated, and soft-spoken sister under her wing, but their father hadn't objected, and Moira had leaped at the opportunity to learn to help others. One day, she would make a very fine doctor indeed, perhaps even take over Mary's position as the most respected healer in the glen.

Moira cut the first stitch, and Sorcha's foot jerked involuntarily. Moira grasped on to it more firmly. "Think of something else, Sorcha. Tell me what it's like to be married."

Married? Was that what she was? So far it had been a state of constant discomfort. More like a Catholic's Purgatory than the Heaven she'd once imagined in her girlish fantasies. Her parents had sparked those fantasies—they'd truly loved each other.

As a young lass, Sorcha had woken often at night to their soft murmurings, which later she came to understand were the sounds of them making love. On the night Mama had died giving birth to a stillborn son, Da seemed to have aged twenty years. He'd been sober and sad for so long. Although after ten years he'd finally taken a mistress, he'd never remarried, and even now it seemed the greatest joy he found was in remembering his wife through their children—especially Moira, who looked so much like her.

"Marriage . . . isn't what I thought it would be," Sorcha said thickly.

"Why is that?"

Sorcha tilted her head back, closing her eyes as she tried to ignore the feel of the thread slipping through her flesh. "I don't know him. Not really. I don't know his likes and dislikes. I know nothing of his past. I don't know if he's a cruel man or a kind one."

"Och." Moira held the knife hilt between her lips as she tugged on the second stitch. She pulled it out and set it on the table. "A kind one, surely."

Sorcha had thought so too, at first. She opened her eyes and pinned her sister with a look. "How can you be so certain?"

"The way he looks at you, of course."

"The way he looks at me?"

"Aye. Haven't you seen it?"

Sorcha shook her head. Moira smiled. "Well, when he came into our cottage that first time we were there after he made the contract with Da, he was searching for you. I watched him carefully—I was frightened for you. And the moment he laid his eyes on you . . . well, I knew it would be all right."

"How?" Sorcha pressed.

"His eyes widened, then grew all softlike. And when he sat and spoke with Da, his voice grew . . . *dreamy* whenever you were mentioned. Even though he was gone so many years and none of us had known him for long, I knew he'd make you an honorable husband. He was besotted with you."

Sorcha clenched her hands together. "That was before, though. When he thought I could make him an honorable wife."

Moira raised her brows but focused on her task. "What is it that makes you dishonorable?"

"You know."

"That was your past. It shouldn't matter to either of you."

"I lied to him about it," Sorcha said.

Moira's gaze shot to hers. "Oh, Sorcha. You didn't."

Sorcha nodded miserably. "I dishonored myself by lying to my husband on our wedding night. I pretended I was a virgin. And now he knows I came to him sullied, not pure as he expected."

"Well, he will soon learn that it's against your nature to be dishonest, and he'll forgive you. And surely he cannot fault you for having relations before your marriage. If he does . . . well"—her sister's blue eyes flashed—"make him promise he's never bedded a willing lass."

"Moira!"

"Well, it's true," Moira said mulishly. "I'm sure he's had many more women than you've had men."

Sorcha stared at her sister in shock. Moira was two years her junior, and as innocent as they came. Or . . .

"Moira," she said, a note of warning in her voice, "how do you come to know so much of the carnal relations between unmarried men and women?"

"Oh, heavens!" Moira laughed. "I wasn't born in a convent. I know as much as you, I'm sure."

Sorcha raised a brow at her sister, and Moira finally had the grace to flush. "Well, maybe not that much."

"Are you still a virgin?"

"Of course!"

"You'd best stay pure until you're married, Moira. I've learned the hard way that it is too dangerous otherwise."

"Finished." Moira patted Sorcha's foot, then lifted it off her lap.

Narrowing her eyes, Sorcha flexed her toes. "I hope that wasn't all a distraction to make me sit docilely while you plucked out the threads."

"Aye, well, it worked, didn't it?" Moira leaned forward to hug Sorcha, squeezing tight. "I love you, Sorcha. I want you to be happy."

"Thank you," Sorcha whispered into her sister's thick russet-colored hair. But how could she attain any semblance of happiness with a husband who constantly rejected her? How long would Alan continue with this painful silence before she cracked straight down the middle?

Moira pulled back and clasped her hand, her eyes searching Sorcha's face. "You should know . . . the men are meeting in a council of war every day to debate whether to march south to join the Earl of Mar."

Sorcha leaned closer to her sister. "Has Alan been attending these debates?"

"Aye."

This could prove Alan hadn't taken a mistress on the mountain. She gazed at her sister, relief mingled with a new kind of fear. "I thought they'd agreed not to go, not until King James lands in Scotland."

"The Earl of Mar has amassed thousands of men ready and able to fight for the cause. They say there's going to be a grand battle in the Lowlands. Most of the men of Glenfinnan believe the king's presence won't be necessary to overcome the government."

"But Alan—"

"He's still hesitant, but his resistance has begun to wane. If every man in the glen decides to rise, their laird won't allow them to go alone. He is asking that they wait till the end of harvest and for the men to return from the cattle markets."

"Oh, Moira. What do Da and James think?"

Moira squeezed her hand. "They want to go. They don't want to wait."

The door opened, and both women looked up.

"Ah, there he is now." Moira's tight expression dissolved into a gracious smile. "Good morning, Alan. I've come to remove your stitches."

Alan inclined his head politely. "Good morning, Moira."

Sorcha gazed at him, thinking of him leading the men of the glen into battle. Her chest tightened painfully.

Charles and James tumbled in after Alan, carrying eggs and the bucket of milk. James set the milk on the table and then moved behind Sorcha, studying her foot as she showed him the scabs. "Does it still hurt?"

"No, not really. It itches and it tickles, but it'll be all right." She glanced up to see Alan looking at James with a deep furrow etched between his brows. As if he didn't like the way James stood so solicitously over her. Almost as if he were jealous.

Sorcha nearly shook her head. That was ridiculous. She and James had always had a special bond, and James, though younger than her, had always stood up for her and protected her from harm. If not for his support, she doubted her father would have allowed her and her sister to learn to read.

James's hand closed over her shoulder. "How are you, Sorcha? Is all well?"

She tilted her head to smile up at her brother. "Very well indeed."

"Is aught amiss?"

"No," she lied. "Nothing at all."

Alan's blue gaze locked with hers.

Moira clapped her hands, breaking the sudden tension. "Well, then. Perhaps you will help me take out Alan's sutures, James?"

"Aye," James murmured, but his fingers tightened over Sorcha's shoulder before he removed them.

Moira directed Alan to the bedroom and instructed him to lean over the mattress so she could pluck his stitches. Sorcha couldn't watch. Hurt, upset, and guilt twisted through her, making a painful knot rise in her gorge.

Alan might go to war. He could be killed by the English, or worse, captured and convicted as a traitor, hanged, disemboweled and cut into pieces . . .

Blinking back tears, she stared at the simmering hearth, listening to Moira's soft commands and James's responses in the other room. Charles wandered back outside, probably to rejoin the animals. He always had a fondness for horses, and Alan owned two of them, beautiful bays brought from England.

They finished in short order, and with a final tight hug between the sisters, Moira and James left.

When they were gone, all was silent for a long moment. A bird called outside, and a gentle breeze rustled the grass. She heard the soft sounds of material as Alan donned his shirt and pinned his plaid.

"Can you walk on it, then?" Alan finally asked. Sorcha looked up from her embroidery to see him leaning casually against the partition separating the rooms of the cottage, and her breath stalled in her throat.

"Aye."

"Would you like to go outside with me?"

Dropping the shawl she was embroidering in her lap, Sorcha blinked. "Really?"

Goodness, she sounded like an overeager child. She couldn't help it, though. Her heart surged with hope.

Alan didn't smile. He just held out his hand to her. She set the shawl aside and allowed him to help her from the chair.

She went to her chest and removed a pair of stockings. She rolled them on, ignoring the uncomfortable way they pulled on her scabs. Then she slipped on her shoes and tied on her kertch.

Alan grasped her elbow as they walked outside. Fresh, cool air hit Sorcha's face, and she swallowed a moan of delight.

Alan glanced at her, his cool, impenetrable mask firmly in place. "You enjoy the outdoors?"

"I'm always most at home when I'm outside."

He took a deep breath. From the corner of her eye, Sorcha watched his broad chest rise and fall. "I prefer the outdoors as well."

Arm in arm, they strolled down the path. About a hundred feet from the door, it branched off in two directions. One fork led to the road to Glenfinnan, and the other to the loch. She paused. "Which way?"

"The loch. I don't think you could travel as far as the village. Not yet, in any case."

It was true—Glenfinnan was more than three miles away. Perhaps tomorrow.

They turned toward the loch, down the short, meandering path that led to the shore. It was a beautiful day: crisp, blue, and clear. The surface of the water rippled in the breeze and glimmered golden sparks in the bright sunlight. Hard to imagine she'd waded through these waters and nearly frozen to death just over a week ago.

The bank sloped gently, the natural lawn ending where the water began. The path spread at the bottom, forming a small beach where they took water for the cottage and the animals. He led her onto the grassy bank. "Would you like to sit for a while?"

Cam had asked her that same question, not six months ago. As Alan settled beside her, she leaned back, remembering.

It had been a beautiful spring day, somewhat like today. She'd told her father she was going up to the shieling with Moira, but instead she'd met with Cam at the top of the hill leading away from Camdonn Castle, in a spot hidden from the sentries and other eyes. Looking magnificent in a cloak trimmed in gold, with his richly tailored breeches, jacket, and waistcoat, he'd pulled her up on his horse to sit in front of him and covered her with a plaid. Much like he had when he'd stolen her from Alan, but on that spring day she'd had no desire to fight him.

They'd ridden down a road, farther west from Camdonn Castle than Sorcha had ever gone. By the time they arrived at the stone cottage on the loch, the sun hung high in the sky, and it was quite warm. "Would you like to sit for a while?" Cam had asked.

She said yes and basked like an otter in the sun while Cam disappeared into the little building—one of his hunting cottages, he'd said—and brought out several plaids, which he'd laid out. They'd feasted on roasted beef and fresh, creamy milk. They'd made love as the sun warmed their bodies, and then they'd talked, mostly of Shakespeare, for Sorcha had been raiding Cam's library, devouring as many of the bard's works as she could find. One of the works they'd spoken of was *Romeo and Juliet*—of how close the lovers had come to finding true happiness before they lost everything.

It was the longest time they'd spent together all at once. It was a beautiful day—one she'd never forget.

She glanced at Alan, whose face was tilted up to the sun. She still hadn't spent that long with him. Instead he found excuses to go riding, to see to his men. And now she knew he had gone to hold war councils in Glenfinnan. Despite the warmth, she shivered.

He had avoided her. He wouldn't sleep with her, scarcely spoke to her, and before today, had hardly touched her.

Yet right now they reclined side by side on the banks of the loch. Perhaps they were making progress. Grass blades tickled the tiny hairs on Sorcha's arms as she leaned back. She gazed at the man—her husband—who was so elusive to her.

"What is England like, Alan?"

Opening his eyes, he rolled onto his side to face her. "What do you want to know about it?"

"Was it so very civilized, as they say?"

Alan's lip curled. "In some ways."

"Are the cities very grand? Are there riches everywhere you look?" A part of her had always wished to visit the place, as irrational as that dream was. Highlanders referred to England and the English with distrust, sometimes loathing, but Sorcha would love to see it and judge for herself.

"Yes, the cities are grand. London is the most wretched, stinking, crowded mass of humanity you could ever imagine. And as for riches, yes, there are many riches. But there is also terrible poverty—in some ways worse than you'd find here, because the English don't help one another like we do."

"Why is that?"

"They have no one who commands their loyalty. There's the king, of course, but even their loyalty to him is in question at the moment." He frowned. "It's not instilled in the English, for whatever reason. Here, we are loyal to our families, our clans, our lairds. Our communities are an integral part of us, as much as the land itself."

"Do they despair of the Hanoverian king as we do?"

He glanced sharply at her. "Aye, but it is different in England, more subversive. There are many Jacobites, but the penalties for treason are severe, and the English don't hesitate to carry out their sentences."

She closed her eyes, thinking again of the severity of the reprisals should the Earl of Mar fail. They were all at risk.

"I wish King James would come," she whispered.

"So do I."

She opened her eyes in surprise, and he gave her a crooked smile that didn't reach his eyes. "We are close to being able to supplant George, but not close enough for my comfort. If King James brought an army, we'd win." He sighed. "Imagine it. Independence from England's yoke."

"You dislike England."

"I do."

"But . . . you lived there so long. And you have English blood in you. Your mother was English."

"Aye."

Alan's father, Doughall, was known as a kind and fair laird, dedicated to his clan. His only shortcoming had been in marrying a wealthy Sassenach lady from London. Even today, it was whispered in some circles that she, in her mad desire to return to England, had killed him.

Sorcha knew the truth, however. Her father had been Doughall's closest friend and confidant, and Alan's parents had been as in love with each other as her own parents were. Doughall MacDonald had loved his foreign wife until the day he died, and she'd felt the same consuming passion for him. She would have stood beside him forever, but when he died, grief weakened her, and she'd gone to her family in England, who received her and Alan with open arms. She'd never remarried and remained in deep mourning for Alan's father until she died.

Doughall's death had left Alan as the absentee boy laird, whose uncle held control in his stead. The Glenfinnan clansmen believed Alan would someday return, and when Sorcha was a child, people speculated endlessly about him. Would he be aloof and foreign, dressed in breeches and stockings in the Sassenach style? Would he refuse to speak the language of his homeland? Wear ostentatious white wigs and adopt the pretensions of a holier-than-thou Englishman in a land of heathens?

When Alan finally came home, the MacDonalds viewed him with wary eyes. But that had lasted no more than a day. He dressed like a Highlander. He returned to the home of his fathers and forebears with praise for the leaders and tacksmen who had run the clan in his absence. When he opened his mouth, the Gaelic that flowed from it was flawless. He was open, intelligent, and generous, with an innate understanding of the inner workings of his people and lands, and it took him no time at all to win everyone's respect.

Again, Sorcha made an attempt to engage him in conversation. "You were gone for many years."

"Almost twenty years, all told."

Sorcha frowned. "But you wished to come back?"

"Aye. I always knew I'd come home." He slid her a glance. "To claim what was mine."

The heat in his gaze settled in Sorcha's chest then spread low in her belly. From the tone of his voice and the warmth in his crystalline eyes, she knew he meant her as well as his lands and lairdship of the MacDonalds.

Closing her eyes, Sorcha lay back on the grass. Coarse blades pricked at her bare arms and the back of her neck, but she didn't care. Hope blossomed inside her, balmy and sweet. Perhaps he would forgive her. Perhaps they could make this marriage work.

CHAPTER EIGHT

Alan stared at his wife lying on the grass, her eyes closed as she basked in the autumn sun. Emotions tumbled through his chest like the stones of a collapsing ancient castle. Did she know how beautiful she was? What madness she evoked in him? How deeply and painfully he ached for her?

Visions crashed through his mind. Kissing that red mouth. Revealing those creamy breasts. Lifting her skirts. Sinking himself into her. Sorcha holding him, clutching him, as he took her to ecstasy.

Pride seemed an inane emotion right now, but it was pride nevertheless that kept him from touching her.

He lay beside her on the grass. Frustrated. Wanting. And yet too proud to give in to her. He knew she wanted it. She glowed with the desire for him to touch her. She constantly taunted him with her wiles, but the hopeful look in her emerald eyes was nearly his undoing.

The temptation to bind himself more strongly to her before he was forced away to war was maddening. He didn't have much time. The surrounding clans had already gone. The MacLeans and the MacDonalds of Glengarry and Clanranald had marched south last month.

Alan had thought his neighbor Cameron of Lochiel would stay put due to his men's hesitance—they feared the nearby Earl of Camdonn and other geographically close supporters of the government. Yet Lochiel had finally gathered his forces and passed near Glenfinnan only days ago on his way to join Mar.

Hearing of Lochiel's march south had roused Alan's own men to a fever pitch. Though their force would be reduced—a group of his most battle-ready men had taken stock down to the Lowlands to sell and weren't due back for another few weeks—the remaining men detested the idea of their countrymen facing battle while they languished at home.

The harvest was abundant, yet he needed the men to bring it in properly, to feed their families and beasts through the winter. It would hardly be advisable to win the battle and then return home only to starve.

God, he didn't think he could bear to leave Sorcha with Cam so close. Yet his clan needed him to act.

He should take her to her father and then lead his men south. But Stewart had failed to protect Sorcha from Cam once, and as much as Alan respected the older man, he hesitated to entrust his wife to him.

Damn it. He couldn't leave her. Not now.

Tentatively, she reached out to brush a finger over the bump on his nose. "Was it broken?"

"Aye."

"What happened?"

Lacing his fingers behind his head, he closed his eyes against the glare of the sun. "A fight."

"Why did you fight?"

His chest rose and fell as he took a deep breath. "They'd sent me to an English school in London, and Cam and I were the only Scots there. The other lads didn't know what to make of us, especially me with my strange ways and language, so they mocked me. A mob of them threw stones at me." His lips twisted. "They called me a devil-worshipping ignorant barbarian heathen bastard. I think I cracked more than one jaw before they overwhelmed me. One of their blows broke my nose before Cam and I fought them off."

"Lord. Were all the lads so cruel?"

"No." He cast her a wry glance. "Not for long, at any rate."

"Why not?"

He shrugged. "You ask too many questions, Sorcha."

"I'm only curious about you. About your past. It's different from anyone's I know."

"Not so different from the Earl of Camdonn's."

"He rarely spoke of his past to me."

Alan ground his teeth. Why he wished to stay beside her, to protect her, was a mystery to him. He didn't love her—hell, he didn't even like her.

Or perhaps he liked her very much. Perhaps, in his uncertainty over their fate, he merely tried to convince himself otherwise.

He opened his eyes and turned onto his side, resting his head in his hand and studying her. She was wearing an *arisaid* of a deep rust color with darker stripes, its ends held together by her silver brooch. Beneath, she wore a buttoned jacket that accentuated her slender waist. Her eyes were closed, her breathing steady. Contrasting against the white of her kertch, wisps of blue-black hair danced around her face in the breeze.

He could find no fault with her appearance, that was for certain. And as for her demeanor . . . since she'd made that one mistake on their wedding night, she'd offered him more than he deserved with her simple, honest repentance in the face of his coldness. He couldn't help himself—his heart was thawing toward her.

Sensing his gaze, she opened her eyes and smiled. "I think there's no more beautiful spot than Loch Shiel in autumn. Surely no place in England could compare."

He stared over the water laid out like a serene blue blanket before him. Across the loch, the mountains rose sharply, their crags ascending into the low-hanging clouds. Great boulders rippled through the green and gold grasses on the steep slopes. Overhead, the sun reached long fingers through the clouds, making the land glow in the colors of spun gold and sparkling gems.

"It's true—there is no place in England like this."

Her fingers curled round his sleeve. "Oh, look."

He followed the path of her gaze. Across the loch, a deer and her dappled fawn stood at the edge of the pebbled beach, drinking. He and Sorcha watched in silence as they took their fill and then loped away.

Alan plucked a blade of grass and studied it as he pulled it between the pads of his fingers, its rough surface scraping his skin. "What of you, Sorcha? The life I plan to lead here is a simple one. Is it what you wanted?"

How could it be, given that she'd lived so long in bustling Camdonn Castle with all its opulence and modern conveniences?

Not to mention that she'd bedded its lord, and perhaps part of the reason she'd done so was out of awe for Cam's wealth. And that was something Alan would never covet. Despite their friendship, Alan had always known to his core that he craved simplicity far more than the riches of the Earl of Camdonn.

She took a deep breath in and then blew it out. "Aye, I always dreamed of a quiet life like this. I love my family, and I was never lonely with them close, but Camdonn Castle was too busy for me. I found a secluded spot near the loch when I needed to escape, and that became my place of solitude from the time I was a child."

He gave her an appraising look. She was six years younger than him. Despite her experiences with Cam, she'd seen far less in her life than he had. She was very beautiful, too, in an unspoiled way. Dark eyebrows arched above the slanted green eyes. Her nose was small and sloped toward deep red lips, stark against the paleness of her face. A light smattering of freckles covered her nose, impossible to discern unless one studied her closely. It was no wonder he'd assumed her to be virginal.

"Where was this place?"

She stilled, staring at him. "I've never told anyone about it. Not even Moira."

He remained silent, finding himself in no position to encourage her to confidence.

Her thick, dark eyelashes swept downward. "A cliff separates Camdonn Castle from the loch."

"Aye. I've been there."

"On the western shore, the cliff isn't as steep as it is everywhere else. If you descend the slope there, at the waterline, you'll find a small impression of earth . . . the beginnings of a cave."

He waited for her to go on. When she did, her voice had a breathy, wistful quality. "That was my place. I'd sit there for hours with the water lapping at my toes. Sometimes"—a pale pink flush spread over the bridge of her nose and fanned into her cheeks—"I would read."

He couldn't hide his surprise. "You know how to read, then?"

"Aye." She nodded solemnly. "The old earl insisted all the lads of the castle were taught to read in English."

He couldn't contain his snicker. "You're no lad, Sorcha."

"No, but my brother is." Her eyes held a wicked gleam, a hint of that passion he'd seen in her that first night. "I merely decided to learn what he did."

"And they allowed it?"

"Not at first. But I pestered James late at night and forced him to teach me what he'd learned, so my father finally gave in. My sister learned too. Later, during his illness, we read to the old earl, and he took great pleasure from it."

"He was an eccentric old man, wasn't he? I never knew him well—only saw him a few times when he came to England." Alan smiled and rolled onto his back. "He stopped in London on occasion to see Cam—or rather, to chastise Cam for his wicked behavior and his lavish spending."

Just as he had begun to relax, Alan stiffened again. How was it their conversations always ended up turning to Cam? The last person he wished to discuss in his wife's presence was the present Earl of Camdonn, and yet he kept bringing the goddamned man up.

He turned his head in the grass and saw her gazing at him. She must have sensed his tension, because her green eyes filled with despair and her fist clenched in the grass.

"I'm sorry, Alan. Forgive me."

"Do you love him, Sorcha?" Each painful word tore at something deep in his gut.

Her eyes glistened with unshed tears. "No."

He clenched his teeth to keep from saying something he might regret.

"I realize I never did. Not really."

Not really? With the guilty expression on her face, she sank the dagger in, and with her words, she twisted it.

"Whatever happened to the honesty you promised me?" he asked through gritted teeth.

"I am being honest. I swear it."

"You don't look honest. Your face tells me you're lying. That it pains you to say you don't love him."

"You're wrong." Her tone hardened, and her expression transformed from distraught to intractable. "It hurts to admit to you that I thought I might love him. It hurts to admit that I was a foolish lass who made a terrible mistake."

"So are you saying that you no longer love him, but you love me instead?"

"I . . ." Her voice dwindled.

"Tell me. Is that what you're saying?"

"No."

"So you do love him."

"No! I don't love him. But . . . I—" She took a deep breath. "I don't think I love you, either."

All the air whooshed out of his lungs as if she'd punched him in the stomach.

She rose to a seated position, and her green eyes glowed with passion. "I don't know you! I have spent too little time with you, and you've been silent and angry for most of it."

He came up beside her. Logic told him she spoke the truth, that he would have laughed in her face if she'd lied and said she loved him. But the truth hurt more than he expected.

God help him, he wanted her to love him, craved her love like he'd never craved anything in his life. He nearly groaned aloud.

"Please, Alan, understand. I want to know you. I want to love you. I want us to make a life together."

And of course she didn't know how, when he was cold and cruel to her. Who would?

Yet he couldn't stop it. He could feel the ice overtaking him again, freezing over his heart, steeling his limbs.

"I must go."

She recoiled as if he'd slapped her. "Where?"

"For a walk," he said tautly. "Perhaps a ride."

Sadness edged into her expression, and he tore his gaze away from her as she nodded. "All right."

He hefted himself to his feet. Some dormant residue of gentlemanliness flared to life, and he held his hand out to her.

Hesitantly, she took it, and he helped her up. "I trust you can manage walking back to the cottage by yourself?"

"Aye," she mumbled.

"Good." He released her hand and turned away. He felt her anguished eyes on him as he strode through the grass, until the bank curved and steepened, and he disappeared from her sight. Taking a deep breath, he stopped and dropped his head into his hands for a long moment. Then, slowly, he turned and peered back round the bend. Shoulders slumped, she picked her way up the path to the cottage, mincing her steps.

Once she'd closed the cottage door behind her, he released a deep breath and raked a hand through his hair. He felt shaken, off balance.

He fought the urge to follow her inside to draw her sweet form against him and apologize for his cruel, cold behavior. Then he'd kiss her, showing her just how much he'd wished to do so—wished all along . . .

Pride, man. Show some pride.

Stiffening his resolve, he stalked back to the clearing and signaled to the hidden copses of shrubs where he'd assigned clansmen to keep watch. Each man returned his signal, confirming they'd seen no sign of Cam or any of his men.

When he was certain all was well, Alan crouched near the back wall of the stables and refocused his attention on the cottage. Sorcha would think he'd gone riding, but today he'd join his men in their vigil. If Cam came for her, Alan would be ready.

Sorcha stirred the fire absently, glancing back over her shoulder at Alan's supper. It had gone cold. She'd have to reheat it when he returned.

She rose and walked to the window. A thick fog had rolled in over the loch, obscuring the mountain peaks on the far side. The air had turned damp and cool.

It was almost dusk. Alan had never come home this late before. Sorcha chewed her lip nervously. What could be keeping him?

Perhaps tonight would be the night he didn't return. Perhaps it was over, and she had lost him forever.

She blew out a breath, steaming the window, then drew curlicue designs in the frost. She had to stop these traitorous thoughts or they would drive her to madness. He had given her reason to hope earlier today. They had actually engaged in a civil conversation, one that might have gone on longer if not for the subject of Cam rising like a specter between them to wrench them apart.

Perhaps she should go look for him. She paced for long moments, wringing her hands. Alan had told her to stay in the cottage. What would he do if she disobeyed him?

The urge to go after him overwhelmed her desire to obey. If she went, she should go now. It would be full dark within the hour. And Alan had gone with no way to light his path. He was less familiar with the landscape than she.

Resolved to go after him, she pulled her *arisaid* over her shoulders, pinned on her brooch and tied on her kertch, and went outside. She hurried down the path toward the loch and picked her way along the water's edge until the bank veered.

There, she stopped, frowning as she stared down at the shallow impressions made in the grass by Alan's shoes. Here the tracks doubled back to the clearing.

With her heart hammering in her ears, she followed the footprints back to the stables. He'd stopped, gone inside, and then . . . back out. She peeked into the horses' stalls and saw he'd taken his gelding, Eachann. But his weren't the only footprints—several others of varying sizes churned the dirt in this area.

Sorcha glanced at the darkening sky. The fog had closed in, and mist hung heavy in the air, casting dark shadows across the lawn separating the cottage and the stables.

Whose footprints were these? Perhaps her brothers' from earlier? She thought not.

A feeling of dread skittered up her spine, raising the tiny hairs on the back of her neck.

Someone was watching her. Eyes burned into her skin.

Lord. Could it be Cam?

She flattened her body against the outside wall of the stables, turned the corner, and slipped back inside. The cow let out a low groaning noise, and the chickens clucked and ruffled their feathers, scattering as she entered their midst.

Sorcha scanned the tools hanging across the inside wall, searching for something to use as a weapon. Her eyes alighted on a rusty scythe hung from a peg. Gritting her teeth, she stepped forward, clutched it in two hands, and lifted it away.

Cam wouldn't catch her unprepared. Holding the curved blade high, she slipped back out the door and returned to the place where the footsteps clustered. With every sense bristling, she studied the steps until she determined a direction to follow. Slowly, stealthily, she picked her way through the grass.

Ahead, a branch cracked.

"Who is it?" she called, her voice shrill, the scythe held at the ready.

"All's well, lady, it's just me."

Sorcha frowned, recognizing the voice. "Bowie MacDonald?"

"Aye." Bowie, Alan's younger cousin, appeared from behind a cluster of bushes, his hands raised in a conciliatory gesture. Bowie was Alan's closest living relative since the death of his uncle. He was armed with his sword and dirk, and even held a pistol in his belt.

"What are you doing here?" she asked sharply. "Where's Alan?"

Bowie looked chagrined. "We're keepin' watch over you, Sorcha."

"What?"

"Aye. Alan—well, he feared the earl might come and try to capture you again. So . . . well, we were watching over you. Just to be sure, like."

Annoyance bubbled up within her. Why had Alan told her nothing of this? "We? How many of you are there?"

Bowie cast an uncomfortable glance past her shoulder, and she looked back to see movement in a craggy rise beyond the barn. "Uh. There's about ten of us tonight."

"Where is Alan now, Bowie?" she asked through clenched teeth.

"Well . . ." Bowie trailed off, and his gaze shifted from hers.

"Well what?" She took a menacing step toward him. Bowie was younger than her, and as the laird's wife, she could command his respect.

"Er . . ." A deep blush spread across Bowie's freckled face.

"Tell me what happened. Tell me where he is."

"I'm . . . uh . . . I'm not certain he'd want you to know."

"Bowie MacDonald." Sorcha kept her voice cool, laced with authority. "You shall tell me the whereabouts of my husband. And you shall do so before another moment has passed."

"He's gone to the mountain," Bowie blurted.

Sorcha cocked her head but otherwise stood very still. Even the air between them seemed to hang suspended.

"Has he, then?"

Her stomach felt like a lump of ice. Lord, she'd told him this afternoon she didn't love him. Had that painful admission driven him to the mountain, where any whore would declare her love for a few bits of silver?

Yet they'd been married just over a week. Surely he couldn't expect everlasting love from her already. Alan seemed too practical for such fancies.

It didn't make sense. If he'd climbed the mountain because of that one comment, he was a vengeful, impulsive fool. If he went because he'd kept a mistress all along . . .

That seemed the more likely scenario.

Sorcha flexed her toes, testing the strength of her scab.

She turned on her heel. With her back ramrod straight, she left Bowie MacDonald standing agape and marched toward the cottage.

Once inside, she found a strip of cloth. Shoving off her shoe and stocking, she wrapped the linen around her foot and then replaced her shoe, forcing the leather over the bulk of the bandage.

At the door, Sorcha pulled another plaid over her shoulders. It would be dark and colder by the time she arrived on the mountain. She smelled snow in the air.

Almost as an afterthought, she grabbed the scythe.

She strode out of the cottage and turned onto the path to Glenfinnan. She ignored the murmuring and footsteps behind her.

Let them follow. It made no difference to her.

Unease hit Alan square in the gut as he scanned the one-room cottage. Large pillows, soft furs, and an ivory silk counterpane covered the plush, inviting bed. Clearly some high personage—probably Cam—had given it to the whore as payment, because it looked like something from a grand castle rather than a poor woman's cottage. It overpowered the room and looked nearly ridiculous in its prominent location on the dirt floor. Beside it, splitting the sleeping area from the eating area, the hearth occupied the back wall. The woman bent over it and poked a stick into the fire. The curve of her rump tilted toward Alan, and he averted his gaze to the single square glass-paned window—another luxury. Crowded with fog, the window revealed just a hint of outside greenery.

Alan turned toward the door to discover his guide, a boy from Camdonn Castle, had slipped away. Slowly, Alan dragged his gaze back to the whore.

The woman rose and turned to face him, and from the languid sway of her hips and swing of her hair, Alan knew immediately she calculated every move for maximum effect. She was older than most of Cam's dalliances, and he'd never known Cam to have a particular affection for flame-colored hair. But it was clear to him now that there was quite a bit he didn't know about Cam.

The woman spoke, her voice low, rich, and smooth, like brandy. "I'm Gràinne." Her wide lips curved into a sensual smile. "And you're Alan MacDonald."

Gràinne. Cam spoke of her often. She'd served as his first teacher of the carnal arts, and Cam held her in the highest regard.

Alan narrowed his gaze at her, looking at her through new eyes. This woman had a long, complex history with Cam. Were they in collusion?

"I'm informed the earl wishes to speak with me. Where is he?"

It had surprised him when the lad approached him this afternoon. Red-faced, the youth had ridden up to him and handed him a message from Cam. The note said Cam wanted to meet with Alan here on the mountain, tonight, to make peace between them.

Alan had agreed to come on the condition that he remain armed. For he intended to shoot Cam in cold blood if he did anything but grovel at his feet and offer a thousand different ways to make amends for the damage he'd done.

"He'll be here soon. Make yourself at home, Alan MacDonald. Perhaps you require a stiff drink, eh?"

"No. Thank you."

"Something to eat, then?"

"No."

"Please. Sit." Gràinne gestured to a fancy chair set across from the hearth. Covered in red velvet, it boasted intricate legs and armrests carved to look like a lion's feet and paws. It looked like something straight from an opulent English drawing room. Cam had probably given it to her as well. Alan eyed it dubiously.

"Make yourself comfortable."

Releasing a harsh breath, Alan stalked toward the chair and stiffly lowered himself into it. Instantly, Gràinne hurried to him, knelt before him, and began to unlace his shoes. He jerked his feet away, and she looked up at him from beneath ginger-tipped lashes.

"Sorry, love. I only wished to help you be comfortable."

"I'm comfortable enough, thank you. How long before Cam returns? I should be home." It was nearly dark, and Sorcha would worry.

Gràinne rocked back on her heels, a smile tilting the edges of her bowed lips. "Cam told me about you. Loyal to a fault, are you? Even when your wife isn't?"

Alan ground his teeth. "What are you saying?"

Gràinne's brown eyes widened. "Surely you know she's in love with the Earl of Camdonn?"

Alan's lip curled. "Surely it isn't any of your business, madam." He sounded more like his English grandfather than himself. But when the woman spoke like that to him, she didn't deserve his Highland regard.

"Och. You're likely right." Gràinne lowered her eyes modestly. "But you're a bonnie man, Alan MacDonald. If you haven't the attention you require from your wife, 'twill be easy enough to find it elsewhere."

He watched her through slitted eyes, wondering if Cam intended to come up at all or if this was some harebrained scheme to—what? Draw him away from Sorcha? The notion was laughable. He was already just about as far from Sorcha as one could be without actual physical distance between them.

He'd been foolish to believe Cam wished for peace between them. This was just another of his manipulations, another means by which to steal Sorcha away. In fact . . .

God. Cam could have brought an army to his house, intending to kidnap her again while the whore distracted Alan.

Alan rose abruptly. Gràinne had turned, but she spun round to face him. Her bodice was open, the laces dangling freely on either side. She wore no shift, and the stiff material of her stays curved around the outsides of her ample breasts. He could see the light blue trail of veins beneath the plump, pale skin, and the stark red of her beaded nipples.

"Not today, eh, Alan?" She rose to her feet with her dress hanging precariously from her arms. Her breasts swayed as she stepped closer to him. Close enough to touch. "Perhaps tomorrow, then. Know I am here for you. Thinking about you, ready to comfort—"

"No," he growled. She was blocking his exit. "I don't know what scheme you and Cam have devised, but it isn't going to work, Gràinne. I am a married man, and I have no interest in bedding you. Now step aside so that I might return home to my wife."

"Your marriage," Gràinne murmured, "isn't a happy one, is it?"

"I've been married only a short time."

"'Tis a challenge to keep hold on your Highland honor, isn't it?" she continued. "When you know your wife is bedding a lord with so much more than you yourself have."

"Leave it, Gràinne." He fought the urge to toss her aside.

She stepped closer. "I can make you happy." She reached out and placed her palm flat against his chest. "I can make you feel again."

He gazed at her dispassionately, but he didn't move. "You make me feel nothing."

Her bow-shaped lips curled into a wicked smile. "Not yet. But I can offer you great pleasure."

With a slight twist of her torso, the dress slipped from her shoulders, baring her naked body. Alan wondered how often she had practiced the movement in order to make it just right.

He smiled, almost feeling sorry for the woman. "You'll not be seducing me, Gràinne. Not today."

She shimmied closer to him, undaunted, her grin widening. "Tomorrow, then, perhaps?"

"No."

Just then, the door to the cottage opened with such force, it banged against the inside wall and rattled the windowpane. Gràinne spun round and Alan's gaze snapped up as a blast of cold outside air collided with his face.

Sorcha stood at the threshold, her face white and rigid, her eyes burning like green flames. In her right hand, she wielded his scythe. Behind her, the first flakes of snow had begun to fall—a peaceful scene in contrast to the woman in the full heat of fury.

Had she walked all this way? On her injured foot? Why the hell had his men allowed her to do such a foolhardy thing?

"What are you doing here, Sorcha?" he growled.

She aimed a deadly look at Gràinne and then focused on him, her teeth bared. She tore off her kertch and tossed it to the floor, shaking her hair out so it gleamed like a silvery black halo.

"Perhaps I should ask you the same," she said, her voice ice cold. "We've been married less than a fortnight, and you already choose to slake your lust upon the first willing whore? Or has she been your whore all along?"

Appearing unperturbed, Gràinne stepped aside, leaving her dress piled on the floor and making him look as guilty as sin. She took a woolen blanket from the bed and wrapped it over her shoulders. Alan saw she was shivering. The crisp, clear day had descended into a bitterly frigid and snowy night.

"Close the door, Sorcha. You're letting in the cold."

Sorcha took a step inside. Using her good foot, she slammed the door behind her, not turning away from Alan and Gràinne, nor lowering the rusty scythe.

"'Tis bad manners to wield a weapon in a countrywoman's home." Despite the disapproval in her tone, a smile quirked Gràinne's lips. "Perhaps you should put it down."

"Aye, Sorcha," Alan agreed. "Put it down."

Sorcha's lips curled into a sneer. "You think I'll let you take your pleasure in a whore? You may not like me, Alan MacDonald, but you've married me. You made a vow before God."

"Aye, I did," he said calmly.

"Yet you have no honor. You're a liar. You pretend anger at me for something I did before I married you, while all along, you were just waiting for the opportunity to come up here to bed someone else!"

She was glorious in her bristling rage. Two bright spots of color splashed over her cheekbones. Her eyes glowed like angry emeralds. Her cheeks were taut, her arms rigid. Alan could gaze at her, watch her rage at him for hours.

"I'll kill you before I allow it to happen again." She raised the scythe higher. "I was a fool. But no longer."

"What do you expect, lass?" Gràinne said. "Do you think he'll merely accept that you love another?"

Sorcha turned furious eyes on the naked whore. "What the devil are you talking about?"

"You're in love with the Earl of Camdonn," Gràinne said.

"Did he"—Sorcha jerked her chin at Alan—"tell you that?"

"And what if he did? He's a man. You're a wee fool if you think a man's pride could withstand such a blow."

Sorcha arched her brows. "Is that so? Are men so weak?"

"But of course they are," Gràinne said sagely.

Not wishing to hear where this conversation would invariably lead, Alan raised his hand. "Sorcha. Lower the blade."

She paused a moment, then granted him a twisted smile. "All right, Alan. Is this what you want?" She opened her hand. The scythe hit the floor with a clunk, and she made a generous motion toward Gràinne. "Then I shall sit quietly in the corner and watch. Show me. Show me how you take her when you ride away from me. From our home."

Her voice was quiet. He stared at her, his gut surging with an odd feeling he didn't know how to interpret. It was all he could do not to take her into his arms and beg forgiveness.

But for what? He'd done nothing wrong. Cam had lured him here on false pretenses, and he'd never possessed a single intention of bedding Gràinne.

Sorcha was the one who had done wrong. She'd made love to Cam. Scores of times. *Cam*, of all the godforsaken men in the world. Then she'd lied to him on their wedding night.

She crossed her arms over her chest. "Show me."

Bemused, Alan stared at her for a long moment, then glanced at Gràinne, who returned his gaze, her brown eyes gleaming. "You want me to take her. While you watch?"

"Yes."

"Why?"

"I want to observe how it is she can make you happy when I do not."

He could shoot back a retort: *Because she doesn't fuck the Earl of Camdonn*. But that would be a lie, and though Sorcha likely didn't know about Gràinne's past with Cam, Alan couldn't bring himself to utter that falsehood.

His wife continued. "I want to see what it is that makes what I did to you so very wrong, while it's all right for you to do the reverse, and worse."

"I never lied to you, Sorcha."

"Perhaps not, but I chose never to ask." She spoke bitterly. "I'm not so great a fool as to demand to know how many women you've had, though that number is likely to be far, far greater than the number of men I've had."

He raised a brow.

"Why must I accept the fact that you bedded half the women of England? Why isn't it considered proper for me to expect *you* to be untouched in our marriage bed?"

"It isn't the way of the world," he said with a shrug. But her words rolled through him like an earthquake. He'd never considered such things before. Women and men lived by different standards set by society. Yet both sexes were capable of thought. They both experienced emotion: the pains of betrayal, the joys of love.

In Oxford and then in London, he'd behaved exactly as people expected. He'd enjoyed his debauchery, knowing all along that the day would come for him to take a woman to wife. Ten years ago, the thought of marriage had made him cringe, and he and Cam both had resolved to take their fill before the dreaded moment of their eternal shackling arrived.

They *had* taken their fill. By the time Alan reached his twenty-eighth year, he'd had enough.

But what of the female sex? They were expected to leap into life-long relationships straight out of the nursery. Without exploring, without experiencing. And if they dared to explore and experiment, they were rejected by society, cast off as loose women and whores.

Alan glanced at Gràinne, briefly wondering what crime she had committed to be relegated to such a fate. Likely nothing that could even come close to his own wicked past.

"The world is mad," Sorcha muttered darkly, "if it is acceptable for a man to visit every whorehouse in England, then engage the services of a whore so soon after his marriage."

Gràinne chuckled.

"Not *every* whorehouse in England." Only every whorehouse in Oxford.

Alan considered disabusing her of the notion that he'd engaged Gràinne's services. *No. Not yet.* Perhaps he was enjoying her anger too much. Not a particularly honorable excuse, but then what part of this situation had aught to do with honor?

Sorcha sneered. "Good, then, Alan. Show me what you've learned, why don't you? Show me how you achieve satisfaction without the services of your rejected wife."

She yanked a chair out from the table and lowered herself in it. Sitting upright, she clasped her hands in her lap and raised an expectant eyebrow.

Smug little wench. Why not give her a taste of what betrayal felt like? What he felt like, knowing she'd spent months in Cam's arms?

He glanced at Gràinne again. Still standing naked and wrapped in the blanket, the whore smiled. A bit like a cat that had just gorged itself on the most delicious bowl of cream. The whore seemed more than willing to continue the ruse, making him certain that she knew more about this situation than she'd admitted.

He slid his gaze back to his wife. A muscle moved in Sorcha's jaw as she ground her teeth, but she didn't speak.

He watched her as he unbuckled his belt and removed his dirk, sword, and pistol. He set the weapons and his powder horn beside the hearth. Rising, he tugged his plaid loose and let it fall from his shoulder.

He held it clasped at his hips. "Are you sure you want this, Sorcha?"

She'd stop him now. All color had drained from her face; surely she hadn't actually believed he'd go through with it. She narrowed her eyes at him until they shot venomous green sparks. "Aye."

It struck him then that despite her stubbornness, she was a terrible liar. A fact he might be able to use to his benefit sometime in the future. If he'd been paying better attention, if he hadn't been so lost in the sweetness of her body, he might've recognized that on their wedding night.

Yet she held her ground and wouldn't give in. She dared him to take it further with a flourish of her hand. "Please. Continue."

He was no coward.

He gestured to Gràinne and kept his voice even. "I know what I'll get from her—do you see? A straight tumble. No messy entanglements. I need not worry about lies and betrayal, because nothing she can do to me can hurt me. Only bring me pleasure. She's quite good at that."

Sorcha gave the other woman a look of supreme distaste. If she'd spat on Gràinne's floor it wouldn't have surprised him.

He pulled his plaid free and tossed it aside. He wore only his shirt, shoes, and stockings now. He kicked off his shoes and bent to remove his stockings. Both women watched him in utter silence. Fury radiated from Sorcha, but what was Gràinne thinking? He looked up at her to see that her gaze had turned speculative. Did she comprehend his motives or did she believe she was about to be fucked while Sorcha looked on?

He rose to standing once more, untied the laces closing the neck of his shirt, and lifted the linen material over his head before tossing it aside into the small pile of clothes.

Generally he wasn't self-conscious before women, and he didn't care about his nudity in front of Gràinne, but Sorcha's gaze dragged over his skin like a rake over hot coals. The prickling intensity of her stare roused his cock from its deep slumber, and it hardened under her scrutiny.

The look on her face barely masked the misery simmering beneath.

She sat very still, her spine straight, every muscle in her body rigid as she perused his form. Her heated look contrasted with the tightness of her features, the sharpness in her expression, and the look of pain deep within her eyes. The very air they breathed vibrated with tension.

The blanket slipped from Gràinne's shoulders, and she stood bared before them both. Her nipples had darkened and tightened into puckered peaks, but the cabin was no longer cold. The heat of their bodies, and of their anger, had warmed it.

Alan pointed at the floor in front of him. "Come here, Gràinne. Come and kneel before me."

Gràinne's eyes flicked to Sorcha, then back to him. For an infinitesimal moment, she appeared indecisive. Then she glided closer and dropped to her knees.

Alan looked down at the whore. The next step was to command Gràinne to take him into her mouth.

Silence stretched.

Goddammit. He couldn't do it. It wasn't *her* mouth he wanted closing over his cock.

Before he could step away, Gràinne's shoulders rose as she took a deep breath. She lifted her hand and ran her long fingernail down the length of his erection. His wayward member jumped, hardening even more beneath her teasing touch.

She leaned forward to press her lips to the head. Alan clenched every muscle in his body to prevent himself from thrusting her away.

CHAPTER NINE

Sorcha's frozen body came alive the second Gràinne touched her husband. She lunged for the scythe, grabbed its handle, and sprinted the short distance to where the whore knelt. By God, she'd cut the bitch in two before she let her have him.

Alan was too fast. He leaped in front of Gràinne, protecting her, catching Sorcha's wrist as she began to swing the long, curved blade, and squeezing tight. Sorcha's fingers opened, and the scythe clattered to the floor.

"I hate you," Sorcha hissed.

She tried to wrench away, but he pinned her body against his. His solid rod pressed against her belly. The cock that was hard for a whore. Not for her. "Let me go!" Sorcha cried, struggling, clawing at him. "Damn you! I hate you!"

"No," he growled into her hair. "You don't hate me, you damned little fool."

"I do," she sobbed. "You and your bloody whore."

"She's not my whore," Alan rasped, still holding her tightly. "She's Cam's."

"What?" It made no sense. She twisted and writhed, trying to escape his iron grip. "Let me go, I said."

"No."

"'Tis true," the whore said from behind him. Sorcha stilled as the woman continued. "I'm not too proud to admit defeat when it's staring me in the face. I *am* Cam's, love. Alan MacDonald doesn't want me. You're the one he wants, and I daresay you want him, too." She made a clucking sound with her tongue. "Our poor earl is utterly wrong. You're not the one for him, not at all."

Alan flicked an icy glance at the whore. "Leave. Now."

"You command me to leave my own house?" She sounded astonished.

"This is my house, and my land. You are merely a tenant, Gràinne. And if you hesitate one moment longer, I will throw you out by the scruff of your neck and never allow you shelter on my lands again."

At that, the woman threw back her head and released a gale of laughter. As Sorcha gaped at her in confused disbelief, the whore's guffaws gentled into hiccupping chuckles, and she collected her clothes. Finally, she grabbed a thick cloak from the hook beside the door and strode out, the door banging softly behind her.

Damn them both. They were trying to manipulate her. She didn't believe a word either of them said. Sorcha rounded on Alan, her rage renewed.

She slid her hand between their bodies, pushing downward until she found what she was looking for. "I'll squeeze your ballocks until they explode, you bastard. Now you let me go."

Alan didn't release her. Instead his hands moved to her face. Cupping her cheeks, he tilted her head up to face him. She met his steely blue glare with equal ferocity.

She curled her fingers, digging them into the sensitive skin encasing his testicles. "I've got you by the balls, Alan MacDonald. I'll make you suffer. I'll make you hurt like you've made me hurt."

"Do you feel the come boiling in my ballocks, Sorcha? That's for you. Not for her. I don't care about the damn whore."

Sorcha tightened her hand. The coarse hairs on the underside of his sac rasped over her fingertips.

"I hate you," she said, but with less conviction than before. Confusion swirled in her chest. Was he deliberately driving her to madness?

"Did you honestly think I'd touch her? Could you really think I'd come up here to seek carnal fulfillment from another woman?"

"What else could I think?" she sobbed. Lord, she was losing her mind. "You leave me every day. She was naked when I walked in. She was going—going to s-suck your . . ."

His fingers moved in her hair, threading into the strands. "I haven't had a woman since I took you on our wedding night."

"You lie."

"No."

Before she could react, he captured her wrist in his hand, and her fingers were no longer wrapped around his ballocks. He closed his arms around her, hefted her off her feet, and tossed her onto the bed.

From the cocoon of softness, she stared up at him in shock.

"I'm going to bed you now," he said, but his voice was more like a snarl.

It was clear enough he wanted her. A filmy bead of fluid dripped from the tip of his thick shaft, and the head of his cock was flushed and swollen.

Sorcha couldn't speak for the tremendous lump in her throat, but she challenged him with her look.

Alan crawled onto the bed. Loomed over her.

"You want me, don't you?" he growled. His hand dove under her *arisaid* and his thumb flicked over a nipple that beaded hard, straining against her bodice. "As much as I want you?"

More, she wanted to say. *A thousand times more, a million times more.*

He reached down and found the hem of her dress. His fingertips brushed over her stockings as he yanked her skirts upward.

His hands slid into the vee between her legs, diving between the lips of her sex, finding it hot and wet. Ready. She arched into his touch, releasing a low moan.

Without preamble, he moved into position above her. And then in a long, hard thrust, buried his cock inside her body.

Sorcha groaned.

There was no tenderness in him tonight. In fact, it wasn't lovemaking. It was fucking, pure and simple. He took her with a savage ferocity, thrusting inside her so forcefully he pushed the air from her lungs. Then he yanked himself out until his head hovered at her entrance and he repeated the motion, burrowing himself as deeply as her body would allow. He rested his weight on his forearms, hovering close enough that his lips brushed hers with every thrust. His breath puffed hot over her face.

Sorcha closed her eyes and curled her stockinged legs around Alan's thighs. His muscles flexed and worked beneath her heels.

Hot and hard and heavy, he dug himself into her and dragged out again. So hard she felt as if he tore her to pieces and remade her—she could feel him in every part of her being, from her skin to deep inside her soul.

She wrapped her arms around him, tightened her legs, squeezed her eyes more tightly shut.

He took her spiraling into a black abyss of pleasure and pain, hot as spun sugar and just as sweet. He rode her body until it clung to him, molded against him, shaped itself to him, took and accepted him.

Sorcha sobbed. Sharp lights exploded beyond her closed lids, and her body bowed and undulated in a rolling motion she couldn't control. All around her, Alan was stiff, as hard as metal molten and then cooled to fit perfectly against her body. His muscles quivered, then quaked, and with a long, low groan and one final, violent thrust, he jerked out of her and poured his seed onto the fine silk bed covering.

Alan came slowly back to himself. Sluggishly, his mind recalled where they were and what had happened. He was slumped over

Sorcha's small body, the thick layers of her *arisaid* and petticoats and shift crushed between them. Her eyes were squeezed tightly shut, and perspiration gave her face a shimmering pink glow in the dim, flickering light of the cottage. He brushed a lock of dark hair away from her mouth and then rolled away, tugging her skirts to her ankles as he did so.

Alan moved down Sorcha's body. Slowly, gently, he removed the shoe from her foot and untwined the bandage from her arch. There was no blood, and the scab was still intact. Despite the small amount of swelling no doubt caused by all the walking, her wound hadn't re-opened.

"Thank God," he murmured, replacing the bandage and her shoe. He didn't say more, though he wanted to reprimand her again for her foolishness in walking all this way with her foot not completely healed.

With a final kiss on Sorcha's shin and a squeeze on her forearm, Alan heaved his body off the bed and strode to the hearth, where he pulled on his shirt and belted his plaid, but left his pistol, dirk, and sword.

He went to the door and saw Gràinne waiting beneath the tiny awning, now fully dressed. Rubbing her arms, she cocked an eyebrow at him. "I hope you're finished. It's bloody cold out here."

He tilted his head in acknowledgment and held the door wider. She marched in and headed toward her small kitchen area, where she set a pot over the fire and knelt over a bucket in the corner.

"Why did the earl put you up to this, Gràinne?" he asked.

She stopped and turned, the ladle she carried dripping milk. "Och, he didn't put me up to it. Not at all. It was my own idea. And"—she glanced thoughtfully at Sorcha, who'd curled herself into a ball on the bed—"a foolish one at that."

Gràinne liked his wife, Alan realized, and an odd feeling panged in his chest. It was strange that the whore would acknowledge a lady like Sorcha after what had just occurred . . . but Alan understood.

The fire in Sorcha demanded respect. He still felt the scorching heat in her eyes searing down his back to the base of his spine.

"Was Cam aware of your plan?" Alan asked Gràinne, his voice hard.

She looked away, licking her lips. Then she met his eyes levelly. "Aye. He was."

He nodded, but his neck felt stiff. The languor of his orgasm dissipated, and his muscles once again hardened and stiffened. The knowledge of what he must do flooded through him, cold as ice. He must end this. Once and for all.

Turning from Gràinne, Alan retrieved Sorcha's kertch from the floor and took it to her. She clasped her knees close to her chest, her body still trembling in the aftermath of his savage lovemaking.

"Sorcha?"

She pried her eyes open. "Aye?"

She shuddered, and he held himself in check, restraining himself from taking her into his arms. Instead he satisfied himself with a soft stroke of his knuckles down her cheek.

"I'll take you home, but first—"

"Your men," she said softly. "They're out in the cold."

"They followed you up here?"

She nodded.

Alan nearly smiled. Of course they had followed her, but his men could manage the cold, or if they chose not to, there were many warm, welcoming beds nearby. "Stay here. I'll be back in a moment."

He slipped into the foggy night and called his men to him.

Gràinne poured a measure of warm milk into a cup and brought it to the trembling woman curled on her bed.

"Come, lass," she said softly, reaching out to take Sorcha's hand. "Here's a posset for you."

Sorcha stared at the offering, her eyes narrow with distrust. "Why did you bring Alan here?"

Sighing, Gràinne sat on the edge of the bed. "I am an old friend of the Earl of Camdonn's. I knew him when he was a youth. He has . . . been very good to me."

He'd saved her, really.

She gazed down at the beautiful young woman lying on the ivory silk. She looked so young, so vulnerable. So hurt and confused.

Gràinne had once been a young bride, too. In love, starry-eyed and optimistic, until her husband showed his true side. He began to flaunt his whores in front of her. Made her watch as he fucked them— sometimes four or five at a time—men and women. He'd tied her to the bed as she sobbed, begging him to release her. Then he began ordering the men to use her, sometimes violently, as he watched.

Before all that began, she'd loved him. Truly loved him. She'd dreamed of building a life with him. A family. But for three years he tormented her, tortured her . . . and finally she'd had enough. She escaped from their rooms in Inverness. She ran and ran until she came to the mountain. The women here, each of whom had her own story, some even more terrible than hers, took her in, showed her how to live, how to be happy. They'd remade her, become her family.

Then Cam, the wide-eyed and innocent English schoolboy, had come to her. He'd come home from England for a holiday, and with a flush rising on his baby-soft cheeks, he'd candidly said he wanted to learn from her. Learn everything. As they spent more time together, she'd grown to know him and to love him—to the extent her jaded heart could love. Ultimately, he was the man responsible for restoring her faith in mankind.

Now, she realized, he'd been led astray, but he was too blind to see it. The young bride lying before her belonged to Alan MacDonald, and though neither of them knew it yet, the laird belonged to her as well, heart and soul.

They would discover it, Gràinne hoped, in time. But she wouldn't interfere anymore . . . not in something that could lead to true happiness between two people whose compatibility shone like the brightest star on a clear summer's night.

Sorcha shook her head and her dark brows furrowed. "You brought Alan here . . . for Cam?"

Gràinne shrugged. "Cam wants you, love."

The poor chit still looked confused.

"I meant to seduce your Alan," Gràinne said patiently. "To show you how men are."

"And how's that?" Sorcha breathed.

Gràinne ticked the traits off on her fingers. "Fickle. Untrustworthy. Lustful. Unworthy. Unfaithful."

"You dislike men."

"Oh, no." Gràinne chuckled. "I adore them, but they're such weak creatures."

"Unlike women?"

"Exactly." She smiled. "We are the stronger sex, my dear, though men spend their lives attempting to convince us otherwise. Only a strong woman, and only the *right* woman, can save a man from his baser nature."

This young beauty was undoubtedly that woman for Alan Mac-Donald. But not for Cam.

Gràinne thought of Cam, how weak he was, how deeply he needed to be loved. In an abstract way, Gràinne wished she could be that woman to him, but she'd never be fool enough to think it possible.

Sorcha huffed. "I still don't understand why you'd wish to seduce Alan."

Gràinne suddenly felt tired. It had been a long day, and a sadness crept through her, lodging deep in her bones. "I care deeply for the Earl of Camdonn, lass. I'd do anything for him. If there was hope for him to find happiness with you, I wanted him to have it. If I seduced Alan MacDonald, it would prove to you that your loyalty to him was misguided."

"You *meant* for me to find you here?" Sorcha asked, her lips parted in shock.

"Well, not tonight, lass." Gràinne smiled. "Your appearance rushed things more quickly than I'd anticipated."

"You meant to develop a liaison with my husband so when I discovered his infidelity, I'd run back to Cam?" Sorcha frowned, then shook her head. "If that happened, I'd be more likely to return to my da and never go near another man for all my days."

Gràinne chuckled.

Sorcha shifted to a seated position beside her and took the warm cup of milk from her hands. Taking a deep swallow, the lass gazed expectantly at her.

Gràinne lifted a shoulder. "I had to try, you see. For Cam's sake." She shook her head ruefully. "But you are cut from the wrong cloth altogether. Cam is not the one for you, Sorcha. Alan MacDonald is. I know men, love, and that one'll have none but you."

Sorcha smiled, the first time Gràinne had seen her lips curl into any expression but a sneer. "I think you are an odd sort of matchmaker," she said over the rim of her cup.

Just then, the door opened and the laird stepped inside. Shaking snow from his shoulders, he cast a soft look at Sorcha, then narrowed his blue eyes on Gràinne.

"Do you have parchment and ink?" he growled. "I must write a letter."

Sorcha rested against Alan's chest as they rode down the mountain. They traveled slowly, for though it had stopped snowing and the moon peeked out from behind the clouds, it was still dark and Alan allowed Eachann to pick his way cautiously over the wet terrain. He had tucked his plaid around them both, and despite the wind whipping at her hair, she was comfortable in the tight cocoon of wool. His strong thighs cradled her behind, and he wrapped his arm solidly around her middle.

For the first time since they'd married, she felt safe.

Sighing, she snuggled more deeply against him, sinking into the feel of his flexing muscles against her body.

Something had changed tonight up on the mountain. Alan wanted her fiercely—he'd wanted her all along and had never intended to betray her. Gràinne had witnessed the flaming passion Sorcha and Alan had for each other, and Sorcha hoped she'd take that message back to the earl.

Alan pulled gently on the reins, and Eachann drew short. For a long, silent moment, they stared down at the valley. Fog swirled over the roofs like swirling tentacles, and in the muted moonlight, the grass shimmered midnight green. Beyond, mist rose from the loch, its waters a deep and fathomless black. The damp air smelled of cut wheat and heather.

"It's lovely," Sorcha breathed.

His hand tightened minutely over her waist. "I was thinking," he said into her ear, "of building a house up here."

She remained silent.

"We are standing on its foundations. It would be a modern stone house, with a proper kitchen, a drawing room, and bedrooms. Servants' quarters too."

"A fitting residence for the laird," she said softly.

"Aye," he said. "To be seen as equal to the rest of the world, we must bring ourselves into this century."

"It would be a beautiful house. In a beautiful setting."

Alan released a breath, and with it, she could feel some of the tension leave his body. "The stables would be down the hill," he said. "Where the cottage is now. The other cottages might house some of the staff."

Gazing down at the small cluster of buildings, she nodded. The fog had drifted away, leaving a clearer view of the thatched roofs.

She could easily picture a house standing in this spot. In her mind's eye, she stepped out the front door to gaze down at Alan exercising his horses in the clearing below. It was a comforting vision.

Alan clucked at his horse, and they resumed their slow walk down toward the cottage. Moments later, they pulled up before the door. Alan unclasped the brooch holding the plaid wrapped over them. Instantly, cold air seeped straight through the wool of Sorcha's jacket, and she shivered.

He dismounted and lifted her off. With a light pat on her rump, he said, "Go on to bed. I must brush Eachann down, but I'll be right along."

Cam paced before the fire in his study.

Again, he'd been an impulsive fool, thinking with his heart rather than his head. Even if Gràinne did succeed in seducing Alan—and in retrospect he doubted she would, knowing Alan and his old-fashioned Highland sentiments on honor and marriage—what then? It was not a given that Sorcha would come running to him.

He pushed his hand through his tangled hair. He felt like a caged lion trapped in this infernal prison of desire. Sorcha was his keeper, and nothing, save her, could set him free.

He needed to formulate a plan to turn her away from Alan. If that didn't work . . .

Hell. He'd kidnap her again. He'd prefer her to come on her own accord, but if there was no way . . . Yes, he'd take her. This time he'd make sure he kept her.

She just hadn't had enough opportunity to grow accustomed to the idea last time. If she hadn't escaped, he would have let her go, and she would have realized he was an honorable man. Just as honorable as Alan.

He stalked to the window, fists clenched. What was he thinking? Was he simpleminded? As if repeating the same mistake would make her love him.

He reeled around and stopped at the fire to gaze moodily into it. No matter what he did now, she would think him less honorable than Alan.

Worse, she was right—he *was* less honorable than Alan. He'd wronged them both. Not for the first time, regret washed through him.

A soft knock sounded at the door, and he jerked around to face the heavy wooden planks. "Come," he barked.

It was Duncan. Standing behind him was a younger MacDonald he recognized as Alan's cousin and current heir. Cam narrowed his eyes. "Yes?" he said in his most disdainful English lord voice.

"Forgive me, milord. But I've brought Bowie MacDonald—he says he has a message for you." Duncan stepped aside so the man could enter.

Bowie's youthful face was completely blank as he held out a folded sheet of parchment. Cam took it and went to stand by the light of his desk lamp to read.

My Lord Camdonn,

As you have breached my honor countless times, I now have no recourse but to demand the satisfaction entitled me as a gentleman. We will meet with swords at the place and time of your choosing.

Alan MacDonald

Cam stood motionless for a long moment, rereading the brief note several times. He didn't know what to think.

How could he fight Alan MacDonald? The man was like a brother to him.

He had forced his friend's hand, given Alan no choice. Of course Alan would feel there was no other way to reclaim his honor. Cam had offended him in the basest fashion—by coveting his wife and then attempting to trick him into adultery. For either one of those transgressions, Alan's honor would demand a challenge.

Drawing in a breath filled with the close, smoky air of his study, he glanced up at Bowie. "Please wait whilst I compose a response."

"Before you do that, it's my duty as the laird's second to determine the source of the misunderstanding and to attempt a reconciliation."

Cam raised an eyebrow at the lad. "Is it?"

"Aye." But the boy had nothing further to offer, and Cam just stared at him.

"So," Cam finally said. "You know it wasn't a misunderstanding, don't you?"

"Aye. I know it well."

"You believe there is no hope for a reconciliation, don't you?"

Bowie shrugged. "Have you any ideas to offer?"

"No. None."

"Very well." Bowie crossed his arms over his chest. "Go on and write your response, then."

Could Alan really trust such a young lad as his second? But Bowie was seventeen, eleven years younger than Alan—man enough to go to war, and man enough to be his kinsman's second. Cam didn't doubt that Bowie would represent Alan with the dedication of kinship and clan.

Before he'd abducted the man's wife, Cam undoubtedly would have been Alan's foremost choice as a second in any duel he fought. They'd even discussed it once and had agreed to back each other up should they mistakenly offend someone.

But who would serve as Cam's second? So entranced had he been by Sorcha since he'd set foot on the grounds of Camdonn Castle upon his return from England, he'd scarcely paid attention to his reputation. It was his own fault the Highlanders kept their distance. He hadn't done a thing to earn their respect, after all. He had only tried to earn Sorcha's—and look how that had turned out.

He'd lost her to his best friend. His rival. The man he most admired in the world.

A sullen part of him thought on how easy it was for Alan to saunter home from England and have the villagers and his few tenants and even his stranger of a wife instantly fall to their knees in loyal adoration. Despite his mother's English blood, Alan was a Scot through and through. He held himself like a Highlander. He spoke like one, his Gaelic fluent and perfect.

Cam had always preferred to speak the more comfortable English. His English ties were what guided him as a child. When he went to England for school, he pretended to be one of them, while Alan stood apart, never feeling the need to shed his plaids or his Highland ways. And when Alan was challenged—rare once people got to know him— he proved his mettle with his fists.

Cam had wanted respect. He'd wanted to fit in, so he'd ignored his background and had used his English title, Viscount Manderly. He took on the accent, the posture, all of their "civilized" ways.

After all that, Cam had only gained the respect of social climbers. Alan earned more friends, more esteem, and more admiration with seemingly no effort. Even Cam's father preferred Alan to his own son. Once when Cam was fourteen years old, his father had come to London. Alan had joined them for dinner one night, and afterward the earl said Cam should study Alan to learn how to behave like a man.

Cam didn't understand exactly what his father had meant, but he did know Alan had lost his virginity to a willing girl just a few months before. So when he'd gone home with his father on the next holiday from school, he made it his first order of business to go to one of the whores on the mountain to learn about the carnal arts. He was certain that his own loss of virginity would turn him into a man in his father's eyes.

It hadn't worked. It seemed no matter what he did or how hard he tried, Cam still wasn't good enough.

And now he realized his father was right. There was no doubt of it: Alan *was* the better man.

Cam suppressed a sigh and pressed his fingers over the bridge of his nose. Hell, he needed to choose a second. He had no close kinsmen left in Scotland—his cousins all lived in England. He had no real friends other than Alan, and that was over, ruined by his own impulsive actions. The only reasonable choice would be the blockheaded Angus MacLean.

He'd prefer young Bowie.

Wearily, Cam walked to his desk and lowered himself into the ornately carved chair behind it. He pulled out a blank sheet and dipped his quill into the ink to compose his response.

Tomorrow, Alan. We will settle this tomorrow.

Relief washed over him. Thank God. It would all end soon.

CHAPTER TEN

Alan brushed his horse's flank and tried to cool his heated blood. His cock was at full stand, eager to claim Sorcha again. He wanted her, and he'd take her again inside the comfort and privacy of his home. But he'd be damned if he'd lose all control this time. He wished to give her pleasure too.

"Alan?"

Alan jerked his head to see Bowie enter, his cropped blond hair standing in damp spikes across his head. "Back already?"

"Aye, and with a response from the earl." Grimacing with distaste, the boy held out a folded, sealed paper between two fingers.

Alan took the letter, broke the wax of Cam's seal, and quickly scanned the contents. Cam had acknowledged his challenge. They'd settle it tomorrow at daybreak, on Glenfinnan Moor. He glanced back up at Bowie. "As I expected. Tomorrow, at dawn."

With tight lips, Bowie nodded. "You must get your sleep tonight, Alan."

"Aye, I will, and you too. Meet me at Glenfinnan by the water's edge an hour before sunrise."

"Aye." With an incline of his head, Bowie strode outside and left him alone.

Alan turned back to Eachann and finished brushing him down. The animal blew out the occasional contented breath between his lips, but otherwise Alan worked in silence. When he finished, he hung the brush and left the horse with some oats.

He went outdoors and strode past the cottage to the loch. Steam drifted across the surface of the water, spreading ghostlike tendrils to curl like clutching fingers over the black pool.

Alan removed his plaid and shirt, gritting his teeth against the frigid air. Dropping his clothes on the grassy bank, he walked in, sucking in his breath at the frozen bite of the water, until he was waist-deep. He ducked his head and scrubbed the smell of horse from his body. Steeling himself against the cold, he waded out, grabbing his clothes on the way to the cottage.

He pushed open the door. Warmth and the smell of burning peat washed over him. Sorcha had stoked the fire, and it burned cheerfully in the hearth. He paused at the threshold of the bedroom. His wife lay on the bed, her dark hair spread over the pillow.

She turned toward him, resting her head in her palm. Her eyebrows shot upward. "Alan! You're naked!" This statement of the obvious was followed by an instantaneous flush.

He couldn't help but give her a rakish grin. "Aye. I stank of horse."

Her surprise dissolved into an impish grin. "You're lucky Shielagh didn't attack you."

"Shielagh?"

"You don't remember?" She arched a brow. "Our wee kelpie."

"Ah." He searched his memory for a recollection of Loch Shiel's evil water horse and found nothing. "Is he so wicked, then?"

"He's never bothered me, but . . ." She shrugged. "Perhaps he prefers men."

He doubted that. "Well, if I were a kelpie . . ." *I'd turn myself into a human and lure you onto my bed of weeds . . .* Rather than finish the thought, he allowed his voice to dwindle.

She bit her lip, looking at him shyly. Then, tentatively, as if she'd built her courage, she held out her arm. "Come. I'll warm you."

Alan took a spare plaid from a peg on the wall, and using it like a towel, scrubbed it over his skin. Then he joined her, crawling under the covers and pressing his cool body to hers, watching her grit her teeth. She let out a hiss of a breath. "Ooh."

"Cold?"

"Aye." But very deliberately, she turned to him, wrapped her arms around his body, and pressed herself against him, draping her leg over his thigh. As surprised as she had seemed to see him walk in naked, she was also completely bare, and they were touching, skin to skin, from head to toe. Her silky heat spread through him, an incredibly satisfying feeling, and his cock responded, warming and growing as her heat stole away the chill.

Slowly, he reminded himself. As much as he wanted to bury himself inside her and stay there, he couldn't. Something continued to hold him back from being himself.

Despite what had happened between them earlier, the still-raw knowledge that his wife wasn't who he thought she was hung in his chest like a heavy stone. She had loved someone else. *Cam.*

And then there was the knowledge of the increasing power she wielded over him. He was treading dangerous ground to become this close to a woman he couldn't bring himself to trust.

"Do you believe in mythical creatures, Sorcha?"

She shrugged. "My da taught us not to place too much credence in the old superstitions. Yet . . . one can't help but wonder."

"Has anyone ever actually seen the kelpie?"

"Oh, aye. I have."

He chuckled. "Have you?"

She nodded, snuggling closer to him. "He's black and shiny, with humps on his back. He has golden eyes. I think he's not interested in me, though, because once he set eyes upon me, he swam away, leaving me frozen in fear up to my knees in the loch."

"How long ago was this?"

"Not so long. Maybe two years."

"Were you dreaming?"

"Maybe I was . . ." Her lashes lowered in lush velvet arcs, and she pressed her palm against his chest. Alan sucked in a breath.

"You're hot as a brand," he said in a low voice. "When you move away, will the imprint of your hand remain?"

"I hope so." An edge of heat tinged her voice.

He didn't respond. By her actions in Gràinne's cottage, it was clear she thought to possess him. As much as logic screamed at him to rebel against that concept, he found it oddly pleasing.

He wished to possess her as well. He'd be damned if he'd share her affections with any other man. He was glad it would end tomorrow. Whether in victory or defeat for him, thank God it would end.

Raising his hand, he smoothed a dark arched brow with his fingertip. She seemed to revel in his touch; her eyes drifted shut. He continued exploring her face, smoothing his fingers over the faint creases in her forehead, brushing across the line of her hair. Moving lower, he descended the slope of her nose, touching each of the near-invisible little freckles. Last, he traced the soft, supple curve of her lip.

His cock was so hard it ached. Throbbed. God, how he wanted her. His little hotheaded wife. His lying, treacherous wife.

He loved her.

No.

No, he didn't love her. He felt strongly because a bond had been formed between them under God, and no man of honor took that bond lightly. He would feel equally strongly about any woman he took to wife. Wouldn't he?

A subtle smile curled the edges of her lips. Her hand slid upward, and he jerked as her fingertip skimmed his chest.

"Do you like being touched there, Alan?"

"Aye," he said, his voice gruff.

Slowly, she circled his nipple then pinched it between two fingers. His cock pulsed in response.

Her fingers dipped lower, down his stomach to graze the tip of his eager shaft. "Oooh," she breathed, smearing a tiny drop of liquid over the head. In an abrupt motion, she burrowed underneath the covers, and before he comprehended her intent, her wet, hot, slightly rough tongue lapped at the moisture.

"Mmm," she murmured, as if it was the sweetest thing she'd ever tasted. And then her mouth closed fully over him, and he groaned low in his throat.

Her lips sealed around his length, beginning a gentle motion downward, then back up. Her tongue swirled across and over the crown as she neared the tip. He reached under the blanket, finding her head and cupping it in his palms, fucking her mouth as if it were her tight sheath, rotating his hips and pushing on her head until he felt the back of her throat touch his sensitive glans.

Clenching his jaw, he directed her movements until his balls tightened and pressure built at the base of his shaft. As if she felt his imminent release, she peppered kisses down the length of him. Taking his sac in her hands, she rolled it gently, tickling the root of his cock with the tip of her tongue.

No one, whore or lady, had ever touched him with such abandon. His shock at her actions was short-lived, however, because her gasps of pleasure combined with the mere thought of her sucking his balls was enough to make him come again.

In a matter of seconds it would be over. With a low growl, he reached down and lifted her over him. Her mouth glistened from her uninhibited actions, and she stared down at him with a feral glint in her eyes. She reminded him of a black and white cat he had seen once, with slanted, feline eyes full of some internal wisdom it refused to share.

By the look on her face, he knew, beyond a doubt, Sorcha was ready for him.

He lifted her, positioning her over him. As she spread her thighs, settling her legs on either side of his hips, the shiny pink of her center flashed in the line of his vision.

She rubbed herself wantonly over him, and the silky heat between her legs slid up and down his swollen shaft.

Bonnie, soft Sorcha. He didn't know what to think of this wanton side she was showing him for the first time.

She gazed down at him, and he stared up at the haze of lust radiating from her eyes. She stilled, and in a blink, the feral expression disappeared from her face. "What is it?" she whispered.

Holding her waist in his hands, he shifted his hips, continuing her wet glide over his cock. "Is this you, Sorcha?" he asked in a low voice. "The real you? Or do you merely pretend?"

"Do I displease you?" A hint of despair colored her voice.

He knew she could hardly be playacting—her peaked nipples and slick cunny were evidence enough of her lust for him.

Perhaps that was the question: Clearly she was lustful . . . but was it for *him*? Him alone? He thought perhaps not.

"No. Your ardor doesn't displease me. It pleases me very much." *But only if it is for me.*

"No pretense." Lowering her lids so he couldn't see the expression in her eyes, she slid forward then back in a hot stroke. "This is me."

His whole body tightened. There was no way he could last long once inside her. "But who is it you want?" he ground out.

Opening her eyes, she speared him with her green gaze. She paused in midmotion, her entrance hovering over the blunt head of his cock. "You, Alan MacDonald. Only you."

In a slow, deliberate move, she pushed her body down over him.

"You," she whispered again, beginning to move in a long, slow glide. "I want you. So . . . much."

She closed over him, hot and clenching, and he tightened his fingers on her waist, trying to hold back. Leaning down, she wrapped her arms around the outside of his head, resting on her forearms on the bed as she ground her body into him, the jeweled tips of her breasts scraping his chest.

It felt so good. So wet and warm and tight. His seed strained for release as her silk gripped his granite length. Hell, he was about to burst. Explode like a dam weakened by a torrential flood.

He heaved her off of him and in a smooth motion, flipped her over, landing on top of her. Before she could move, he slid downward, closing his mouth over a taut nipple. Below him, she whimpered. "Alan."

He didn't respond, instead moved to the other side, laving it, worshipping it with his mouth. She smelled of sweet lusty woman, and her skin tasted of heather and wheat.

When her steady breaths degenerated into gasps of pleasure each time he nipped at her skin, he traveled farther down, blazing a trail with his tongue. He kissed her soft belly before settling himself between her legs.

Pushing her thighs more widely apart, he simply stared at her for a long moment. Black curls hid her quim, and using his thumbs, he opened her outer lips. Her clitoris was swollen, glistening pink, and he blew softly before touching the tip of his tongue to it.

She gasped and jerked, but he held her still as he tasted her. Here, her taste was more concentrated, more musky and feminine, but yet with that underlying sunshine sweetness he had secretly craved since their wedding night.

He pulled his mouth away from her. "Touch yourself, Sorcha."

"W-what?" she gasped.

Her hand clutched at the blanket. Gently, he unfurled her fingers, opened her palm, and pressed her hand over her mound. "Touch yourself."

She didn't move. He propped himself on his elbow to give himself a clear view of her face. "Don't tell me you've never made yourself come."

A pretty flush crept up her neck. "Oh . . . I—"

"Have you, then?"

"In the cave I told you about," she admitted.

The image flickered through his mind. Sorcha nestled in the cliff behind Camdonn Castle, facing the dark waters of the loch, her skirts lifted past her waist, showing off her garters and pale thighs, her fingers diving into the curls between her legs and rubbing furiously. He took a measured breath in an attempt to control the heat that surged through him at the thought.

"But never with anyone else watching."

"Good." Perhaps it was one of the few things he could enjoy with her that Cam hadn't already.

He ground his teeth. It was a mistake to think of Cam now. Best to thrust away any thought of the man he conjured.

He focused on Sorcha's plump, pink nether lips just beneath her fingertips.

"Do it," he gritted out.

"Why, Alan?" she asked, her voice tentative.

"Because it will please me."

With a deep breath, she slipped her fingers between her moist lips, pushing downward until they brushed over her clitoris. She gasped.

"That's it," he coaxed. Her slick juices coated her fingers as she slid even lower. "Touch yourself for me. Show me what feels good to you."

She touched the tiny pearl again, then circled it, arching her hips upward, pressing more firmly.

"I'll help," he murmured. He brushed her opening, rimming it, then slipping two fingers deep into her, pushing against the resistance of her channel. She cried out.

He began to stroke her inner walls, using his fingertips to find the most sensitive areas inside her.

"Ah!"

"Does that feel good, *ceisd mo chridhe?*"

There was an infinitesimal pause as they both registered the endearment; then Alan pushed his fingers deeper and Sorcha rubbed herself harder, arching up in a rhythm that matched his thrusts.

He felt the ripples against the flesh of his digits first, and then her thighs stiffened under his shoulders. He raised his head to see her beautiful face. She was staring down at him, witnessing firsthand the erotic tableau, her eyes alight with passion, her lips parted. Spots of red flamed high on her cheeks. "Oh, Alan," she whispered, "I'm going to come. Please—"

"Yes, *mo chridhe*," he murmured. He moved his free fingers to the puckered rosette of her arse, painting soft little circles around it. "It's all right. Beautiful Sorcha. Come for me."

Her hands clenched and her body shuddered all around him. Her channel tightened over his fingers, then spasmed like a clenching fist.

His cock throbbed as her cream dribbled to the base of his fingers. Slowly, she relaxed. He kissed the top of her hand, stroked her thigh, and finally pulled away from her body.

He crawled up beside her to look in her face. Her eyes squeezed shut, she tried to turn away from him, but he held her pinned to the bed.

Sorcha wanted to curl away, but his hand tightened over her shoulder, and she couldn't fight him. Alan did something unique to her. The way he'd walked inside, tall and muscular, with water droplets glistening all over his hard body, and then the way he'd looked at her with those deep, blazing blue eyes . . . It had made her leap right out of the demure shell she'd hidden behind when she believed Alan wanted her to be innocent.

"Look at me." The command was quiet, forceful, and Sorcha couldn't do anything but obey.

She opened her eyes and faced him. Whatever happened, she wouldn't cower.

"Why do you turn away from me?" he asked, his voice low and rumbling.

"I am . . . embarrassed."

"Why?"

"You said I was shameless, and you're right. I haven't behaved as I should. As a lady. As a—a wife." Her lower lip began to tremble, so she closed her teeth over it. Hard.

His eyes widened minutely. "And how is it do you think a lady and a wife should behave, Sorcha?"

"With more reserve."

"Do you think I'd prefer a cold fish beneath me in bed?"

"I don't know. Seeing you walk inside like that—I got carried away . . ." And now he would undoubtedly think she was so wanton she'd jump into any man's bed without a qualm. No doubt he'd think that was why she'd done so with Cam.

A smile curved Alan's handsome lips. "I asked you to touch yourself, remember? I don't fault you for your enthusiasm."

"No?"

"No."

Still, she eyed him warily. She couldn't shake the feeling her enthusiasm had gone too far.

"Here, *mo chridhe*, let me show you."

My heart. He called her "my heart." And he had before as well, in the heat of it.

His hand skimmed down her arm, his fingers entwining with hers. He brought her hand between his legs. His shaft burned her fingertips, so heavy and hot and hard, she gasped.

"Do you see? This is what you do to me," he said in a low voice.

She curled her hand around the steely length. She stroked it as he guided her movements.

His face twisted with pleasure. "That's what I want, Sorcha. Touch me. Squeeze hard."

She tightened her fingers and increased the length of her stroke. He groaned.

"You don't believe I am too wanton?" she murmured into his ear.

"No."

This was what she'd dreamed of ever since she'd escaped Cam to return to Alan. To touch and be touched by him. To make love to him again. To have him show her things Cam never could, because she hadn't loved him. Now, perhaps, Alan was on the road to forgiving her, and in time they might achieve that closeness she craved.

She wanted to kiss him again, down there, as she had before. To run her tongue over the silken length, trace the outline of his veins as they traveled up, then swirl over his foreskin, lightly grazing the swollen crown she knew was so sensitive. As she began to slide downward over the bedsheet, though, Alan stopped her.

"Turn over," he said, his eyes deep as a fathomless ocean. "On your hands and knees."

A bolt of lust sped directly to her center. Trembling, Sorcha rolled and drew her legs beneath her as Alan positioned himself behind her. For a long moment, he didn't touch her. She finally looked back at him to see him stroking his shaft lightly as he stared at her backside.

He didn't look at her face; instead he reached his free hand to stroke down the crease between her cheeks. He paused at her most private place, and she lowered her head, shivering, as he lightly applied pressure there.

"Did Cam take you here?" His voice was gruff.

"No," she whispered, though her mouth was so dry she was surprised she was able to gasp out the word.

Did men really take women there? Though she'd never thought about such a thing until this moment, she wished Alan would. She wanted to feel what it would be like to have his cock invade her and to feel that connection with him in her most secret of places.

She drew in a shaky breath.

"Good."

She could tell by his tone he was pleased. Alan was so reserved and respectable, it seemed a mad thought that he would even conceive of such a thing. And yet the fingertip pushed inexorably against the taut ring of resisting muscle.

"Alan!" It came out as a half cough, half groan. She fisted the bed-clothes and dropped her forehead to the blanket.

"Not tonight," he whispered gruffly. But his tone promised soon, very soon, and she shuddered as he pushed in a fraction of an inch deeper. Below his questing fingertip, her sex trembled and hummed with need.

He pulled away and within a few seconds the head of his cock pressed against her arse, traveling the same course as his fingers had moments ago, from the top of her crack, then lower, until it hesitated at that forbidden entrance. After the slightest pause, it descended again until it was lodged in the welcoming notch of her sex.

In one smooth-as-satin motion, he thrust in. Sorcha groaned, arching her back. Almost beyond her control, she balanced her weight on one forearm while she reached to touch her needy, aching, sensitive nub.

Alan thrust again, just as Sorcha found what she was looking for. She exploded like a gunshot, her body tightening and releasing in a glorious, powerful explosion. Alan's hands wrapped around her waist, pulling her tight against his body as she came down, whimpering.

He followed close behind. Moments later, he tensed around her and, with a low groan, he yanked out of her. Thick, warm semen landed on her lower back and slid down into the crack of her bottom as he came.

Pushing her knees from under her, Sorcha dropped to her stomach, then turned to face Alan, who had lowered himself at her side. His arm came up to her waist, stroking idly.

"I'll get you a cloth to wash." He turned away, but Sorcha caught his arm.

"No. I want to leave your seed on me."

Alan's eyes flared—but she could not read into why. She hoped it was a flare of possession. He'd marked her like some primitive creature, and the last thing she wanted to do was wash it away.

She wanted to be his.

* * *

Awakened from a deep sleep, Sorcha opened her eyes drowsily. It was still dark, and Alan hovered over her, nudging her legs apart. He pushed himself into her without preamble, and Sorcha released a gasp as her body adjusted to his size.

They made slow, sweet love, and when it was over, Sorcha trailed her fingers through his seed on her belly before she pressed her body against his.

Nobody had ever made her feel like Alan did. Never had she felt so absolutely perfect in someone's embrace. Never had she felt so at peace.

Everything was going to be all right. They would live in the cottage until their house was built up on the hill. They'd be happy.

She had cared for the Earl of Camdonn. She'd been infatuated with him, perhaps. She'd certainly lusted for him. But those feelings combined were nothing compared to her feelings for the man who held her safe in his strong arms.

Earlier today she'd told him she didn't love him. But so much had happened since then. So much to burn away the cloak of fear shrouding her heart. Now the truth was exposed, and it was so sweet.

She loved Alan MacDonald.

Love was a beautiful thing, swelling her heart so full, she thought she might burst with it.

With a peaceful smile curving her lips, she fell into a dreamless sleep.

When she woke hours later, it was still dark. All was quiet. And Alan was gone from her side.

CHAPTER ELEVEN

Perhaps he hadn't been able to sleep and had gone for a walk, Sorcha rationalized. Yesterday had been a trying day for both of them.

She checked the clock and saw it was nearly dawn. Knowing she wouldn't be able to fall back asleep—not without Alan—she washed up, stoked the fire, and headed outside to check the stables. She released a sigh of disappointment when she saw Eachann's empty stall.

She turned away and leaned against the stable's doorframe to stare out across the loch. The predawn light spread across the water, giving it a sparkling, pearly hue.

She gazed up the dark hill at the plateau where they'd paused last night on their way home from the mountain—the spot where Alan intended to build his grand house.

Alan was softening toward her—dare she even think he was beginning to love her? She could only hope. And pray.

Surely the Earl of Camdonn would soon move on to other pursuits. Surely he understood that his continued obsession with her would only bring more pain to all of them.

Having an earl look at her the way Cam had once looked at her was a girlish fantasy come to life for a brief time. But things would have never worked between them—they were far too different from each other. Clearly Cam had always known that—at least before he'd abducted her on her wedding night—otherwise he would have stopped her marriage to Alan before it happened. Deep in his heart, Cam knew that this was the life destined for her. The life that could fulfill her.

Yet there was still so much uncertainty. The uprising loomed on the horizon like a dark cloud. Soon it was likely Alan would lead the MacDonalds to war. He'd never send his men to battle without a leader.

She closed her eyes, afraid for them all.

"Sorcha!"

Startled, Sorcha turned toward the sound of her sister's voice. The door to the cottage was ajar, and she saw a flash of dark material as Moira searched for her inside.

What in Heaven's name could her sister be doing here so early? She picked up her skirts and hurried to the cottage. "Moira? I'm outside."

Moira, pink-cheeked and flustered, appeared at the door just as Sorcha approached it.

"Thank the Lord you're all right," Moira burst out; then she looked down at Sorcha's feet. "How is your wound?"

Alarm bells shrieked in Sorcha's head. "My wound?"

"Your foot. You haven't reopened the cut, have you?"

"No, no, I haven't." She grabbed her sister's hands. "Why are you here? What has happened? Is it Alan?"

Her sister's freckled face turned grave. "Oh, Sorcha. Da forbade me to come, but I thought Alan might keep it from you. I came as soon as they all left."

"What are you saying? Keep *what* from me?"

"Alan has gone to duel with the Earl of Camdonn. They are to meet at the loch's edge at dawn."

Sorcha stared at her sister. "How do you know this?"

"You know how quickly word travels in the valley. Bowie Mac-

Donald told his friends before he left to serve as Alan's second, and they spread the word, starting with our own da."

Sorcha's mouth dropped open as her sister continued. "Everyone has gone down to watch."

"No," Sorcha whispered. *No, no, no.*

The thought of Alan hurt, of Cam hurt, of either of them killed by the other . . . She couldn't stomach it. She brushed past Moira, who spun around and followed her into the cottage.

"What are you doing?" Moira cried as Sorcha pushed her feet into her shoes.

"If I run, I might be able to stop them." God knew nobody else would. Curse men and their bloodthirsty nature.

"You must not! Your foot, Sorcha!"

She glared at her sister as she shoved her second foot into her shoe. "You just try to stop me, Moira Stewart! I am going to prevent my husband and the Earl of Camdonn from killing each other. And you tell me I shouldn't go because I've a scratched foot?"

Moira bit her lower lip and wrung her hands. Sorcha buttoned her jacket and pinned her *arisaid*. As she reached the door at a run, Moira rushed to follow. "Wait! I'm coming with you."

"Then hurry." Sorcha picked up the pace, lifting her skirts. Already wet from the dewy heather, they slapped heavily against her bare calves.

It was freeing to run. To glide over the cool, damp landscape, exhaling puffs of steam with every breath.

She felt the slight tear when the wound on her foot reopened, but she didn't slow her stride. Moira could sew it back up later. Sorcha glanced behind to see her sister following at a distance, her face red with exertion.

She would catch up. All that mattered was that Sorcha reach Glenfinnan Moor in time to stop Alan and Cam. She leaped over a rock and sprinted toward the glen.

* * *

The location Cam had selected was a flat plain bordering the loch at the mouth of the valley near Glenfinnan. Alan, standing knee-deep in heather, smiled at Bowie, who glanced over at Cam taking practice swings at an imaginary opponent. The wide, sweeping arcs of his broadsword whistled through the air.

A strange peace had settled over Alan. The past ten days had perhaps been the most difficult of his life. His honor had been crushed under the Earl of Camdonn's heel, but he was about to reclaim it and rebuild it into something stronger. Win or lose, at least he would be a man once again. Worthy of the name of MacDonald.

He scanned the crowd of men from the village and Camdonn Castle who had gathered to witness the duel. It didn't surprise him that they'd come, but it unsettled him to see the grave looks on everyone's faces. The crowd was quiet, waiting with bated breath to see who would be the victor . . . and whether quarter would be given at the last.

He'd give Cam quarter. He did not intend to murder the earl, only to achieve satisfaction, and he didn't need to kill to do that.

But seeing Cam this morning, Alan wasn't sure of the other man's intentions. Cam was dressed in dark breeches and a white shirt, and his scalp already shone with perspiration from his practice. He made a show of his preparation as Alan stood by his horse, sipping water and occasionally speaking in low tones to Bowie.

Alan glanced at the sky. It was as bright as it was ever going to be. Time to get this over with.

"Alan?"

"Aye, Bowie. It's time. Go on and speak with the earl's second."

Taking a deep breath, Bowie straightened, then jogged across the grass to speak with Cam's second, Angus MacLean, whose broken gut had apparently healed quite nicely. From the distance, Alan saw the giant nod as Bowie spoke to him, then they both approached the earl.

Bowie jogged back to him. "We'll begin in two minutes."

Alan leaned against the spindly tree trunk. He shut his eyes and cleared his mind. It seemed like only seconds passed before Bowie tapped him on the shoulder.

"Alan?"

"Aye, lad."

"They're waiting."

He nodded. His mouth dry, he took a long drink of plain water from the flask he had brought. He checked both his broadsword and his dirk one final time. Then he moved to the center of the circle formed by the onlookers.

It was all a blur. First the giant spoke and then Bowie, but Alan didn't hear a word they said. He gripped his hilt and waited until both men moved aside, leaving him face-to-face with Cam for the first time since his wedding night.

With a dark, intent expression, Cam reached for his sword. Someone shouted, signaling the start of the duel, and a whistling noise sounded from both men's sheaths as they drew their weapons.

Immediately on the defensive, Alan raised his broadsword to block an arcing thrust aimed for his chest. Cam swung around, reaching for the other side, but Alan blocked again. The swords clashed in the crisp early-morning air, startling a flock of birds from their perches in nearby shrubs. They rose, wings flapping, squawking with annoyance.

Alan's senses sharpened. Though he was aware of the birds and the gasps of the crowd, his focus riveted to the earl. It was almost as if he could predict Cam's next moves from the subtle hints of muscles tensing behind the billowing white shirt.

He blocked a low jab, then a high one, and finally was able to offer his own attack, a sweep to the side, which the earl parried instantly.

Cam danced forward, pushing Alan back until they skirted the edge of the crowd. The clang of their swords echoed in Alan's head. A drop of sweat rolled down the side of Cam's face.

He blocked and parried ten times for every one of his own slices at Cam. But he took solace in the fact that each of his swipes was carefully placed and powerful. If Cam faltered once, it would be over.

The sweeping arcs of Cam's sword, on the other hand, were fast but light. If struck, Alan would be scratched but able to continue.

Nevertheless, Alan couldn't count on Cam faltering. Neither of them was a fool with a sword—it was why he had chosen this particular weapon. And though sweat cooled his skin, Alan knew Cam possessed the endurance of two men.

Cam's sword whooshed through the air. Low then high, right and left. It developed into a pattern, and it was Alan who grew lazy. Two sweeping slashes from the right threw him off guard, and on the third swipe, Cam's sword sliced through Alan's shirtsleeve and scratched his arm.

It hurt more than Alan could have predicted. Tears sprang to his eyes, but he blinked hard to make them go away. He tightened his fingers over his hilt and concentrated. Though Cam had struck him, he had not paused in his assault. To lose concentration now would be Alan's undoing.

He tried not to think of the blood dribbling down his arm. How he wanted to clutch the wound to staunch the bleeding and soothe the sting.

No sooner had Alan regained his focus than Cam took him by surprise again. He slowed, adding power to each thrust and swipe of his sword.

Alan realized that whatever had happened before was merely a warm-up. Now Cam was serious.

As soon as Alan comprehended that, Cam struck again.

Sorcha heard the loud clang of swords long before she could see them. A sob tore through her chest and she sprinted hard down the hill before she reached the flat of the moor, ignoring the hot pain now pulsing through the bottom of her foot.

Cam. Alan. Cam. Alan. Her mind cried the name of each man with every stride.

She drew up short as she reached the clearing. Alan and Cam slashed at each other in the center of the crowd of men. Alan's arm dripped blood. Oh God, he'd been injured.

"Alan!" she cried, rushing forward. But strong arms grabbed her and yanked her back. "Alan!" she screamed again, only to have a meaty hand close over her mouth. She bit down with all her might.

With a roared curse, her captor pushed her away. "Bitch!"

She didn't look at him; instead she sprinted once again onto the clearing. Somehow, she had to stop them. She could only pray she wouldn't distract one of them only to have the other take the advantage . . .

"Alan," she called. "Cam!"

Both men paused in midmotion. But then, once again, male hands grabbed at her. She fought with everything she possessed, trying to twist free. This time, though, there was more than one man, and one of them was her father.

"Sorcha!" he snapped, his face ground into a furious mask. "Do you want both of them to die? Stop this madness at once!"

"No, Da, no! Alan's hurt. Please, make them stop."

Her father's callused hands rounded over her cheeks. "Look at me."

She opened her eyes and gazed into his. People always said they had the same eyes. But his were older . . . and they had always struck her as so much wiser. She'd always obeyed her da. It was one reason she'd gone to such lengths to keep her affair with Cam a secret. As reckless as she'd been, she'd not wanted her father to know. He'd be so disappointed in her.

"You must let them finish this, lass."

"No." She cringed as somewhere behind her the swords clashed again.

"Listen to me," he said in a low voice. "Alan needs this. A chief must retain his honor. There is no other way."

"They'll kill each other!"

"Better that way. Better to be a dead man with honor than a living man without."

"That's stupid," she spat. But even as she spoke, she understood with all her heart. In either man's position, she'd have done the same.

"It is your choice," her father murmured, his eyes hard. "I'll have the MacDonalds drag you away from here, or you can remain and keep your fool mouth shut."

She glanced beyond her father's shoulder where a group of Mac-Donalds glowered at her, annoyed at being torn from their entertainment. They gave her no choice.

"I'll watch," she ground out.

By the clanging of the men's swords, she knew the duel continued. She wrenched out of her father's grip and straightened her spine. Holding her head high, she turned away and limped back to the crowd, pushing her way through the men. Her foot bled profusely, soaking her shoe.

Alan's shirtsleeve was also soaked in blood—his injuries appeared much worse than her own, but the motion of his sword was strong and precise. If he felt pain, he didn't show it.

Moira finally appeared. She pushed in beside Sorcha, but Sorcha ignored her wheezing sister.

Blood dripped from Alan's sleeve. Still, he fought with complete control, heedless of the injury. He blocked two quick jabs aimed at his stomach, then went on the offense with a high, powerful swipe of his blade, which Cam parried easily.

Clenching her fists at her sides, Sorcha watched, aware of the men surrounding her, aware of her father hovering behind her, all of them ready to haul her away if she so much as made a peep.

You caused this, Sorcha. They've the killing rage in their eyes. You will be responsible for the demise of one of these men. Just as she ignored the throb in her foot, she ignored the tear that leaked from her eye and began a slow, hot descent down her cheek.

This was her fault. The blood on Alan's arms was her fault.

She would never forgive herself if one of them died.

Please, God, she begged. *Forgive me. Let them live. Whoever is the victor, make him offer quarter . . .*

Cam lunged forward, taking a low slice at Alan's leg. The sharp point of his sword cut through the wool of his plaid and Alan grunted as the blade nicked his thigh.

Sorcha stood on wobbly legs, her fists clenched at her sides. She would not let them die. Either one of them.

With a growl emerging from low in his throat, Alan spun away from another of Cam's jabs, ending a step behind him. Cam misjudged a powerful thrust aimed for his torso, and instead of parrying, leaned toward the oncoming weapon. Alan's sword sank deep, and Cam cried out hoarsely.

Alan yanked his blade from Cam's side. It was slick with blood. Cam's blood.

Cam raised his sword to parry again, but when he lunged forward, he swayed. Alan stepped back toward Sorcha, as if in shock.

Blood poured like a waterfall from Cam's side, and he lurched drunkenly. His free hand went to his side. Blood gushed between his fingers. Ever so slowly, he sank to his knees. Then he toppled over like a rock.

Oh Lord, no.

CHAPTER TWELVE

Sorcha sprinted to Cam and dropped onto her haunches when she reached his side.

He trembled all over. Sweat sheened the pale skin of his face, and blood stained his shirt a deep crimson. The pink of the gash in his flesh gaped through a long tear in the linen. His eyes rolled back in his head, and he blinked, struggling to maintain consciousness.

He focused cloudy eyes on her. "Sorcha?"

"I'm here." She pressed her palm to the wound. She didn't know how else to staunch the flow of blood.

"Sorcha. Please stay with me."

"Aye, Cam. I will."

His lids fluttered closed. Sorcha bit her lip hard, staring at the unsteady rise and fall of his chest. He had only fainted, thank God. But he wouldn't survive for long if she didn't stop the blood from pouring out of him. Her hand was doing nothing.

She glanced behind her and saw Alan on his knees. A man was wrapping a handkerchief round the wound on his arm. The slit in his plaid exposed his thigh.

She searched the faces swarming around her. "Moira! Where's my sister?"

"She's here, lass," someone said, and in a moment the crowd parted to reveal Moira standing alone, her face blanched, wringing her hands.

"He's too badly injured," Moira whispered. "I can't—"

"You must." Sorcha gave her sister a hard look. "Come help me. We have to stop the bleeding."

"Call for Mary MacNab!" The shout came from behind her, and she didn't turn to see who it was. "The earl's in a bad way. Hurry!"

A boy standing across from her turned and ran, pushing past the men blocking his path.

Moira sank to her knees across from Sorcha. "Pressure. There must be more pressure on the wound. I need a bandage."

Heedless of the people surrounding her, Sorcha lifted her dress and took the skirt of her petticoat between two hands. The screeching sound of tearing fabric seemed to quiet the murmurings of the crowd as she tore strips of linen and handed them to Moira.

"Will you help me turn him over, Bowie?"

Bowie, kneeling beside Moira on the other side of Cam, nodded.

How odd that it was Bowie, Alan's second, who helped now. What had happened to that giant, MacLean? She rapidly scanned the gathering, and her lip curled when she spotted him. Even at a distance, he towered over the crowd. He stood alone, shoulders hunched, with a handful of pebbles he was using to pelt at a nearby tree.

She turned back to Cam. He deserved better friends than that.

Alan stared at his wife's back, at her bloody shoe. God, she'd probably run all the way from the valley. She'd hurt herself to chase after him. She needed help. She needed a doctor. She needed to be home and stitched back up . . .

All he could think of was Sorcha and her injury, for it was bleeding more profusely than his own scratches. But the men surrounding him made it impossible for him to go to her. Finally the bandage was tied off on his arm, and Alan pushed through his clansmen and hurried to his wife's side.

It was then he saw Cam.

His friend lay limp on the ground, his eyes closed, his face pale as death. His shirt was more red than white. Alan's slicing sword had gone deep. Deadly deep.

Alan swallowed as grief overwhelmed him. Hell, he didn't want Cam to die. Not the man who'd defended him from the boys who'd broken his nose. Not the man who'd stood by him, who supported him, who'd helped him survive Oxford . . .

The thought of Cam dying made his stomach twist.

Kneeling across from Sorcha, he took the earl's limp hand in his own. *Goddammit.* Cam had never failed to block that kind of attack before. Alan had intended to try to cut him, to end the duel, nothing more.

Their hands covered in blood, Sorcha and her sister focused on Cam with a single-minded determination. Alan just watched, locked in a mire of fear and regret, as they worked to save the man's life.

Within minutes, Mary MacNab marched up and gave everyone hell for participating in a foolhardy, pointless duel, but she praised Moira for stopping Cam's bleeding. Alan asked her to see to Sorcha's cut after she was done with Cam, and she snapped at him that it was her duty to see to all injuries, not just to the high-and-mighty earl's.

As a cart arrived to carry Cam back to Camdonn Castle, Cam clawed back to consciousness. His eyes locked on Alan's.

"Honor restored?" he gritted out from behind bloodless lips.

"Aye." Alan realized he still gripped Cam's hand, and he released it gently.

"Good." Cam let out a shaky sigh. Still staring at Alan, he whispered, "How long do I have?"

"You're not dying. You'll be with us a long time yet." Alan's voice sounded more confident than he felt.

"I wronged you." The words were so quiet, Alan had to put his ear near Cam's mouth to hear.

"You did."

"Forgive me."

"It's over."

"Alan—" Cam released a low, grating sob. "Stay with me. Stay with me till it's over."

"Goddamn you, Cam. It's not over. You're young and hale, and you'll mend."

"Please, Alan. Please don't leave me. Don't go."

There was no choice, really. In the end, there was too much history between them. Alan still loved the damned fool.

"Aye," he said gruffly. "I'll see you home."

Mary MacNab shooed Alan away and presided over loading Cam into the cart. She and Moira rode with Cam, but Alan lifted Sorcha onto his horse, and they followed close behind.

They rode in silence for the first mile, but then she turned to face him. "You will stay with him?"

He nodded. "I won't leave him until I am certain he'll be all right."

His hand rested on her stomach, holding her against him, and her palm closed over it. "You're a good friend."

Of course she was thankful—it was clear she still cared for Cam. Far more than made him comfortable. Alan bit back his rising jealousy, but a part of him wondered how he'd endure setting foot in Camdonn Castle knowing Cam and his wife had loved there.

It was late, and Sorcha felt close to falling over from sheer fatigue. Mary MacNab had left in a huff hours ago, after disagreeing with the castle surgeon. As she and Moira worked on Sorcha's foot, she'd stated that Cam's chances of recovery were "grim to fair," whatever that meant. Sorcha diligently refused to think too much on it.

Now Moira sat on the other side of the bed, her shoulders drooping and her auburn hair hanging limply, a sweat-slicked strand stuck to her cheek.

Cam had faded in and out of consciousness all day. When dusk fell, he woke long enough to look at Sorcha in surprise and ask her where Alan was.

She had to admit she didn't know. Once they'd entered the living quarters, he'd remained outside to take care of the horses. She hadn't seen him since.

"He'll be back, won't he?" Cam asked through white lips before drifting back to sleep.

Sorcha glanced at her sister over Cam's sleeping body. "You should go," she said in a low voice. "Bowie will take you home."

"I don't want to leave you here alone with him."

"Alan is close by. In any case, Cam is too ill to touch me, much less besmirch my honor." Sorcha's lips twisted. "Any further, that is."

"Oh, Sorcha." Her sister looked as though the words had physically harmed her. "I'm so sorry. I should have stopped you—"

"No, Moira. You should have done nothing. I made many mistakes, but I wouldn't exchange the time I spent with Cam. And Alan—" Lord . . . how to explain the intensity of her feelings for Alan? She pursed her lips.

A rustling sounded at the door, and Sorcha whipped her head around to see her husband standing at the threshold. The wool of his clothing brushed against the doorframe, and he wore a clean shirt and plaid. Heat suffused her cheeks, and she pressed her palms against her skin to soothe it. How much had he heard?

Ignoring her, he smiled at Moira. "You've done well, lass. You should go home. Your da will be worried."

Moira chewed her lower lip. "I don't know . . ."

Alan stepped deeper into the room. "Bowie's already waiting."

Moira still hesitated. "But . . ."

"You're tired, Moira. Come. I'll walk you downstairs." Alan's voice brooked no further argument. He strode over to Moira and helped her from the bed.

Moira looked at Sorcha with pleading blue eyes. "Maybe it's best you come with me."

Sorcha tightened her hand on Cam's arm. Sweat beaded on his brow, and she took the cloth at the side table and dabbed it away. She wanted to stay with Cam. Who else would sit beside him if not her? She'd only leave his side if Alan forced her to.

"I'll be staying."

Still, Moira lingered, hovering over Sorcha. "Go, sister," Sorcha said in a low voice. "I'll see you soon."

Moira bent down to give her a kiss on the cheek. "Be careful."

Be careful of what? Sorcha wondered. How could things get any worse? Alan might've killed the Earl of Camdonn. The repercussions of murdering the earl would be enormous. He'd probably have to leave Scotland as a fugitive to escape the noose.

Her affair with Cam seemed so meaningless when stood up against the fact that he might die as a consequence.

She sat alone at his bedside. No friends or family came to comfort him. The servants and doctors came and went, as was their duty. But she was the only one who cared about him enough to sit beside him. Her and Moira. And Alan.

Poor Cam. All her life, Sorcha had been surrounded by her loving family, and there wasn't a soul in the glen who wouldn't stand behind her as a woman of their clan.

But Cam? Who did he have? Nobody. The MacDonalds had never quite trusted the Earls of Camdonn, and for good reason. Their ties to the government of England and the hated Campbells, led by the powerful Duke of Argyll, were strong as steel.

When Alan and Moira left, Sorcha wiped the sweat from Cam's brow, resolved to remain at his side. As she went to the basin to rinse the cloth, she glanced around Cam's familiar bedchamber. Colorful tapestries hung on the walls, well-kept relics from the last century woven in colorful patterns depicting scenes from the Bible. The floor was carpeted in thick wool, imported from Italy, as was the carved furniture made from deep-grained russet-colored wood. Cam's bed, dressed in a downy-soft mattress and luscious green and black silk curtains, was magnificent. A maid had folded down the matching counterpane and taken a fur away, leaving him covered by comparatively plain woolen and linen blankets.

Yet for all its richness, Cam's bedchamber was cold.

Sorcha pulled one of the carved Italian armchairs beside the bed and lowered herself on its mustard-colored velvet cushion. Chewing her lip, she studied Cam. Two pink spots flared on his otherwise pale cheeks. His skin was warm to the touch, but gooseflesh covered his bare arms. Did that mean he was feverish? She should have asked Moira before she left.

And why wouldn't he wake? He'd been out for hours now, with only an occasional stir. The castle surgeon had given him a diffusion of foxglove before seeing to the wound—perhaps that was what had caused him to sleep so steadily through all the noise and bustle.

Sorcha slipped her hand into his, studying his pale but still handsome face. His eyelashes were dark against his skin, and a shadow of a beard had formed across his jaw. His lips were full and firm, the bottom one slightly plump. She remembered how she'd loved kissing it. Sucking it between her own lips and teeth, nipping and licking.

Sorcha released a ragged sigh.

"Sorcha?"

Stiffening, she glanced up at Alan's soft voice, but didn't remove her hand from Cam's.

Alan entered the room and pulled a plush striped armchair to the opposite side of the bed, and they sat in silence for a while. Then, in a low voice, Sorcha asked the question that had been forming in her mind for hours. "Why did you agree to stay with him, Alan? Earlier today, you wanted to kill him. I don't understand why you don't wish to kill him now. You've had ample opportunity."

Then again, it wouldn't be honorable for Alan to kill Cam in such a way, would it? She shook her head. Death was death, but for some unfathomable reason, the delivery of it seemed to matter.

"I never wanted to kill him," Alan said in a low voice. "But the duel was necessary. He called himself my friend, but then he took what was mine. He knew exactly what he was doing."

"I still don't understand." The frayed edge of exhaustion roughened her voice. "It was all over. You'd won. You and I were finding happiness together. Why should it matter what came before?"

He stared down at her hand covering Cam's, then looked up at her, his eyes pale blue slits. "Were we finding happiness, Sorcha? Have I won?"

"Yes." Sorcha tried to swallow away the lump of emotion lodged in her throat.

Alan shook his head, his face hard. "Understand this, Sorcha. It was the way—the *only* way—for both of us to redeem our honor. We couldn't continue living as enemies. Neither would have survived it."

Cam groaned and shifted, his eyes fluttering. Grooves formed on his forehead as he attempted to force his lids to crack open. He squinted, trying to focus on Alan even as his fingers curled weakly around Sorcha's hand.

"Alan?" he rasped. "What happened? Where am I?"

Alan took a deep breath. "We dueled, and I wounded you with my sword. You're in your bed at Camdonn Castle."

Cam's brow furrowed. "Why didn't you kill me? Shouldn't I be dead by now?"

He might yet die. Sorcha eyed Alan, clamping her lips together so the sob gathering in her throat wouldn't emerge.

Before Alan could answer, Cam's gaze came to rest on her. "Sorcha. Why are you here?"

"You asked us to stay with you," she said.

"But why are you here?" Cam asked again, clearly confused. "Why are you both here?" He struggled to raise himself up on his elbows, but gave up, groaning in pain.

"Shh." Sorcha stroked his arm, feeling helpless but wanting to ease his suffering.

Alan answered Cam gruffly. "I considered you my brother once, my lord. I wouldn't leave you to suffer alone."

Could it be true? Had Alan forgiven his one-time friend of his sins? Alan was an enigma to her. But the depth of his caring, for both her and Cam, shone in his eyes. Some strong emotion surged through her, and a new hope swelled deep within.

"I want you here," Cam said. "Both of you. Please stay."

Alan inhaled deeply. After a long moment of silence, he said, "Of course we will."

A slight smile touched Cam's lips, and a hint of color returned to his cheeks.

"Your injuries?" he asked Alan.

Alan shrugged. "They're nothing. The leg is a scratch, and Moira bound my arm but it didn't require stitches."

Sorcha blew out a breath of relief, and Cam's lips curled. "First time you bested me so thoroughly, Alan."

"It was," said Alan, his expression sober. "And hopefully the last."

The smile bled from Cam's lips and his eyelids drooped. "Am I going to die, then?"

"No," Alan said, though there was no way he could know, not having been present earlier when the doctor and Mary MacNab had argued about the course of treatment for Cam's terrible wound.

"We'll both stay with you, Cam," Sorcha said as Cam's lids drifted shut. "We'll help you through this."

She met Alan's eyes over Cam's chest. Sorcha and her husband stared at each other, the surrounding air thick with emotion.

Something grew between them. A rare and precious understanding, something Sorcha never would have predicted. Would the man who had torn them apart now help them come together?

If only she could trust Alan. If only he would trust her.

It hardly seemed likely with the source of all their troubles lying flat on his back between them. And yet . . .

"Love you," Cam whispered, his eyelids fluttering as he slipped away. "Love you both."

Sorcha woke to the dim light of a tentative dawn trickling through a crack in the curtains. The room was stifling hot, and she brushed beads of sweat from her upper lip with the back of her hand.

Alan still sat in the armchair on the other side of the bed. His head rested against the wing of the chair, and he'd somehow curled his large body into a comfortable-looking position and appeared fast asleep.

Shifting in the hard chair, she looked down at Cam. The dark shadow of beard on his jaw had grown thicker, and his cheeks were now stained pink, though his skin appeared dry of sweat, unlike her own. Tentatively, she stroked the backs of her fingers down his cheek.

He was burning hot.

Stifling a whimper of fear, Sorcha rose and slipped through the door to rouse the doctor.

CHAPTER THIRTEEN

Fading in and out of delirium, Cam dreamed of Sorcha. Oddly enough, only occasionally did she appear naked. Only once in a while did she moan in ecstasy as he held himself over her, driving himself into her willing body again and again.

In truth, in most of the images his mind created, she was dressed in a beautiful English gown that displayed the creamy mounds of her breasts rising over the top edge of the bodice.

And Alan was at her side.

Even more strange, when he saw them together like this, he didn't feel like pushing Alan away or drawing his sword to kill him. Instead, he gleaned an odd sense of comfort from dreaming about them together. Watching and hearing them interact.

He knew in the depths of his consciousness that the soft discussions between them weren't products of his imagination. Sorcha and Alan were really there, beside him, caring for him. Both honestly worried he was going to die.

Dying didn't sound so bad. He hurt. His whole body raged with pain, centered at the scorching fireball in his side.

Everything would be easier if he died. Alan and Sorcha wouldn't have to worry about him. They'd be happy together, without him pushing himself between them.

Wasn't that what he ultimately wanted? The two people he cared for most on this earth to be happy?

Yes.

How long had this been going on? Days? Weeks? How long could a soul lie in bed on the brink of death?

A sort of peace drifted over him, and he sighed. The pain seemed muted, and in his mind's eye, the two most beloved people in his world appeared. Alan and Sorcha. But this time, they were both naked. In their little cottage making love. Alan's body gleaming bronze in the firelight, his muscles rippling as he moved over his wife. Sorcha gripped her husband's shoulders hard enough to leave white imprints from her fingers when she moved her hands. Her pale legs wrapped around Alan's arse as it flexed and released with every thrust into her.

Cam watched it all. This time, though he was aroused as he'd been on their wedding night, his cock painfully hard, he didn't feel the jealous, possessive rage he'd experienced that evening.

This time, he didn't want to pull them apart.

He wanted to join them.

Day and night, Alan stood beside her, took care of her as well as Cam. When Sorcha was so exhausted she couldn't see straight, it was Alan who carried her to the pallet he'd had placed beside Cam's bed. It was Alan who comforted her, who talked to her, who proved to be more than just a husband, but also a friend.

Cam was dying. The doctor said so. He insisted on bleeding him yet again as a final effort to revive him.

"No," Sorcha whispered. Cam had lost so much blood to begin with . . . how could these bleedings help?

"I must," said the doctor, a reed-thin man with a dour disposition and a nose like a hawk's beak. "The inflammation at the site of the wound must be controlled. It is his only hope."

Sorcha's eyes stung. She stood stiffly near the far wall of the room, watching the leeches grow fat as they clung to the blanched skin around Cam's wound. Alan stood behind her, his hands cupping her shoulders, lending her strength.

Would Mary MacNab bleed Cam to death? Sorcha didn't think so. The doctor was wrong. The bleeding wasn't Cam's last hope. Mary and Moira were. If they couldn't help him, nobody could.

"I'll go fetch Mrs. MacNab and Moira," Alan murmured in her ear as if he'd read her mind.

The near-bursting leeches began to fall away, and the doctor removed them from Cam's chest. He nodded at Sorcha. "I doubt that'll help, but it's the best I can do. Please inform me if there's any change."

"I will," Sorcha murmured. "Thank you."

She didn't know why she thanked him. Nothing this man did seem to help Cam.

Nodding brusquely, the doctor followed his beaked nose out of Cam's bedchamber. The two maids who had helped him shuffled behind, one of them carrying the bucket of fat leeches.

Sorcha stared at Cam's still body. He hadn't moved once or made a single noise of complaint throughout the whole procedure. Was he so far gone he couldn't even feel the leeches pulling away his lifeblood?

Suddenly, Cam's body arched upward, and he began to twist and convulse.

Sorcha lunged toward him. Cam's head whipped back and forth. His body undulated on the bed. She grabbed on to his hand and gripped it for all she was worth, even though he flailed away. "Cam," she cried, "you must stop this!"

As his body fought the fever, she went on, her voice lowering to a murmur. "You must live. Please live. I need you. I love you. Alan needs and loves you. Your people need you too. They need your kindness, your depth of feeling, your care. Please, Cam. Please don't go."

She continued to speak of love and need and passion, and how great a loss to the world it would be if he died. She tore off the blankets and swabbed his furnace of a body with cool water as she murmured her gentle words.

Much later, the convulsions settled and Cam's body stilled. Sorcha took his pulse and found it quick and irregular. But he was alive, his breaths weak and shaky. His body as hot as a burning lump of coal.

Exhausted, she crawled into the bed beside him, wrapped her arms around him, kissed his burning cheek, and slipped into a fitful doze.

"Damn fool doctors," Mary MacNab muttered as they approached the living quarters of Camdonn Castle. She snorted. "Bleeding a man who's already nearly bled to death. And those idiots think themselves so damned superior."

Moira, who appeared nearly a foot taller than the old woman, smiled at Alan over her head. Alan couldn't help but to smile back.

He understood Mary MacNab's old medicine—at least in theory. He'd seen with his own eyes what it could do. Passed on by oral tradition through generations of women, this knowledge was something he couldn't deny. Some of Mary's ancestors, he knew, had been burned at the stake for using their forms of medicine, but such a thing would never happen to Mary. Even the old Duke of Argyll had called on her to administer to his son when he had once taken ill as a boy.

Alan carried Mary's medicine chest, an ancient-looking wooden box filled with herbs and medicines and special pagan concoctions made by Mary with Moira's help.

They walked into the living quarters. None of the servants so much as batted an eyelash as they trudged upstairs in a line, Mary in the lead and Alan following Moira. When they reached the landing, Mary turned to him.

"Which way?" she snapped. "I've forgotten."

"To the left, Mrs. MacNab."

Mary turned down the hall and paused at Cam's closed door, cocking her head against the smooth wood planking.

"Doctor's gone," she murmured. "Least I can't hear his damn fool blathering."

"Good." Alan pushed open the door.

He froze when he saw Cam and Sorcha on the bed. Their arms were wrapped around each other and both slept like babes. Something panged heavily in his heart, and the resulting tremor rumbled through his entire body.

Mary MacNab chuckled behind him, and Moira gasped in horror.

"Don't fret, lass," Mary said cheerfully. "Naught is amiss. She comforts him, as is her wont."

Alan's eyes widened as he stared at the bead of sweat rolling down the side of Cam's face. His heart pounded with excitement. "Has his fever broken?"

Mary marched up to Cam and slid her hand under his shirt, pressing her palm to his chest. "Aye," she confirmed. "He's cool."

Alan blinked hard in relief, and Sorcha stirred on the bed, stretching and yawning.

And then her eyes opened, and her gaze alighted on the three of them. She yanked her arms away from Cam and shot up to a seated position. "He was—" She looked down at Cam, then at Alan. "Oh, Alan. He was shaking . . . and . . . and . . ." Her lip quivered and teardrops hovered on her lower lids.

Alan strode to his wife and gathered her into his embrace. "His fever's broken, Sorcha."

"What?"

"His fever. It's gone."

She went limp in his arms. "Oh Lord. I thought—I thought . . ."

He stroked her back and she clung to him, her body heaving with emotion. "He was trembling and shaking. I thought he was dying, Alan. I—I talked to him. I told him how much we all cared. I begged him not to die . . ."

Alan comforted his wife as Moira and Mary administered to Cam. Mary ordered water from a maid and spent several minutes dabbling in her chest as Moira crouched beside her, focused and following each direction with precision. Side by side, the two women thoroughly cleaned Cam's wound and applied a warm healing poultice.

Sorcha turned to watch them. "Has his fever truly broken?"

Sweat beaded on Cam's forehead then rolled in streaks down his face, matting his hair to his skin.

"Aye, lass." Mary didn't bother to turn from her work. "He'll need liquid, lots of it, to recover. Make certain he drinks plenty, and not too much of it whisky, eh?"

Sorcha took one of the towels on the bedside table and climbed back on the bed. She pressed the soft linen against Cam's sweaty face. She turned back to Alan, her green eyes shining. "It's true. The fever is gone."

Cam groaned softly, and his eyes fluttered, but he didn't wake.

Mary MacNab rose and turned to Alan. "Give him this when he wakes. It's made from silvered water." She thrust a foul-smelling brown liquid concoction beneath Alan's nose, and he fought to keep from gagging. The wrinkles in her face deepened. "Damn fool that he was for dueling to begin with."

She narrowed her little eyes at Alan. "And," she continued. "Feed him fresh bannocks soaked in cream. It'll help him heal."

"Aye, Mary," Sorcha promised from the bed. "Thank you. Thank you so much for saving him."

Though, Alan thought, Mary had done little to save him. And Alan was fairly certain the doctor hadn't done a damn thing, either. He gazed at his wife as she clasped Cam's hand, her eyes shining with relief . . . with love.

Cam would live because of Sorcha—her sweet words and her healing touch.

Cam woke to the sound of birds chirping and Alan's light snore. Turning toward the direction of the noise, Cam saw with surprise that

Alan slept in a pallet beside his bed. He didn't remember the bedding being placed there.

How long had he been ill?

"Good morning."

Cam swiveled his head at the sound of Sorcha's voice. Too quickly. He had to close his eyes against the onslaught of dizziness.

"Ungh," he groaned.

She chuckled softly.

"You're still weak. But the fever's gone."

There was relief in her voice. A lightness he hadn't heard since long before her wedding. Before their affair, for that matter, when he'd first returned to Camdonn Castle to find his factor's daughter full-grown and desperately alluring. When she'd looked at him with those fiery green eyes, his skin had prickled from head to toe. He'd wanted her instantly. Only later had he grown to love her.

He opened his eyes to see her gazing down at him, her smile so wide, a deep dimple appeared in one cheek.

"How long?" he whispered, his voice rough from disuse.

Her smile faltered. "Five days. We've missed the festivities of Samhain."

Good God. "You've been here five days?"

"Aye. Alan and myself both."

Cam let his eyes drift shut again, lest she should see the emotion swirling in them. They had remained by his side as the fever gripped him. They were the only ones who'd stayed beside him—the only ones he would've asked for before he'd damaged everything between them.

"Did you sleep here?"

"Aye. Alan had the pallet brought in." She cleared her throat. "It isn't wide enough for both of us, so we take turns at night. I wanted one of us awake at all times, in the event . . ."

Her voice dwindled, but Cam knew. In the event he grew sicker. In the event he died.

"Thank you" was all he could murmur.

What had he done to deserve the forgiveness of these two people? As much as he claimed to care for them, he had betrayed them both, hurt them both. In return, they restored his honor, then remained by his side in his darkest hours.

Opening his eyes, Cam glanced at Alan, remembering how Alan had called him brother before he'd fallen into delirium. After all that had happened, once honor had been restored, he treated him as no less than a kinsman.

He turned to Sorcha. Even now, he couldn't look at her without wanting her. The attraction was a fierce pull in his chest, in his groin. Just the sight of her made his cock grow beneath the blanket. It didn't matter that he'd spent days on his deathbed and all he could smell was the stench of his own sickness. He wanted her.

But the devil himself would take him before he'd touch her again. Without Alan's permission, that was.

A vision of Alan watching them together, a benevolent smile on his face, flashed through his mind, and he almost laughed out loud. Only in his debauched dreams.

"How do you feel?" she asked.

"Tired," he answered honestly. "But you must be tired too."

She shrugged, but he saw the light blue-black circles beneath her eyes.

"Do you want to go home?"

She hesitated. "We'll go home if you wish it. But I'd rather stay until you're on your feet again."

He exhaled in relief. "I'd be honored if you stayed. Both of you."

Sorcha looked past him, her smile faltering slightly, and he turned to see Alan stretching on the narrow pallet.

"Good morning," Sorcha murmured.

Alan rose to a seated position, arching an eyebrow at Cam. "So you're awake, are you?"

"Yes. And lucid, I suppose."

A smile skittered over Alan's face before the resident seriousness returned. He swung his legs over the side of the pallet and stretched. "It's been a difficult few days. We thought we might lose you."

Cam's side thudded, a reminder that he was facing the man who'd injured him—who'd almost killed him. Yet he couldn't blame Alan. Nobody could. Alan had only defended his own honor, and his wife's.

"How is your wound?" Alan asked, his features carefully schooled.

"Hurts," Cam said. His side throbbed in agreement. It didn't burn like it had in the past days, but damn, it hurt. If he stretched or turned or moved in any way, it complained. Loudly.

Alan nodded, but no sympathy edged into his expression. Both he and Cam knew he deserved whatever pain Alan had wrought upon him with his broadsword.

"I'm so sorry," Sorcha whispered.

Cam frowned at her. "Why?"

"I—I didn't wish this upon you."

"I know, Sorcha." There was a long, pregnant pause. "But we all know it was justified. You must hate me for what I did to you."

"No," she said. "I was angry, yes. But I never hated you."

"I think she's incapable of hate," Alan said.

Flushing, she glanced at her husband and something passed between them. "Maybe so," she admitted. "Even when I claimed to hate you, it was a lie."

Alan's lips curled. "I know."

Sorcha bowed her head, and Cam turned to Alan. "Thank you for staying with me."

"It was the least we could do."

Humbled, Cam said, "I'll have the servants prepare the state bedchamber for you." He found it difficult to form words, he was so tired. But they needed their privacy. It was ridiculous to ask them to stay as close as they had, sleeping on that uncomfortable pallet. Both Sorcha and Alan looked exhausted.

He felt Sorcha's hand close over his. "Rest, my lord. We'll be here when you wake."

CHAPTER FOURTEEN

Days passed. Cam recovered quickly—as a healthy man in his prime, he wasn't easily cowed. Within the week, he was walking the castle grounds.

He stood at one of the stall doors in the stable, looking down at a newborn foal wobbling as it tested its weak, spindly legs. He could empathize—he'd never felt as weak as he had in the past few days.

Sensing a presence beside him, he turned to see Alan gazing at the foal.

"He'll be a beauty."

Cam smiled but didn't answer. Alan cast him a sidelong glance. "You all right?"

"Yes. I feel fine. Considering."

Alan nodded. "Good."

He stared at Alan, assessing the other man. "Don't you wish you'd killed me?"

"No," Alan said easily. "I'm glad you're alive. Honor has been redeemed, and I didn't have to kill my friend in order to do so."

"After all I've done . . . how can you still consider me a friend?"

Alan gazed at the foal, which was nuzzling up to its mother, one of Cam's finest mares. "Aye, you've tested my limits. But we had a long history prior to the past few weeks. You must have suffered a lapse in your memory." Alan turned back to Cam. "But can you remember all those years now?"

Hell yes, Cam remembered. Standing up to the English . . . they used different methods, but together, they'd survived. It had been the two of them against the world. And then later, at the university, explorations into adulthood. Experimentation, mistakes, close calls. Just about everything that formed them into the men they were today, they'd experienced together.

"You're right. I did forget." He sighed. "I'm sorry for it, man. Forgive me for betraying you."

His behavior had far surpassed the limits of acceptability, but Alan and Sorcha showed him the true meaning of friendship. Of love. He'd never forget. Not this time.

Alan clapped him on the shoulder. "It's over. It's time to move forward."

How? Cam wanted to ask. It was a stupid question, because deep inside, he knew the answer. He had to take a scrubbing cloth to his mind and heart, and scour away all trace of Sorcha MacDonald.

But was he strong enough?

Alan struggled to keep his jealousy in check. It was clear Sorcha cared deeply for Cam, had always cared deeply for him.

Working and living beside her as the days went by, Alan's affection for her grew, along with the painful realization that she loved another man. Alan now knew she would remain faithful to him, but at what cost? Would they both be miserable knowing the object of her desire lived mere miles away in Camdonn Castle?

Sorcha treated Alan with deference and respect. She slept with him in the big state bed at night. He held her close, but he didn't touch her beyond that.

However, he did observe her touching Cam, and each time her skin made contact with the earl's, Alan saw the spark snap between them. Their attraction for each other was palpable, and yet out of their loyalty to him, neither acted upon it. He trusted both of them not to act upon it now.

Alan knew Cam, knew how humbled he'd been by their show of solidarity during his illness. And he was beginning to understand Sorcha. Her beauty—which he'd originally thought of as mere surface—came from deep inside. She was fierce in her loyalties, resolute in her personal divisions between right and wrong. She was dedicated, honest, and fair.

Alan didn't know what to do. His love for his wife was growing, but how could he live with a woman who loved someone else? More confusing, when he saw the arousal between her and Cam, Alan felt the spark resonate within himself. A humming heat that lit a fire in his groin. Against his will, he lusted after the idea of watching Sorcha make love to Cam, even while his mind rebelled wholeheartedly against it.

He leaned against the carved headboard of the elaborate state bed in the tower room where Cam had insisted they sleep. Alan would have been just as happy making a bed above the stables, but he'd humored Cam by agreeing to stay here.

Sorcha stood across the room washing in the basin. Her slender arms moved as she dried her face and then reached back, her shoulder blades squeezing together, to braid her silky black fall of hair.

Beautiful Sorcha. He couldn't really blame Cam for being unable to resist her pull. Her body sang to him, the sweet song of a siren. She didn't seem to notice how she affected him, which made her all the more alluring.

He and Cam had always shared a similar taste in women, Alan thought with a sigh.

It was time to discuss the inevitable. Cam was nearly well.

"We must return home soon," he said in a low voice. "My men have been watching the valley for me, but there is much to do, and I can no longer avoid this rebellion."

Her hands faltered, but then she started braiding again, one strand over the other. "Yes. Cam is on the mend. He's no longer at risk."

"Unless, of course, you'd prefer to stay with him."

She was quiet as she finished, using a small ribbon to tie off the braid. Her shoulders rose and fell as she took a deep breath, then slowly turned to face him.

"I don't wish to stay with Cam. I wish to stay with my husband."

"I won't abide a wife who's in love with another."

Her lips parted. "Is that what you think?"

"What should I think, Sorcha?" he asked quietly. "I see how you've cared for him. How you touch him."

"I'd care for and touch my brother in the same way if he were injured."

Alan didn't think so.

He pushed his fingers through his hair. Goddammit. He wished he could believe her, but how could he ignore the meaningful looks and touches and intimate conversation that passed between his wife and the earl?

"Which of us do you want, Sorcha?" he finally ground out.

"You." The answer came instantly, almost overlapping his question. "Only you."

"Because I happen to be the one the minister married you to."

Her lips firmed. "No."

"Why, then?"

"Because you are the man I'm *meant* to be with."

He couldn't see how that was any different.

With her chest rising unevenly, she pulled on the ties of her nightdress, revealing the creamy skin between her breasts. She pulled apart the edges of the gown. "When I'm with you, I'm overwhelmed. By desire. By pleasure. By the need to please you, to earn your love."

She'd already earned it, but he kept his mouth shut, watching.

The thin garment slipped off her shoulders and pooled at her feet. She stood there, staring at him. Shivering. "I never felt this way with anyone else. You've settled into the deepest recesses of my soul, making me hungry for more. Being separated from you would be like being torn in two."

She looked at her toes, crossing her arms over her chest. Alan stared at her curvy, feminine form, hardly containing the urge to jump out of the bed, lower her to the floor, and take her right there.

But it was more than that. He felt an aching need to have her beside him, to listen to her voice, to know her in every way.

Blast. Somewhere in the midst of this disastrous beginning of a marriage, he'd fallen in love with her.

"I need you. I miss your touch. I miss—" Her breath caught, and she tried again. "I miss the feel of you moving inside me." She took a step toward him. "It has been so long, and I'm so afraid. Afraid you don't want me. Afraid you'll go to war and I'll never see you again."

She swallowed down a sob, and her heartbeat pulsed wildly in her neck.

How could she entertain the thought that he didn't want her? He was nearly mad with need to bury himself in her sweet body.

But then he remembered his pride. Even now, a vestige of it remained. Seeing her with Cam had caused him to rebuild the barriers in his heart. His pride was what kept him from touching her.

He didn't say a word, just studied her. The swell of her bosom, brimming over her thin arms. The flare of her hips. The dark triangle at the juncture of her pale legs.

Her lower lip trembled, and she spoke again, her voice a mere whisper. "I haven't been able to stop thinking about . . . last time. How you touched me. Everywhere."

He raised a brow. So she'd liked his experimental play, had she? Not all women found such things erotic. But then again, this was Sorcha. Nothing should surprise him when it came to his wife's wantonness.

"You want more," he said. It was a statement rather than a question.

Pressing her lips together so tightly they turned white, she gave a jerk of a nod.

She dropped her arms so her breasts bobbed free, and she clenched her fists at her sides. "I want . . . I want you to possess me. I want you to show me that I'm yours."

Anguish clawed at him. How could he when she'd belonged to another first? How could he claim her when she'd already been claimed?

"I want to be yours. Please make me yours."

"Nobody else's?"

"Aye," she agreed breathlessly. "No one else's."

His face still, Alan stared at her as he climbed off the bed. Ignoring the discomfort of his cock as he rose, he stepped toward her.

"Very well." He led her to one of the carved wooden posts at the foot of the bed and pressed her back to it. "Stand here."

He turned to fetch one of her stockings, then carried it back to her. "Clasp your hands behind you."

She obeyed instantly, her chest heaving, her eyes shining.

He couldn't resist. Still holding the stocking, he cupped her breast in his palm, bent down, and brushed his lips across the rosy tip. She tasted so sweet, so good. He took the other breast in his other palm, weighing it, kneading it as he laved and suckled and nipped at her delicate skin until she released each of her breaths with a low sob.

Goddamn. He had to stop. He pressed his mouth against her soft flesh; then he moved around her, deftly looping the stocking over her wrists and tying it securely.

"Alan?" she murmured.

"Do you trust me, Sorcha?"

After a short pause, she whispered, "Aye. With my life."

"Good. Stand here until I return." He tore his gaze from her glistening nipples to her face. Sometimes he could read her like an open book. Now was one of those times. She was aching, arching into him, needy with lust. It was exactly how he wanted her.

And now she would wait.

She couldn't believe he had left her. Sorcha pressed her thighs together and wiggled her hands. Alan hadn't bound her too tightly, but the wool scratched at the delicate skin on the insides of her wrists.

How long had it been? She glanced at the clock on the mantel. Ten minutes, at least. Where had he gone? What if he didn't come back? Would he leave her standing here, naked and cold, all night long?

She would do it. For as long as she could stand, if it would only prove her devotion to him.

She knew Alan still doubted her feelings toward him. How could he not, after all the attention and affection she'd showered upon Cam for the past several days? Cam was a broken man. He was hurting—mind, body, and soul. Her heart reached out to him, and she felt compelled to show him that despite all he'd done, she still cared for him. Yet she hadn't meant for her devotion to Cam to be at Alan's expense.

She'd sensed him watching her and Cam together. Sometimes she caught a thoughtful expression on his face, a look she couldn't decipher. Was he hurting or angry? Did he fear she still possessed feelings for Cam? At times she thought it might be something else. Some sort of attraction, fascination at seeing her and Cam share a touch? Surely that couldn't be right. Nevertheless, a low hum resonated between her legs whenever she sensed Alan staring at them in that way.

It didn't matter. Even if seeing Cam and her together aroused Alan, it certainly also hurt him. And she wanted nothing more than to erase that hurt.

Alan was the most honorable, most caring and selfless person she'd known. He was masculine, handsome, wise, caring, honorable, strong. Everything she'd fantasized about in a man as she'd discovered her body in the cave below Camdonn Castle. Everything she needed to feel content. To feel whole.

Her teeth chattered in the lonesome coldness of the room, but Alan had stoked a simmering fire between her legs. She crossed her thighs. If her hands were free, she would have felt compelled to touch herself, to soothe the burn.

She closed her eyes and leaned her head back against the hard wood of the post. She'd stand here and wait. As long as he wanted her to. Resting her weight against the bed, she tried to relax and clear her mind.

Perhaps he would come deep inside her tonight. He never had to this point, and yet she found herself craving it. His choice to spend outside her had become symbolic of the break in the bond they should share as husband and wife. One she wanted to mend.

And if he did get her with child . . . yes, she feared giving birth, feared the horror her mother had gone through, but the prospect of her stomach increasing with Alan's child made her chest clench with some sweet new emotion she'd never experienced before.

"Sorcha."

Her eyes flew open. Alan passed in front of her holding a small jar. He set the jar on the shiny wood surface of the table beside the bed. Coming to stand before her, he cupped warm hands over her shoulders.

He traced down her arms, then traveled the sides of her body, the roughness of his fingers gently scraping her sensitive skin. He stopped when his hands reached the inward dip of her waist. She glanced downward, marveling at how large, how masculine, his hands appeared against her body.

She looked into his blue, blue eyes. "I waited for you, as you asked."

He smiled. "So you did."

"I would have waited longer, if you'd wanted. All night." It sounded silly, but she wanted to let him know.

"Would you?"

"Aye."

He reached around and flicked at the knot binding her arms behind the bedpost. Immediately, the tightness against her wrists released, and he pulled the twisted stocking away.

As soon as her hands fell free, he took her into the warmth of his embrace, lifting her. She burrowed into the heat of his chest as he carried her to the side of the bed and sat her on its edge.

He pushed his plaid off his shoulder, and she reached up to untie the strings closing the neck of his shirt. He allowed her to work the ties free, and he lifted the shirt over his head.

Now his muscular torso was bare, as were his legs and feet. He wore only the green and black tartan plaid belted about his waist. A telltale bulge showed from between the pleats.

"Do I do that to you?" she asked with a long upward sweep of her fingers. His cock was hard beneath the wool, solid as stone.

"Aye, Sorcha. Just looking at you, I—"

She licked her lips and raised her hands, exploring the sides of his body just as he'd explored hers moments ago. "You're so beautiful."

Her fingers traveled the line of hair that led from his belly button down to the top edge of his belt. Lust flared in his eyes as they narrowed and took on a silvery gleam. He took a step back, out of reach.

"On your feet," he growled.

Shaking with anticipation, she obeyed instantly.

He curved his palms over her shoulders and turned her so she faced the bed. Then he nudged her upper back. "Bend over."

She bent at the waist, lowering her upper body on the bed. The blanket rasped against her sensitive nipples. Resting her weight on her forearms, she turned her head to look back at him.

He discarded his belt and plaid, revealing his cock jutting proudly out, flushed dark. She gasped at the sight of it, knowing it would soon join the two of them together. She wouldn't be able to stand it if he didn't take her soon. Every inch of her body ached for his touch.

"I want you," she murmured.

His fist curled around his shaft and he gave it a hard tug. "Is this what you want?"

"Yes." She wiggled her backside in invitation. "Yes, please, Alan."

The callused tips of his fingers traveled down her back, down the crack of her behind until they met the moist heat of her sex.

"Oh," she murmured as his fingers danced and played between her outer lips, teasing and taunting her.

She tilted her hips even more and spread her stance in a silent plea.

The head of his penis nestled between her plump, blood-filled lips, and she groaned in pleasure at the feel of him, hot and hard, finally touching her, pushing against her.

Slowly, he burrowed in, crowding the air from her lungs.

He bent over her and planted a hard kiss against her neck. "You feel so damned good around me."

Her channel tightened over him, grasping on to him as he began to pull out, as if to reach for him, to hold him deep. They both moaned as he tunneled back inside. Sorcha reached behind and clasped his thigh, urging him deeper.

His hands rested on her lower back, forcing her down against the bed, and his thumbs played in the upper crack of her arse. He removed his hands, but she barely noticed, lost in the feel of the slow, long glides of his cock.

His fingers returned, slipping between the cheeks of her bottom, and she stiffened at the feel of the cool, creamy substance he smoothed over her skin.

"Do you trust me?"

"Aye," she choked.

"Then relax, *mo chridhe.*"

He pulled his cock from her body. His fingers moved lower until one cool digit pressed against the rosette of her arse. "Is this what you want?"

She squirmed, but he held her firm, anchored under the weight of his palm.

Oh Lord. He felt so good. It felt so wickedly good.

"Yes," she groaned. "Yes."

"Touch yourself, Sorcha. Stroke yourself."

She obeyed, slipping her hand between her body and the bed and cupping her mound.

He leaned over her again, pinning his hand between them, his weight pushing the tip of the digit into her.

"Grind your body into your palm."

She complied, gasping at the torrential rush of sensation. Every nerve between her legs was alive, aching, needy.

His body heaved against her, and he rose, simultaneously pressing his finger all the way into the resisting hole.

Sorcha cried out, and her sex spasmed under her hand. She curled two of her fingers, burying them between her slick lips until they brushed over her clitoris.

She felt the prod of a second finger against her backside, and whimpered.

"Too much?" Alan murmured.

"Yes. No," she gasped. She felt like a skittish animal, unable to keep still.

Alan pushed the second finger inside her, and she pressed her cheek against the rough wool of the blanket.

"Oh. Oh."

As she lay there, overwhelmed with sensation, he worked her arse with his fingers. Nothing existed but his movements and her own, and the flaring heat curling between her legs.

All of a sudden, he removed his fingers, but just as suddenly, they were replaced by the head of his cock.

Surely it wasn't possible. Surely he was too big . . .

Slowly, with painstaking care, Alan pushed inside.

Sorcha squeezed her eyes shut and grabbed the blanket in her fist.

"Relax, love."

"Alan," she sobbed.

"Relax." His arm curled beneath her body, lifting her slightly off the bed, and soft lips pressed against her neck. "Let go, Sorcha. You're so tight. Let go, *mo chridhe*."

Sorcha focused all her energy into loosening the tight ring of muscle and allowing him entrance, even as he pushed deeper into her. Finally, everything released and he slid home, his balls brushing against her fingertips, which were still buried between her legs.

They hung there for a long moment, perched on the edge of something unfathomable. Alan's breath brushed in her ear, his exhalations whispering against her lobe.

"Are you all right?" he murmured.

"Aye," she said on a gulp of air. She was standing on a cliff with one foot poised off the edge. Alan had lit a torch deep in her body, and she leaned back into the heat, not wanting to fall. Not yet.

Slowly, experimentally, he moved out slightly, then pushed back in. Her body undulated beneath him, completely out of her control.

"Oh, Alan . . . I don't think—" But he moved again, and the words died in her throat.

He slid in and out of her, kneading her breast, his breath hot on her neck. Sorcha's body shuddered and bowed, but she couldn't control the spasms, couldn't contain the sobbing moans that emerged from between her lips, couldn't stop the furious rubbing of her fingers over her sex. It was absolutely necessary for her to touch herself. Her quim needed to be touched, her sensitive nub required flicking and pinching.

Alan's breaths turned harsh. He released her, allowing her to sink onto the blanket; then he gripped her shoulders and rode her hard.

Sorcha was being torn apart. It hurt, it was fire, but it was the most exquisite, beautiful pain and the sweetest heat she'd ever experienced. The torch inside her body lit a hot blue blaze to each nerve ending.

She raised her arse to meet every one of Alan's thrusts, and when his balls slapped against her quim, she ground herself into her hand. It was an instinctive motion, occurring without thought, without effort, and her whole body participated, down to her toes, which dug into the carpet, and her fingers, some of them plunging into her dripping channel, the others curling in the coarse blanket.

Alan began to shake. Even as his movements became jerkier, his thrusts deepened. Sorcha's mouth opened in a silent scream as she was rent in two by Alan's thick, long cock.

She twisted and writhed, each movement taking her higher, pushing her closer to the edge. Squeezing her arse tight around Alan, Sorcha ground her body into the bed, into her hand.

Leaning forward now, off the cliff into the crisp Highland breeze. The loch stretched out below her, gleaming a fathomless blue mirrored by the clear blue sky above. Golden heather whispered in the breeze. And Sorcha didn't plummet to the earth—instead she spread her wings and glided through the air as Alan held her steady, keeping her safe from harm.

As if from far away, she heard his low groan. Gripping her hips, he thrust twice more, then buried himself as deep as he could go.

She flew higher. Air rushed past, rippling and streaming over her body. Alan was with her, and together they reached the heavens and then drifted slowly down, as light and gentle as a pair of feathers twisted in a lover's embrace.

Sorcha slumped against the bed, all the tightness in her body releasing in a rush. Seconds later, she felt Alan relaxing similarly, but he kept his weight on his forearms so as not to crush her.

Gently, he pulled out of her, as careful as if she were a delicate piece of lace. And then he left her.

With great effort, Sorcha turned her head as he walked over to the basin. She should get up, move, climb into bed, do something. But she couldn't garner the energy. She simply stayed there, flopped over the edge of the bed.

Alan returned moments later with a damp cloth, and he stroked the cool material between her legs.

"Mmm." It felt wonderful—the cool contrasting against the blazing inferno she'd felt there just moments ago.

She smiled against the blanket. He'd come inside her for the first time. Not in the way she'd imagined, but it was meaningful, nonetheless.

He left to discard the towel and returned, gathering her in his arms and lifting her up onto the bed, arranging her beneath the covers.

Her eyelids felt like dead weights, her muscles languid and soft. Alan extinguished the single burning lamp on the bedside table, then turned to tuck her against his side.

Just as she drifted off into a sweet slumber, she heard a low murmur. "I love you, Sorcha."

Had she dreamed it?

CHAPTER FIFTEEN

C am shifted uncomfortably to adjust himself. His cock was hot and hard, pressing painfully against the material of his breeches. He hardly felt the movement in his injured side.

Sorcha and Alan sat on the chaise longue across from him in the receiving room adjacent to his bedchamber. Alan's shoes were off and his legs were propped on the cushions. Sorcha sat firmly wedged between his thighs. She sipped from his glass of whisky and made a face. Alan laughed at her and kissed her lips.

Cam moved discreetly again, trying not to call attention to his raging erection. He eyed the tumbler on the sidebar. It was more than half empty.

After the deadly fever, his injury had healed so quickly the doctor said it was a miracle. Cam had thus far kept the state of his near-perfect health from Sorcha and Alan. The truth was that he didn't want them to go.

It was becoming apparent that he was nearly well, though. There were certain truths a man couldn't hide. Although neither had broached the topic, he knew they'd return home soon. Leaving him alone once again.

This time, he'd manage on his own. He'd have to.

Staring at the two of them, it hit Cam square in the gut that it was time for him to change. He'd inherited an earldom, for Christ's sake. He could squander all he had to offer . . . or he could use his friend as an example and exploit his power and wealth for the betterment of his corner of the world, including all the people in it. Hopefully, that would someday include a family. But he couldn't think on that now. Each time he gazed upon Sorcha MacDonald laughing up at her husband, a sharp blade of pain pierced his heart.

He'd had a chance with her. She'd been on the verge of falling beyond lust and into love with him. Yet he'd treated her like a mistress, never as someone who could be anything more. He hadn't given her what she deserved, had never offered marriage but dismissed the idea due to some foolish notion of impressing the English with a noble heiress. What a bloody cur he was.

He'd do it all differently if he had the chance. But it was too late.

She raised a dark eyebrow at him. "Penny for your thoughts, my lord?"

Cam smiled. "I was just thinking of my plans for buying more stock once I'm up and about a bit more." He looked at Alan. "And giving the herds to my MacLeans. Do you think they'd take them on?"

"Oh, aye," Alan said in an offhand manner, yet Cam saw the spark of interest light up in his eyes. "Your herds are aging, and fresh beef is a strong motivator for the MacLeans. And if you don't want them lifting half the Inverness stock, it'd be a fine idea to keep them occupied with yours."

Cam smirked. "A more legal option, in any case."

"They're fine men, on the whole. I'd rather not see blood shed," Alan said.

"I agree." Cam leaned back into the velvet comfort of his favorite chair. "It seems cattle raiding is the least of everyone's concerns at the moment, however."

Alan's face instantly shuttered, and Cam's senses sharpened. It had to be something to do with the rising.

"What is it?"

Sorcha seemed to sober a bit, and she scrambled out of Alan's lap to face him. "What has happened?"

"Bowie and a group of clansmen came to me this morning." Alan sat up straighter and swung his legs over the edge of the chaise. "Have you heard from Argyll?" he asked Cam.

Cam had received a message from the duke, who, as his neighbor and ally, considered it his duty to keep Cam informed, just yesterday. "Still holed outside Stirling. He believes conflict is inevitable and he has been scouting the lay of the land in the area."

Alan nodded tersely. "Mar plans to move from Perth soon. My men wish to leave in three days to join him." He took a deep breath and met Cam's eyes. "If they go, I must lead them south."

Cam's chest tightened, but he gave a sober nod.

Sorcha spoke first. "Can't you stop them, Alan?"

Alan shrugged. "They are free men and may do as they please."

Bloody hell. Alan would never allow his men to go into battle without their leader—not if it was for a cause he believed in. "Just tell me," Cam asked, "do you honestly wish to have the Pretender on the throne of Great Britain?"

Alan stared at him, his expression like steel. "I want what is best for my country."

"You believe James is best? I've heard he is a careless, coldhearted man." Cam flicked a piece of dust from the arm of his chair, then bent forward. "And I ask you, why hasn't he joined Mar? Brought reinforcements from France? Agreed to fight with the thousands who've risen to stand for him?" He leaned back again. "I would question such a leader. He'd gladly take the throne . . . but only after forcing his underlings to suffer for the cause, while he sits back, grows fat, and reaps the benefit."

"And yet my people are poor and live in hovels. Some are starving." Alan's voice was flat, and Cam fought a flinch.

Everything felt so calm, so normal. Relaxed, even. But in three days' time, Alan might be headed for the Lowlands at the head of his men, his life at risk. Abruptly, Cam rose and strode to the sidebar, noting with a little regret that his side didn't pain him at all. "More whisky?"

"Aye." A smile fringed Alan's tone as he said, "Sorcha drank the last glass."

His tension eased, and Cam grinned at Sorcha. "Shall I pour you some, too?"

"No, thank you," she said primly. Then she gave a low laugh. "I'll lift more sips from Alan."

"Do you fancy my whisky?"

She hesitated. "It's quite . . . *harsh* . . . but then again, I could never resist a challenge."

Alan chuckled, and Cam walked over to hand him a new glass. "You've hardly a limp anymore."

Tell the truth. Cam took a deep breath. "I'm quite healed. I'm lucky your sword pierced no organs . . . and once the fever passed the wound closed quickly."

Cam had refused the help of Mary MacNab and Moira since he'd awoken from the fever. Mary MacNab was an old shrew. And Moira— the knowing way she looked at him made him uncomfortable. She must despise him for what he'd done to her sister and Alan.

"Well," Alan said after a long pause. "Sorcha and I should head home in the morning. If I go south, I'll leave her in a safe place." His blue eyes flashed at Cam, daring him to comment.

Sudden pain flared in Cam's side, as if the knowledge that Alan still didn't trust him to keep his hands off Sorcha had prodded him directly in the wound.

Alan kept his gaze fixed on Cam. "If I join Mar, will you try to stop me?"

Cam hesitated, thinking of his peer Argyll leading the government's force. If Argyll were in his place, he'd do everything he could to prevent Alan from joining the rebels. Undoubtedly, Argyll would even go so far as to kill him.

"No." He tried to keep his voice even as he continued. "Neither of you have aught to fear from me."

"Haven't we?" Alan asked in a low voice.

"No. I will never . . . *interfere* in your lives again. It was wrong of me, and I am sorrier than you'll ever know."

"We have already forgiven you, my lord," Sorcha said quietly. "Surely you know that."

Cam sank back into his chair, his glass in hand. "But please understand I will stand by you . . . and your marriage."

He took a long, fortifying drink. As much as he believed to his core that what he was saying was right and true, something in his heart rebelled, and he could only hope the whisky would quell that small point of contention.

Sorcha snuggled against Alan and pressed her lips to the rim of his glass. He tilted it, and she drank. When he pulled it away, she gasped. An appealing pink flush spread upward from the neck of her bloodred bodice.

Alan swallowed the rest of the amber liquid in one long draft. He set the glass on the floor, then clasped Sorcha's waist, settling her on his lap.

The movement caused her cheek to brush his face. Alan took advantage of the contact, turning his head to capture her lips with his.

Cam stilled, watching as their mouths locked together and they fell into the kiss, seemingly forgetting his existence.

Alan's hands ran erotically up and down the buttons of her dress as she arched her back, encircling his neck with her arms.

Cam couldn't tear his eyes away. The sounds of their contact filled the room. Rustling fabric, the puffs of their breaths, a soft moan from Sorcha. Tendrils of her dark hair curled around her ear, brushing against Alan's cheek.

Oh God. Cam would sell his soul at that moment to have her lips on him. To have her kissing him with the enthusiasm she showed Alan. To nuzzle his face in her hair and smell her fresh, sweet scent.

He'd had that once. He'd given it up, idiot that he was.

A log popped loudly in the hearth. Sap sizzled, and Sorcha and Alan broke apart abruptly, blinking, brought out of the lustful haze. They stared at each other for a long moment before their heads swiveled toward him.

Cam didn't move, but Alan must have seen the lust swirling in his gaze, because he laughed gruffly. "Wish it were you, my lord?"

Cam hesitated. It wasn't often that Alan called him by his formal title. The moment was charged, full of something Cam could hardly decipher beyond the sudden heat humming in the air.

But God, how he wanted Sorcha. Every drop of blood in his wretched, godforsaken body ached for her.

"Yes," he rasped. "Yes, I do."

"She's mine," Alan growled.

"Yes," he agreed, staring at Alan's hand curved possessively around her waist.

"But you took her nonetheless."

"Forgive me," Cam pushed out. It seemed Alan might outwardly forgive him after his honor was redeemed in the duel, but it would always stand between them, a solid brick wall preventing them from being as close as they once were.

Alan shrugged. His hand tightened around Sorcha's waist, and Cam saw the knuckles whitening.

"She still wants you," Alan said in a low voice.

Sorcha gasped. "Alan!"

Alan took her chin in his hand, turning her face and forcing her to look at him.

"Do you? Remember your promise to me, Sorcha." He shook her lightly. "Remember your vow never to lie to me again. Tell me the truth."

"Alan, please," she whispered. "It is you I want."

"Very well. Since you refuse to answer my question"—Alan's hold loosened on her chin. His voice was calm, almost serene—"tell me how he fucked you."

"No!" Sorcha choked, casting Cam an alarmed glance.

"Alan. Stop," Cam said quietly. Why would the man torture himself? Clearly he hadn't let any of it go—he was still full of rage and betrayal over Cam's seduction of Sorcha. "It is past. Don't dwell on it. It's over—we all agree it won't happen again."

Alan turned to Cam, and this time Cam did wince at the sheer look of tortured pain in his friend's eyes. "Tell me what it was like for you that first time. When you took her innocence."

The scene seemed dreamlike, as if Cam were back in the haze of the drug the doctor had given him during the fever. The room swirled around him, and the air thickened. And there were only Alan's pained eyes, staring at him in anguish. How many times could he say he was sorry?

"You must tell me, Cam . . . since you stole from me what was by rights mine. The least you can do is tell me what she was like the first time you took her."

"Why?" Sorcha asked on a whimper. "Why is that important?"

Cam understood. He would always be the one who'd possessed her first, who'd always hold that part of her within himself.

Alan didn't answer her. Instead, he stared at Cam, willing him to respond.

"She was sweet," Cam whispered. "Just as she was each time afterward."

"No, Cam," Sorcha moaned. "No. Don't."

Alan nodded. "What else?"

"She cried out . . ."

"Did she say your name?"

"Yes. She stiffened in my arms." Cam closed his eyes, remembering. Their first time coming together, like so many of their subsequent meetings, was furtive and brief. But that first time had sealed it for him. After that, he'd been well and truly addicted to her. Her ripe, peachy softness. Her true abandon in bed. He seldom bedded a female who loved him back with such passion, such fervor.

Yes, he had been obsessed. He still was, but by God, he was fighting it with every ounce of strength he possessed.

"Tell me more. Were you on top?"

Cam stiffened in dismay. He'd watched Alan take her in what he'd thought was her first time. He'd been so gentle, so careful, so mindful of her pleasure, whereas Cam had been an impatient rutting beast.

The words emerged dry, emotionless. "We were on the floor in the closet leading from the countess's rooms, and, yes, I was on top." Those rooms had been unoccupied ever since Cam's mother died when he was a toddler. Cam had dragged her in there on a prayer that they wouldn't get caught by some unsuspecting maid.

Sorcha released a sobbing breath.

"I see," Alan said.

"I did nothing to prepare her," Cam confessed. "Again, I am sorry, Sorcha."

She didn't answer, just gazed at him, her eyes glassy.

"Did he hurt you, love?" Alan asked Sorcha.

Cam clenched his jaw.

"Aye," she said, still staring at him. "But I knew it would hurt. It hurts all women, or so I am told. And"—she took a fortifying breath—"it faded more quickly than I thought it would."

"How many times after that?"

She turned to Alan, her eyes questioning. "What do you mean?"

"How many times did he fuck you?"

"Alan . . ." she choked out.

This was a new side of Alan, one Cam didn't know how to approach. He did know he didn't like what it was doing to Sorcha. She looked horrified, scared.

"Tell me." Alan's voice was flat.

Sorcha closed her eyes. Perhaps all Cam needed to do was answer the damn questions and Alan would cease this torturous line of conversation.

"Many times," Cam supplied in a low voice. He clutched the arm of his chair with his free hand. "I don't believe either of us kept count."

A muscle ticked in Alan's jaw, and his lips flattened to a thin line. Beneath his shirt, his biceps flexed and tensed.

"Alan, you must stop this," Cam murmured. "Neither of us wishes to cause you more pain."

Sorcha bowed her head.

"You misunderstand," Alan said. "I needed to know. It's important I know about your past."

"Why? How is it important?" Sorcha cried. She looked as if she wanted to throw herself at him and wrap her arms around his stiff body, but she held back, too uncertain, too afraid.

Seeing her misery, Alan gathered her in his arms and kissed the top of her head. "Let me manage this in my own way, Sorcha. It isn't hurting me. It's healing me." His eyes met Cam's over her head. "It is good for me. It's better that everything be out in the open between us, otherwise how can we go on?"

Sorcha nestled into Alan's chest, kissing the vee of his shirt, his neck, his jaw, murmuring endearments at him, and it occurred to Cam that she must be more than a little drunk. Hell, *he* was more than a little drunk, and he hadn't had much more to drink than she had. And Alan—he'd had quite a bit too.

Dangerous? Volatile? Hell, yes.

Cam knew he should go. Walk out of here and leave them alone to do what it was clear they both wanted—and badly. But he was too weak, damn his soul. Cam realized his own fingers had fallen over his pulsing cock and were stroking lightly. Gritting his teeth, he removed his hand and gripped the velvety arm of his chair.

When Sorcha finally pulled away, her eyes glistened with unshed tears. She ran a knuckle down Alan's cheek. "I don't ask you about the women in your past."

Touché, thought Cam a little smugly. He leaned back against the soft cushion, studying Alan.

Alan's features relaxed, and he cupped her cheeks in his palms, kissing her nose, the sides of her lips.

"What would you like to know, love?" Alan's voice had gone from gruff to silky.

"Nothing," Sorcha stated flatly. "Why would I want to?"

"I want to know about your past because I seek to learn more about you. Don't you wish to learn more about me?"

"I plan to learn through discovery." A hint of challenge crept into her voice. "I needn't know anything about how other women pleased you."

He glanced at Cam, then back at his wife, a wicked flare in his blue eyes. Cam tensed, sensing what was to come.

No. Don't, Alan. Don't do it.

"Did you know we took them together, *ceisd mo chridhe?*"

"Cam . . . said . . ." Her voice came out as little more than a squeak.

"Cam didn't lie. We took women together. At the same time. Both he and I found it quite satisfying."

Sorcha's breath hitched.

"Alan," Cam snapped in warning, sitting up straighter.

"One of us would take her arse and the other her sweet cunny."

In an abrupt motion, Cam rose from the chair. Alan was trying to lure them into a trap. This had to stop.

Alan's lips twisted into a cunning smile, and his hands nearly spanned her waist as he tugged her closer toward his body. "Or one of us would take her mouth while the other took her arse or cunt."

Sorcha's eyelids dipped, and she shuddered. "Why?"

"Because, as fucking goes, it's quite satisfying, *mo chridhe*," Alan murmured. "For all parties involved."

She was so pale, Cam thought she might faint. "Alan." He took another step forward. "Enough."

Sorcha sighed raggedly. She was furious at Alan—but her traitorous body rebelled against her anger, refused to jump up and run away when the sober part of her mind commanded it.

A blooming heat spread through her, centering between her legs, blossoming ever so slowly into a crawling, aching need. Alan and Cam . . . at the same time? The mere thought alone was so arousing, so erotic, it was almost too much to bear.

Lord, she was beyond hope. Even now, when she committed herself entirely to Alan, she could still think of Cam in a carnal way. But was it her fault? She stared at Alan. He had prompted her arousal with his wicked words, his smooth, satiny voice.

Damn him.

"Why are you doing this?" she whispered.

He was so close to her. His essence of musk and leather filled her senses, warm and masculine. He enveloped her in a sensual cocoon, made her itch for relief.

"You understand, Sorcha," he said quietly. "I see it in your face." His hand drifted down her leg until it reached the hem of her gown. His fingers lifted her skirts upward, grazing her stocking until he played with her garter. His thumb edged beneath it, stroking the sensitive area above her knee. "I feel it on your skin. The idea excites you, doesn't it?"

Would he hate her if she admitted it did? It didn't matter, ultimately. She couldn't lie to him.

It was all so confusing. The haze of lust, the strange sensation of the whisky swirling within her. Alan physically enveloping her, Cam nearby, his loving gaze stroking over her, soft and delicate as a feather. She was lost.

"Do you want it, Sorcha? Do you want us both?"

She couldn't lie. She'd promised not to.

"Aye," she sobbed.

CHAPTER SIXTEEN

E ven now, she couldn't lie to him. Alan blinked against the onslaught of emotion he felt upon seeing his young wife's confusion. She was overwhelmed by lust but beset by fear. That he inspired such strong feeling in her made his body quake with the need to have her, to possess her entirely.

Jealousy simmered somewhere in the background. The knowledge that she also desired Cam was a dark spot of poison on a rampant flowering vine. One he could ignore . . . for the moment.

Because, by God, the idea of both of them taking her at the same time made him want to come under his plaid. He glanced at Cam again. The dark lust in his friend's eyes shone back at him. It had been there since Cam had awakened from the fever, but kept dormant, thrust aside. Now it was clear Cam had let it go, to grow and overpower his tightly held reserve of the past several days.

They'd always been able to communicate this way, he and Cam. It was part of what made them work well together. They could be silent but still-communicating partners, giving a woman the most pleasure possible.

"Stand." Alan gave Sorcha a tiny nudge.

Cam nodded, but he blew out a nervous breath. Alan understood. This wasn't some nameless whore. This was Sorcha, Alan's wife.

Alan couldn't think ahead, refused to acknowledge what would become of them after this night. Hell, in three days he could be headed south. In five, he could be dead.

There was only now. One woman and the two men who loved her. Who wanted her.

Sorcha rose, facing Cam.

"Turn around, Sorcha," Alan commanded. "Toward me."

Sorcha complied, turning until she was looking down at him, her chest heaving and her pulse beating in her throat like a frightened rabbit's as Cam rose from his chair and came to stand behind her.

Tentatively, Cam's hands closed over her shoulders. He moved her hair aside, and his mouth descended to her neck. All the while, he kept his gaze fastened on Alan.

It was a test, Alan realized. Would seeing his friend touch her make Alan insane with jealous rage? Did he mean to follow through with this mad plan?

Clenching his fists, Alan watched Cam's fingers knead her shoulders. Cam's lips pressed to the side of her neck, nipping gently. In his arms, Sorcha trembled from head to foot, flushed, needy, and more afraid than he'd ever seen her. Her fingers twitched in her skirts.

"Rest easy, *mo chridhe*," Alan said in a low, soothing voice contrary to the tumultuous emotion roiling in his chest. "Cam and I seek only to please you."

"Are you sure, Alan?" she asked, her voice pleading, even as she tilted her head to give Cam better access to the pale column of her neck. "Please tell me you are certain about this . . . please . . . I don't want to . . ."

He rose and stood before her, taking her upper arms in his hands and squeezing gently. "I'm sure. We all want it."

He spoke the truth. Cam's long fingers played against her neck, stroking the place he'd just kissed. His eyelids were heavy with longing.

Sorcha was flushed, panting, and Alan knew if he slid his fingers between her legs, he'd find her wet and ready for them.

And Alan himself . . . God help him, but his dissolute, debauched soul *enjoyed* seeing Cam's hands on her. Craved it. Made him ache for more. For Cam to take more of her. He wanted to watch Cam's cock shuttle in and out of her body. Wanted to see the look on her face when Cam took her. When he and Cam took her together.

A part of him bellowed a warning, telling him he was drunk and not thinking straight, but he squelched it ruthlessly as he raised his hands to the front of her bodice. Cam stood behind her, plucking at her laces. When he pulled the strings apart, Cam pushed her gown from her shoulders. With it went her stays and shift, and working together, the two men helped her shimmy out of the confining fabrics.

Finally she stood bare, wearing only her stockings, garters, and shoes, her pert breasts heaving with every breath she took.

Alan glanced at the door to the adjoining bedchamber, then cast a questioning look at Cam, who nodded. Lifting Sorcha in his arms, Alan pulled her close, her cool flesh pressing against his chest.

"Are you cold?" He brushed his lips against the silk of her hair.

"A little." Snuggling closer into his body, she wrapped her arms around his neck.

Moving ahead of them, Cam opened the door to his bedchamber. Alan paused at the threshold, staring in at the familiar, cavernous room.

Sorcha and Cam had made love here.

He strode toward the bed with determination. It would never happen again. Not without him there. Watching. Participating. In control.

Sorcha burrowed her face into Alan's sleeve. He carried her as if she weighed nothing, and when he reached the bed, Cam pulled back the curtain and counterpane before Alan set her gently down. From her position on her back, she stared up into their hungry eyes. One light, one dark, both tall and so masculine, gazing down at her like she was the only woman in the world.

Alan wanted this. His expression was fierce with desire. Her own desire crested and peaked just by observing his need. If he wanted this, so did she. Anything that would please him would please her a hundred times over.

Cam walked around the bed, shucking his shirt and loosening his breeches as he moved. Sorcha followed him with her gaze, her mouth watering when his hard torso came into view. His muscles weren't as large as Alan's, but each one was well defined and tight, and there was no excess fat on any part of him.

She looked back toward Alan as the bed dipped with his weight, and he moved beside her.

Without hesitation or preamble, he cupped her breast in his hand and set his mouth over it, suckling her nipple so deeply, she could feel the pull all the way between her legs.

Cam pressed in behind her, and his erection settled in the crack of her bottom. Concern flared for his injury, but as she turned to question him, he curved his arm around her hip and touched the mound of her quim. Sorcha stilled as his fingers slipped lower to brush over her outer lips, gently parting them. Cam had never before moved this slowly with her.

Alan plucked her nipple just as two of Cam's fingers tugged on her clitoris, and she shuddered, feeling the men all through her. Their warmth, their hard masculinity, their need. She threaded her hands through Alan's thick hair and pressed him tighter to her breast as she wedged her backside more firmly against Cam's groin.

Alan pushed her onto her back. Cam rose up onto his knees and bent to her free breast. His mouth closed over her nipple.

It was almost too much to stand. Sensation barreled through her, hot and sharp, and she squirmed against it. One of their hands—she couldn't tell whose anymore—pressed on her hip bone, pinning her to the bed.

"Alan," she gasped. "Cam." She looked at the two heads—Cam's cropped black locks and Alan's thick blond curls, both knelt in worship over her body.

Fingers—Cam's, she thought, because she couldn't remember him ever removing his hand from between her legs—began stroking her in earnest. Sliding through her slick folds, circling her entrance, teasing the sensitive pearl above.

Alan curled his fingers around her breast, squeezing hard enough to make her gasp, but not quite hard enough to hurt.

With one final lick over her taut, aching nipple, he raised his head, meeting her gaze.

"I'm going to fuck you now, *mo chridhe*." The statement was blunt, said in a rasping voice, but it made her arch her back in anticipation.

Please.

Cam's damp hand grazed her belly and kneaded the breast Alan had abandoned, and Cam's teeth closed over her flesh as Alan rose to settle between her legs.

Holding his cock in his hand, he gazed at the top of Cam's head for a long moment as Cam tortured one of her breasts with his mouth, the other with his fingers. Sorcha watched in fascinated anticipation as Alan's fingertips brushed lightly over the long length of his erection, pushing the foreskin upward, and then pulling back down to reveal the blunt, swollen cap.

She licked her lips, remembering how the tip of his cock felt—warm and soft, but so very alive—and Alan's gaze rose to meet hers.

"Do you want me, Sorcha? Do you want this?" A whispered growl.

She did. And yet— "Only if you do, Alan. I only want what you want." Her voice sounded smooth to her ears, like honey, so quiet she hardly heard herself beyond the lust roaring through her body. Cam paused at her breasts for a breath, and then he swirled his tongue around her nipple and lifted away. She closed her fingers on his shoulder.

Alan, however, didn't move. His eyes clouded, and his lids lowered as if he were considering the options. His hand tightened over his cock, but stopped its languid motion.

Sorcha wanted to bite her tongue for making him question himself.

"Please, Alan," she whispered. "I want this. I want *you*. So much."

Alan leaned over her as Cam faded into the background. She still felt Cam's skin beneath her fingers, though, his muscles rippling as he moved to give Alan room.

Alan adjusted his cock at her entrance, and she groaned as it nudged her open, forcing her body to conform to its girth.

He didn't push all the way in, though. Lodged halfway inside her, he stopped, his jaw clenching with restraint.

He bent low over her and whispered into her ear, his voice a silken brush over her lobe. "I want to watch you suck Cam's cock."

She could only whimper as the words sent her arousal soaring higher. She bit her lip. It was all she could do not to grind her body down over Alan's erection.

Yet she didn't understand why he wanted to watch her with Cam. She still sensed a simmer of animosity under his skin. Perhaps he suspected that she desired Cam more than him. The emotion wasn't blatant, but she could sense it, smell it, like a lingering dampness in the sun after a storm.

She feared what would happen if she did this. And yet her husband had commanded her to.

Worse, far worse, she wanted to. Since the last time she and Cam had made love, she'd thought hundreds of times of taking his long, satiny cock in her mouth. She loved his taste almost as much as she loved Alan's. Lord help her.

"Are you sure?" she managed to gasp. "Please, Alan . . ." *Please tell the truth. Don't ask me to do this if it's going to hurt you.* Because as much as she wanted Cam, she didn't want to hurt Alan. She'd rather die than risk their marriage again.

"Goddammit, Sorcha." He raised his head, searing her with his hot blue gaze. "Do you think I'd suggest it if I didn't find it arousing? If it didn't make me want to fuck you harder, to come all over you? Over"—he shoved his cock balls-deep, making her cry out at the rush of sensation—"and over?"

Cam's hand traced down her arm, and his fingers laced in hers and squeezed, but he remained silent, allowing her and Alan to work it out between them. She loved Cam for his silence, knew that one word from him might spark a fire none of them would be able to contain.

"I don't—I don't know, Alan—" She was so afraid. So, so frightened of what might happen when this was over.

Slowly, he drew out, and then just as fast, just as hard as the first time, he sank deep inside of her.

"Oh!" Sorcha cried, shaken to her toes by the violence of the motion. She gripped his forearm, digging her nails into the skin. He paused, his groin flush against hers, and rose up onto his knees, adjusting Sorcha's body to move with him and giving Cam room to edge close. She didn't look Cam's way, but saw him in her peripheral vision, felt his heat, his warmth.

"Take him in your mouth, *mo chridhe*," Alan commanded.

The blunt head of Cam's cock nudged her cheek, and she turned her head, pursing her lips. Gently, he bumped against her closed mouth as Alan stroked inside her again. Sorcha shuddered. She felt like she'd been laid out on the rack. With the merest effort, these men could tear her apart, either bringing her exquisite pleasure or ultimate, deadly pain.

To think they had such power over her—her whole body reacted, every muscle spasming, even the one circling the channel in which Alan's cock was now lodged. Clearly feeling the undulating pressure, he growled low in his throat.

Cam's cock brushed her lips again, smearing a drop of fluid over them. It took all her will to resist licking it off.

"Open, Sorcha." Alan's order seemed to come from far above her.

Instantly, she opened her lips, moaning when Cam's cock stretched her mouth wide, his male taste heady against her tongue. Just as Alan's cock stretched her, pulsing inside her. He was close, but he moved as slowly as she did, holding back from bursting inside her. She could feel his restraint in the trembling muscles of his forearm.

Cam was tentative at first. With his fingers wrapped in her hair, he allowed her to set the pace. Cupping her palm under his ballocks, she nudged him forward until his crown tapped the back of her throat.

Alan made a small noise above her and matched her pace, settling deep against her womb. She arched her hips to meet him, still gripping his forearm with her free hand.

Cam slid out, and so did Alan. It wasn't long before they'd settled into a rhythm, both shuttling in and out of her wet and willing passages. Something coiled tight in Sorcha, wound like a ball of yarn centered low in her abdomen. She arched her back and tugged on Cam's sac to encourage them to move faster, harder. She wanted to be taken, to be pummeled. She wanted them to hold on to her by a thread and let her unravel, because she couldn't bear the aching tension. Not for much longer.

But they resisted her pull, even as she felt them both grow harder inside her. Cam's veins pulsed on her tongue, under her lips. Alan's cock stretched her even wider, making her gasp over Cam. Each of their thrusts made her groan in sweet agony.

And then, suddenly, it changed. As if the men had silently communicated. Or perhaps they had spoken to each other and she simply hadn't heard, too lost in sensation. But Alan's fingers tightened over her hips. Cam's fingers tightened in her hair. And their thrusts deepened, hardened. Quickened. Cam took over completely, forcing her head forward in time with thrusts of his hips. She had no choice but to take him all, so deep she could feel the hairs at the base of his shaft tickle her lips.

Alan pummeled her channel. She tightened even more, closing around him, milking him with her muscles even as her lips tensed around Cam's cock. Her hips tilted and her legs wrapped around Alan, encouraging him as deep as he could go. Cam's fingers tugged at her hair as he pulled her away from his cock until his head rubbed at her lips, and then they dug into her scalp as he pushed her to the base again, her lips feeling every inch of his steely length encased by softest satin.

Every part of Sorcha screamed in aching sensitivity, from her curling toes to the roots of her hair. Her body was not her own. Surely someone else was making those mewling noises. Surely someone else's body was undulating wildly on Cam's bed. She certainly wasn't knowingly doing either. Yet she still felt everything, every nuance, from the soft sheets under her to the bite of Alan's fingers in her side to the cool air brushing over her tender nipples. She noted her lack of control with distance, yet acceptance. She was completely ruled by the two men, and moving on instinct.

The ball of tension within her coiled tighter, and her whimpers became cries.

Still controlling the movement of her head with one hand, Cam's fingers traced the shell of her ear, then traveled down her neck, her chest, and came to rest on her breast. He palmed the tight, aching peak. Sorcha sobbed over his cock.

Oh Lord, she was going to come apart at the seams.

And then Alan moved his hand from her waist to take control of her other breast. In synchronized motion, both men thrust deep, simultaneously pulling hard on her nipples.

She fell over the edge. Cam held her tight, her lips touching the base of his cock, and as if from a distance, she felt his seed splash against the back of her tongue. Tasted his familiar tang.

The hot coil inside her burst open. Exploding in her core and branching through her limbs like dazzling bolts of lightning.

She might have truly flown apart, but both men held on to her, keeping her grounded and sane. Cam's fingers tight against her scalp, Alan's palm rounded over her hip, holding her steady.

Slowly, she returned to earth, rejoining her body on the bed. Her muscles twitched, still full of the beautiful, tingling buzz of sensation her orgasm had produced. Her mouth was still full of Cam's cock, and now crowded with his come. She swallowed convulsively, and he gently pulled away, loosening his fingers from her hair.

She looked up at him for the first time in what seemed like hours. He smiled down at her, his brown eyes soft and full of love. "Thank you." He stroked a lock of sweat-drenched hair away from her face.

She swallowed again, savoring the residue of his release coating her tongue and relishing the thought that she could make him look at her like that. Such . . . *devotion*.

"Good, Sorcha."

She glanced up at Alan, feeling a little guilty, for he hadn't yet achieved his release. Yet he didn't look angry in the least. He looked as she'd felt mere moments ago, dazed with lust, longing, and need.

"Very good," he whispered. "You pleased him. You please me too."

He pulled out and thrust deep again. She'd thought the tissues between her legs sensitive before, but now they were finely tuned to the most miniscule movement. When he brushed against her inner walls, sparks crackled through her. When the tip of his cock nudged the entrance to her womb, she shuddered from the fiery heat that flared through her belly. And when the lower part of his abdomen pressed against her clitoris, it fanned the flames.

She squeezed her eyes shut. "I can't," she murmured. "Oh, Alan, I—"

"You can," he rasped. "You can and you will."

After a long moment of white-hot pleasure-pain, Alan slipped out of her, and she opened her eyes.

Pale fluid leaked furiously from his cock, and she looked up at him in alarm. Alan froze on his knees, eyes shut, clearly willing himself not to come. Sorcha scrambled up in front of him, taking his cock in her fist and licking away the creamy liquid. She nearly groaned at his taste. Her husband's taste, warm and bittersweet, tore through her.

Hers.

Gripped in a fiery clutch of possessiveness, she wrapped her arm around his lower back, bent her head to his cock, and took Alan's manhood fully into her mouth.

Mine, mine, mine, her mind sang to her with every lick, every deep suck. *This man is mine.*

With strong arms, he held her at arm's length. "Not yet," he gasped, his chest heaving. "Soon, but not yet."

He turned around and lowered himself to his back, lifting Sorcha over him so her legs straddled his body. Sorcha glanced at Cam, still on his knees in the corner of the bed, watching them with hooded eyes. His cock had risen again, and he curled his fingers around it.

"Fuck me, Sorcha." Alan's hands curved around her waist, coaxing her over his cock. "Take me deep inside your body and wrap yourself around me."

She took his still-pulsing iron-hard rod into her hand and guided it to her entrance. She hovered above him for a long moment, savoring the feel of his cock head tickling her sensitive outer tissues. He moved impatiently under her, and a complaining noise emerged from his throat, but she smiled a secret smile of feminine power. *She* did this to him. Made him nearly mad with need, with lust. For her.

Ever so slowly, she lowered herself over him, sighing at the stretch of her body to conform to him once again. Once seated all the way, she planted her hands on either side of his head and began long drags over him, pulling out just to the verge of him falling out of her, then pushing down until she ground herself against his body with a roll of her hips.

His body stilled beneath her, and he allowed her complete control. Power.

She closed her eyes and moved against him, reveling in the slow, sweet build of her orgasm.

She hardly took note of the movement of the bed as Cam shifted his weight, but she groaned when she felt his warm, big hands settle on her lower back.

Alan's fingers squeezed her thighs. "I don't want Cam in your cunny, *mo chridhe*. That belongs to me now. Do you understand?"

"Yes," she breathed, locked in dark ecstasy. "Yes."

"I want him to take your arse."

Her eyes flew open, and she faltered in her rhythm.

Oh Lord. They would both be in her. At the same time. Close together.

Cam's arm curled around her middle as if he recognized her hesitation. "I want to be inside you, Sorcha. One last time." His voice sounded odd in the world she'd reserved for herself and Alan alone, but it was not unwelcome. She took comfort in the warm, solid feel of his body behind her.

And the thought of him deep in her bottom just as Alan had been last night made eager gooseflesh rise all over her body.

Alan raised his hands to cup her cheeks. "Look at me."

She blinked at him.

"Tell us. Do you want this?"

"I—I don't know. Will it—will it hurt?"

"I wouldn't hurt you," Cam said, his hands moving lower, now palming the globes of her behind. "I'd never hurt you, Sorcha. Only bring you pleasure."

Her channel clenched around Alan's cock, and her shoulders shook with a bone-deep shudder.

"Aye," she whispered. "I . . . want it."

Cam released a breath. "Just relax," he murmured. "Relax, and make love to your husband."

She lowered her body over Alan's, nestling her head in the space between his chin and shoulder, breathing into the curve of his neck. She moved up and down over his cock, but more slowly now, almost languidly. He wrapped a strong arm around her waist, limiting her motion.

Cam's fingers slid between the cheeks of her bottom, but now they were cool, likely covered in the same grease Alan had used. She gasped as he circled around the tight hole, then in a smooth motion, buried a slick finger deep inside her.

Oh. She could feel it. So strongly. She could feel him pressing against Alan's cock through the thin membrane separating her two entrances. Her body began to tremble as he pulled out and pushed two fingers deep into her, working to stretch the tight ring of muscle.

When she thought she couldn't take another second of it, he pulled away, and she took a great gasping breath. Her sex trembled and pulsed over Alan's cock.

"Ah, God, Sorcha," Alan whispered into her hair. "Goddamn."

Gently, Cam used his fingers to separate her cheeks, and she froze, trembling, when the crown of Cam's cock pressed against her entrance.

"Relax." His hands stroked her back. "You're so beautiful. So tight. Enjoy it, Sorcha. Savor it."

She pressed her teeth together, and he began to push in, forcing the tight muscle to open for him.

Her mouth opened as a cry hovered in the back of her throat, but she buried her face into Alan's neck. As Cam thrust deeper, the muscles all over her body grew tighter.

No more! She wanted to cry. It wasn't pain . . . it was the intensity. Too much. Too overwhelming. She couldn't take any more.

Just as she was about to scream for him to stop, the muscle released the slightest bit, allowing Cam to slide all the way in, and all that emerged from her throat was the tiniest whimper.

He stayed there for a long moment, lodged deep inside her spasming passage. Below her, Alan's breath rasped in his chest as he held her tightly against him, his palms pressing on her upper back.

Slowly, almost experimentally, Cam withdrew and then sank into her once again.

A shudder worked from deep inside her, fanning outward. And as Cam and Alan began to work in and out of her body rhythmically, all thoughts fled from Sorcha's mind. There was only her and Cam and Alan. And how they felt against her, in her. What they did to her. How they made her feel.

She shook from head to toe as they held her pinned, working her deep, Alan sliding out as Cam slid in and vice versa. The burning lust streaking through her body sizzled every nerve ending as she trembled in their arms.

Both men picked up the pace. Their muscles flexed all around her, and sweat slickened their bodies. Sorcha's mouth rounded in an O against Alan's tense, vibrating shoulder.

Their flesh made slapping noises as they connected hard, then retreated. Over and over again, until Sorcha was drowning in a sea of white-hot sensation.

Then Alan went rigid beneath her, and with a whoosh of air from his lungs, he lifted her off him, then pressed his shaft between them. His cock contracted with a jerk, and a warm rush flowed onto her belly. It seemed to go on forever, torrents of come flowing from his cock. Cam fucked her harder, burning her arse as he thrust with everything he had. She was helpless to the onslaught. She was being blissfully torn apart, ripped open and bared.

Alan's cock flexed and pulsed against her skin as Cam battered her behind.

Her orgasm came so suddenly and with such fury, she was unable to brace herself for it. It took her tumbling, rolling into a black abyss of sheer, raw pleasure, fraying her consciousness.

With one final, piercing thrust, Cam gave an agonized groan and he poured his orgasm deep into her bottom.

Wet heat. Contracting, pulsing. Sorcha reeled away from a conscious state and into a deep, warm bed of pleasure.

Moments later, her eyes fluttered open. The men's hot, slick bodies pressed in on her everywhere, comforting. She took a deep breath. A carnal smell washed through her senses, and she breathed in again, taking it in like a drug.

Murmuring softly, Cam pulled away from her. Water sloshed from the basin at the bedside table, and when he turned back toward her, he pressed the cool cloth between her legs just as Alan had last night. It felt like heaven on the sensitive, overheated flesh, and she murmured her approval, rolling to settle in the crux of Alan's arm. He smiled down at her and pressed a kiss to her forehead.

"Sleep, *mo chridhe*. Sleep."

But her eyes were already drifting shut.

CHAPTER SEVENTEEN

Alan woke to a hand on his shoulder and a pounding head-ache. Disoriented, he squinted his bleary eyes. It was still dark. Where the hell was he?

He shifted in bed, his body brushing against the smooth, soft flesh he instantly recognized as his wife's. His vision came into focus, and he froze.

Sorcha was lying beside him, but her naked limbs were tangled with Cam's. As if they were lovers.

And, of course, they were.

The events of last night came rushing back to him, and his gorge rose as the dam within him broke, allowing all those emotions he'd kept tightly bottled in the past days to come pouring through.

Damn fucking hell.

"MacDonald?" It was the merest breath of a whisper in his ear. He whipped his head around to see Duncan hovering over him.

Duncan MacDougall—God, that another had witnessed this scene made it even worse.

Alan breathed tight, fast breaths, trying to reel in his nausea, try-ing to contain the fury threatening to erupt.

"Sir, your kinsmen are downstairs." Duncan paused. "I'm sorry to disturb you, but it's urgent."

"Aye." His voice came out in a scratch of a sound.

Ignoring his body's protest, he pushed his legs over the side of the bed. Quietly, he rose and found his clothes on the floor at the bedside.

Alan pulled on his shirt and plaid in quick, jerky movements, trying to control the shaking of his hands. Trying to stop the pricking tears from seeping out of his eyes, he stared at the door to prevent the image of Sorcha in Cam's arms from assaulting him. Last night, that image had filled him with lust. Now it incited a killing rage.

He'd been sotted. They'd all been sotted. But not too far gone to forget what had happened. He remembered every detail, every nuance.

He had told her to do everything she'd done. Everything had been his idea, from the beginning. He'd commanded her to suck Cam's cock, encouraged her to take him in her back entrance.

Both she and Cam had resisted in the beginning, but their resistance was weak, a pretense. It wasn't hard to convince them to make love.

And while his cock hardened as the image of Sorcha sucking Cam flickered through his mind, he also hated himself with a passion. Hated them, for being so eager to comply with his drunken requests.

He ran a hand through his matted hair, wincing as pain slashed through his temples. Holy hell, he was a damned wreck. Inside and out.

He couldn't face this right now. His men were here, and they needed his undivided attention. They wouldn't have come so early unless something serious had happened.

He nodded to Duncan. "Take me to them, please."

"Aye, sir," Duncan whispered.

With one final glance at the two lovers sleeping face-to-face, their lips just a hairsbreadth apart, he steeled himself, turned away, and followed Duncan out of the Earl of Camdonn's bedchamber.

Sorcha stretched languidly. Warmth encompassed her and she sighed in contentment. With the arms and legs touching her, surrounding her, she felt so . . . cherished. She opened her eyes to see a late-morning sun searing through the curtains and Cam gazing at her, his brown eyes soft.

"Mmm," she murmured.

His wide lips tilted into a rakish smile, and he snuggled closer to her. His erection brushed against her leg.

She sent her hand behind her, searching for Alan. She craved his touch too. But her seeking fingers only encountered the blanket, so she turned away from Cam to find him.

His side of the bed was empty. He was gone.

Her heart began to throb against her rib cage. She turned back to Cam. "Where is Alan?"

Cam rose to a seated position, rubbing his eyes before resting a hand on his wound and wincing a little. "I couldn't say. He might have gone in search of some breakfast."

"Is your injury paining you?"

"It's all right."

She scrambled to the edge of the bed, frowning as she pressed fingers to her forehead to counter the dull pain in her head. "Alan took his clothes."

"Do you wish me to go after him, Sorcha?"

She cast a faltering smile at Cam. In truth, it was disconcerting to be alone with him without her husband nearby. She wouldn't have thought Alan would leave them together.

Fear curled in her gut.

"Yes, please. But I'll come with you. Let's find him."

An hour later, Cam's arm was wrapped around Sorcha's waist as they rode upon a galloping horse. It was just like when Cam had stolen her from Alan, only this time a cold sun shone down on them and they were speeding away from Camdonn Castle, not toward it.

They were headed to Alan and Sorcha's home. Sorcha squeezed her eyes shut as she held herself stiffly in Cam's embrace.

Please let him be home. Please . . .

When Duncan had told her Alan had departed from the castle just before dawn, the panic in her chest welled and bubbled over. She'd turned to Cam, her lips parted, but she couldn't push out the words from her crowded throat.

Alan's message was crystal clear. He was abandoning her. Leaving her to Cam, when all she wanted, all she *needed*, was her husband.

Last night had been wonderful. Alan had been so accepting of her and of Cam. Forgiveness had flowed between them, healed them. Or so she'd thought.

It was Alan she wanted beside her when she woke this morning.

In response to Duncan's announcement, she'd stared at Cam for several long moments, tears pricking behind her eyes. Nothing had surprised her more than Cam's response to her beseeching look.

"I'll take you home," he'd said softly.

She'd lurched backward as if someone had punched her in the stomach.

"If he's not there, we'll go into the village and ask the MacDonalds. We'll find him, Sorcha."

"Thank you," she'd whispered, overcome.

The valley drew closer, the low thatched roofs emerging through the shrubby trees. Sorcha's heart sank when she saw no smoke curling from the cottage's chimney.

She couldn't feel his presence. Surely he wasn't there.

When Cam drew up to the door, he called Alan's name. No response. The only sound was a horse's heavy breathing.

Cam dismounted, then lifted Sorcha off. His hands lingered on her waist, his eyes questioning.

"Let's look for him," she said.

"I'll search the stables."

She nodded and turned to go inside. After a cursory search, she found the cottage just as they'd left it. He hadn't come home. She returned outside and met Cam emerging from the outbuilding shaking his head.

"I'll take you to Glenfinnan."

"I—I can walk."

"Nonsense. It'll cost you an hour. I can have you there in a quarter of the time."

Still she hesitated, knowing what the villagers—what her family—would think if they saw Cam's horse approach with her upon it, Cam's arms wrapped around her waist.

Cam blew out a breath. "It wouldn't look proper, would it?"

She shook her head mutely.

"Very well. I'll drop you outside and you can walk the remainder of the way." His frown deepened until furrows bracketed his lips. "But everyone knows you and Alan have been with me. I hate the thought of leaving you to them."

"No one in Glenfinnan will harm me. But I will go to my father's first."

He nodded, but the lines around his mouth didn't soften.

In silence, they rode the distance to Glenfinnan. When they reached the village's edge, Cam lifted her and deposited her on the boggy earth.

Sorcha gazed up at him, taking a deep breath of air fringed with the smell of the peat fires burning in the nearby cottages.

"Thank you."

His lips eased into the ghost of a smile. "Go now."

She turned and hurried down the path, which curved into the village, looking back only once to see Cam waiting, reins in hand, a wistful expression on his face.

The next time she looked, he was no longer in sight.

* * *

Duncan hurried from the direction of the living quarters as Cam dismounted at the entry to the stables. He handed the reins to a groomsman and turned to his servant, whose disapproving frown seemed at odds with his wringing hands.

"What is it, Duncan?"

"Milord. There is a woman here—a red-haired wench of"—his hands twisted together—"well, of dubious reputation. She refuses to leave and demands to see Mrs. MacDonald."

Gràinne. It had to be. Though Gràinne had never before stepped foot upon the grounds of Camdonn Castle, and Cam couldn't fathom the reason she'd come now. He frowned. "Did you tell her Sorcha is no longer here?"

"Aye, my lord."

Cam sighed. "Where is she?"

Moments later, Cam entered his drawing room. Gràinne sashayed toward him, and he crossed his arms over his chest. "Gràinne. I thought I told you never to come here."

She flashed him an unrepentant smile. "I do apologize, love. But I've come to see the MacDonald chit. Regarding our dear laird."

"Alan?"

"Aye."

"What of him?"

Gràinne gave him a sly look. "'Tis a matter between women."

Cam's arms tightened across his chest. He stepped deeper into the room, and the door closed with a soft click behind him. Gràinne turned away and glided through the room, studying the carvings on the mantel, the paintings on the walls, the rich green fabrics covering the chairs, the silk damask on the windows, the dark Italian furniture.

"Like another world," she murmured with a sidelong glance at him.

Cam followed her gaze with jaded eyes. He had been to the village and hill so often, he scarcely thought of the differences between his home and the primitive dwellings of the people outside Camdonn Castle anymore.

"Aye, it is," he agreed, his tone flat.

What the hell could she have to discuss with Sorcha? Cam felt like taking her shoulders and shaking the information from her, but as always, Gràinne proceeded at her own pace.

She stared at a cushioned armchair upholstered in a velvet of deep forest green, and the pink tip of her tongue swept across her top lip. "May I?"

"Of course."

She sank down, sighing softly, and draped her arms over the sides. "Like sitting on a cloud."

Cam stood still, studying her. Waiting patiently as she settled back in the chair, eyeing him shrewdly with her rich brown gaze. The way her fiery waves fanned out over the silk of the chair back sparked a carnal memory, and his cock surged to life.

Her lips curled into a smile. "Very well, then, love. Since she's not here . . . Alan MacDonald spoke with Sorcha's father this morning."

Resisting the urge to demand where Alan had gone, Cam raised a questioning brow. "Whore's gossip?"

Gràinne shrugged. "I learn the most fascinating things by keeping an open ear, love."

"And what did you learn this morning?"

"Alan MacDonald believes his woman's heart is shackled to yours."

Cam's throat went dry and he remained silent for a moment. If Alan believed Sorcha loved Cam, would it make it so?

No. Of course it would not.

"He's wrong," Cam pushed out. "Her heart belongs to Alan."

"Aye, I know. 'Twas written plain on both their faces when I saw them together." Gràinne narrowed her eyes at him. "So why, then, does he believe differently? Did you tup her?"

"Ahh . . ." Cam spun around and headed to the sidebar. He needed a drink. A stiff one. "Would you like some wine?"

"So you did." Gràinne clicked her tongue. "I'd have thought better of you than to debauch a married woman."

He poured Gràinne some claret and himself some whisky, though by all rights it was too early in the day for it. "It's far more complicated than you might think."

He handed her the goblet. She turned the glittering crystal in fascination before she looked over the rim at him, her lips twisted. "What's complicated about it? You know the man far better than I, love. But from the little I've seen of him, I can guarantee that neither his pride nor his honor will accept a woman who takes pleasure from another man."

Cam resisted the urge to grind his teeth. Goddammit. Alan himself had demanded it of them. . . .

Nevertheless, he knew Gràinne spoke the truth. Alan, damn his soul, had been testing both him and Sorcha. Between her naive efforts to please Alan, and Cam's wayward and rampant lust for her, they had both failed.

He gazed at the amber liquid swirling in his glass and then tipped his head back and swallowed it in one gulp, savoring the burn as it traveled down his throat.

He thumped the empty glass on the sideboard. "What am I going to do?"

"Let her go." The simplest answer, spoken softly as if the bearer of the news knew how difficult it would be for him to accept. He looked up into Gràinne's face, and the brittle cynicism he usually found there had softened into compassion. "You must let her go, Cam. You love them both, I know you do, but you are tearing them apart. If you destroy them, in the end you will destroy yourself. Sorcha was never meant for you, love."

He stared down at his empty glass, blinking hard to push away the liquid filling his eyes. "There is no one like her."

"Of course there is."

He shook his head mutely, thinking of the governess who had abandoned him.

Once again, he was completely alone in the world.

Gràinne set her glass of wine carefully on the polished side table. She rose from the chair, stepped toward him, and enfolded him in her arms. "There is someone better," she murmured into his shoulder. "Someone who fills the emptiness in your soul and makes it overflow. That woman is out there, my love. She will make you a perfect countess. Your task is to find her. But to do so, you must let Sorcha go."

He sank his face into Gràinne's sweet-smelling hair. "How can you be so confident there is someone else?"

Her chuckle resonated through her body. "I am a woman who has known many men. There are few as worthy of love as you."

"You are a good friend, Gràinne."

"I will always be your friend." Her voice softened as her gentle fingers sifted through his hair. "And so will Alan and Sorcha Mac-Donald. Everyone has heard how they stood beside you during your illness. Few would be so loyal, you know, after your betrayal."

Again Gràinne spoke the truth. He sighed into the top of her head. "As much as you go on about honor biting you in the arse, Gràinne darling, you're one of the most honorable people I've ever known."

She didn't speak, just continued combing her fingers over his scalp.

He had to let Sorcha go. Once and for all. It was the only way to keep both Alan and her in his life. What had transpired last night could never occur again. No matter what happened between the three of them, he must keep his hands off Sorcha MacDonald.

Acceptance swept through him, a cool mist that seeped into every pore and left a keen sense of devastation in its wake. He'd expected devastation, but he didn't expect the other feeling the acceptance awakened within him: hope.

They hadn't abandoned him forever like his governess had. Not yet. If he continued to push, they would leave him permanently, but if he simply accepted their friendship and offered his own, they would grant it.

It wasn't too late for him. But it was his responsibility to bring them back together, to convince Alan that he was the one Sorcha loved. The man must be blind not to have seen the way his wife had gazed upon him last night. Love for Alan had seeped from every pore in her body, had encased Cam's bedchamber in a soft, hazy glow.

Then again, Cam knew from experience, jealousy could be a blinding beast.

Gràinne's voluminous bosom pressed against his chest as her fingertips skittered over the hair-roughened skin of his cheek. Her lips followed, grazing his jaw, and her voice settled over him, soothing as a balm. "Now you must prove to them that you can be a friend in return."

"I know," he murmured, catching her face in his hands. "But first I want to give you something." He paused uncertainly. "If you'll accept it."

"What's that, love?"

"May I take you to bed? May I pleasure you?"

He felt a small shiver resonate through her. "Aye," she said gravely. "I'll be here for you. My body is yours whenever you wish. Until you find what you're searching for."

"You're good to me, Gràinne."

She gave him a wicked, knowing smile. "I care for you. And shocking as it may sound coming from someone of my reputation and skill, it's not all a farce with you, love. Our carnal arrangement pleases me."

Sorcha passed a cluster of cottages. The village was so still today, it was almost uncanny. Likely the MacDonalds were spread through Alan's lands, preparing the livestock—and themselves—for the men's departure in two days.

She turned into the small yard of her father's cottage. A chicken clucked condescendingly at her, but she ignored it and pushed open the door.

The room was unnaturally quiet. Her father looked up from his book when she entered. She instantly saw the lines of strain around his eyes, and she slowed to a stop just inside the door, her hand still curved around the smooth wooden edge. Her father's green eyes glittered with regret.

Good God. What had happened? What had Alan done?

CHAPTER EIGHTEEN

Gràinne began to untie the bow at her bodice, but Cam placed his hands over hers to still them. "Come with me," he said quietly. "To my bedroom."

Her arms dropped to her sides, and after a long pause, she nodded.

Twining his fingers with hers, he led her upstairs to his bedchamber, casting an acerbic glare at Duncan, who had lingered in the hall but scurried away upon seeing Cam's expression.

He closed the door behind them, then turned to Gràinne to study her. Behind the jaded, cynical mask, she was a beautiful woman. Maturity only intensified her beauty.

But it wasn't only her beauty that drew him to her. There was a selflessness about her. A kindness. If she didn't care for him, she wouldn't have come today. He wanted to show her how thankful he was for her friendship.

He reached toward her and began to undress her. He'd rarely taken such pains with any woman, much less Gràinne.

Touching her flesh whenever possible, he slowly stripped off her skirts, stays, and shift, and then lowered himself to one knee to remove her garters and roll down her stockings. She sucked in a breath as his fingers brushed her calves. How many men had caressed her there? Very few, he imagined.

He took her into his arms and carried her to the bed, just as Alan had carried Sorcha to the bed last night. The action pulled at his injury, but it was just a twinge, nothing he wouldn't survive.

He set her gently on the bed and looked down at her. "You're a beautiful woman, Gràinne."

"Your bed feels like heaven." She grinned up at him and held her arms out. "Come. Join me."

He peeled off his clothes, and within moments climbed beside her and pressed his body against her warm, supple flesh.

He stroked her all over, crawling downward as he did so, finally insinuating himself between her legs. Lying on his stomach, he touched her mound and stroked through the bronzed hairs to her clitoris. She gasped when his fingers feathered over it.

Inhaling lemon soap, he flicked his tongue out to swipe at the taut bud between her legs. Above him, Gràinne gasped again, and her legs tensed around his ears. "I've never . . ."

He looked up at her, brows raised. "But you've had many men—"

"Not . . . like that," she choked, her brown eyes wide.

Cam dropped his head and set about enjoying her thoroughly, using his tongue to stroke and prod in her most sensitive places. He kept his hands on her thighs, pressing them apart.

She tasted like lemon cream, sweet and tangy. He swirled his tongue around her swollen bundle of nerves, and then brought his hand to the opening just beneath his mouth. In one smooth motion, he slid two fingers inside her. Gràinne bucked wildly, but he held her down with his other hand.

"Cam!"

She was already coming. Her passage squeezed him, the rings of muscles tightening and releasing spasmodically over his buried fingers.

He took her clitoris into his mouth and sucked harder. She groaned, and the squeeze of her orgasm intensified.

He held her there for several long moments. Finally, satisfied it was over, he gently removed his fingers. Kissing and nipping along the way, he traveled up her body, smiling at the dazed look on her face.

"Did you like it?" he murmured.

"Oh" was all she seemed to be able to say.

Her shocked expression was something he'd never seen, not once in all the years he'd known Gràinne. It made his cock pulse angrily, eager to explode. And he damn well would be inside her when that happened.

"I'm going to take you now," he warned.

Still unable to speak, she simply spread her legs to welcome him.

He pushed in, seating himself in one thrust. Gràinne arched her body to meet his.

He began a slow glide. He forgot Sorcha and Alan. There was only Gràinne and her lush, willing body and the pleasure she gave him.

Long moments later, his cock gave way to the overwhelming pressure and he exploded, releasing in long, agonizing jets deep within her body as she cried out her satisfaction.

"Gràinne," he murmured as he collapsed on the bed beside her. "Sweet Gràinne."

For long moments, he stared up at the whorls and rosettes on the ceiling molding as a plan formed in his mind.

He must go to Alan and Sorcha, explain that beyond anything, he wanted their friendship, their presence in his life. He would give up his love for Sorcha and try to find another, though he wasn't as confident as Gràinne that there was another woman who could fulfill him.

He'd been reckless; he'd risked earning the enmity of the two people he loved most in the world. By their continued forgiveness, they'd proven to him that they were deserving of his highest regard.

He'd never fail them again.

Turning his head, he smiled at Gràinne, who stared drowsily back at him, her eyes half lidded.

He rose up onto his elbow. "You may stay here as long as you wish, Gràinne. I've some business to attend."

Her lips curled into a wicked smile. "I daresay you've a pair of lovers to reunite."

He returned her smile, then swung his legs over the edge of the bed and reached for his breeches. "Exactly."

Sorcha tamped down the feeling of alarm rising from her chest. Along with the panic, twisting like a vine around it, was shame. That, she squelched ruthlessly. Everyone might treat her with derision now. They might think she should be ashamed of her affair with Cam. But she wasn't. Her past with Cam was a piece of her, entwined in her soul. Without it, she would be only part of who she was today.

No, she wasn't ashamed. She only wished it hadn't hurt her husband.

She straightened her spine. "Good afternoon, Da. Have you seen Alan?"

Slowly, her father marked his page, then closed the ledger and set down his pen.

"Good afternoon, lass. Aye, I saw him at dawn. When he led his men southward."

"What do you mean? The men are planning to leave day after tomorrow."

Her father shook his head. "A message came from the Earl of Mar last night, entreating them to make haste. Mar is on the move, and the confrontation will occur any day. The MacDonalds gathered and decided to march at dawn, with or without Alan. A few hours before sunrise, Bowie MacDonald and two other men rushed to Camdonn Castle to deliver the news to Alan."

"No."

No. Alan had left without saying goodbye, without rousing her and Cam to tell them what was happening. It could only mean he regretted what they'd done last night, that he was angry at them.

And she loved him. She loved him so much. Had she never told him that?

"James too?"

Her father nodded.

"They might die," she whispered.

"Aye," her father said bluntly. "That is war."

Sorcha's vision swam. Her knees buckled, but her father moved forward quickly to support her waist. "Sit down, lass. Would you like some wine?"

He led her to a chair and pressed her into it.

Tears slipped over her lids and streamed down her cheeks, and her shoulders shuddered as quiet sobs racked her body.

How had the beauty of last night turned into something so devastating? She'd thought what happened had been healing to them all. When she'd awoken this morning to see Cam's smiling face, she'd been certain of it.

And now Alan had gone to war without saying goodbye.

She'd done exactly as he'd commanded last night. She thought she had given him pleasure.

Her father patted her shoulder awkwardly. "Hush now." He passed her a handkerchief and she clenched it in her fist, crossed her arms on the table, and lowered her head on them. Misery overwhelmed her for many long moments. Her father moved about, but she was aware of little else besides the sharp talons of pain that gripped at her heart.

Finally, she raised her head to find her father seated at the opposite side of the table, watching her. He pushed a cup in her direction. "Have some wine. It might help."

She stared at the glass. Slightly misshapen and cloudy, it was so different from the cut crystal she'd sipped from last night.

"I'm surprised at your reaction," her father said.

"Why?" She struggled against another onslaught of tears. She clutched the cup in both hands but made no move to drink.

"You knew Alan would join his men."

"But not like this." Not without knowing how much she loved him. Not without saying goodbye to her, or promising he'd return.

"He cares for you, Sorcha. Very strongly. It's carved all over his face when he speaks of you. Yet he cannot abide the dishonor of sharing your affections with another."

She looked up at him, her chest tight. "Alan is my husband," she said slowly. "He makes me happy, and I want only him."

"Despite the earl taking you into his bed?"

A hot flush crawled up Sorcha's cheeks. "Aye," she choked out. "I love Alan."

"Well, then, you must tell him."

"Yes. Yes, I must. I have to make certain he knows . . . before the battle . . ."

Her father captured her wrist, holding it gently but firmly against the table. "Is this what you want? Be certain, daughter. I won't advise you to chase after Alan only for you to betray him later."

A tear slipped down her cheek. It was devastating to know her father now held her in so little regard. Before this disaster, he'd trusted her.

"I swear by everything holy that it's what I want. I'd die before betraying Alan."

A worry niggled at her heart as she remembered Cam making love to her last night. She didn't consider it a betrayal, but it seemed clear Alan did. Even though he had encouraged her every step along the way . . .

She shook her head as if to fling off the confusion. All that mattered was her husband. She had to reveal her heart to him before the battle. If he died thinking her in love with Cam . . . God, she would never be able to survive that.

"I must return to Camdonn Castle." Abruptly, she rose, pushing the chair back over the flagstone floor. "The Earl of Camdonn is the only person who will be able to take me to the Lowlands in time."

* * *

They encountered Cam a mile out of Glenfinnan on the wide path leading to Camdonn Castle. On foot, Charles and Moira flanked Sorcha. Cam rode alone, reining his horse when he drew up to them.

He dismounted, his forehead furrowed in confusion. "Where is Alan?" he asked Sorcha. "I was coming to find you, to speak with you both."

"Alan's gone." The words were painful to say aloud, even to push out in a tone higher than a whisper. Moira squeezed Sorcha's hand in support.

A crease appeared between Cam's brows as he frowned. "What do you mean?"

"Mar's men held a council of war. He's already leaving Perth." Charles eyed Cam distrustfully. Her brother had obeyed their father by accompanying Sorcha to Camdonn Castle, but he didn't like Sorcha's plan, and he hesitated to ask the earl for anything. Before they'd seen Cam approach, he'd been attempting to devise a way to take Sorcha south himself. But he possessed neither the horseflesh nor the funds to deliver her south quickly. Cam was the only man who had enough of both.

"The Glenfinnan men marched at dawn," Charles continued as Cam's frown deepened. "Bowie rode to Camdonn Castle early this morning to inform Alan of their plans. Of course he agreed to lead them."

"Of course." Cam's soulful eyes met Sorcha's, and she saw the pained understanding in them.

"Cam—" She broke off, struggling for the words. How to say them in the presence of her brother and sister.

Cam thrust a hand through his short-cropped hair, then lowered it to his side, fingers balled into a fist. "You'll come with me," he said in a low voice.

Charles gripped the hilt of his dirk and took a menacing step forward—as if to protect Sorcha should Cam attempt to toss her over his shoulder.

Sorcha grabbed her brother's arm and yanked him back. "Stop, Charles. He means no harm."

Still, Charles bristled. His lip curled as he stared Cam down, his blue eyes narrowing. "I've no understanding why my sister chooses to defend you when you've done nothing but cause her harm."

"You're wrong," Sorcha breathed.

"No." Cam's brown gaze focused calmly on Charles. "He speaks the truth. But you all must understand, I now intend to remedy the mistakes I have made. There will be no more confusion about my intentions. I'll take your sister to Alan MacDonald so she might reconcile with him before the battle."

Sorcha stood in stunned silence, her lips parted. Cam had finally let her go. There was no need to beg him to take her south. Her relief was so acute, her shoulders lifted as if a great weight had melted from them.

Charles pushed out a harsh breath. "How can I be certain you speak the truth? How can I be sure you won't abduct her again?"

Sorcha cast Cam a helpless glance, then squeezed her brother's arm. "He won't, Charles."

"How can you know?" Moira asked quietly.

Sorcha turned to her sister in surprise. "I trust him."

"But why?"

"I've nothing to offer but my word," Cam replied, his voice solemn. "I know it's not worth much, but I vow I'll treat your sister with honor and take her to her husband in the most expedient way I know how."

"I'll travel south with you, then," Charles said.

Sorcha shook her head, inwardly cringing at the thought of Charles anywhere near a field of battle. She feared as much as her father that her brother would leap into the fray and get himself killed.

"No, lad." Cam's voice was gentle. "Your clan needs you here."

Charles huffed.

Cam inclined his head and held out his hands, palms up, in a gesture of supplication. "Your desire to protect your sister is laudable,

Charles, but I ask you to pass that task along to me. I seek redemption. Forgiveness. Can you understand that?"

Sorcha pressed her lips together to hold back the emotion wrought by the sincerity in Cam's voice, but Charles merely bristled.

"We'll leave this afternoon. We'll try to intercept the army before they engage."

Cam looked exhausted. The muscles of his face had tautened into an expression of resignation, and his brown eyes shone with emotion. He was letting her go, but it hurt him. Sorcha hated his pain, despised that she had to be the cause of it. But some things were necessary.

He was such a passionate man, inside and out. The woman who won Cam's love would be a very lucky woman indeed.

She released her brother and sister and stepped toward Cam. He enfolded her in a warm, brotherly embrace. "Thank you," she whispered, clinging to him. "Thank you, my lord."

CHAPTER NINETEEN

They were too late.

When Cam and Sorcha reached the remnants of the soldiers' camp on the edge of the village of Auchterarder three mornings later, exhausted from hard riding and little sleep, smoke no longer trickled up from the fire pits, but the place smelled of burned wood and peat with overtones of scalded porridge. Cam's heart sank as they rode into the abandoned camp.

A woman stood at the doorway of a crude shelter as Cam drew the horse to a halt, its hooves spraying mud. She was a haggard-looking, scrawny matron, who introduced herself as Jane Farquarson. Friendly and hospitable, she herded them inside, where they huddled around a smoldering fire as she fed them barley broth. She explained how she and her husband, a trooper, had been on the march with the Earl of Mar since he'd raised King James's standard in early September. Yesterday morning Mar had ordered the men to head south to take possession of Dunblane. She hadn't heard any news since.

Sorcha turned to Cam and placed her hand on the horse's pommel, ready to be lifted into the saddle. "Let's go, then."

Cam shook his head somberly and stiffened his resolve. "No, Sorcha. I'll not allow you to step foot on a battlefield."

Her jaw set, and her pretty lips pressed into a mulish line he knew well. "I must."

"No. I'll not risk your safety. You will remain here with Mrs. Farquarson."

Sorcha opened her mouth to protest, but he wouldn't give in. She was so bent on finding Alan, she'd risk everything to reach him—even her own life. Cam knew Alan wouldn't want her within miles of a battle. He pressed two fingers to her lips to stop her from speaking. "You may stand here and argue with me all day, or you can agree to allow me to go find him to deliver your message."

Seeing the decision had been made for her—she was not fool enough to persist in the argument when he'd made up his mind, and they had no time for quibbling—she acquiesced. "You'll hurry?"

"Of course."

She buried herself in his embrace. "Bring him back to me."

"I will."

He held her tight for a long moment, but then she released him and gave him a little push. "Go. Before I leap up on that beast and find him myself."

He mounted and turned toward Dunblane. "Stay here," he ordered over his shoulder. "I'll be back."

She just looked at him, her green eyes filled with fear. "Hurry."

His heart surging, he prodded the horse into a gallop.

Cam rode for miles in the cold without encountering a soul, but he finally passed through a village and was told the rebels had spent the frigid night on the edge of Kinbuck Moor. One of the villagers was kind enough, given a small purse, to change his horse for a fresh mount. Cam sped to Kinbuck, arriving at the encampment long past noon. Losing hope he'd intercept Alan in time, he followed the trampled ground southeast from there.

As soon as Kinbuck Moor disappeared behind him, he began to hear the sounds of battle from beyond the sparsely forested rise ahead. Gunshots, like the clatter of pebbles against a window. The low boom of cannon fire. Soon after, shouts, grunts, the clank of steel on steel. Worst of all, and rising above the rest, were the ear-splitting screams of dying men and animals.

The borrowed mare was no war-trained horse, and under his knees, Cam sensed her rising tension as he urged her forward. They crested a rise, and he looked down onto the moor spread out below.

Thousands of men and horses had trampled the pale autumn yellows of the grass and bracken. Argyll's men swarmed over a low rise in the distance, but it looked as though Mar's forces drove them back just as quickly. Beyond the rise, framing the scene, stood a line of long hills. Different from the craggy, steep mountains like those that surrounded Cam's home on Loch Shiel, the gentle autumn greens and golds of the grass-covered Lowland hills sloped gently toward the low-hanging gray clouds.

On the field, men and horses moved so quickly, the line of battle blurred, like a wide smudge in an otherwise detailed painting. Fanning out between the main action of the battle and Cam, hundreds of Highlanders moved steadily forward. He could not see the entire width of the army because the ground was too uneven and the smoke too thick, but from the look of it, he must be near the right flank of the Jacobite army. The stench of gunpowder mingled with mud and blood rose from the soil far below, and Cam fought to keep from gagging.

Fear gnawed in his gut. Good God. He hadn't wanted to be involved in any part of this confrontation. How was he to find Alan in this mass of men? And how could he do it without getting himself killed in the process?

He spurred the horse down the hill toward a clump of dismounted officers engaged in heated conversation at the bottom. One of the men he recognized as the Earl of Mar himself, dressed in a tartan jacket and trews with blue garters. He looked up as Cam drew near.

"Camdonn! What in blazes are you doing here?" he bellowed, his buggy eyes bulging more than usual. His wig was dirty and askew, and his actions jerky, as if he was in a panic. As Cam dismounted, the earl's hand dropped to his sword hilt.

"Rest easy, Mar," he said mildly, though loudly enough to be heard above the din. "I'm not here to fight, but to deliver a message to a friend."

"A Highlander?"

Cam nodded. "A MacDonald."

With narrowed eyes, Mar gave him a once-over, then looked away, apparently satisfied he told the truth.

"A message?" said another officer. "What in God's name could be so important as to interfere with a man on the field of battle?"

Cam shrugged. "It's a private matter, sir. I must find him."

"The MacDonalds are here in the right flank," said yet another. "But they're in the front lines, in the heat of the fight."

Cam swallowed. He wasn't surprised. All this was surely a trial from God himself, meant to test his fortitude.

"Well, then." Mar's voice sounded a hundred furlongs away. "Go find your man, Camdonn. I've a battle to win."

Cam turned back to the earl and inclined his head. "Of course. I'll leave you to it."

Licking his dry lips, he stared in the direction of the fray. Could he do it? Ride into a mass of men in a killing rage, with no intent to engage but merely to find a sole man? Even if he did venture into the midst of the battle, what were his chances of finding Alan? The smoke and dust were so thick, he'd hardly be able to see his hand in front of his face.

Not to mention that he wasn't a rebel. He was a supporter of the government among insurgent ranks. What if one of them recognized him? What if the government troops mistook him for a Jacobite and cut him down? How could he defend himself against the very men he tacitly supported?

He held the reins steady. God. It would be so easy. A flick of his wrist and he'd be headed toward safety. Toward Sorcha and home. But he imagined her disappointment—no, her heartbreak—if he failed to bring Alan to her. The thought sent a pang of pain through his chest.

He continued questioning himself as the mare plodded forward, as nervous as Cam. They forged ahead despite both horse and rider's obvious reluctance.

The odor of grime and fresh blood grew stronger and mingled with the acrid smell of smoke, making Cam's stomach roil. He gritted his teeth and, bunching the muscles in his arms, forced himself to draw his sword.

Bloody hell. How had he gotten himself into this? He didn't know what he'd do if he happened to encounter Alan. Pull him aside to deliver Sorcha's message and then let him jump back into the battle? The entire scenario seemed ridiculous.

Sorcha. Alan. His beloved friends. His companions during his darkest—and lightest—hours. The two people who had seen him at his worst and still stood by his side.

He must do this. For them. Above all, they deserved the happiness he knew could be theirs.

If he succeeded, it meant his redemption.

Baring his teeth, he plunged into the confusion. Jagged lines of Highlanders dressed in shirts and short jackets, their plaids cast off at the beginning of the battle, dodged from the inconsistent step of his jittery horse. It was all Cam could do to keep the mare from bolting, and his healing side, already pushed to its limits from the hard travel for the past few days, throbbed with a dull, deep ache.

The noise assailed his ears, as powerful as a physical blow. The clash of weapons was so intense, even the gunfire seemed distant and unreal in comparison. Yet the screams sliced through it all, death knells that chilled him to the bone.

A red-faced man, wearing a coat to match the hue of his cheeks and a blue bonnet sporting Argyll's crest and the Hanoverian cockade, rushed at him swinging a broadsword and cursing in English.

Argyll's man. God in heaven, Cam didn't know if he was friend or foe. But when the man, his eyes wild, raised his sword to slice at Cam, Cam's response was instinctive. He turned the horse, which shied, nearly unseating him, as he raised his own sword to block.

The tip of the man's sword collided with Cam's boot. His smallest toe smarted as the blade cut through the leather and nicked the toenail. Just a scratch, but it felt like his foot had burst into flames.

Men rushed by, weapons raised, shouting, "Huzzah! Huzzah! It's a rout! Close in!" They sprinted past in a blur. Cam recognized none of them. But then, close by, a young, dark-haired Highlander trotted after the masses. The boy wore the MacDonald clan badge, the sprig of heather, beside the white cockade on his bonnet that marked him as a rebel. "MacDonald!" Cam called.

The boy turned, and though his cheeks were caked with mud and blood, Cam saw the resemblance to Sorcha in the slanted green eyes. His breath released in a whoosh. *James.*

"Aye?" James panted at him before recognition flared in his expression. "My lord?"

For a moment, Cam was distracted by keeping his frightened horse in line. "James," he said when he had his mount back under control. "Do you need anything, lad?"

"Me, my lord? No." His mouth twitched ironically as he glanced at the mare's no-doubt crazed eyes and terrified face. "Looks like you might need some help, though."

"Have you seen Alan?"

"Aye. We were fighting together moments ago." He pointed up the rise. "He went that way, chasing after some wee English cowards."

"Thank you, lad. Good luck to you."

But James had spun round. Cam winced when he saw the boy had engaged another of Argyll's—a young man who looked like he could have been James's brother.

The horse tossed her head wildly as Cam pushed her to move behind James's opponent. The mare leaped forward, and as he rode by, Cam aimed the butt of his sword at Argyll's man. He toppled like a crumbling tower of bricks. As Cam struggled to regain control, he heard James calling his thanks.

The mare plunged into a thick clump of fighting men. Red coats and multicolored Highland jackets swarmed together in a confusing mass of bodies engaged in violence.

Fear pounded at Cam's spine, made his bowels turn to jelly. For Christ's sake, he'd never wished to be anywhere near a battle. Yet here he was, in the midst of the worst of one.

A sharp shout came from behind him. Cam glanced back to see a government soldier sprinting at him, sword raised. He spurred the horse, but just as she lunged ahead, the man's sword swooped down, slicing her rear flank.

She reared high, and Cam lost his grip on the reins. His body slammed to the earth. The air rushed from his lungs. He lay still, gasping for air as his horse pounded away.

He hurt from head to toe, but he wasn't seriously injured. His sword lay in the muck a few feet away, and he reached for it. Slowly, he came to his knees, the world spinning around him . . . or perhaps he was the one spinning like a child's top. For a moment, he wasn't sure.

He struggled to his feet, swaying. Blinking hard, he raised his sword into a defensive position. But all the men surrounding him were deep in battle.

Alan. He had to find Alan.

Cam pushed forward. He could scarcely see a body's length ahead of him. Cannon fire boomed loud and resonated in his skull. Brushing the back of his hand across his eyes, he saw a flash of blond curls sway beneath a blue bonnet.

He lunged toward the man, but he turned, revealing a cherubic face and brown eyes. Not Alan.

God. Where could he be? Cam limped, stumbling over injured men, defending himself when necessary, trying to achieve the impossible end of staying alive without harming anyone on either side.

Dropping to his knees on the boggy earth, he pushed on the shoulder of a prone Highlander, pressing his lips together when he saw the man's glazed eyes. It wasn't Alan. Thank God.

Then, just ahead, he heard a familiar grunt. He looked up. Alan had eschewed tradition and kept his plaid on to combat the cold on this frigid day. His bonnet was perched gaily on his head, the sprig of heather framing the rosette of the cockade. He'd just delivered a deadly blow to an Englishman and was now doubled over, taking in gulping breaths.

Two soldiers shouting in English rushed up the slope behind him, bayonets raised. A loud boom echoed close by, and thick, black smoke billowed around them so suddenly Cam could hardly see Alan or the men attacking.

"Alan!" Cam screamed, sprinting toward them. "Behind you!"

Alan spun around and managed to raise his shield to deflect a blow that would have sliced through his neck. Cam leaped to his feet to assist him as yet another English soldier advanced.

"I don't think so, you bastard," Cam snarled. "Alan's busy."

The man faced him, his bloodshot eyes wide. He swung his sword wildly, but Cam jumped aside and drove his weapon into the man's belly. The soldier fell to his knees, a shocked expression on his face, but Cam didn't have time for him. He dodged past to help Alan.

One of the Englishmen had circled around Alan. Busy staving off his other opponent, Alan didn't seem to notice him hovering behind him in the smoke.

With a howl, Cam dove at the Englishman just as the soldier poised to sink his bayonet into Alan's spine. He head-butted the man in the side, and they both tumbled to the ground, Cam on top. Pinning the man to the earth, Cam punched his face until blood sprayed from his mouth with every blow.

Cam took in a big gulp of smoke and coughed. Besides the burning in his lungs, he felt nothing except a sharp pain in his side where Alan had wounded him in the duel. It seemed like a lifetime ago, and yet it hurt like hell. A dim part of his mind registered that it had probably reopened. Warm fluid glued the fabric of his shirt to the skin on his stomach, confirming it.

Finally, the Englishman's eyes rolled back in his head as he fainted.

Gasping for breath, Cam looked up at Alan, who stood inches away and stared down at him, openmouthed.

"Cam, what the hell—?" But a Hanoverian trooper swooped past, aiming a boot at Alan's skull. Alan's neck twisted awkwardly, and he crumpled to the ground like a deer shot in the heart.

"Alan?" His gasping breaths turning to sobs, Cam crawled to his friend. Just as he reached out and grasped Alan's arm, a blinding pain swept through his head. Stars flashed brightly in his vision. He collapsed on top of Alan. And then everything went dark.

Sorcha paced the muddy encampment, glancing frequently in the direction Cam had gone. Just after dusk, a mounted man arrived, informing Mrs. Farquarson the battle was over and her husband's squadron had retired a few miles south. He bore news that Mr. Farquarson had survived and all were in good spirits, their right flank having routed the government's left.

Unsurprisingly, he bore no news of Alan, Cam, James, or any of the MacDonalds of the Glen.

Mrs. Farquarson took one look at Sorcha, and her face softened in sympathy. "Can ye walk, lass?"

"Aye."

"Come, then. 'Tis no matter it's nearly full dark. We'll go to Blackford and see to your kinsmen for ye."

"Thank you," Sorcha said, relieved to have the company. Even if Mrs. Farquarson hadn't suggested it, she would have gone on her own. If Cam and Alan were all right, they would have returned to her immediately. Panic whispered in her blood. She feared she wouldn't find either of them in Blackford.

Over an hour later, they arrived at the encampment, wet, cold, and tired. As Mrs. Farquarson reunited with her husband, Sorcha searched the exhausted ranks of the rebel army.

She nearly burst into tears as she recognized a small group of Mac-Donalds huddled round a fire. When they heard the choking noise emerge from her throat, they stared up at her in shock.

"Have you . . . have you seen Alan?" she managed.

Bowie rose from his position on his haunches at the fire. Taking two steps toward her, he said, "Sorcha . . . milady, what in God's name are you doing here?"

"I . . ." She could barely get the words to emerge from her squeezed chest. "I need to find Alan. To tell him . . ."

Bowie shook his head. "It was chaos. None of us have seen him since midafternoon, in the thick of it."

"You . . . you've *lost* your laird?"

"Appears we have," said one of the older men glumly.

Bowie gave the man a hard look and then turned back to Sorcha. "He disappeared in the confusion," he said in a low voice. "There were four of us guarding him. A cannon misfired near us and set off a small fire, and when the smoke cleared, we couldn't find him."

"What about James?"

"We haven't seen your brother. We were separated from the rest. We think they've already started home. But we"—he gestured to the four other men—"have decided to stay and continue to fight with Lord Mar."

"Have you seen the Earl of Camdonn?"

Bowie raised a brow. "Last I heard, he was safe at Camdonn Castle."

One of the other men smirked. "Not one for grand battles is our wee earl, now, is he?"

Turning from them in despair, she went to seek out Mrs. Farquarson, who was nursing a man with a bloody arm.

"I'm going to the field," she said, kneeling beside the older woman.

Mrs. Farquarson made a clucking sound with her tongue, but kept her focus on the bandage she was wrapping. "It's quite a distance from here, my dear. Perhaps you should wait till morning."

"No. If they're alive, if they're injured, I'll not have them freezing to death overnight in this cold."

"Aye, lass, I understand. I'd be ill at ease too, if my Colum hadn't come home yet." Mrs. Farquarson rose, withdrawing a glinting object from the folds of her skirt. "Well, then. Take one of your MacDonalds with you, and also take this."

She pressed the hilt of a dirk into Sorcha's hand.

Sorcha gasped. "I don't know how to use this!"

Mrs. Farquarson's lips twisted. "Well, you will know if you need it, won't you? Go on, then, and may God go with you." She turned back to the man whose wound she'd nursed, who was staring at Sorcha with bright, dazed eyes.

Sorcha had nowhere to stow the weapon, so she just gripped it in her hand as she returned to Bowie, who lounged against a pile of rocks.

"I'm going after them," she said softly.

Bowie cracked open one eye to gaze up at her, and groaning softly, scrambled to his feet. "Aye, Sorcha. We'll come with you." He turned to the big man who'd been reclining beside him and kicked him in the ribs. "Up, Malcolm, you lazy sod. We've got to help Sorcha find Alan and James."

"And the earl," Sorcha murmured, her heart panging for Cam.

Bowie managed to borrow a pair of horses from the kindly Colum Farquarson, and they picked their way out of the camp, away from the resting and wounded men and the people scurrying around to attend them.

The recent traffic of men made their progress toward the battle-field easier, but it was dark as pitch save the blanket of stars overhead casting a meager light over the trampled fields.

They scaled a short rise a few hours before dawn. Sorcha gripped

Bowie's waist from behind, Mrs. Farquarson's dirk still in hand. The temperature had fallen below freezing, and Sorcha clenched her teeth to keep them from chattering.

"Sherrifmuir's just over this ridge," Bowie murmured.

At the top, they hid behind a copse of thick brush and gazed down at the battlefield. It looked like the whole area had been burned, but in fact most of the blackness was only churned earth. Debris from the battle was scattered everywhere—overturned carts, abandoned plaids and weapons, sacks of grain, even crates of ammunition.

A few men wielding lanterns—English and Lowland Scots, Sorcha realized from their accents—searched the area, shouting to one another whenever they found a spoil. She, Malcolm, and Bowie watched as they dragged a near-dead rebel to a wagon filled with prisoners.

How could a Campbell, the Duke of Argyll, have done this to his own people? It seemed so wrong.

Beside her, Bowie shuddered.

"You can't go down there," Sorcha forced herself to say. "You'll be arrested. I must go by myself."

"No, Sorcha."

"Likely to be some sights down there not fit for a lady's eyes," Malcolm muttered.

Ultimately, neither man possessed the power to stop her, not like Cam did. "I'll pretend to be the wife of one of the governmentals from Stirling. My English is good enough. And if I find Cam—" She swallowed. "The fact of the matter is that I'll be in far less danger than the two of you. You wait here. I'll bring them back."

Bowie and Malcolm provided no further argument as she broke from the bushes and stepped onto the road leading down the rise.

A hand closed over her arm. Malcolm. She looked up into his fleshy face. "Go to the southernmost corner of the field," he advised. "'Twas where we were fighting."

She nodded, and he disappeared back into the brush after helping her to light the lantern they'd brought. Keeping her back straight, the lantern in one hand and Mrs. Farquarson's dirk in the other, she headed down the hill. She told herself to be systematic. She'd scour the field from the southern corner fanning outward. She'd keep her already-cramping stomach and breaking heart out of it. Until she found one of her men.

A group of soldiers pointed at her, discussing her, but she stared daggers at them until they looked away, apparently deeming her unworthy of further attention.

She blinked back tears when she found the first body. Clearly an English soldier, with his red coat and black hat lying on the ground nearby. She tried not to stare at the blood drying on the back of his coat.

Her breaths began to stutter in her chest as she passed more carnage. Finally, after long minutes of striding through hell, she saw a familiar body splayed awkwardly on the ground. Silky black hair under a blue bonnet.

She stopped, frozen, and then she dropped both lantern and dirk as she lunged forward, falling to her knees beside the body. A wail of despair broke from her chest.

James stared up at her, his blue eyes cloudy in death.

CHAPTER TWENTY

Alan awoke to a low groan. Not his own, he realized as he clutched his aching head. His fingers grazed a sensitive, plum-sized goose egg on the side of his skull.

He opened his eyes and blinked away the fog to stare at a frigid, star-studded sky. Hell, he didn't think he'd ever been this cold.

He turned with effort toward the source of the groan.

Cam! Alan's eyes widened as he took in the other man. Cam knelt on his knees, clutching his head in a similar fashion as Alan, his teeth chattering. Blood caked his coat, pasting the wool to his side.

"Cam," Alan murmured through his scratchy throat and a mouth that felt coated in thick velvet. "Are you all right, man?"

Slowly, Cam swiveled to face him. A faint smile twitched his pale lips. "Thank God you're alive. I thought the bastard broke your neck and then I finished the job by fainting on top of you."

"Hell if my neck doesn't feel broken." Wrapping his arms around himself, Alan forced himself into a seated position. A discarded plaid lay within reach, thick with icy mud, and he pulled it over his shoulders. "Though we probably kept each other from freezing to death."

He turned his head to scan the area. The battle was over. Darkness blanketed the field. A woman sobbed nearby and men shouted in

English. He stared at a clump of red coats moving along the ridge above them. Did this mean the Jacobites had lost?

He glanced back at Cam, frowning. "What in the hell are you doing here?"

"Came . . . for you," Cam said tightly. One hand moved to his injured waist.

"Why?"

"Sorcha."

Alan's heart surged against his chest. "Sorcha . . . what?"

"She wanted to tell you . . ." Cam rubbed his brow as Alan scrambled to his knees. Cam's face was white and his shoulders trembled. "She wanted to tell you she loves you."

"We need to get you some help," Alan murmured. "But only the English and Argyll's men are about."

"Yes . . . well, Argyll's a friend of mine, you know." Cam smiled faintly.

"Aye." Alan struggled to his feet and reached down to help Cam up. But beyond his friend's kneeling body and just down the rise, he saw a sight that made his hand go limp. His wife, her arms flung around a man lying on his back in the muck.

What in God's name was she doing here?

"Sorcha?" he whispered. Then louder. "Sorcha!"

Alan scrambled to her, fighting back nausea and dizziness.

Sorcha blinked at him. Her face was as pale as if she'd just seen a ghost. Her near-invisible freckles stood out in relief across the bridge of her nose.

A tear trembled on her lower lash, then tumbled over, forging a path down her smudged cheek.

"You're alive, praise the Lord." She stared down at the body beside her, and Alan saw, with a lurch of his heart, that the man lying there was James Stewart.

"But my brother . . . my brother is dead."

* * *

By the time the battlefield lightened with dawn, Cam had received medical attention. Not Mary MacNab–quality—they'd have to wait until they arrived home to the glen for her cruel yet competent care— but English quality. The wound in his side had reopened, and a medic wrapped it with a dirty rag. His bound head was a twin to Alan's, and by the pained look in his eyes, Cam didn't doubt that Alan's head screamed just as loudly as his own.

Cam's worst injury, however, was the cut to his small toe. The "scratch" was in actually a deep slice to the bone, nearly severing his toe. The busy medic had finished the job quickly, cauterized it, and gave Cam a stick to use as a crutch.

During this time, Cam engaged in a cursory conversation with the Duke of Argyll, who arrived at dawn to survey the field. Despite knowing Alan and the two men who'd joined him were rebels, Argyll told Cam to return "his men" and the body of James Stewart to the glen and assured him that they wouldn't be harassed. Argyll even offered them lodgings and said they could borrow a servant, a team of horses, and a wagon for the journey back to the Highlands.

Cam wanted nothing more than to leave this cursed place and return home at once. To the serene beauty of Loch Shiel and the comfort of Camdonn Castle.

Leaning heavily on his crutch, Cam limped toward Sorcha and Alan. They'd sent the two Glenfinnan men back to Mar's encampment, but neither Sorcha nor Alan had left James Stewart's side. They sat close together with their hands clasped, murmuring quietly to each other.

They turned their attention to him as he approached. He told them about his agreement with Argyll, and Alan nodded. "You didn't have to protect—"

"Yes, I did," Cam said quietly. "You know I did."

"Thank you." Sorcha looked up at him, and his chest tightened at the grayness of her complexion and the lines of grief at the edges of her mouth and eyes. "I've never met anyone more selfless or honorable than you have been these past days."

He shook his head. "No. I'm none of those things."

"You are. You are a true, dear friend."

In a rush of contentment, he realized if that was all he could ever be to Alan and Sorcha, it would be enough. When he smiled at them, his relief and gratitude were genuine.

Alan rose, helping Sorcha to her feet beside him. He glanced over the field of battle, where the English were still gathering the spoils, including the Earl of Mar's rebel supply wagons, and he sighed heavily.

"Let us leave this place," Alan said. "It's time to take James home."

To Alan, the long trip home was like an extended nightmare. Cam's toe developed an infection. Every step the horses took pained him. Sorcha was mentally exhausted, distressed by what she'd seen, and devastated by the loss of her brother. It seemed the matter of their marriage was the least of their worries.

Alan felt like the rope holding everything together—a rope that was rapidly fraying and in danger of coming apart. His minor head injury had healed quickly, but he was exhausted, worried for his wife and friend, and frustrated by the uncertain outcome of the battle. Why had Mar chosen to withdraw when he had?

The rebels vastly outnumbered the English, and Alan was convinced if they'd continued fighting, they would have won. Instead, Mar had withdrawn, using the darkness as an excuse, leaving the field in the hands of Argyll. Though Mar claimed victory, Argyll had taken most of the spoils, including scores of prisoners who would be tried for treason.

There was nothing Alan could do about it, however. All he could do was focus on keeping his family together and his friend from falling into a fever yet again.

Days later, they reached Glenfinnan at dusk. Men ceremoniously took James's body from the cart and moved him to a shelter to be prepared for his funeral. Sorcha dismounted and huddled with her family.

Hell. Stewart's grief was so palpable, Alan couldn't even look him in the eye. He prayed he'd never have to experience the loss of one of his own children.

He stepped up to Sorcha, whose arms were flung round both Charles and Moira. "Sorcha?"

"Aye?" She turned to him, but her glazed green eyes hardly seemed to register his presence.

He knew what she needed, though it pained him to be separated from her in her fragile state. "I'm taking Cam home. Will you remain with your family until I return?"

She nodded and turned back to her loved ones. Moira, especially, seemed to have taken the loss of her brother hard. Sobs racked her frame, and without Charles propping her upright, she surely would have fallen to her knees.

Alan plodded back to the horses. He was bone weary, and by the drawn expression on his pale face, Cam fared no better.

They hardly spoke on the road to Camdonn Castle. When they reached the path leading to the castle gates, Cam inhaled what felt like the first clean breath he'd taken in a week.

"Why are you riding with me?" he asked Alan. "Why not stay with Sorcha?"

"She needs her family now." Alan kept his gaze focused straight ahead. "They need one another. I'd merely interfere."

Cam shook his head, too tired to argue. They reached Camdonn Castle in a slow walk, and after the groomsmen came to take their horses, they dragged their weary bodies into the living quarters. Cam ordered up a bath for both of them, and Alan raised a brow. "Should you be bathing your injuries?"

"I don't care," Cam said. "I have to wash that place off my skin."

Alan didn't respond, and Cam knew he understood. There was no need to discuss it further.

* * *

Finally clean and feeling more energized than he had in days, Alan went to the drawing room only to interrupt Mary MacNab berating Cam. Not for taking a bath, but for the filthy condition of his wounds.

"I'm going to have to scrub out the dirt and poke more thread into yer beleaguered body! Do ye think your skin enjoys that kind of treatment, you damn fool?"

"I know I don't," Cam mumbled.

Mary harrumphed and ambled to a table where her medical kit sat and began to rifle through it, taking out bottles of unguents and powders. She glanced at Alan and rolled her eyes heavenward. "Devil take it, another one. And what's wrong with you?" she snapped.

"I'm well." Alan offered her a small smile.

She was unaffected by his gracious look. "Well, get out of my way, then. I've a patient to attend."

"Of course." Alan sidled past her to stand by Cam.

"Sorcha sent her," Cam murmured.

Alan nodded. "Good. You need her help." The thought of Cam falling into another deadly fever made his stomach twist. The first infection had weakened Cam, and he was exhausted by the days of travel and battle while he still should have been recovering. Alan doubted he'd survive a second bout of fever.

Mary trudged back to Cam, her hands full of bottles, which she thrust at Alan. "Make yerself useful, then."

"Happy to help, Mrs. MacNab."

She withdrew a long, glimmering needle from a fold in her skirt and waved it in front of Cam's face. "This will hurt."

Cam nodded. "I know."

She thrust the sharp end at his nose, and he drew back quickly, narrowly escaping being punctured by the pointed tip.

"Is that idiot of a doctor returning?" She made a disgusted noise in her nose. "His damn fool medicine was why ye fell ill the first time. I'll not have the bastard fouling up my work again."

"I won't call on him, Mrs. MacNab. I promise," Cam said. "God knows I don't want that to happen again."

"Yes, well, none of us do, ye know," she mumbled, turning away.

Alan's eyebrows shot toward his hairline, and Cam glanced at him with an equally astonished expression. Had Mary MacNab just expressed approval of the Earl of Camdonn? Alan gave her an appraising look. Perhaps Mary watched people more closely than she let on.

Alan dutifully passed the concoctions to Mary when she ordered them. At the same time, he plied Cam, who was gritting his teeth and blinking hard in a valiant effort not to faint, with whisky.

When she was done cleaning, stitching, applying bandages to both Cam's wounds, and had finished performing her pagan healing rituals, she clapped her hands together in satisfaction. "There now. Ye'll be right as my leg in fewer days than ye can count."

Cam slumped back in his chair, his eyes half lidded and his mouth drawn in a tight white line as Alan showed Mary out and arranged an escort to return her to the glen.

When he returned to the drawing room, Cam pushed his eyelids open and pinned him with a stare. "When will you go back to Sorcha?"

Alan sighed and sat in the seat across from Cam. "Soon. I wished to speak with you first."

The look of muddled exhaustion bled from Cam's face, leaving him wide-awake and concerned. "What of?"

Alan pressed the bridge of his nose between two fingers. "Nothing has been resolved. I cannot fathom what possessed either of you to pursue me all the way to Sherrifmuir."

"First you might wish to explain what drove you away without a word."

Alan fought back the urge to clamp his lips shut and walk out—all the way back to Sherrifmuir if necessary. He'd rather avoid difficult or uncomfortable topics, and this one was perhaps the most challenging he'd ever have to face.

But running away again would achieve nothing. They all needed to understand what had happened between the three of them.

He took a deep breath. When he spoke, his voice was hoarse. "I was in my cups, Cam. We all were."

"Not enough to forget what had happened," Cam pointed out.

"No."

Cam's lips twisted sardonically. "Come, now. You cannot tell me you didn't enjoy that night. I was a witness to it, after all."

Alan shrugged. "It wasn't that. I—" He pushed his breath out. "It was when I awoke, apart from Sorcha. I looked over and saw the two of you . . . embracing. And I knew—" He broke off abruptly.

"What did you know?" Cam asked. "What wisdom did seeing Sorcha and I touch bestow upon you?"

"You love her."

That ruffled Cam. He leaned against the velvet cushions, and the tall chair back cast a dark shadow over his face, rendering it unreadable.

Finally, he steepled his fingers beneath his chin. "I do love her," he murmured thoughtfully.

At Cam's blunt words, a possessive rage shot up through Alan's body like a geyser. Just as it was about to burst, Cam added, "But she is not for me."

"No?" Alan's voice was a near growl.

"No." Cam dropped his hands to his lap. "I made a deadly error when I took her from you that night, Alan. Sorcha belongs to you. She's yours, my friend."

"Why?" Alan demanded. "If you love her, and it's clear you want her, then why?"

Cam sighed heavily. "I care for you both. I look at you and see a love match—one that I meddled with using my personal poison. Not to mention"—he leaned forward awkwardly, hampered by his bandage—"the fact that she loves *you*, Alan MacDonald. Not me."

Alan shook his head. God, he wanted to believe Cam. But what if Cam was wrong? Alan's injured pride couldn't take another blow.

"Why did you come to Sherrifmuir?" he asked quietly.

"It was as I told you on the field. She wanted to reveal her heart."

"But . . . why?"

Cam hissed out a breath. "She didn't want you to face death believing she didn't love you."

Alan just sat, staring at Cam. All his bottled-up jealousy drained from him like water through a sieve, and his heart resurfaced once again.

She did love him.

The truth of it melted the final vestiges of the ice he'd packed around his heart on the night of their wedding.

After studying him for a long moment, Cam asked, "When will you speak with her?"

"She needs time to mourn—"

"Don't be an ass, man. All she needs is you."

It was snowing lightly as Alan and Sorcha made their way down the sloped path leading home. They'd covered the distance from Glenfinnan on horseback, and they had hardly exchanged a word the entire way, both of them lost in their own thoughts.

When they reached the cottage, Alan dismounted, then lifted her off. When her feet touched the ground, he smiled down at her, still clasping her waist in his hands.

She smiled back. It was the first time she'd smiled in days, and it felt good. Healing.

He released her, and she went inside the cottage while he took care of the horse, promising to follow soon.

A few moments later, Sorcha turned from the hearth to see Alan standing at the threshold, his gaze fastened on her. She took a shaky step toward the door and leaned on a supporting post in the center of the room.

They were home. Well and truly alone for the first time in many days.

"Do you want to be here with me, Sorcha?" he asked in a low voice.

She shook her head, confused. "You must know I want to be with you, Alan. I'd follow you anywhere."

Alan's brows pressed together, and a deep line appeared between them. "I've been a damn fool."

"How can you say that?"

"I was jealous. I couldn't stand sharing your love."

"I care about Cam." She licked her lips. "He's essential to who I am, like my brothers and sister and father. I'll always love him. But you're different. More. You're my husband."

His face tight, he nodded.

"Why didn't you say goodbye that morning?" she asked quietly.

"Duncan woke me before dawn. I looked over at you and saw you tangled in a lover's embrace with Cam, and I couldn't think. It nearly killed me to see the two of you like that. I felt—" He raked a hand through his hair. "I felt *alone*."

Emotion lurched in her chest, but she remained silent.

"I was too sick of mind and heart to confront you at that moment. My men were waiting for me downstairs. It seemed so much easier to go to them than to wake you . . . to let you see how"—he glanced away—"hurt I was." He inhaled deeply and met her eyes once again. "I went down to meet with Bowie—it was just him and two others. They'd risked the men leaving without them to come fetch me, and Bowie told me they planned to depart at dawn, whether I was there or not." A guilty look crossed over Alan's face. "I should have gone up to tell you what was happening, to reassure you all would be well between us. But I took the cowardly way out. I left."

"I didn't mean to hurt you," she breathed. "You must know that."

"I do now. I think I might have realized it later that day when we were on the march. By then it was too late to go back and say goodbye."

"And now?"

"You came after me," he said simply. "You and Cam drove to exhaustion to reach me in time, and when you didn't, you searched for me among the dead in a field of battle. What further proof do I need?"

She pushed herself from the post and stepped toward him. "I love you, Alan. Can you see how much I love you?"

"I—" Alan gazed at her. She stepped up to him and rested her palms on his shoulders. "I fear what you might do to me."

"I would never hurt you."

He shook his head. "I know you wouldn't—not purposely. But still . . ." His voice dwindled.

He was afraid she'd hurt him again. Because he loved her and had given her that power over him. "I lied to you once," she said, "and I will never forgive myself for that. But I have never lied to you since. I love you. If we are open and honest with each other, as you said on the first night of our marriage, how can there ever be anything else?"

His thumb grazed her cheek and she closed her eyes. The mere touch of his finger nearly overwhelmed her. She continued in a low voice. "I didn't know what it was, at first, this feeling in my chest whenever I looked upon your face and saw the wariness there. I hurt, because I'd hurt you. And I am so sorry for it.

"And then I hurt you again, with Cam that night. But everything I did was to please you. The greatest joy I experienced during that night was in thinking how I'd pleased you. How close I felt to you."

"I manipulated you," he said softly. "I tested you."

Pain clogged her chest. "And I failed. I'm sorry." She dropped her head, but his fingers found her chin and pressed it up so once again she stared into his eyes.

"No, it is I who am sorry. I misled you, *mo chridhe*. Into failing me so I'd have an excuse to run away. It was a sham to disguise my own cowardice." Alan paused for a long moment, his fingers still holding her chin, but she felt a slight tremor in them. "It was because I'd fallen in love with you and I was too cowardly to acknowledge it. I was afraid of the pain you could cause me. Afraid if I opened my heart to you, you'd destroy me by returning to Cam."

"Never."

His fingers stroked her hair behind her ear. "I love you, Sorcha. So much, it scares me. Forgive me for being a . . . well, in Cam's words, an 'ass.'"

"I forgive you," she murmured. "We both made mistakes."

"Aye, we did."

She wrapped her arms around his muscular torso and buried her face in his chest. They held each other for a long moment, and then she whispered, "I miss my brother. So much."

"I know, *ceisd mo chridhe*."

"He's gone, and I will never know what kind of a man he would have become."

Alan continued stroking her hair.

"If—if I had lost you as well—" Tears gathered behind her lids. "I couldn't have borne it, Alan."

"I'm here. I'm beside you, and I'm not leaving again."

"You are the most important thing in the world to me, and I thought I might lose you without you ever knowing it. And . . ." She swallowed down the thick emotion crowding her throat. "I wished . . . I wished I had given you all of myself, and I realized I never really had."

His fingers stilled over her ear. "What do you mean, *mo chridhe?*"

"I want to have a family. With you." She glimpsed at him to gauge his reaction. His face was blank and she forged on, breathless. "You, me, and maybe a son or daughter for us to raise . . . in our new home up on the hill."

"What about what happened to your mother?" he asked softly.

"I'm not afraid of death anymore. I've seen enough of it in the past few days. If my mother's fate should befall me, at least I will die knowing I tried to give you a child."

He cupped her cheeks in his palms. "Are you certain?"

"I've never been more certain of anything."

"Ah, Sorcha." His lips descended on hers, soft and light. She wrapped her arms around him and returned his kiss.

It had been so long. She tried to keep it slow, to refrain from devouring him, but a long, agonized groan emerged from her throat.

He gathered her tight against him. In all her life, she'd never felt so content, so loved. So right.

She pulled away. "Does this mean yes?"

He chuckled. "I say we begin right now."

Gathering her close, he carried her to the bed. Their bed. He laid her down, removed his belt and plaid and then joined her, unclasping her brooch to release her *arisaid*, then plucking at her laces until her petticoats and stays gaped open. Then he grasped the edges, and she shimmied out of the garments as he tugged them from her body.

"It's cold outside," she whispered, shivering a little.

"Aye, it is."

She slipped her hand beneath the hem of his shirt. "But you're warm."

"I am." He smiled at her. "Warm for you, Sorcha."

They finished undressing each other, and Alan kissed her again.

He *was* warm. His body was like an oven, and she pressed herself into it, stealing his warmth onto her own cool skin. And when he entered her, she gasped as his heat speared through her.

He gazed down at her as he began to move inside her body.

"Look at me," he said in a low voice.

She opened her eyes and stared at him, allowing her love for him to pour out of her. In return she opened herself up to his offering of love, taking everything he had to give. As if, before this moment, they were empty vessels and now they were filling each other with care, trust, affection . . . and love.

She would remember this moment, perhaps even more than the moment the priest had bound them together. Because while God had accepted them as one on their wedding day, it had taken Sorcha and her husband a little longer to understand their joining.

She now knew it would be forever. Nothing could part them now.

She arched up into him. He penetrated her so deeply, and she squeezed so tightly around him, his shaft seemed to stroke her everywhere. She came, a sweet piercing orgasm that made her gasp and cling to him even tighter. And just as her peak receded, Alan's body began to quiver. He thrust hard, and she cried out as she felt him pulse deep inside her, releasing his seed against the mouth of her womb.

A new tremble began in her core and then spread until she shook all over. Alan lowered himself beside her and pulled her close.

"Cold again?" he murmured. "So soon?"

"N-n-no," she managed, trying to keep her teeth from chattering.

"What then, *mo chridhe*?"

"I—I'm happy," she whispered. "So happy."

He pulled her closer, and she pressed herself against him. Finally, when she could speak again, she asked, "Do you think we created a child?"

"There's no telling," he said, a smile in his voice. "We'll just have to keep trying until we're sure."

"Ooh," she murmured, her words muffled against his body. "Can we try again right now?"

Alan's chest vibrated as he laughed. "I said on our wedding night my wife was wanton."

"Did I ever deny it?"

He chuckled again. "You tried."

"That I did," she admitted softly, and then she frowned. "I can't seem to remember why."

In one smooth motion, he turned her so she lay on her back and he hovered over her.

Smiling as their love pulsed around and through them, they both had their wicked way with each other. Again.

EPILOGUE

Ten Months Later

Sorcha knelt in her little garden, plucking tiny weeds from the newly sprouted herbs she'd planted. In the distance, she could hear the noise of hammering and stones clacking. Alan was up the rise, supervising the progress of their new home.

A new sound emerged—the unmistakable clomp of a horse's hooves. Shading her eyes from the sun, she looked up to see Cam approaching on horseback, looking dashing in his traveling clothes.

Sorcha rose, brushing the dirt from her hands. She glanced up to see Alan striding down the hill to greet him.

Cam stopped at the cottage, dismounted, and tied the tethers to a post before turning to her, removing his English hat. She allowed herself a secret smile to see that he still refused to ride in a wig.

As she approached, he held out a gloved hand, and she took it, squeezing the buttery leather.

"You said you weren't leaving till next week."

"I'm ready to go, Sorcha. The rebellion is over. Alan is prepared to watch over my lands while I'm gone. Everything is in order."

There was a sadness to his smile that made her heart pang. Now that the rising had been quashed and all was peaceful once again in the Highlands, he was returning to England, to look for, in his words, "a proper wife." And hopefully a love like Sorcha and Alan had found.

"I'll miss you," she whispered.

"As will I." Alan strode up to them and took his position beside her.

"And I will miss you both," Cam said.

Sorcha glanced at Alan, and he nodded almost imperceptibly. "Cam . . ." He cleared his throat. "Sorcha and I . . . well, we have something to tell you . . ."

Alan seemed almost embarrassed, and Sorcha couldn't help the grin that spread her lips wide. "I'm—"

Cam laughed and squeezed her hand harder. "With child?"

She gasped. "Yes—in the spring. But how could you know?"

"You're glowing, my dear." He leaned forward to kiss her cheek. "I'm happy for you. Happy for you both."

"Oh, Cam."

She began to sniff, blinking back tears, and Alan rolled his eyes heavenward. "She's become a veritable waterfall since we discovered her condition."

"Oh, stop." She swiped the back of her hand over her eyes.

"Be well, dearest Sorcha," Cam said in a quiet voice, handing her a handkerchief. "Don't cry too much, all right?"

She nodded, blinking to clear her blurred vision. "I'll try," she said on a choked laugh.

Alan clapped Cam on the back. "Come home soon, my friend."

"I—we—hoped you'd be home in time to be the child's godfather." Sorcha dabbed the handkerchief over her watery eyes.

Cam sucked in a breath, and his lips twisted a tiny bit, belying his outwardly smooth appearance. "I'd be honored," he said with a tilt of his head. "I'll endeavor to return in time."

He leaned forward to kiss Sorcha again. He and Alan exchanged a brief hug; then he turned and strode to his horse. He mounted and reined the horse toward them. "Goodbye," he said, touching the brim of his hat.

"Goodbye," Sorcha said breathlessly. She doubted he even heard her as he turned and rode away.

Alan's hand slipped into hers as Cam disappeared behind a clump of juniper trees. "It won't be the same here without him."

"No," she agreed. "I hope he finds what he's looking for."

"He will," Alan murmured. "He's a man of dedication and passion. He won't accept anything less."

Sorcha merely nodded. Still, she'd never stop worrying for him. Not until he found that woman who understood him, who completed him. She took a deep breath.

Alan touched a hand to her stomach, and concern deepened his sapphire eyes. "How are you, *mo chridhe?*"

"Better," she said. "It feels good to be outside."

His voice lowered. "May I have the honor of taking you . . . inside?"

She smiled. Alan made her feel so desired. Even through the awful sickness she'd suffered for the past few weeks. This new, sometimes frightening, experience of her pregnancy had brought them closer, if possible.

She placed her hand over his, and both of them pressed gently against the new life they'd created that was growing inside her.

"You may, Alan MacDonald. You may have the honor of taking me . . . whenever and wherever you please."

PHOTO BY RENEE BOWEN PHOTOGRAPHY 2005–2009

Dawn Halliday has degrees in Computer Science and Education, and before she became a full-time writer, she held various jobs from bookselling to teaching inner-city children to acting in soap operas. When she isn't locked in her office reading or writing, you can find her playing video games or posing as a baseball mom in California, where she lives with her husband and three children. You can learn more about Dawn Halliday on her Web site at www.dawnhalliday.com.

The Earl of Camdonn's saga continues
in Dawn Halliday's next passionate tale . . .

HIGHLAND
SURRENDER

COMING FROM SIGNET ECLIPSE

IN APRIL 2010

Turn the page for a sneak peek . . .

Cam urged his horse to a canter. Ears pricked, the animal willingly obliged, sensing its rider's eagerness. From the gentle hills of Hampshire to the craggy mountains of the Highlands, Cam had followed behind the two black lacquered carriages rumbling sedately toward Camdonn Castle. Today, however, on the final leg of the journey, he'd stopped to greet one of his tenants, and the carriages had drawn ahead.

He must catch up to them—since they had left England, he'd clung to a vision of leading his bride-to-be and her uncle through the gates of Camdonn Castle. He wanted to make it clear that he was back to stay this time, and he intended to keep his primary home here. He planned to finally become the leader his Highlanders needed. A rider had gone ahead this morning to bear the news that they would arrive this afternoon—and Cam had indulged in imagining the staff lined up along the road leading through the castle gates, smiling and cheering as they welcomed him home.

Only a few miles to go—they now rode through the pass in the forested mountains bordering the southern side of Loch Shiel. Cam took a deep breath, and the sweet, fresh smells of pine and heather—of *home*—washed through him. From somewhere in the brush, a male capercallie tapped and gurgled an aria in an attempt to lure a mate. Cam hoped Elizabeth would grow to love the Highlands as quickly as he had.

He thought she might. Lady Elizabeth was young, titled, and rich. A proper, innocent English lass, and a perfect wife, politically speaking, for Cam. Even better, though she was beautiful and alluring and would be no hardship to bed, she didn't rouse him to all-consuming lust, a state Cam had promised to avoid at all costs.

He hardly knew her, but that didn't matter. Cam had gone to England in search of someone precisely like Elizabeth. He was glad his quest hadn't taken too long. He'd been in England for only five months, but already he ached for home—for his Highland castle.

His horse rounded a bend in the wide path, and a faint commotion ahead drew Cam from his thoughts. Cam frowned and leaned forward in the saddle, straining his ears. Men shouting? Suddenly, the crack of a gunshot resonated through the air, and Cam's horse surged into a gallop.

What the hell? Cam gave the animal its head as another gunshot sent a flock of birds bursting from the branches of a nearby pine.

Within moments, the road opened into a clearing, where men on horseback surrounded the larger, gold-trimmed carriage—the one bearing Elizabeth and her uncle. The men all wore black, and scarves covered the lower halves of their faces. The second vehicle carrying the servants in the duke's employ was nowhere to be seen.

Cam's lips twisted in fury. *Highwaymen.*

As Cam thundered closer, the sole man on foot yanked Lady Elizabeth from the carriage. She didn't make a sound, nor did she fight back. The poor girl was petrified with fear.

Protective rage swelled in Cam's chest, and he yanked his pistol from his belt. "Let her go, damn you," he bellowed, heedless of the fact she'd hear his foul language.

All four men swiveled in his direction. Good. If he diverted their attention away from his helpless family-to-be, perhaps he could keep them safe. He focused on the bastard whose filthy, callused hands wrapped around Elizabeth's tiny waist.

"Release her!" he snarled, leveling the pistol at the man, though he didn't dare risk shooting and injuring Elizabeth.

Astonishingly, the man obeyed. He shoved her to the side of the road. She stumbled backward, tripping over her voluminous skirts and into a gorse bush blooming with a flower that complemented the yellow silk of her dress. The villain glared at Cam as the three others on horseback turned toward him. Someone tossed the man on foot the reins of a riderless horse, and he mounted quickly.

Looked like they all intended to come after him. Good. He'd draw them away from Elizabeth and the duke.

Garbled shouting came from inside the carriage, and Cam's attention snapped to the rig. The coachman, gazing wide-eyed over his shoulder, raised the reins.

"Ho! On with you, then!" the man shouted, whipping the animals into a frenzied gallop. The carriage lurched forward, leaving Elizabeth stranded in the bush.

None of the highwaymen pursued the carriage or paid attention to the bright yellow flurry of Elizabeth's skirts—all four focused solely on Cam. It was him they wanted, he thought grimly. *So much the better.*

But they were closing on him.

He aimed his pistol at one of the bandits and fired. The man toppled from his horse, but the rest lunged closer, weapons drawn. Three guns aimed directly at him.

Turning away from them, Cam bent low over the mare's elongated neck and dug in his heels. A bullet whizzed past his shoulder.

Air streamed through his hair as the mare leap smoothly over a fallen tree. Brilliant, he thought with pride. Another excellent acquisition from his trip to England. As with Lady Elizabeth, he hadn't spent a fortune on this animal for her beauty alone.

A man shouted behind him, and his enemies' horses drew nearer. Cam unsheathed his sword with a whoosh of steel against leather.

He had been on the move for the greater part of the day. It was the only reason their horses could outrun his. As one approached his rear flank, Cam held out his sword as if he were jousting. He yanked on the reins, turning in a tight circle only a well-trained and well-bred horse could manage. The abrupt motion sent the animal just behind him catapulting past. The weapon skewered the man, jerking him off his horse. Cam yanked his sword away, and the man fell to the ground, screaming hoarsely, blood pouring from the tear in his tattered black coat.

The second bandit was suddenly upon him. This one Cam jabbed in the shoulder. The horse shied, and the man hunched over in the saddle, clutching his wound.

The final man chasing him had time to slow his mount, and Cam caught a glimpse of the barrel of a musket pointed at him. Again he made a tight turn and spurred his horse, leaning low. The animal leaped ahead, passing through a thick screen of greenery.

Just as he decided he was safe, the loud report of a gunshot shook the trees, and fire exploded in Cam's body. He jerked, yanking on the reins, and the mare reared. He toppled from her sleek back. Bracken and moss softened his fall, but he felt nothing, really, besides the all-consuming pain.

God help him. Finally, just as he was about to turn his life to rights, he'd been killed. And worst of all, he'd left the sheltered, innocent Lady Elizabeth all alone in the wild Highlands of Scotland.

Elizabeth crawled from the awful, thorny bush, praising God her uncle couldn't see the ungainly way in which she performed the awkward action. In fact, she thought as she yanked her sleeve from a bramble and grimaced at the screeching sound of fabric tearing, she'd like to see him attempt to accomplish the feat with more grace. First she'd strap him in her stays and her stiff stomacher, and then she'd watch in satisfaction as he floundered helplessly in the thorns.

Finally straightening on the dirt path, she shook out her skirts and gazed regretfully down at her dress. Only moments ago, it had been a beautiful yellow silk sack gown, pleated at the shoulders, trimmed with lush embroidery and the finest lace, but now the nasty leaves and branches had snagged the expensive material, tearing her skirts and leaving lace bits to dangle haphazardly from her bodice and bell-shaped sleeves.

Elizabeth took a deep breath and glanced up and down the path. Thank God Cam had driven those awful men away. Heaven forbid he see her in such a state.

She sighed. Her thoughts just went to show how jaded and dissolute she truly was. If she were truly innocent, if she were truly a lady, she'd be terrified. She'd be a shaking lump, utterly petrified by fear. Instead, she worried about her dress.

It was sad, really, that a masked stranger had pulled her from her uncle's carriage and could have killed her, and she couldn't bring herself to feel the requisite terror. She tilted her head to search her emotions, but they were a blank slate. At this moment, she didn't feel a bit of fear—or much of anything else, for that matter.

She was no fool. If another soul stood nearby, she'd put on a show of it, just so they wouldn't grow concerned for her sanity. But since she was all alone, there was no need to school her actions. She could be herself.

She could thank Uncle Walter for her strange, improper reaction, she supposed. Had this been his goal? To eradicate her ability to feel? To eliminate the instinctual response to fear for her life?

And then she did feel a little something. A tiny flicker of fear. Not of the highwaymen, though, nor for her life. Of Uncle Walter himself.

A bird cackled nearby, and she cast an acerbic glance in the creature's direction, then scoured the edge of the path until she found a sharp stick to use as a weapon. Who knew what kinds of wild beasts could be roaming this wild place?

Perhaps this was where she belonged, after all. It was wild. Just like her. She smiled a little at the thought.

Suddenly, the clomp of a horse's hooves sounded behind her. Gripping her stick tightly, she stilled, not knowing whether she'd face her husband-to-be or one of the criminals come back to ravish her. Or hold her for ransom. Or both.

It was neither. A tall, dark-haired man approached her on horseback. He wore one of those Highland plaids that gave the men in this region such an untamed, scandalous appearance. Young Scotsmen in their plaids always made her stomach tighten with pleasant appreciation. Even this one, who wore a tartan of a most appealing shade of blue but was particularly wild-looking, made her stomach flutter, when instead she should be scared to death—or at the very least on her guard.

Instinctively, she knew he wasn't involved with the attack or the highwaymen. She couldn't imagine how she could know such a thing. Perhaps it was in his bearing, or in the horse he rode—a much finer animal than the short, skinny Scottish hags the highwaymen had ridden.

As he came closer, she straightened her spine, lowered the stick, and took position in the center of the path, adopting her Lady Elizabeth look. Her uncle approved of this particular air she affected—said it made her look as haughty as a queen. Over the years, she'd refined and polished it until it shone like one of the golden Roman statues adorning the Duke of Irvington's foyer. Until it solidified into stone, as hard as one of the Greek alabaster statues in the library.

The horse's back legs sprayed mud as it halted before her. For a long moment, the man's light brown eyes perused her. Assessed her. Then one corner of his mouth twitched upward. "Who are you?"

His rumbling accent sent a chill of awareness down her spine, but she hid it, knowing full well her visceral reaction to him was utterly ridiculous.

She lifted her chin and narrowed her eyes, doing her best to look down her nose at him, though his position on the horse put him several feet above her. Anyone who knew anything about manners would have dismounted before speaking to a lady of her status.

"I am Lady Elizabeth Grant. The Earl of Camdonn is my intended. My carriage was attacked by bandits. Surely you heard the gunshots."

The man quickly scanned the area. Finding nothing, he asked, "Where are they now?"

"The earl chased them away," she said primly.

The man seemed to do a rapid mental calculation, then he dismounted smoothly. An expert horseman, she deduced. Not a peasant, certainly. She imagined the majority of the population of this poor country had no idea whatsoever how to handle a horse.

He bowed his head. His hair was dark—the color of coffee with just the barest touch of cream—but not as dark as Cam's. "Robert MacLean."

She nodded coolly. Keeping her stiff composure, inwardly she indulged in a brash smile. Here she stood in the wilds of Scotland with a scandalously torn dress, alone on an abandoned path and at the whim of a young and handsome stranger, and they were exchanging introductions. Days ago, she could never have imagined such an absurd scenario.

Robert angled his head at the horse. "It is my duty to deliver you safely to Camdonn Castle, then. You'll ride with me."

She was surely mad. Any of the girls back home would be terrified, but Elizabeth . . . no, again she wasn't frightened in the least.

"I will not," she huffed. "I shall walk. I do not know you, and I do not wish to. Camdonn Castle is not—" Before she had the opportunity to command he return the way he had come to find Cam, his hands encircled her waist, lifted her, and set her upon the horse. Then he mounted and settled behind her in the saddle. The rough wool of his plaid scraped the delicate silk of her gown, and when she inhaled she smelled him. Clean hay and leather. Shockingly, deliciously close.

He adjusted the reins and wrapped one hard arm around her waist, presumably to keep her from toppling off the animal.

She looked over her shoulder, directly into Robert MacLean's eyes. Not quite brown, not quite gold, they reminded her of autumn. No, of caramel, the most deliciously sweet caramel she'd ever tasted. She found them as absorbing as a whirlpool. He didn't meet her gaze; instead he stared steadily ahead. Nevertheless, she read something in the dark gold depths. Dislike, perhaps.

She turned forward again and stared straight ahead at the rutted path as Robert coaxed the horse into a walk. It didn't matter. As delicious as he appeared—coffee hair and caramel eyes, indeed!—it was certainly for the best if he didn't like her. In any event, she wasn't a very likeable person. From her uncle to her frivolous peers to her lady's maid to the lowest scullery maid, nobody much seemed to like her. Which was perfectly fine, really.

Cam, however, did seem to like her. He was infinitely polite, infinitely solicitous in her presence. But did he like her as a person, as a human being, as a woman, a future companion? She thought perhaps not. Maybe someday he would. That would be ideal, of course, but ultimately she didn't care. As long as Cam didn't hate her, nothing else mattered.

All she wanted was freedom from her uncle.

But what if one of the gunshots she'd heard had hit Cam? Elizabeth squeezed her eyes shut and pictured Cam with a hole torn open in his chest. Taking gasping, wheezing breaths as his lifeblood drained from him . . .

She would be sent back to England with Uncle Walter.

She turned to Robert MacLean. "Stop immediately. You must go back to search for Lord Camdonn. I'll continue on foot to the castle and inform them that the earl's missing. But if he's in dire need, you might find him first and save him. If we delay any longer, we might be too late."

Robert MacLean didn't respond. He didn't even deign to look at her—instead his eyes focused unerringly on the uneven surface of the path.

"Stop at once. I insist." She pushed at the arm clasped round her waist, but it wouldn't budge.

"No."

She sat in rising frustration as the horse plodded forward. When she arrived at Camdonn Castle, Uncle Walter would have taken control, and she would be impotent as usual.

Desperation surged through her. She didn't trust her uncle to help Cam. If Cam was hurt, the Highlander sitting behind her was her only hope.

When she spoke, it was with her quietest, most lethal voice. The voice that made her servants at home blanch in fear. "You must obey me."

"Why?" He seemed mildly amused.

"Because I am the niece of the Duke of Irvington, of course."

"Aye, and the soon-to-be wife of the Earl of Camdonn. You'll find the high-and-mighty titles to mean a wee bit less to Highlanders."

Highlanders. The word rolled off his tongue carnally, and her stomach fluttered even as she clenched her fists in her skirts. How dare he dismiss her order so lightly? She ground her teeth, hating him, hating even more how her body responded him. Still, her desperation to help Cam overwhelmed it all. Tears pricked at her eyes.

"I could have you horsewhipped."

The threat sounded as though it came from the mouth of a petulant child—no, she sounded as horrible as her uncle, and shame thundered through her like a flashflood.

If Robert MacLean hadn't hated her before, her words certainly sealed the impression. He didn't make any move to obey her; instead, his arm stiffened about her waist, and an angry steam seemed to billow from his body. He was so warm, she struggled not to sink into him like the softest of down quilts. Even though he was hard as stone.

They continued down the mountain in rigid silence. All along, the raw strength of Robert MacLean simmered behind her, and regret for her rash, childish outburst bit through her like scampering mice.

A group of guards eyed them warily as they approached the castle, but then relaxed when they recognized the man riding behind her.

led to Robert in Gaelic, regarding her with a glimmer in their
t curdled in her stomach.

ert dismounted and cocked his head in her direction. He spoke
ish, likely for her benefit. "This is Lady Elizabeth Grant, his
p's intended. I found her on the road back a ways."

e men glanced at her, then looked away, none of them offering
onable semblance of an obeisance. Elizabeth kept her expression

he gate swung open with a loud squeal.

Vithout looking at her, Robert strode forward, leading the horse
ss the narrow length of the spit, then up a winding, narrow path
1e castle grounds.

People crowded the graveled courtyard in a disorganized mass.
n shouted orders, but nobody seemed to be listening, and Robert
de a disapproving sound low in his throat. She agreed with his as-
sment but sat tall and revealed nothing.

As they approached, a group separated from the rest and came
1shing at them. Elizabeth immediately recognized her uncle's white
ig amongst the darker heads of the Scots.

"Elizabeth," he bellowed, breaking from the crowd. He reached up
o pull her from the horse. Her feet hit the ground with a jolt, and her
uncle's embrace smothered her.

From the corner of her eye, she saw Robert take up the reins and
lead the horse away. She knew better than to stare, and she tore her
gaze away from the Scot as Uncle Walter ushered her toward a long,
rectangular building with a square tower rising from one end.

She'd felt utterly safe with Robert's arm locked around her body.
With his legs encasing her behind. As he left her, so did that warm,
sweet sensation of security.

She looked up at her uncle, saw the silvery glint in his eyes as he
slanted his gaze at her, and steeled herself against the panic threatening to consume her whole.